Wolf's

Louis
Hillary
Park

RUN

This book is a work of fiction. DeLong, Mississippi and Cattahatchie County,
Mississippi, are fictional locales. All of the characters, situations and events depicted in
this book are the product of the author's imagination, other than historic events,
which are used fictitiously.

ISBN: 0982735405
ISBN-13: 9780982735404
LCCN: 2010927186

This book is dedicated to my wife, Joyce,
who has taught me the meaning of grace
and dignity and committed love.

Thank you for your faith in God and your faith in me.

The Lord does not look at the things man looks at.
Man looks at the outward appearance
but the Lord looks at the heart.

1 Samuel 16:7

Prologue

Los Angeles, April 1969

ନ୍ତ

Holly Lee Carter felt herself being snatched upward, her face rising in a dizzy trajectory toward two uncovered flourescent lights on the ceiling. One flickered like a flare dying in the night jungle somewhere away from the coast, beyond Da Nang. She blinked – once, twice, again – trying to get her bearings, trying to shake herself from a dream of fire and noise and blood-spattered elephant grass.

"What the —?" she gasped, her startled heart thudding against her ribs.

Now, just as suddenly, she was falling. Tumbling out of control toward the tile floor. Fast. *Too fast!* Holly wanted to scream but the lambskin straps cinched across her chin and forehead held her face so snugly that she could not really open her jaw. She gritted her teeth and scrunched her eyes, praying for the spinning to stop, but it didn't until the whole five-foot-ten-inches of her was past horizontal and her brain was trying to fly out the top of her head. She gagged on the bile thrown into her throat before she finally felt herself settling back to even keel. She heard the aide slide the locking pin into place to secure the old Stryker-style frame she had been sandwiched in for almost three weeks.

Holly had begged the hospital aides not to turn her so quickly. Now it felt like the full weight of her brain was resting on the back of her eyes. They throbbed as she opened them again and tried to focus. Her arms slipped from their straps and dangled below her. She watched a salty drop of perspiration — or was it a tear? – trickle to the end of her nose and tumble free. It fell and fell until it crashed soundlessly onto the hospital floor.

She'd had plenty of time to study, to memorize every line in that floor and the maze of pipes that snaked across the ceiling. Four hours on her back, four hours on her stomach, four hours on her back, four hours on her stomach, four hours — hour after helpless hour inside the creaking steel frame that gripped her. It wasn't even a real Stryker, not like the one the medical team had used when the *Los Angeles Chronicle* had flown their hotshot young photographer back from Vietnam in '65. No, this was a cheap copy, put together like a kid's erector set, full of wobbles and loose screws. But the basics were the same, like a Ferris wheel with a narrow cot mounted at the fulcrum between the two circular rails. Once her damaged back was on the padded, reinforced canvas, a matching canvas frame was slid down on top of her and screwed into place. Two straps kept her head immobile, and two small slings gave her a place to hang her arms.

"Like a sleeping bat," Holly more than once had remarked.

When the pounding behind her eyes eased a bit, she rubbed the small guitar calluses on her fingertips against her palms, and flexed her arms. The muscles in her shoulders and upper back were oversized and hard from miles of laps done religiously in the pool behind her house and the simple effort of everyday life as a paraplegic. With no use of her legs, she had to heave her one-hundred-and-thirty-five pounds from bed to wheelchair, wheelchair to toilet, toilet to chair, chair to car, car to wheelchair; then she had to push that chair wherever she needed to go, hauling the dead weight of her hips and the long legs. Legs that once could scorch a man from across a pasture or a dance floor or a Saigon street.

She thought of Senator Haughton Wellingham III, who had visited her a week earlier. Wellingham represented her hometown of DeLong in the Mississippi legislature, and was her brother's attorney – at least for the purposes of Tom purchasing the fifty-one percent interest their father had left her in the family's twice-weekly newspaper.

"Awwww, Miz Holly, I do hate to see you sufferin' so many trials," Mr. Wellingham had crooned in his melodic, cotton-soft drawl. He unloaded a massive bouquet of roses into the arms of an aide. "But you are a treasure. Just as gaw-jus as the night you won the Miss Cattahatchie County crown.

"That was nineteen-and-fifty-nine. Ten years ago. I remember it like it was yesterday. For your talent you sang *Faded Love*. Marvelous! It gave me goose flesh," he'd gone on, then sighed dramatically. "And my gracious, you just haven't changed a tad. It's truly an amazement."

Haven't changed? Holly thought.

It had been a straight-out lie and so enormous under the circumstances that Holly remembered having to fight the urge to laugh – or perhaps to cry. Yet it was the sort of genteel shading of the truth for kindness's sake that she missed about the South, the very Deep South where she'd grown up.

"My dear," he'd said, "as you know, I'm not here as an elected official of the great state of Miss-uh-sissppi. I'm here about your father's estate. I'm here representing your brother Tom and a group of investors. And, Holly, I hope I'm here as your friend."

The day of T.L. Carter's accident, Tom, Holly's older brother by nearly seven years, had tried to reach her at her home in Pacific Palisades, then finally at the community college in Malibu where she taught photography. College officials had referred him to the Los Angeles hospital where Holly was undergoing surgery to further stabilize her spinal column and ease the scorching pain she often endured in her lower back. It had gotten so bad since Christmas that at night she could no longer lift herself from her wheelchair into bed. Had it not been for one of her students — her best student, Eve Howard — moving in and helping her for a few weeks, Holly did not know what she would have done.

No, there was no way she could come home for her father's funeral, she had told Tom. Holly explained that she'd just had surgery and would be immobilized in the frame for several weeks and it would be at least a month after that before she would be strong enough to travel.

Silence.

"Tom, it's not like I timed this surgery so I couldn't come home for Daddy's funeral," she finally had said. T.L. Carter's drowning death in the Cattahatchie River was a shock to everyone.

Still, her brother was having none of it. "Aw'right, I guess we'll just have to go on without you. Just like we always have."

Starting with the age difference, Holly and Tom had never been close, but he now was the only significant family she had and the words had stung. Yet in a strange way, they had made Holly smile. In many ways, Tom Carter was every inch T.L. Carter's son.

Now Senator Wellingham's roses were faded and dying on a nearby table.

A nurse appeared in the door. "Holly, you have visitors."
From the corner of her eye, Holly recognized the spotless white shoes and firm calves of Nurse Frederick. "Rhonda, who are they?"

"I don't know. But one sounds like another friend from the South. Another bigwig, too, I suppose. The hospital director walked them down."

Holly hated the notion of anyone seeing her bolted into the contraption that held her, but any break was a relief from the tedium of staring at the ceiling, then the floor, then the ceiling, then ...

"Rhonda, would you please hand me a wash cloth?" she asked.

Holly took the damp cloth and washed the portions of her face that she could reach, then ran it over her arms to wipe away the salt sheen of sweat that her dreams of Vietnam always boiled to the surface – as if she'd actually just returned to the humid jungles and million horrors of that place. Her long, auburn hair mostly was hidden by the frame, but it felt to Holly as if her head had been dipped in cooking oil. It had been seventeen days since she was able to wash her hair. There were four more to go before she could have a shower, a real shower, instead of the sponge baths that she was given while laying naked, motionless. Helpless.

Nurse Frederick led the men to the door. One wore suit trousers that hung perfectly over a set of expensive, perhaps handmade wing-tips. The other had on faded jeans that bunched atop hard-used work boots.

"Miz Carter?" said wingtips, the drawl definitely Southern but not from Mississippi. Maybe the Carolinas.

"Yes, I'm in here somewhere. Half woman, half machine."

Both sets of feet shifted with indecision.

"There's a blanket and some pillows in the closet over there. You can spread them on the floor and stretch out." More awkward shifting. "Look, whoever you are, I'm not going to have a conversation with your feet. Either lay down where I can talk to you face to face or come back in about four hours when they flip this pancake."

"I'm sorry," said wingtips, squatting beside her. "How rude of us."

Holly shifted her eyes — the only part of her face she could easily move — and saw brown hair and a square jaw. It was only mid-afternoon but wingtips already had a five o'clock shadow creeping across his chin. "I'm J.L. Burke," he said, extending his hand. Holly took it. It was strong but soft. "I'm the United States Attorney for the Northern District of Mississippi." Work boots was spreading the blanket, throwing down pillows. "This is Reverend Clemmer of the National Coalition for Justice."

"We're based out of Ohio," said Clemmer, extending his hand – a nice hand that did harder work than simply turning pages in a Bible. Still, he didn't try to use his handshake to impress her with his masculine muscle. Though sturdy, Clemmer was not a big man. Maybe one-hundred-and-sixty pounds, including his tight Afro and granny glasses – *a la* John Lennon.

"I know what the NCJ is. And I think I know what a U.S. Attorney does," said Holly, as the men positioned themselves shoulder to shoulder on the blanket. "The big question is, what are you two doing getting cozy on my floor?"

Burke smiled, the caps on his teeth perfectly aligned. *Cozy?* he thought. Judging from the background report and photos his staff had put together, he would have enjoyed getting very cozy with Holly Lee Carter — at least before she packed her cameras and went to Vietnam. Her face was more mature, stronger, the tiny start of sun lines at her temples, but still beautiful – her brows as thick, her lips as full as when she was photographed for the Cattahatchie High School annual, Class of '59. But the black-and-white couldn't capture her eyes. They were an amazing, luminous green, flecked with gold.

What a waste, he thought.

"You're as sharp and down to business as Gerald Yards said you'd be," offered Clemmer.

Gerry Yards was chief of photography for the *Los Angeles Chronicle.* He'd been Holly's boss, her mentor, her lover – briefly – and still was her friend. On more than one occasion, he'd asked her to be Mrs. Yards, but Holly thought that was mostly guilt talking. Guilt for taking her with him into a war zone. She'd only been twenty-three when they landed in Saigon. Guilt because she was a woman, and a woman's place ... but they both knew being a woman had nothing to do with what had happened. If it hadn't been her, it would have been some other young photog who climbed onto that chopper bound for Ia Drang Valley. Like the GIs, reporters and photographers take their chances in a war zone. She knew it. Gerry knew it, but he couldn't let go of the guilt. Now they enjoyed a melancholy friendship and the occasional good bottle of California chardonnay on the back deck of her home, watching the cars pass below on the Pacific Coast Highway in waves nearly as ceaseless as those of the ocean beyond.

"Sounds like you two have been making the rounds," said Holly. "Now what can I do for you?"

The men looked at each other, deciding who should take the lead. Reverend Clemmer started. "It's about your father's newspaper."

"What about it?"

The men shared another glance. "We've come to ask you not to sell it," said Burke. "At least not to your brother and the people who are financing him."

Holly looked from Burke to Clemmer and back. "I'm sorry, gentlemen, you're too late. I signed the papers this morning," she said, motioning to a large brown envelope next to a Bible on the seat of her wheelchair parked in the corner. "Nurse Frederick is going to mail it for me when she goes off duty."

Clemmer's brown eyes brightened, unfazed. "That doesn't mean anything, Miss Carter. As long as you haven't mailed the documents, you can just tear them up."

"Why would I want to do that? My father was a wonderful journalist, but he was a lousy businessman. Considering *The Current-Leader* is in very shaky financial shape, Tom has made me quite a generous offer."

"How do you think he can afford such a generous offer?" asked Burke.

"He has backers. So what?"

"Do you know who they are?" asked Clemmer.

"No. Tom says they'll be silent partners. He'll remain publisher and the paper will stay in the family. Just as it has been for a-hundred-and-thirty years."

Burke pulled a piece of paper from an expensive briefcase. He handed it to Holly, and she felt the eyes of the men on her as she read. There were five names. All were prominent Cattahatchie County citizens. All were major advertisers. They were men she knew to be sometime poker buddies, occasional allies but most often enemies of her father. All but one had expressed an interest in *knowing* her before she left Cattahatchie County, even though she'd been barely eighteen. But it was the final name that caused the breath to tighten in Holly's chest. Cecil Weathers was a backwoods politician who'd married into the DeLong family and over time gained control of sprawling Chalmette Plantation, which had been in his wife's family since the early nineteenth century. He'd been elected to various state offices throughout the 1930s, '40s and '50s on a "segregation then, segregation now, segregation forever" platform. As governor in 1962, he'd sworn no black would ever set foot in a Mississippi university "except as a janitor." It had taken a troop of U.S. Marshals and a show of force by the Army to prove him wrong. Four people died and dozens more were injured in the three days of rioting that Gov. Weathers instigated.

For reasons unknown, T.L. Carter never had taken Weathers on in print. In private, they detested each other. *How could Tom take that racist idiot on as a partner?* Holly fumed inwardly, then steadied herself. "How do you know this?"

"We have our sources," said Burke.

"You're going to have to do better than that. What kind of sources?"

"All I can say is that it came up as part of the FBI's effort to monitor Ku Klux Klan activity," he told her.

Holly hesitated. It was no secret to anyone who grew up in DeLong that Weathers pulled the strings in the Kattahatchie Klavern of the so-called Invisible Empire. She knew Tom always had held Dixiecrat segregationist views – egged on by his blue-blood wife, Mary Nell – *but to go into business with that pompous, backward megalomaniac?* She had to clench her jaw to keep from cursing. From cursing Tom and Weathers, and the timing of these men on the floor beneath her. Another two hours and the sales contract would have been in the mail. Within a week, there would be a seven-figure check in her mailbox. Much of it would go to hospital bills, old and new. But it also would pay off the mortgage on her little house above the ocean. Then it would be all hers. A safe place, completely modified so that even in a wheelchair Holly would need no one's help to get to every inch of it. There would be enough left over to convert the garage into a photo studio where she could augment her teaching salary doing family portraits and kids' birthdays. Not glamorous. Not the stuff of Pulitzer Prizes. Not like covering a war. But it would help put gas in her car to fuel her all-night drives, and keep her in wine and cheese and strawberries, and big bowls of buttered popcorn – her secret passion.

"Miss Carter, if you mail those documents, you'll be signing your father's legacy over to the Klan," pressed Clemmer.

Holly didn't want to deal with this bombshell. After a twelve-year roller coaster of reckless behavior that finally had landed her in a wheelchair, paralyzed from the waist down, she simply wanted to be able to live quietly, comfortably – with her cameras, her dog and sunsets that melted into the Pacific.

"You know, Reverend Clemmer, *The Current-Leader* always has maintained a white news only policy," tried Holly. "And Daddy never directly took on Weathers or his crowd. We fought about it more than once."

"That's true," said Burke. "But I had the pleasure of meeting with your father several times. He was a pragmatist, not a racist."

"In any case," said Clemmer, "while *The Current-Leader* may never have come out openly against the segregationists, it never supported them. Your father's editorials always emphasized that there was a political process in place and that violence on either side was unacceptable."

"By Mississippi standards, that nearly made your father a Bobby Kennedy Democrat," said Burke. "Do you think T.L. Carter would want Weathers in control of the paper he put forty years of his life into?"

Holly was so angry with Tom, and with herself, that she felt the same bile rising in her throat that she had when the aide had carelessly spun her onto her chest. Maybe she had known deep down that Tom would get in bed with men like Weathers as soon as their father died. Maybe that's why she hadn't asked about his backers. She hadn't wanted to know. She'd been afraid to know. Now she forced a steadiness into her voice that she didn't feel. "I'll talk to my brother, but this is a family matter. I'm sorry."

"You're wrong, Miss Carter. This is *not* just a family matter," persisted Reverend Clemmer. "A federal judge has ordered Cattahatchie schools and other public facilities integrated by September. With local elections coming up this fall, the NCJ is planning the county's first-ever black voter registration drive over the summer."

Holly wished she could turn away, run away, but the metal frame felt as if it were tightening against her chest. Said Burke, "With Cattahatchie his home county, Weathers has used all his wealth and political power to keep it segregated. It's the last county of its kind, even in Mississippi."

"A lot of the old-time Klan crazies see this as their last stand," Clemmer went on. "Weathers already owns the county's only radio station. If he controls the newspaper, too, there'll be no voice of reason or moderation. Things could get very ugly, very fast."

Burke could see they had shaken Holly Lee Carter, and he moved in with the precision of a seasoned prosecutor playing to the jury. "Miss Carter, your father had a big plaque on the wall behind his desk – 'A newspaper is the conscience of a community.' What sort of conscience do you think *The Current-Leader* will be for DeLong if its soul is mortgaged to Weathers?"

Holly wasn't looking at Burke or Clemmer. She was gripping the steel frame, looking through them, into her past and her future. Clemmer gently covered one hand with his. "Why do you think your father left you controlling interest in the newspaper?"

It was a question Holly had asked herself a hundred times since Tom called and angrily gave her the news that Thomas Lee Carter Jr. had bequeathed to his daughter the family's country house, Wolf's Run, and fifty-one percent of the newspaper. Tom had worked at *The Current-Leader* since he was old enough to run copy from their father's desk to the hot lead typesetters in the backshop, and had spent his entire adult life trying to keep it solvent as the company's vice president and general manager. More than that, ever since their mother abandoned the family – disappearing when Holly was eight and her brother was fifteen – Tom had been her father's verbal punching bag. Some of the assaults at the dinner table, in the newspaper office or even on a public street were so vicious and degrading that a leather strap or brass knuckles almost would have been kinder. Tom took it stoically, but Holly would hear him crying when she passed his door. At first, she tried to go in and comfort him – or share comfort as children physically abandoned by their mother and emotionally abandoned by their father. But Tom always would shut the door and shut her out. After a time, he took to locking it.

Part of it, perhaps, was Holly's appearance. Born with her mother's tawny complexion and fine French features, even as a child she was arrestingly beautiful. As she grew, the resemblance to her mother became almost uncanny.

Holly also was born with her mother's Cajun temper. By age twelve, she had mastered the French phrase *"embrassez mon âne (kiss my ass),"* and used it with frequency. By fifteen, she had moved out of the family's two-story Victorian home in DeLong and into what was then her grandmother's house, Wolf's Run. During the late spring of Holly's senior year, her Meemaw Carter died. Twenty-two minutes after her high school graduation, Holly pointed her white Corvette toward the West Coast, punched it up to eighty-five and barely slowed down until she was walking barefoot in the surf at Malibu.

Since her evacuation from Vietnam, Holly and her father had begun to correspond here and there and occasionally talked on the phone, but when word of the accident came, she had neither expected nor wanted anything from the estate.

"What am I supposed to do?" she asked. "Refuse to sell my half? Let the paper go into bankruptcy? Because without some new financing, that's where it's headed."

"Of course not," said Burke, who had been waiting for the right opening. "We've found another group willing to purchase your fifty-one percent. Not at the inflated price that Weathers' bunch is offering, but a fair price. Well into the mid six figures."

"Cattahatchie County people?" asked Holly.

"No. No one in that part of the state is willing to go up against Weathers," explained Burke. "One man is from Kentucky, and two are from Indiana."

"What about Tom? Would he remain as publisher?"

Burke and Clemmer shared a look. "The men we're talking about certainly would try to work with Tom," said the U.S. Attorney.

"But their views are lot more, well, forward thinking. If they couldn't come to an understanding on *The Current-Leader's* editorial policy – "

"With fifty-one percent, they could force Tom out," said Holly. "No, gentlemen, I'm sorry. I won't – I *can't* do that to my brother. *The Current-Leader* is Tom's birthright. Lord knows, he's earned it. I won't help you steal it from him."

Clemmer tried, "Please, Miss Carter –"

"No!" she interrupted. "Now please go."

There was nothing in Holly Lee Carter's eyes or the tight set of her lips that allowed for further discussion. J.L. Burke and Ron Clemmer rolled off the pillows. Clemmer picked up the blanket, folded it and returned it and the pillows to the closet.

"Thank you for your time, Miss Carter," said Burke.

Holly watched wingtips and work boots head for the door. She said nothing, inwardly furious with Tom. She shifted her eyes to the envelope with her future inside of it, and Tom's. Tears of frustration burned her eyes.

"Miss Carter, there is one other alternative," Reverend Clemmer said from the door.

"Please leave. I've heard all I want to hear."

"You could go back and run the paper yourself," he persisted.

Holly laughed. "Forget it, Reverend," she said, quickly wiping her eyes with the backs of her hands. "I have a life here. I have a house where I don't need legs to get around. I can see the ocean from my porch. I have flowers I can take care of and a little dog that loves me. I have a job, and students who respect me.

"Most of all, I have friends who have never seen me without a wheelchair. They don't look at me with pity, remembering who I used to be."

The silence hung deep and long between them. They could hear the sound of nursing shoes squeaking on the floor and the elevator doors opening and closing down the hall. The pastor's eyes moved around the dimly lit room as he searched for words to change Holly Lee Carter's mind. Then they stopped in the wheelchair in the corner.

"I see you keep a Bible close," he said. "I've heard from others that you've become a woman of faith. Before you mail that envelope, would you pray about it?"

Holly drew in a long breath and let it out. "Reverend, I pray every day about things large and small, but I don't need to pray about this," she told him. "I'm never going back to DeLong."

After several moments, she saw Clemmer's work boots turn to go. She didn't intend to speak, but she heard herself say, "Be careful, Reverend. Cattahatchie County is covered with steep hills and thick woods. The swamps are wide and the river is deep. If you don't know your way around, it can be a dangerous place. An easy place for someone to disappear."

"Thank you, Miss Carter," he said. "I'll remember that. I don't want to die in Mississippi."

"Neither do I, Reverend Clemmer. Neither do I."

PART I

Chapter 1

Mississippi, July 1969

∞

Vietnam killed my older brother in the fall of '66. By the following autumn, Momma had grieved herself into the ground. Since then, Daddy had been drinking hard and daily, trying to follow them down into the black soil of our Cattahatchie County farm south of DeLong.

At the open kitchen window, I lowered my coffee cup and drew in a long breath, wanting to hold within me the dark, cool minutes just ahead of morning when the world is at its quietest and crops stand in their orderly moonlit rows like acres of green, freshly washed crystal. Daddy's deep, drunken snoring soured the moment and my stomach. He snored when sober, but the potent red-corn whiskey lowered the tone until it became a rasp, capable of grinding away my best moods and making rough even the most pleasant mornings. Alone in the kitchen that had been so well used and loved by my mother, Denise Wallace – "Neesie" to her friends, and they included nearly everyone in Cattahatchie County – I told myself I shouldn't let myself get worked up … again.

Moments ahead of first light I pushed through the screen door and let it slam. On the front porch I listened as the ring of the door spring died away, buried in the noise from Daddy's bedroom. No awakening. No concern that maybe an intruder was endangering the comfortable home he'd built on land handed down from his grandfather. The farm was in near ruin, but he didn't care. He didn't even change cadence.

It made good sense for a farmer with two sons to hint of splitting the land between them. The policy made considerably easier the task of keeping both interested during the tedium of plowing and other repetitive, mechanical chores that made up the bulk of farm life. And I'm sure I would have gotten a decent share of our 520 acres. But from early on it was obvious Steve, who was my senior by eight years, was a born farmer. After Steve, my mother had had a hard time getting pregnant and carrying a child – there were three miscarriages – so I was a born surprise. Steve had our father's touch in the fields and I had our mother's love for books, and world events and history. He was stout and handsome, in a wind burned unpretty way, and had an ability that was little short of magic to urge a sturdy bean plant or a tall cotton stalk out of the soil. What magic I made was in spiral notebooks, writing on both sides of each page until the books were filled with stories set anywhere other than a farm.

Steve quietly encouraged me the only way he knew how — with his hands, building the large bookcases that covered one entire wall of my room. Sometimes when I was missing him the most, I ran my hand along the shelves and could almost feel his sweat and see the smile he wore as confidently as his Army fatigues. *How could he be dead?*

Still, my writing was seen as nothing solid. Not a bean plant or a cornstalk, like the green legions that stood at attention at the edge of my headlights as I bounced toward the highway. Back in the spring, Daddy had managed enough sober days to guide me and some part-time laborers in getting the seeds into the ground. Then about the middle of May he began a solid drunk and dumped the whole farm in my lap. There was no other lap to drop it in. Certainly not Steve's. After my brother leaped from a helicopter onto a land mine, he lived for thirteen days with both legs and most of his pelvis blown away. Then he stopped.

When the half of Steve that remained was returned to us ten days later, Brother MacAllister, the minister of First Denomination Church where mother had been a member for forty-odd years, stood beneath the large oak tree set alone in the middle of our acreage. Like a massive umbrella, the ancient tree overspread and shaded the Wallace family cemetery. Over stones that dated back to the eighteen-fifties, Brother MacAllister intoned – "It's better that the Lord took Steve to sit at His right hand rather than leave him to *cra-a-awl* this earth. The Lord spared Steve that humiliation. Now let us kneel here on this good ground Steve so loved - took so much from, gave so much to - and give God thanks for the merciful sleep He granted your Steve."

But Mama didn't kneel and she didn't give thanks, and she never went back to First Denomination. She figured, I think, that if God was all that merciful, He would have had Steve hop off that Cobra gunship about a foot to the right. But it's funny how things work out. Two-

and-a-half years later and heading into my senior year, I was all but engaged to Brother Charles Everett MacAllister's youngest daughter, Patti. Everyone, except her folks and me, called her "PattiWac" - because it rhymed with Mac and because she could be a bit – well, "wacky" would be the kindest word.

By the time I reached the intersection of Highway 27, the last of Saturday night's quarter moon was as white as my Sunday shirt and set off in a blue-black belt that was tightening on the western horizon. I looked south, then north, then south again. Highway 27 was the main artery of travel and commerce through Cattahatchie County, running as it did all the way from the shrimp boat docks of the Misssssipi Gulf Coast, through dozens of small towns like DeLong and deep into Tennessee. On most days it was thick with traffic – pickups loaded with vegetables for sale on DeLong's town square, eighteen-wheelers roaring through and people in their used cars headed for jobs in New Albany or Tupelo. But this was Sunday morning and in the far distance I saw only two sets of headlights cutting through the day's first pink-purple light. Sunday was the one day that most of the county let itself sleep. But I hadn't because I knew my best friend, Cutter, would just now be winding down from another Saturday's worth of work at a Tennessee juke joint called The Gin.

Slapping the long neck of the floor shifter into first, I swung north off the gravel of Pleasant Ridge Road and onto the damp, gray pavement that loosely followed the contours of the Cattahatchie River's east bank and the railroad tracks that ran beside it. Next stop, DeLong and the Cotton Café.

DeLong was the county seat and the largest town within 40 miles. Population 1,991. An active set of fall births and a moderate number of autumn deaths at the old-folks home would send DeLong brimming over 2,000 before the next decade arrived in January. It was something to shoot for. Something – anything – in a little place like DeLong was better than nothing. We had plenty of nothing already.

Had it not been for perpetually bald tires and a suspension that was irreparably warped – accounting for the tires, I could have dropped my hands from the wheel and let the experienced old Chevy find its own way to the café on River Street. The Cotton, after all, was a tradition ingrained in the county's farmers, merchants, lawyers, cops and kids who daily moved through its booths and tables on a schedule as regular as factory shifts. Miss Winona St. Julian, a small, bent black woman from across the river, had cooked for three or more generations – depending on how prolific the family. She had stayed on through two changes of ownership, four husbands and a pair of world wars. Her breakfast biscuits, fried chicken lunches and chicken-fried steak suppers were what really kept people coming back.

Changing gears, I was eager to cover the 8.7 miles between the highway intersection and The Cotton. Cutter probably would beat me to the café, be at our usual Sunday morning spot at the counter, drinking black coffee from behind even blacker aviator shades. He was always a step ahead or a flash quicker. Not just of me, but of every teenager straining the reins of manhood at Cattahatchie High School.

At six-foot-three, two-hundred-and-thirty-two pounds, Cutter Carlucci would have been a blue-chip, nationally sought-after college running back/linebacker prospect had he played anywhere except at a little high school in Mississippi's smallest sports division. But it wasn't just his size. Dodge McDowell, who played right guard, and Gary Vernon, the left tackle, were bigger. Truck Jamison, our center, was two hundred and fifteen. But that was all just grunt-and-push muscle. Cutter had an extraordinary mix of pure speed, lateral agility and something Coach Pearce called "football vision" – the ability to see running lanes before the holes opened. Defensively, he was a brutal linebacker who played every down with that quality of barely tempered insanity that coaches admire above all others. "Reckless abandon," they call it.

Driving four miles south of DeLong I was eager to hear from Cutter what adventures had transpired the previous night in his oh-so-exciting and independent life. At least, that's how his life seemed to me heading into our senior year. Cutter had left home almost four years earlier, and between farm, construction or mechanic'ing jobs worked as a bouncer, bartender and waiter at a notorious roadhouse just above the Tennessee line. The Gin was famous - or infamous, depending on how hard you thumped your Bible - and the closest place within 20 miles of bone-dry DeLong to legally get a cold beer. Of course, some of the Cattahatchie County's more enterprising bootleggers made rounds as regularly as milkmen. Dodge McDowell's dad, "Shootin' Sam," stopped by my house twice a week delivering gasoline-colored home-brew in pint-sized Mason jars.

With all that on my mind, and my eight-track player blaring The Stones' *Beggar's Banquet* from the four speakers behind my seats, I didn't hear or see the two vehicles racing up behind me until they practically were on my bumper. Their lights exploded in my rearview mirrors. I felt my chest tighten, my eyes widen and I had to fight my instinct to hit the brake. If I had, the big, four-door convertible would have plowed right into me. Instead, it shot into the passing lane as a green Ford sedan tried to cut it off. Both cars went by me doing what had to be close to a hundred. It happened so fast, I didn't get a look at either of the drivers, but I knew I wanted to see who was racing this time of the morning so I floored my old truck and got it all the way up to sixty. I couldn't come close to catching them, but maybe I could watch from a distance. It was the first Lincoln Continental convertible I'd ever seen up close. Even for the couple of seconds it took to blow past me.

When I rounded a curve into a long straightaway that led to the Yancy Creek bridge south of the fairgrounds, I saw the sedan banging door to door with the baby blue Lincoln, trying to push it into the ditch – and succeeding. Two wheels were off on the shoulder and – *ohh, shhhit!* – the concrete bridge abutment was coming up. Fast!

Turning my face half away, I was prepared to see the convertible shatter against the end of the bridge – metal and limbs flying in all directions, propelled by a fireball. At the last instant the cars separated. The Lincoln disappeared into the wide ditch on the right as the driver of the green sedan shot across the bridge without ever touching the brakes.

A moment later, I slid to a stop at the foot of the bridge and ran around to the edge of the road, expecting to see the car upside down and torn apart. Maybe even burning. But the driver hadn't let the nose climb up the steep bank, where it would have snagged and rolled. Instead, he – *no she!* – had held it in the flat of the ditch, letting the water, mud and the thick stand of cattails slow the big convertible like a safety net. The water from Yancy Creek flowed just under the front bumper.

Quickly, I hustled down the ditch bank and came up on the back of the car.

A little white ball of fur leaped over the shoulder of the black woman in the front passenger seat and onto the luggage that was scattered in back. It began to yap.

"Easy," I said as the little dog barked and snapped and bared its black gums. "I don't mean anyone any harm. I saw what happened. I wanted to see if anyone was hurt. If I can help."

Without turning around, the white woman in the driver's seat said, "Charlie, *régler après à moi.*"

The dog gave me one more hard look then hopped over the front seat and lay down. I pulled my feet through muck to the front door.

"Whatever you told it, that dog sure seems to mind," I said, but the woman with the long auburn hair and Wayfarers didn't respond. She was still gripping the steering wheel with both hands and staring straight ahead. I looked her over and there was plenty to see – lots of curves even under a tie-dyed T-shirt and pair of well-worn Tuff-Nut overalls. Especially as she drew in one deep breath after another, her chest rising and falling. The pretty black woman with the big Afro and pullover blouse was holding her hand over her mouth as if she might throw up. Then I saw it. The hand control beside the driver's knee. I had never seen one up close before, but I knew what it was – that it allowed someone without use of their legs to control the brakes and the gas. I glanced into the back seat and saw the handles of a wheelchair sticking up from a pile of luggage that had slid atop it. The woman behind the wheel was Holly Lee Carter, my new boss.

"Miss Carter, my name is Nate Wallace. I work part-time for *The Current-Leader*. Are you –?"

"Nate Wallace, yes. You write high school sports," she said, still without looking at me.

"Yes, ma'am. Miss Carter, should I go get an ambulance or a doctor or somethin'?" I tried again, and the questions finally seemed to bring her into the moment and loosen her grip on the wheel. "Are you two okay?"

She flexed her fingers then ran her hands along her thighs. She still hadn't looked at me. "It's kind of hard to tell, but I think so. Eve, are you all right?"

The woman nodded but didn't remove her hand from her mouth.

It was then that we heard another vehicle on the bridge, and it crossed everyone's mind at the same moment that the men in the sedan had come back. "They had a gun," gasped the black woman, real fear in her eyes.

My heart started to race. If they had a gun and decided to use it, it would be like shooting fish in a barrel. I exhaled an audible sigh of relief when Cutter leaned over the rail. Flustered and embarrassed by my own fear, I swallowed and tried to force my voice to be steady. With limited success, I asked, "What are you doing here?"

"I went by the Cotton and you weren't there. I thought one of those may-pop tires you ride around on might have seen its day," he said. "I expected to find *you* in the ditch. What'cha got?"

"Two men in a green Ford ran these ladies off the road," I told him. "Nearly ran 'em into the end of the bridge."

Cutter pulled off his Ray-Bans for a better look. His eyes were so light blue that they were nearly clear. From our bottom-of-the-ditch angle it seemed you could look straight through the back of his head and up into the morning sky.

"I didn't see a car on this stretch."

"You think we're making it up?" demanded the black woman, her voice quivering with anger and a residue of pure fear.

"Nope. You ladies clearly had a run-in with somebody. I expect your green Ford turned off on Buena Vista Road. That's why I didn't see it," he said. "Are y'all hurt?"

"No broken bones," said Miss Carter, pulling off her sunglasses to take a look at the man twenty feet above her. Her eyes were the same sunlit green as the wet fields that spread out around us, her hair the color of smoked copper. "You're Cutter Carlucci. I've seen your picture in *The Current-Leader*."

"Cutter," he said, not angrily but firmly. "Just Cutter'll do. I've seen yours, too – Miz Carter."

"Your mother was my homeroom teacher my junior year. How –"

"That was a long time ago."

Holly took the hint and changed the subject. "This is my friend, Eve Howard."

Cutter nodded – "Miz Howard."

Except for the pinging of the engine and the splash of a fish jumping in the creek we all were silent for several long moments. Finally, Miss Carter said, "So ... The good news is, we didn't hit the bridge."

"The bad news is, you're stuck in that ditch," said Cutter, continuing to look the situation over. "If that soft-top limo of yours'll crank, I might be able to winch you out with my jeep. Try it."

Miss Carter turned the key once, twice – on the third turn the big eight-cylinder caught. Within five minutes Cutter had the jeep swung around and a cable secured to the Continental's frame.

"Nate, you climb on out and run the winch," he said. "I'm gonna stay here and see if I can't rock the back a little. Get us some traction. Just make sure, if we can't winch this big ol' thing out of this ditch, we don't winch my jeep into it."

Cutter went to the driver's door. "Can anybody drive this car?"

"Sure. The floor pedals work."

"Then maybe your friend should do this. I don't want to get run over."

"I've driven this car nearly every day for the last three years," Miss Carter told him. "And over the last three days, I've driven it most of the way here from L.A. I assure you, I can back it out of this ditch without inflicting any fatal injuries."

He looked her over skeptically but said, "Aw'right, then. You go forward when I say. Backwards when I say. And *stop* when I say. And be careful. If it catches, it'll probably want to fishtail."

Holly Lee Carter saluted.

Cutter went to the back quarter panel and gave me the sign to wind the winch. He put all of his weight over the right rear tire. Two minutes of rocking the car forward-and-back, forward-and-back seemed to be doing no good. Then the muck let go of the Lincoln with a sucking sound and Cutter pushed out of the way, muddy from his shoulders to his work boots. While I winched the convertible on out of the ditch, he walked down to the creek, peeled off his black T-shirt with The Gin logo on the front, washed it in the stream and then used it to get the mud off his arms and face. He rinsed it again and pulled it back on.

When Cutter climbed out of the ditch, the T-shirt clung to his chest and abdomen and made his upper body look as if was forged from black steel plate. His arms, neck and face could have been smelted from bronze and his short black hair shined like wet coal. As always, his Levi's fit like they were sewn on.

Miss Carter and her friend shared a look. I had been around Cutter and girls – and not just girls but *women* – enough that I'd seen the look many times. Finally the spell broke and Miss Carter began digging in her purse.

"Look guys, we really appreciate this," she said, pulling out two bills. "If you two hadn't stopped, there's no telling how long we'd have been down there."

"Well, it looks like you swapped some paint with that Ford, but otherwise this big ol' tank fared pretty well," I said as I took the twenty she offered. "Riley Pressman does good body work if you want to get the dings smoothed out and get this side of the car repainted."

"Thank you, Nate," she said, extending her hand toward Cutter. He turned away.

"I don't want your money," he said getting into the jeep. "I only did what I'd do for anybody I found off in a ditch. But, Miss Carter, we don't need any more of your kind in this town."

"Cutter!" I exclaimed, shocked, at least by his directness. But he ignored me and went on. "Maybe you should take this for what it was – a warning – and high-tail it back to California before you end up in even worse shape than you are now."

Before anyone could speak, Cutter threw the jeep in gear, barked the tires and headed toward DeLong. For several moments we stared after him, saying nothing and listening as the gears changed.

"Nice guy, huh?" grunted Eve Howard.

"He usually is," I said. "He just has a real blind spot."

"For what? White folks with black friends?"

"No. For, uh, for –"

"Cripples?" Miss Carter asked softly.

I looked at her, at the handles of the wheelchair poking up behind the car seat, and back at her. I started not to answer, then considered lying, but decided there was no point denying the obvious to my new boss. "Yes, ma'am," was all I said. It was all I needed to say.

Chapter 2

༄

In DeLong, Highway 27 swung slightly east, away from the Cattahatchie, and kept to a shallow valley. Sitting on a long ridge to the east were DeLong's elementary and middle schools, and the county's only high school — for white kids, that is. Behind it, the big antebellum and Victorian houses of Hill Street looked down on the rest of town, including the plateau directly above the river where the courthouse stood, surrounded by faded brick storefronts.

I took one turn around the square to see if any of our friends were sleeping it off in the parking lot beside the Rebel Theater. None were, which was unusual. I turned down the hill at Commerce Street and went the one block to River Street, where The Cotton Café overlooked the Cattahatchie. A string of cotton warehouses painted green or red, tin grain silos and the depot for Weathers-McLain Trucking Company lined the other side of the river and mostly screened "Roseville" from view by the town's white residents. There the unpaved streets nearly were devoid of trees, cut for building material and burned for firewood long ago. But from spring to late fall, the place was overflowing with wild roses of every type and color, planted there in the 1890s by the women of the DeLong Garden Club in an effort to "brighten the lives of the unfortunate." While the plants had added lively hues to the mostly dilapidated neighborhood, over the decades they had bred and mixed and tangled to create a sea of thorns on nearly any plot of land larger than a gravesite. Nonetheless, blacks maintained their small businesses, clapboard churches, low-slung schools and street row of shotgun-style houses. All were roofed in tin that was rusting away in myriad shades of weather-worn disrepair. And for most of us — that is to say, those of us born with white skin — Roseville nearly was as distant as the spot on the moon where Apollo XI was scheduled to land later in the month.

As soon as I turned my truck onto River Street I knew something was up, and that it probably wasn't good. Sheriff Floyd Johnson's unmarked cruiser was parked behind a row of Cadillacs, Buicks and new pickups – its red dash light flashing.

I parked and got out of my old truck and stomped as much mud as I could off my only pair of good shoes. The twenty Miss Carter gave me would have to go for a new pair of oxblood penny loafers at Handley's Department Store up on the square. As it was, I'd have to hustle back home and get my tennis shoes and some clean socks. Patti and the rest of the MacAllisters would not look favorably on tennis shoes in the grand sanctuary of First Denomination, but after my Good Samaritan efforts it was tennis shoes, work boots or barefoot.

Stomping around some more I noticed that one of the vehicles was the spotless Chevy pickup former Governor Weathers had been driving around town for the last eleven months. Weathers had a deal with Kamp Motors. Each August, he got the very first pickup of the new model year that came onto the lot. And always in white, with a red interior.

"The ol' Guv, he thinks he's keepin' 'the common touch' by drivin' a pickup around town," Daddy once said. "Ever'body knows he does his Memphis business and visits his fancy Delta planter friends in a chauffeur-driven Rolls. But that's like puttin' a dirt clod in a velvet sack. It's still just a dirt clod."

When I pushed through the double glass doors into the air-conditioned comfort of The Cotton Café, it was as if someone had found the volume knob on the room and turned it down to a whisper. A hand or two raised to wave in my direction, and another few heads nodded my way, but no one spoke, not wanting to break the quiet that let them hear the bits of raised voices coming from the restaurant's side room.

Paula Simpson walked to the end of the counter. "Mornin', Nate," said Paula, whose family owned the café. She was in the same Cattahatchie High class with me and Cutter. On Sunday mornings, she worked the counter so her parents could sleep in one day a week.

"What's goin' on? How come everybody's bein' so quiet?"

"Big confab goin' on in the Rotary Club Room," she told me. "From what it sounds like, the Klan was out doin' their dirt last night. They burned a cross out by Willy Slater's Grocery."

"Klan, huh?" I said, wondering if some of the Klux could have been in the car that ran Miss Carter off the road.

"Yep. Seems like the hotter this summer gets, the busier and meaner they get."

"There must be two or three county supervisor cars out there. The mayor's Caddy. Seems like a big meetin' for –"

"The cross burnin' wasn't the worst of it," said Gary Williams, who was working on a plate of bacon and buttered grits on the stool closest to us. "I heard they shot up a bunch of houses out at Pickens Ferry, up on the Moccasin Slough."

"Is that right?"

"My cousin, Phil Ward – you know, he's a dispatcher down at the jail?" Gary went on as I nodded. "He talked to his daddy, Uncle Claude, this morning. And Uncle Claude told Aunt Ezzie, who told momma, that Sheriff Johnson came back to the jail hoppin' mad. That he called a whole covey of our civic leaders and told them they could meet here or in a jail cell."

"You think he's actually got something on 'em?" I asked.

Gary shrugged.

"Nate, you want coffee?" asked Paula, who played the flute in the CHS band.

"Sure. Have you seen Cutter?"

"Only in my dreams," she said, sighing theatrically. "But your stools are open. Say, Nate, how come Cutter don't date nobody from around these parts?"

It was a question I got on fairly regular basis and my answer was always the same. I shrugged. "I guess he hasn't found anybody around here he likes that way."

Paula leaned forward propping her elbows on the counter as she looked directly into my eyes. The top three buttons of her uniform top were open. I fought with limited success to keep my gaze from tumbling into the deep valley of her cleavage.

"If Cutter would give me half a chance, I bet I could make him like me," she said, and I felt the warmth rising in my neck and spreading into my cheeks. "I'd do anything," she said, running her tongue slowly around her lips. I felt a warmth and a stirring begin in the front of my pants. "Anything."

Paula Simpson held my gaze and a realized I'd stopped breathing.

"Miss Paula, could I get some coffee down here?" called John-Ned Renfro from down the counter.

"Sure thing, John-Ned," said Paula over her shoulder as she straightened. Then to me, "You tell Cutter I said that. Okay?"

I took a breath and cleared my throat. "Yep," I croaked, lifting the coffee cup to my lips as Paula turned away. I hoped she didn't notice that my hands were trembling.

Except for the clatter of plates and the sizzle of bacon frying, the main room of The Cotton remained quiet as the ten or so early Sunday morning regulars strained to hear what was going on behind the folding panels that closed off the back part of the dining area. We caught a word here or there from a raised voice, but mostly it was just a rumble. Like the time Daddy took me and Steve camping and canoeing up in Arkansas. You could hear the sound of rapids around a bend in the river before you ever saw them, and you knew there was trouble ahead. In DeLong, we'd been hearing the rumblings for a long time. I thought of what I'd just heard and what I'd seen this morning out on the highway and wondered if we finally were rounding the bend toward something dangerous and inescapable.

Floyd Johnson had been my father's boss when they were on the Memphis police force after World War II. Daddy had spent most of five years in Europe as a paratrooper with the famous 101st Airborne, and when he came back he had no desire to settle again on the farm. So, he got on with the Memphis P.D. and Lieutenant Johnson, who also had family roots in Cattahatchie County, took the young officer under his wing. Daddy proved to be a skilled and able officer, and quickly rose to the rank of detective sergeant. But Momma hated the city. She wanted to be back closer to "her people" in Cattahatchie County. When Grandpa Wallace's health failed in '52 and he could no longer handle the farm, Momma talked Daddy into moving back and taking it over. So, my father watched the detective shows flicker across our black-and-white TV screen, regret in his eyes but never on his lips, because Momma was happy. More than anything else in this world, that's what had mattered most to Billy Wallace. I think that hurt Daddy as much as Steve's death itself. The day the grim-faced Army sergeant turned into our driveway, the light went out of Momma's eyes and no matter his best efforts, Daddy never was able to make it shine again.

I sniffled and wiped my nose with a napkin. Why I was thinking about that, I wasn't sure. Sometimes thoughts of Momma and Steve, and by extension Daddy, just came on me that way.

In any case, when Captain Johnson retired from the Memphis police in '61, he moved back to Cattahatchie County. He opened a bait shop and boat dock on the river south of town. When Sheriff Moore decided not to run again in '65, Floyd Johnson defeated Governor Weathers' hand-picked candidate, Highway Patrol Sergeant J.D. Benoit, by sixty-one votes.

Sheriff Johnson had developed a reputation for relatively fair treatment for poor white folks and even blacks, but he wasn't naive. Thanks to systematic intimidation by the Klan and government officials high and low, less than three percent of the county's black population voted. The power in the county resided on Hill Street and out at Chalmette Plantation, and it was all white.

The phone rang on the wall behind the counter. Paula picked it up, listened for a moment and said, "I'll tell him right away."

She went to the sliding panel and cracked it open. "Sheriff, Doctor Garner just called. He said the little Hayes girl is ready to go."

"Thank you, Paula," said the sheriff as he came out, pushing open the partition.

Inside the room were a dozen of the county's most prominent citizens, including Tom Carter and Brother MacAllister, my future daddy-in-law, I hoped.

"Sheriff, where do you think you're going?" demanded Frank Powell, the president of the county board of supervisors.

"I'm going to lead the ambulance to Memphis."

"May I remind you that you're not authorized to take a county vehicle across state lines unless you're in hot pursuit," said County Prosecutor Jimmy Epps.

Floyd Johnson had been a frequent visitor in our home until Daddy took to drink so bad that we no longer had visitors. Sheriff Johnson was normally an even-tempered man, but his cheeks were flushed now, and I could see he was fighting to keep control. The sheriff took a deep breath and reset his gray fedora. "Funny, Jimmy, you didn't mention that last year," he said, "when your mother had her stroke, and I cleared the way right to the emergency room doors of Baptist Hospital."

Mr. Thomas cleared his throat. "Well, that was –"

"A white woman from a prominent family," said the sheriff. "I know. But let me tell you gentlemen something. I've looked the other way while your bunch has marched around in your bed sheets and burned your crosses, because that's the way it's always been here. But I'm warning you, setting fire to those two colored churches last month and now this? Shooting into occupied homes with automatic weapons?

"It's only pure, dumb luck your thugs didn't kill somebody up there at Pickens' Ferry. As it is, Dr. Garner says Roy Hayes' little girl may lose her sight from the flying glass. If she does, I intend to put somebody's ass in Parchman Prison. And it may be more than one.

"Mr. Bradshaw ... Mr. Hadley ... *Governor* Weathers," he said, fixing each man with his gaze, "you better get those hooded clowns under control. If you don't, I will."

Sheriff Johnson stormed out and most of those who had been in the side room did the same. Suddenly, Brother Mac was standing over me, looking down at my shoes. "I hope you're not planning to come to church like that."

"Uhh, no, sir," I told him, standing. "I was going to go home and –"

"Those shoes are ruined and you smell like river muck. What have you been up to?"

I hated to tell him the truth. T.L. "Tom" Carter IV was a deacon at First Denomination and his wife, Mary Nell, taught the Young Teen Girls Sunday school class. As far as Brother Mac and his flock were concerned, Holly Lee Carter had somehow stolen the newspaper from Tom with the help of the "integrationist race-mixers." But if Miss Carter reported the morning's bumping and grinding to the sheriff, the whole town would know the details soon enough.

"Miss Carter," I said. "She's back. Somebody ran her off in the ditch down by Yancy Creek."

"Huh!" he snorted. "Holly Lee Carter is a well-known liar, harlot and consumer of spirits. I would proffer that it is a great deal more likely that she was simply imbibing alcohol and ran off in the ditch."

I started to tell him I'd seen the whole thing, but there was no point.

"Still, I suppose I can't chastise you for being a Good Samaritan. Especially considering her invalid condition."

Invalid condition? I thought of the curves under Holly Lee Carter's overalls, those eyes and the way she'd handled that big car in the ditch, but there was nothing to be gained by mentioning my observations. Brother Mac was going on – "In fact, Nate, I continue to have deep reservations about you staying on at *The Current-Leader*. Satan can take on many guises, and that of a Jezebel can be among his most dangerous."

"Yes, sir. I know! But like you say, she is an invalid now. And I promise, I'm gonna be on my guard every minute," I reassured. "Anyway, I'm just a part-time sportswriter. I report to Mr. Rainy, the sports editor. I hardly ever even spoke to Mr. Carter. I'm sure it'll be the same with her."

"We'll see. Now you better get on home and change your shoes. Shall we go?"

When we walked out the front door, Cutter was angling into a parking spot across the street. "Brother Mac, I need to speak to Cutter for a minute."

He looked down his nose in the direction of the jeep. "Very well, Nate, but I expect you to be in your Sunday school room on time."

"Yes, sir. I –"

"And, Nate, don't forget, goal posts are no substitute for the cross."

"Nope. No, sir. I sure won't forget."

How could I? I wondered. It was one of C.E. MacAllister's favorite catch phrases and I'd heard it at least a hundred times.

"This whole town's just too football crazy," he repeated. I'd heard all this many times as well. "This county has put that boy on a pedestal, like an idol, like a golden calf. But you mark my word, his feet are made of clay, and one of these days they'll crumble."

Cutter was a sore subject between me and Patti and her daddy. When I made no response, Brother Mac headed for his new Mercury and drove away. I crossed the street. "Where've you been?"

"I pulled down Convict Road and changed clothes behind that big stand of oaks. What was Brother Daddy doing here of a Sunday mornin'?" he asked, teasing me about my would-be father-in-law.

Cutter propped against the Jeep and listened as I related, like the good reporter I hoped to someday be, everything I'd seen and heard inside the café. Every ugly and exciting and worrisome detail. As was his way, Cutter let me talk, taking it all in and saying nothing.

"So, what do you think?" I prodded as Cutter walked to the back of the Jeep and began unlocking the metal footlocker bolted into the bed.

"I think you need new shoes."

"Shoes? I'm not talking about shoes. What do you think about what the Klux're up to? You think it was them that run Miss Carter off the road?"

"I don't think about it one way or another. Mainly, I think it's not my fight," he said, keying the trunk's padlock and sliding it out of the eyelet. "I'm not a politician or preacher. And I'm not a policeman. I'm just a guy who plays football and tends a little bar."

"But – "

He pushed up the trunk lid and pulled free from an elastic strap a set of new black cowboy boots with white stitching and silver toe caps. "Here," he said, handing them to me. "They're too small for me. But you might get some wear out of 'em. I'd planned to pass 'em on the next time you dropped by camp, but it looks like you could use 'em now."

"Wow!" I sighed, smelling the fresh leather. "Where'd they come from?"

"I stopped in the Cone & Cream the other night for a milkshake, and they were on the seat when I came out."

Such unexpected and unrequested offerings had become part of his life. And though I knew he understood it at some level the way the town – the whole county, really – had adopted him since he left home, he never grew comfortable with the odd way in which his Jeep often was treated like a four-wheeled shrine by football-worshipping pilgrims. Their gifts usually had more significance to the giver than to Cutter, but he accepted them in the spirit of mysterious dignity with which they were offered.

A watch, waterproof.

Pies of all sorts, and cakes with every flavor of frosting.

A box of rubbers – 200 count.

A mask and snorkel.

Boxes of shotgun shells.

A black-trimmed wallet with "Cutter #13" sculpted into the tan hide.

Pocket knives were popular.

Bushels of butter beans and black-eyed peas.

Several hand-made fishing lures and a number that weren't.

Gallon cans stacked with fresh peaches.

Watermelons appeared so regularly we'd taken to calling them "jeep eggs." We didn't call the steaks anything but "great" each time a Styrofoam ice chest showed up loaded with T-bones, top sirloins and rib-eyes.

Bottles of good bonded liquor, a limitless amount of homebrew and cases of beer appeared to help wash down the meals. Six-packs of Coke came, too.

Several Bibles.

Four pages from a Baptist hymnal.

A worn-out collar for a dog named Jess.

Tickets to various college sports events and Memphis concerts.

A nice ratchet set.

Then there were the rolls of cash that sometimes materialized under the seats.

All of it was left more or less anonymously, except for lingerie that often had a phone number written in the crotch or cup.

And there were more odds and ends that Cutter mostly passed along to teammates. I worked out as a scrawny third-string wide receiver on a Cattahatchie Wolves team that had only two real strings. On football Friday nights, all I ever caught was the clipboard Coach Pearce tossed my way. But I was Cutter's best friend.

In any case, he could keep only so much tribute. Everything he owned had to fit into the old jeep he'd rebuilt from the ground up. And it did.

On the back bumper, I sat and slipped off my ruined penny loafers. Cutter tossed me a pair of white athletic socks.

"You comin' out to the camp tonight?" he asked. "Me and Dodge are gonna throw some steaks on the fire."

"Sounds good. I'd love to. But me and Patti have practice for the youth choir until eight. I'm hopin' Brother Daddy'll let us go ridin' around for a while after."

"Out Palmer Road? To that little cutback behind Josh Knowles' barn?"

I felt my cheeks flush a little pink. "If I'm lucky," I said as I pulled the second boot on and stood. "Nice! These are beauties. Thanks."

"I'm glad to see somebody get some use –"

Cutter snapped the phrase off in mid-sentence like an icicle breaking under its own weight. His lips tightened and his gaze was as easy to follow as a strand of cold barbed wire. Cutter's father, Tony Carlucci, was turning onto River Street. He was in the passenger seat of a green Ford sedan driven by Highway Patrolman J.D. Benoit.

The car slowed to a crawl before approaching in the narrow street. My friend's body tensed then uncoiled in the same way it did just before kickoff. Cutter stepped to the driver's side of the jeep and popped his shotgun from its dashboard mount and laid it across the seats. "Nate, step back," he said, but I was frozen in my new boots.

"They're probably just looking for Weathers," I offered, my voice suddenly brittle with a charge of nervous adrenalin.

Benoit was the ex-governor's state-provided bodyguard and Cutter's father ran the machine shop that took care of all the trucks, tractors and various other pieces of motorized equipment on Weathers' sprawling farm west of town. He and Weathers had been war buddies down on the Gulf Coast where Tony was sent to recuperate after losing his leg when his B-17 bomber was shot down over Holland. At least, that was the story told by the former prizefighter and street thug raised here and there but mostly near the Philadelphia docks. Cecil Weathers had been a major in charge of a supply depot in Gulfport, and rumor had it that Carlucci and Weathers did some shady dealing with the New Orleans mob involving spare auto parts that should have gone to the war effort in Europe. Nothing was ever proven, and in 1946 Tony arrived in DeLong on the heels of Weathers and a young and trusting nurse's aid named Jennifer Ambrose Cutter. Tony went to work supervising Chalmette's big machine shop and, some said, as an enforcer of Weathers' will among the dozens of black sharecroppers and poor white sawmill and gin workers who earned a living on the big farm. It was a meager living to be sure, and Weathers intended to make sure it stayed that way. Less for them, more for him, and for old Senator DeLong, while he was still alive, which he wasn't for long after Weathers returned from his military service. In '47, a starry-eyed, I-know-I-can-redeem-him Jennifer Cutter defied her family's most strident objections and eloped to Memphis to become Mrs. Anthony J. Carlucci. Now the son produced by that union stared into the car as his father and Benoit passed by slowly.

"Don't stop," Cutter warned Benoit, his hand on the twelve-gauge in the jeep.

This was a battle that had been brewing since the first punch Cutter ever could remember seeing his barrel-chested, hammer-handed father deliver to Cutter's 105-pound mother. He told me once, his eyes bright with moonshine, that it had been a right hook and that he'd heard his mother's rib crack. By Cutter's recollection, that was at least a decade and a half ago.

Tony stared straight ahead, refusing to look his son's way. Benoit sneered and thumped his cigarette butt at Cutter's feet. But he didn't stop.

Cutter warily followed the sedan's progress along River Street until it turned right onto Commerce, allowing us a view of the passenger side. I shook my head as the adrenalin stiffness drained out of my muscles. Their arrogance was at once astonishing and unsurprising, driving the vehicle through the middle of town, its side dented and scraped and streaked with baby blue paint. They thought they were invincible, untouchable – protected by Weathers' vast wealth and political clout, and embraced by the Invisible Empire of the Klan. The truth I had learned growing up in Cattahatchie County, the truth I knew in that moment was that they probably were right.

Chapter 3

∾

Holly Lee Carter crossed the old iron bridge north of DeLong without slowing down any more than the sharp curve and steep hill on the west side demanded. It was the spot on Blue Mountain Road where her father's car had gone into the river. But she couldn't allow herself to think about that now. She kept her eyes straight ahead, glad to be getting close to Wolf's Run. It was the place where she had spent many happy weekends and summer days before finally moving in with her grandmother a few weeks shy of her fifteenth birthday. Even during the pain, anger, confusion and chaos of Holly's high school years, Wolf's Run was a refuge because Meemaw Lois filled it with so much music, life … and love.

No longer the rich, reckless girl in the white Corvette, Holly took the turns carefully on the unrailed switchback road that climbed the face of Blue Mountain in an S. Her muscles ached with fatigue and her arms were like weights on the big steering wheel and the hand controls, but her pulse still was strumming in her neck after the near disastrous encounter on the highway.

By the standards of California and many other places with a more craggy geography, Blue Mountain would not be a mountain at all – more like a big hill. But at 746 feet, it was the second highest point in Mississippi. It was called Blue Mountain because of the gas released by the tens of thousands of pines that grew on and around it. When the setting sun struck the gas just right, it created a blue halo over the mountain. On a plateau three-hundred feet above the river, Wolf's Run was cupped in the palm of two enormous limestone hands gloved in wild grape and kudzu vine.

Holly turned off the gravel road between two leaning brick posts that anchored a wooden fence badly in need of whitewashing. Under a canopy of big pines, maples and pecans, the driveway sloped down to a U-shaped clapboard house with a steep tin roof and a wrap-around porch. There were long rust stains here and there on the roof and the whole place needed fresh paint. Off to one side was a brick building that served as a garage and past it a dilapidated greenhouse. Many of the panes were broken out of the glass walls and roof and what plants remained were running wild.

Charlie was standing up in Eve's lap and looking around. "It needs some work, but it is beautiful," said Eve. "I might even call it 'idyllic' if I didn't know it was built by slaves. Maybe even my own blood."

"It is what it is, Eve. You knew that when you asked if you could come with me and help. Don't start in on me now," said Holly. "I've got enough on my mind without you layin' the old-Southern-family guilt trip on me."

Eve looked at her teacher, mentor and friend. "Yez'zum, Miz Holly. I'z mighty sorry, Miz Holly."

"Stop it!" Holly said more sharply than she intended. Her nerves and Eve's were frayed and sparking like electrical wire scraped down to the copper by three days on the road and the two-man welcoming committee that had fallen in behind them at the county line.

Eve opened the door and stepped out, arching her back and stretching. Charlie hopped down into the pea gravel and began sniffing everything in sight. "I guess we're both still shook up about what happened out on the road," offered Eve. "You drove most of the night. You have to be exhausted."

"I guess I am, but that's not it."

"So clue me in?"

"What do you see?" asked Holly but didn't wait for a reply. "More precisely, what don't you see?" Eve looked around, shrugged. "You don't see any ramps up to the house or any of the walkways I asked Tom to have installed in the yard."

Eve slumped back into the car seat. "Crap," she sighed. Then put into words what Holly was trying not to think about. "It's almost like he didn't expect you to get here," she said. "When you called your brother from San Antonio, I heard you tell him we were going to drive all night. That we'd be here early this morning.

"That's why you didn't want to report what happened to the police, isn't it?"

"No," she said but there was little conviction in her voice. "Tom could have casually mentioned it to any number of people, and before you know it, everyone in town would have known. Or it could have just been bad luck. A white woman and black woman traveling together in a big car at night? It would have been enough for a couple of Ku Klux liquored up and looking for an excuse for meanness."

Eve groaned. "You don't really believe that, do you?"

For the first time since the green sedan fell in behind them during the last minutes of the night, Holly looked rattled. Her chin quivered, she sobbed and a tear slipped from behind her sunglasses. "I have to believe it," Holly told her. "The Carlucci kid is right. I'm *not* wanted here. Not by anyone. Least of all, my own brother. I guess I'd hoped –" Holly wiped her nose on the sleeve of her T-shirt. "I've wished a hundred times that Mr. Burke and Reverend Clemmer had never shown up at the hospital. Never asked me to pray about my decision.

"Why God worked on my heart to bring me back here, I don't know. I wish He hadn't. We nearly got *killed* out there!"

Eve reached across the seat and rested a hand on her friend's shoulder. "But we didn't," she comforted, gently kneading her friend's taut muscles. "You were great. You kept your cool. Mario Andretti couldn't have done any better."

Holly laughed softly, sniffing back more tears.

"And we are here," said Eve, looking around at the grounds and the house. "Now all we have to do is figure out how to get you inside. Those steps are steep. I doubt I can get you up them in your chair."

"I know," said Holly, putting the car in gear and wheeling around the gravel circle that surrounded a disused fountain and planting area in front of the house. "When Grandma Lois was alive, this spot was filled with flowers. She started them in the greenhouse and then moved them here."

"I'm sure it was beautiful," said Eve.

"Back then Wolf's Run was so full of life," said Holly as she stopped with the driver's door as close to the front steps as she could get it. "Grandma Lois was amazing. She could play piano and organ. There was always music in the air.

"At one time or another, Lois Carter was president of every woman's civic or church group in the county. So people were always in and out of the house. She was like sunlight in a bottle. Everyone wanted to be around her. And she loved this place so much."

"I can see why," agreed Eve. "But – you know, I never thought to ask – why is it called Wolf's Run?"

Holly swung her door open and Eve came around. "Get me under my arms, and ease me down. Okay?"

Eve came around and hooked her arms under Holly's. "Ready. One, two …"

"Three," they said together as Eve lifted Holly off the seat and sat her in the driveway next to the steps. Holly propped on her hands and Charlie ran over to lie in the tiny gravel beside her. She stroked Charlie's head. After a moment, the little dog rolled onto its back and offered its pink-and-black belly in an act of pure love, complete submission and absolute trust. Holly scratched it and Charlie actually seemed to smile.

"Let me get your chair set up on the porch," said Eve, swinging open the dented back door of the Lincoln convertible. Eve shoved the displaced luggage out of the way and propped a guitar case against the back fender. Holly studied the scabs of green paint that streaked the Lincoln's baby blue paint job and eyed a variety of dents, but said nothing. The car still ran; the doors still opened. A few dents and scraped paint were the least of her worries. She bit her lip. No matter how Holly tried to play it off to Eve, or to herself, it was true – *they'd nearly been killed!*

Eve unfolded the wheelchair on the porch and placed a special cushion in the seat as Holly tried to refocus, tried to push that dreadful reality from the front of her thoughts. "It's called Wolf's Run," she said, "because when my ancestors built their first rough cabin on this plateau in the eighteen-twenties, there were loads of black bear, fox, deer, bobcat and wolves all through these hills. There was a trail – well, there still is a trail, very steep and narrow, that leads down the cliff face to the river.

"Packs of wolves used to come running through here on the way to that trail, and the name stuck."

"Makes sense. Chair's ready."

Holly reached behind her and lifted her hips onto the first step, then the next and the next.

"So are there still wolves around here?" asked Eve as she held open the screen door.

"No. Unfortunately, they and the rest of the big game – bear and such – were hunted out by the nineteen-thirties," said Holly, lifting her hips onto the porch, her long legs trailing, the heels of her leather moccasins dragging.

Holly rested on her arms, looking at the sprawl of yard rising up to the road. A breeze stirred the leaves of the nearby pecan trees as Charlie scampered onto the porch and began a thorough investigation. "I swore I would never come *crawling* back to DeLong. Never! But look at me now."

Eve eyed her with hands on hips. "Girl, you're not crawling. You're scooting. There's a difference."

Holly smiled at her friend, aide and protégé, glad to have Eve and her sense of perspective and humor nearby. "Now I remember why I asked you to come on this adventure, this mission, this odyssey, this – fool's errand? I just hope I haven't gotten you into something that – well, that –"

"Holly, I'm not a child. I've been a big girl for awhile now. I came here for you, yes. But you know I came for my own reasons, too. So, let it go," she gently told her. "I'm here and I'm staying."

Holly smiled, nodded. "Okay, 'big girl'. Help me get my big butt into my chair before I end up with a row of splinters in my backside."

Chapter 4

❧

Once inside, Holly felt almost like a little girl again. Pushing through Wolf's Run in her wheelchair, she was about the height she was when she went running through the house at age eight or so. Countertops, cabinets, furniture, a multitude of pictures, the fireplace mantels, even the beds were as she remembered them at that age. The twelve-foot ceilings, coupled with exhaustion, made her feel as small and fragile as she had back then. The year her mother left.

Holly had chosen Grandma Lois' bedroom because it was the only one in the house with a bathroom large enough that she could maneuver her wheelchair. It also had a massive claw-foot tub in which her grandmother would take her bubble baths surrounded by candles, the voice of Frank Sinatra or Nat King Cole crooning from a nearby record player. Sometimes she'd pull Holly in with her. Clothes and all. Holly smiled at the memory as she ran her hand along the edge of the tub. But of more importance now, the tub was of a height that would allow Holly to easily transfer into it from her wheelchair. Those were the sort of practical considerations that had become a part of Holly's everyday, even moment-to-moment thinking since Ia Drang.

Grandma Lois' bedroom also held the most good memories. Memories of snuggling together under blankets in the big four-poster bed and watching snow fall on winter mornings. Sitting together in front of the fireplace as corn kernels popped inside a metal basket. Propping with her guitar on the sill of the open eight-foot windows on summer nights and quietly picking out chords while her grandmother reclined in a La-Z-Boy reading her Bible. Grandma Lois knew Holly had a wild and angry side, but never judged or condemned. Unlike many in town who gossiped about Holly and occasionally dared to whisper their complaints and concerns in Lois Carter's ear.

Grandma Carter's standard response was, "I *know* that Holly's heart belongs to the Lord, and that's all I need to know."

To Holly, she would say, "We all have our share of rough roads to go down. Sometimes those roads lead through dark places in this world. And to dark places in our heart. Sometimes we have to go through those dark places to learn the lesson that we need to learn in order to grow closer to the Lord. All I can do is pray that the Lord will guide you safely back to the light in His own good time."

Sometimes Holly would talk with her grandmother about her runaway mother.

Veronique Dupre of New Orleans and Grandma Lois had been very close. It shocked and hurt Lois Carter terribly when "Miss Vee" disappeared. In fact, Holly's grandmother had kept in place at Wolf's Run a large portrait of her daughter-in-law. As Holly's body began to show its curves, her lips gained their full shape and her hair took on a glow like that of smoldering fire, the resemblance between the woman in the picture and her daughter became striking – almost eerie. After a time, Holly had come to accept that her very appearance was painful to her father. When she was fourteen she'd tried changing her hair style, cutting it short and dying it blonde. Thinking, perhaps, if she didn't look so much like her mother … but T.L. Carter only ridiculed her effort. So, it was better if they saw each other as little as possible. That's when she left the house in DeLong and moved, full time, to Wolf's Run.

Through the long series of French doors that formed the interior hallway of the house, Holly saw Eve standing on the porch that wrapped around the slate-covered courtyard. She pushed through an open set of doors.

"Malibu's got nothing on this," Eve said without looking Holly's way. "This is some view!"

From the porch they could see for miles down and across the Cattahatchie Valley. Holly's eyes followed the golden-brown curve of the river sparkling in the morning light and the emerald quilt of the summer crops that spread away from its steep banks. To the east were the Tennessee & Gulf Railroad tracks and Highway 27, and beyond that a long row of green, thickly wooded hills.

"I'd almost forgotten how beautiful it is," said Holly, resting her arms on the railing as Charlie explored the porch. "At night, off in the distance, you can see the glow from town. But there's not much man-made light out this way, so the stars are amazing. And the moon? Sometimes it looks as if it'll fill the entire valley."

Holly smiled at the memory, then slowly let her eyes refocus closer in. The two arms of Wolf's Run embraced a large stone fountain that was clogged with leaves from the previous fall. Perhaps several previous falls. The same was true of the thirty-foot-long pool near the patio's edge. It was one of only three in-ground swimming pools in the county. Lois Carter had it put in during the late forties after she began suffering with arthritis in her knees and ankles. Now its walls were stained black with algae and only a few swampy inches of green water stank in the deep end.

"It would be nice to have dinner over there on the edge, by the pool," said Eve.

"It will be nice as soon as I can get a pool service from Memphis to come down here and clean out that mosquito pit," said Holly. "That's something else I asked Tom to please call about." She was both hurt and angry by the way in which her brother had apparently ignored her simple requests. And if he had sent those thugs after her ... *No!* ... She wasn't going to think that.

"Is your room all right?"

"It's great. It's just, well, not quite like I pictured it."

"Not like in *Gone with the Wind,* huh? Well, Wolf's Run really is a glorified hunting lodge that's been added onto for the last hundred and thirty years," said Holly. "To get the 'Tara effect,' you've got to visit the top of Hill Street in DeLong or visit Governor Weathers' fiefdom, Chalmette Plantation. Ex-Governor Weathers, I should say."

Eve walked around the porch and propped on the rail next to Holly. "Well, Wolf's Run may not have the big white columns out front, but it's certainly a mansion compared to some of the places we saw on the road. Like that place we passed on the right, before we got to the river. Rusty tin roof. Hasn't been painted in my lifetime. The whole place leans. To think that people have to live that way just because of the color of their skin," Eve said angrily, shaking her head. "I just – I guess I don't understand you people."

"Eve, I love you as a friend. But growing up in the Malibu Colony with both your parents in TV – well, it allows you to make some pretty easy assumptions."

"What's that supposed to mean?"

"Look, there is no doubt that a lot of black folks here – for a lack of education or jobs or opportunity – live in deplorable conditions. But, sadly, there's plenty of poverty here to go around. Don't assume it's limited to black people. For instance, that house you're talking about is the one Cutter Carlucci grew up in."

Eve stared at her. "You're kidding! Mr. Mean-and-Handsome?"

"Yes. Although it could have been different for the Carluccis. Their poverty is of their own making. Or, at least, the making of Cutter's father, Tony," Holly explained. "That old farmhouse and hundreds of acres around it were Jennifer Cutter's inheritance from the Ambrose side of her family. In this part of the world, that much land is worth a small fortune. Unfortunately, Tony Carlucci is a drunk and a womanizer. And a gambler. Not to mention a wife-beater and leg-breaker for Weathers.

"Anyway, to pay for his habits, Tony has been selling off the Ambrose acreage here and there since I was a girl."

Eve cocked her head to one side. "How do you possibly know all that?"

Holly thought of MeeMaw Lois. "A very wise woman once told me, 'At one time or another in Cattahatchie County we've all seen each other's underwear hanging out on the clothes line. Holes and all. There are no secrets here, only lies we live with'."

Eve studied Holly for a moment. "What lies are you living with?"

Holly drew in a long breath as she looked out onto the disused courtyard and the valley, and then at the old house surrounding her. "I wish I knew," she said. Then, pivoting her wheelchair – "Come on. Let me show you the rest of the house."

There was a formal dining room with a twelve-place table hewn from one of the giant maples that once stood on the property. Grandma Carter's dinner parties were legendary from Memphis to Tupelo and from Oxford over to Iuka, and invitations were much sought-after. Into the late nineteen-forties and for a hundred years before, candidates for governor and senator, and even a handful of would-be presidents, had dined at that table while seeking the blessing of *The Current-Leader*, Holly explained.

"This was my room," she said as they reached the corner where the north wing almost pushed up against the limestone ridge. She opened the door and felt her breath catch. The room was empty except for three cardboard boxes lined up under the window that faced onto the front yard. The wallpaper, which had been a sunny yellow with pink-and-baby blue flowers of indeterminate genus, was whitewashed over. Dozens of large white drops and hundreds of smaller drips speckled the heart pine floor and roller marks stained the tongue-in-groove ceiling. Holly pushed over the threshold and looked at the white shoe-prints scattered here and there.

"Looks like Daddy didn't waste any time erasing me from Wolf's Run," she said, studying the room. "He didn't even bother with a drop cloth."

Holly flipped open the lid of one of the boxes and on top was an eight-by-ten photo of her dancing with a young man at some long-forgotten party. He was in tails and she was wearing a green satin formal, with white gloves that stretched above her elbows. Her high heels made her slightly taller than her date. She recognized the ballroom at the Peabody Hotel in Memphis, but there had been so many parties and dates, and so many satin formals. She turned and opened the door in the corner. Her closet once had been filled with them. Now it was empty. Nothing of the girl she had been remained.

Eve felt for her friend. Their emotions already were raw from what had happened on the road. She said, "People change. Don't forget, in the end your father wanted you to have this place and the newspaper."

"Yes, well, it's yet to be seen whether that was Daddy's final gift to me, or his final punishment," said Holly, crossing the room and pushing past Eve and into the hall.

Holly moved quickly past several guest rooms and a shared bath that she nodded to but didn't bother to open. This stroll – no, *roll*, she reminded herself – down memory lane was quickly becoming more painful and wearisome than she was ready to deal with. Whatever reserves of adrenaline she'd had were tapped dry playing demolition derby with the Ford. All she wanted to do was to climb into Grandma Lois's bed and sleep … sleep until she felt strong again. Until she felt able to face Tom and Mary Nell and the many *Current-Leader* employees who would see her as a usurper. Until she was ready to deal with the redneck politicians, advertisers and so-called "good ol' boys" who would resent a woman running the county's only news-paper. Until she felt strong enough to face others who would figure that since her legs were paralyzed, her brain also must be impaired. And still others, like Cutter Carlucci, who would assume that because she used a wheelchair she would be an angry, manipulative sympathy junkie – like his father.

Near the end of the hall, Holly grabbed a set of brass handles and pushed open a set of double doors.

"This is the library," she said pushing into the home's largest room. A catacomb of bookshelves and picture nooks flowed away from a sprawling fieldstone fireplace and wrapped around three walls, from the room's floor to the edge of its eighteen-foot ceiling. The head of a snarling wolf was mounted over the fireplace. Several deer heads and that of a boar and black bear looked down as well. The furniture was dark and heavy, a testament to leather and testoster-one. There was a felt-top card table in the center of the room. At one end was an antique billiard table and behind that a ten-slot gun case fully loaded with shotguns and rifles. At the other end of the long room, a window at least ten-feet wide arched from floor to ceiling. A chess table with jade pieces ornately carved in an Asian style sat in front of the window along with two chairs. A large telescope stood to one side.

"Wow! This is – impressive," said Eve, crossing past the sofa to the window. She checked the panoramic view of valley. The room almost hung over the bluff and Eve took a quick step back. "Impres-sive, even if a tad spooky," she added, motioning to the animal heads.

"They take a little getting used to. I used to have names for all of them," said Holly. "But it's all part of the house's history. Back to when it really was a hunting lodge."

Eve crossed the room and rolled a ball the length of the billiard table. It silently kissed the rail and stopped. "Nice. Now I see how you became such a pool shark."

Holly pushed over and ran her hand along the perfect surface. "The lessons MeeMaw Lois taught me on this table kept me from going hungry more than once when I first got to L.A."

Holly smiled vaguely at the memory but Eve saw that her friend's eyes were fixed on one of the few empty spots on the room's walls. The space to the right of the fireplace was about three feet by four feet. "Is something wrong?"

"My mother's portrait," Holly told her. "That's where it always hung."

"You've told me that your parents' split wasn't exactly on friendly terms. When you dad moved back up here, he probably took it down. Or burned it."

Holly seemed lost in thought, then – "You'd think that. But no. In one of Daddy's last letters to me he wrote that he could hear 'a cold spring rain pecking at the library window.' That he was sitting beside this fireplace, looking at mother's portrait and wondering how different all our lives might be had she not – not …"

Eve could see how hard this was on Holly and she didn't let the moment linger. "Maybe your brother took it," she suggested.

Holly bit her lip. It was a natural thing to say for someone who did not know Tom. If anyone held more resentment for Veronique Carter than her jilted husband, it was her son. In the late nineteen-forties and early fifties, runaway wives and divorce were uncommon and frowned upon, especially in the Bible Belt South. Grandma Lois had protected Holly from the worst of the gossip, but as a teenager and then university student, Tom was forced to deal with the full weight of the social stigma. Had Mary Nell Poindexter, of the grand ol' Vicksburg Poindexters, not gotten pregnant while she and Tom were dating, she never would have married into "a family with a history of instability" – as she often reminded her husband. "But I shouldn't be surprised. Newspaper printers are little better than tradespeople."

Holly smiled at the memory in spite of herself. Mary Nell's pretentious ways would be comical if they weren't so hurtful to Tom, and so poisonous to their son and daughter. Holly's nephew and niece.

Lies we live with, thought Holly as she pushed over to the wall. She touched the spot on the dark wood paneling where the portrait had hung. Like her mother, it was simply gone.

"I guess I'll add this to my list of things to ask Tom about," she said, not wanting to get into the serpentine intricacies of Carter family dynamics. Then, "Come on. Let's get unpacked. I'm dying for a bath," she said as she pushed close behind the huge sofa on the way to the door. A crunching sound under her left tire caused her to stop, pivot. "*Shhh*-ooot! What was that?"

Eve and Holly saw a circular piece of glass now fractured into dozens of pieces. "Go through that door over there," said Holly, pointing to a corner of the room. "That hall connects to the bedroom my father was using. There's a bathroom and closet on the right. There might be a broom and dust pan in one of them."

While Eve searched, Holly studied the bright fragments against the hardwood floor. The glass from a small picture frame, maybe? But it seemed too thick for that. Maybe part of a broken whiskey glass?

"Found them," said Eve, returning. She squatted beside Holly and swept the fragments into a dust pan and headed for the waste basket she saw beside the door.

"No, wait!" said Holly as Eve prepared to dump the pan. "I saw some envelopes in the desk there by the window. Put it in one of those."

Eve cocked her hip and stared at her friend. "I beg your pardon?"

"Please."

"Why?"

"I don't know." It was the truth, and the only answer Holly had. "But, please, just humor me."

"Okay," said Eve, crossing the room. She pulled an envelope from a cubbyhole next to the typewriter on a secretary built into the wall. "But my brother is right. White women *are* crazy!"

Chapter 5

❧

Most people would say Cutter and I grew up rough, just tumbling toward manhood with little direction or notion of when or where our wheels would stop. Like many of the thirty-one teenagers who played Wolves football during our previous 13-1 season, we spent the summer between our junior and senior years in the fields each weekday, and more, working hard in the relentless sun. At night we ringed our tubs with the day's sticky remnants, then picked up our dates and ringed the town square with our pickups and second- and third-hand cars.

At the center of the square was the three-story Cattahatchie County Courthouse. It was by far the largest public building in town, and we orbited it as regularly as planets able to turn at right angles around a yellow-brick sun. Circled it until we were dizzy, then parked on River Street and watched the river run, and commerce flow and the in-out tide of people through the doors of The Cotton Café. Some went in for Cokes and burgers before walking up the hill to the Rebel Theater on the square. We all went parking, and on weekends many of us went north, some twenty miles, just across the Tennessee line, to roadhouses on the main highways and whorehouses down dusty, unlit back roads.

Cutter, Dodge McDowell and I shared a problem in common, and perhaps it was what bonded our odd trio. We were without homes.

For Dodge and I there were structures – beams, brick and wood. Beds to call our own and soft places to put our heads. But to one degree or another, we already were making our decisions about which way to turn in life, for better or worse. Our parents had lost their interest, their will, their freedom, their minds or their lives – or some combination thereof. But since the smoke and lead and ear-ringing echo of a shotgun blast punctuated a final falling-out with his father, the only consistent roof Cutter had over his head was the tent he kept in his jeep. Dozens of families in football-mad Cattahatchie County gladly, gleefully, would have taken Cutter into their homes, but he preferred keeping to himself – sleeping wherever the wheels of his jeep stopped turning on any given night. His favorite place was a cleft in the rock of Blue Mountain. The spot was known locally as The Well.

Located off Blue Mountain Road, The Well was an artesian spring that boiled up from a limestone shelf hanging over the river a couple hundred yards north of the Old Iron Bridge. The spot, which was shaped like a set of huge stone jaws, would have been the most popular parking place in Cattahatchie County had it not been located at the end of a narrow, heavily rutted dirt road that snaked desperately along the river's edge where the bank fell away thirty feet into the water. Poor, most often drunken judgment, allowed the Cattahatchie to claim a car or two annually. But for those of us who chanced The Well often, it was a refuge as secure as a fortress – guarded, as it was, on three sides by the river, the current holding the rock outcrop in the crook of its twisted elbow. It was further screened by a curtain of languid willows and low, thorny brush that gave way around the rocky platform where Cutter made his camp. At the center of the space, the spring boiled in cold silence. The water stewed slowly in the teardrop-shaped pool before streaming away and tumbling over a cut in the stone lip. Depending on the time of the year and the depth of the Cattahatchie, the small waterfall formed a perfect, if horrifically bracing shower.

Summer twilight had just crossed over into full darkness when I rattled my pickup in behind Cutter's jeep. It was Wednesday night and I'd been to a prayer meeting at First Denomination with my girlfriend, Patti. Dodge McDowell and Cutter were propped by a fire built to the side of the well. Their hair and shorts were still wet from plunges into The Well – to cool off on a hot July night and to retrieve beer tossed in for chilling.

I looked down at two tin plates from Cutter's mess kit. All that was left was the T-bones from what looked to have been – three? no, four steaks – and the skins of four potatoes baked in the coals.

"They must have been good," I said.

"They were," said Dodge, who produced a long, slow belch to punctuate his culinary opinion.

"We're out of bakin' potatoes but there're two more steaks over there in that ice chest," said Cutter. "Throw one on the fire."

"Thanks. I will. Between gettin' my butt off the tractor and to church on time, I didn't get a chance to eat," I said, and lifted out a thick-sliced steak. I squatted and laid the meat on the metal grate resting atop a natural fire pit in the rock. "You should have heard Brother Mac tonight. Preachin' about DeLong being infiltrated by whores and race-mixers. Miss Carter comin' back to town sure has got him wound up."

"Nate, you cain't hardly tolerate Brother Mac as it is," said Dodge. "How you reckon you're gonna live with him as your preacher-in-law?"

I sat and pulled off the boots Cutter had given me and started unbuttoning my shirt. "It'll be different when me'n Patti go off to college. We won't be home much. I'm gonna get my journalism degree and she's gonna make a teacher. When we're finished, we're not comin' back to Cattahatchie County. There're good papers in New *Or*-leans and Miam-uh. Heck, maybe we'll even go north. Maybe I'll even get a job with the, by gosh, *New York Times*."

"I wouldn't count on it," said Dodge. "Haven't you ever noticed how all of Patti's sisters live within a long walk or a short car ride of Brother Daddy?"

I ignored the question as I stood and undid my belt. "Dodge, how come you don't like Patti?"

" 'Cause she's a snotty, two-faced little kiss-ass, and she treats you like cow flop."

Cutter saw me gritting my teeth. "Don't pull any punches there, Dodge, just 'cause she's Nate's girlfriend," offered Cutter.

I dropped my pants and kicked them to one side as my steak started to sizzle in the grill. "You don't know her," I told him.

"No, Nate. You're the one who don't know her."

I'd had enough. "Go to hell," I told him. Dodge only chuckled. "Patti loves me and I love her, and as soon as we can, we're getting' married. She knows I'm not stayin' in DeLong, Miss'ssippi."

"Her sister Melody promised to love, honor and obey Ray Wilbanks. He's got him a good job offer at the shipyards down on the coast. But Melody won't go. Don't want to leave daddy. I hear they're about to bust up over it."

"You're a liar!" I snapped and instantly regretted it. Dodge McDowell might be a bootlegger's son and beer hall tough, but he was as honest in his word and his promises as the day was long. Dodge sat up on his sleeping bag and looked at me, hard. Neither he nor any of his clan were given to let an insult pass unchallenged. I swallowed hard, knowing that if Dodge sprang to his feet he likely could break me into several pieces before even Cutter could stop him. The steak spit and sizzled above the fire as I stood there in my Jockeys glancing around, wondering which way to run.

"Hey, Dodge, come on," said Cutter, trying to distract the big lineman. "It doesn't do any harm for Nate to dream. And he might as well dream big. For him and PattiWac. I mean, wouldn't it be somethin' if he really did become a writer for the, by gosh, *New York Times*? We could all say we knew you back when."

Dodge grunted and lay down, cupping his hands behind his head. "Yeah, back when he was a scrawny kid who ran off at the mouth too much. If you're gonna make a writer, Nate, you need to be more careful how you choose your words."

The fear that had been thumping in my chest a moment earlier drained away. I was aware that I'd dodged a bullet – or more accurately, a fist that would have landed like a nine-pound hammer. I knew better than to demand an apology from Dodge, but I wasn't going to offer him one. The moment dragged on.

"Nate, are you gonna get us some beer or just stand there lookin' pretty?" asked Cutter, nodding toward the cold, silent boil of The Well.

I stepped off the rocky edge.

An almost electrical shock crackled through my nerves as I passed down into the spring, my balls darting like quick, round fish in search of the warm bay behind my pelvis. Inside the earth I gasped but held it inside myself, every part of me tingling, throbbing with the liquid fire of total sensation that comes just before the numbing.

Once inside, The Well was a world unto itself with its own atmosphere, and geography and twisted physics.

During daytime expeditions, the water felt so pure and weightless that it seemed not to be water at all, but the barely liquefied air of a blue-white winter morning. And suddenly you could fly. It was so clear that it did not bend light in brittle angles, it merely melted it into pastels and added texture. Yet when seen through the full twenty-six feet of water, the light was never the same. It could pour into the mouth of The Well and swim there like liquid gold in a white porcelain bowl, or float on the surface in an animated jigsaw of colors, a cathedral window onto the summer sky.

At night, The Well lurked. A black, open mouth leading to a throat that some swore constricted and changed in the darkness. Tightened to swallow them. Despite the knowledge that The Well's flow was up and out, some shaken "divers" emerged certain that there was a current pushing them down. That the water took on weight and the slushy heft of black, crystalline mud. Over the years some people had become so disoriented that they bolted sideways or even down in a frenzied try at coming up. The rock walls were ridged and unforgiving, and though no one in our generation had drowned, there had been some close calls – stitches, broken bones and the direction of several noses forever changed. But for those of us who regularly tossed in beer by the case and made a game of who could bring up the most cans, The Well was not a pit constricted by claustrophobia. It was a challenge and a test, and there was care to be taken. For me, at least, it was a door into space – the space between my ears. In the minute-like seconds and hour-like minutes of floating downward it was like being adrift in the vast blackness beyond the earth. I imagined it was how the astronauts felt when they walked in space. Weightless, yet in control at the edge of danger with a mission to accomplish. Every sense alive and tingling. Every moment dreamlike. The moon their scarred lighthouse, just as for our veteran corps of night divers it was the compass point that guided us safely up.

"Five!" I yelled as I broke the surface, gulping air, arms upstretched, holding two cans in each hand. Another was stuffed in the front of my underpants. "Five!"

By the time the big steak had filled my belly, Dodge was snoring. Cutter was lying on his side, propped on an elbow with a *National Geographic* in front of him, reading by the light of a kerosene lattern.

"Everybody's on pins and needles at the paper," I said by way of conversation. "Miss Carter is supposed to make her grand entrance tomorrow morning. She told Jimmy Fuller and his dad that she expected the ramps and such to be done at the office by seven a.m. even if they had to work all night."

Cutter turned a page. "I reckon she plans to pay 'em, doesn't she?"

"Sure. But that's not the point. She's already had them bustin' their tails puttin' in ramps and fixin' up stuff at Wolf's Run since Monday," I told him. "I didn't think so down there on the road the other mornin', but now? She does come off as mighty high-handed.

"I heard she read Mr. Tom the riot act about not having things ready for her when she got here. Cussed him worse than a red-headed stepchild, from what Miss Mary Nell told Patti's momma. And this afternoon she made Mr. Tom move out of the publisher's office and into a little room down the hall. Wouldn't even let him go back to the general manager's office downstairs. The room she put him ain't much bigger than a closet." I shook my head in long slow movement, exaggerated by the three beers I'd consumed in rapid succession. "Why do you suppose she came back anyway?"

Cutter studied a diagram of the lunar-lander, the Apollo space capsule and the huge Saturn V rocket that was supposed to propel them and three astronauts to the moon later in the month. "It don't seem to me to take too much supposin'," he said without looking up. "If somebody left you a newspaper and a big ol' place like Wolf's Run, wouldn't you come back?"

I tried to make my mind focus. "Yeah, I guess I would," I conceded. "But it's all mighty curious, the way her daddy changed his will just a few weeks before he died."

"Maybe she talked him into changin' it by makin' him feel sorry for her," Cutter suggested with no enthusiasm for conversation. "A cripple'll do that, you know? Work you that way. 'Ohhh, po'r me! Po'r, po'r me!' I saw it a thousand times with Tony."

Cutter could be right. It could be that simple but – "A lot of people think there's more to it than that," I said. "I heard through Brother Mac that Governor Weathers is havin' that Greenwood lawyer looked into. The one who drew up the will. The word is, he's known to do work for the colored crowd. And one of the partners in his law firm is a Jew."

"And?"

"And … Mr. Carter goes off in the river. So, that U.S. Attorney, Burke, and that colored preacher and their bunch see a chance to steal the paper out from under Mr. Tom, so he can't speak up against the race-mixers. They get that Greenwood lawyer to dummy-up a phoney will."

Cutter looked up at me where I was propped against a log. "I hope you and Patti do hurry up and go off to college because you're soundin' more like Brother Mac every day."

"Just because he's wrong about you, doesn't mean he's wrong about everything."

"The problem is," said Cutter, "Brother Mac doesn't think he's wrong about *any*-thing. From God's lips to his mouth, to hear him tell it."

"Well, he sure does pray and read his Bible a lot."

"Good for him," said Cutter returning to the *National Geographic*. The subject of Brother Dr. C.E. MacAllister and the whole First Denomination crowd was a sore one with Cutter. Even though he and his sister Rose carried in their veins the intermingled blood of some of the county's oldest families, the black hair, full lips and olive skin they gained from their father had made them targets early in their lives. Even their name. To the best of my reckoning, Carlucci was the only one in the county phone book that ended in a vowel. But all that changed when a pee-wee league coach handed Cutter a football and the whole town discovered he could run faster and harder with it than any kid they'd ever seen. Now, if anyone had anything bad to say about Cutter, they mostly kept it to themselves or to a whisper. Everyone except Brother Mac.

It was time to change the subject. I took a sip from a very cold can of Miller, and I had just enough of a buzz on to let my curiosity turn into words. "How come you never date anybody from the high school?"

At first, I didn't think he was going to answer, which was not unusual. If Cutter thought a question silly or intrusive, he felt no obligation to respond. Then to my surprise he said, "I like having time to myself and a place where I can be alone. I don't want a bunch of little girls showin' up out here. Nor their daddys with shotguns."

"But, Cutter, you could have *anybody* at –"

"Nate, I don't want just *anybody*. I want – I want – ?"

He shook his head, always judicious about revealing the parameters of his private life, even to his friends. I was buzzed, but not too buzzed to hear in his voice that his retreat to silence was not a decision he'd made to withhold his thoughts. It was a question for which he had no answer. So I let it drop, but the intermission didn't last long. Whenever I had a few beers in me, I needed conversation nearly as badly as air.

"Is that a good one?" I asked about the *National Geographic* Cutter was reading.

"Nah. Not a single naked Indonesian in the whole thing."

"Why do you pretend that you only look at the pictures?" I asked, letting tumble out another question I'd wondered about for a while. I knew that Cutter actually read everything he could get his hands on concerning science, math, mechanics and architecture, and a novel here and there. He had three or four library cards and was a frequent borrower, but not in Cattahatchie County or nearby towns. "I mean, you could make straight A's but –"

"What is this, Nate? Twenty questions?" Cutter asked, a little testily. He was not one to engage in what he considered meaningless conversation, especially about himself. But he looked over at Dodge and listened for several moments to his snoring as if weighing something. Then he returned his eyes to me and said, "Because smart kids scare coaches."

The answer caught me off guard. "What do you mean?"

"Coaches may say they like smart players, but that's bull. The only things they really care about are size and speed, and having somebody who will do *exactly* what they're told. The last thing a coach wants is a kid who's smart enough to ask, 'Why?'"

"I guess," was the most intelligent response I could come up with. I'd never thought about it. But Cutter had. I suspected he had thought about an awful lot of things I'd never thought about. Had to think about them just to survive.

Cutter slipped his long, powerful legs out of his sleeping bag and stood, dressed in black-and-red CHS gym shorts and a snug white T-shirt that glowed against his skin. We all expected those legs to make him a star at Ole Miss – the University of Mississppi – and carry him all the way to pro ball.

When he walked over to the edge of the stone outcrop, I followed. He took his penis in hand and pissed into the river below. I eyed the huge expanse of stars above us and the moon climbing over the eastern hills. Its pale glow illuminated the mile or so of cotton stalks between the river and the Old Ambrose Place. All the bottom land in that direction for as far as I could see should have belonged to Cutter one day. Now the worn-out old farmhouse was only a dark silhouette against crops that would profit someone else. The only light came from Cutter's sister's room at the northwest corner. I knew Rose slept with it on because no matter when I awoke during a stay at The Well, it was always there – pale and gray through dingy glass, but always on. I knew it was some sort of a signal for Cutter. What exactly the light meant I wasn't sure, but I was afraid of what might happen if it ever went out.

A fish jumped in the river nearby and somewhere past the old Old Iron Bridge an alligator grunted deep and long. My best friend tucked himself back into his shorts and paid them no attention. I finished and did the same as Cutter studied the inheritance that was no longer his. In the moonlight the muscles of his chest and shoulders, his high cheek bones and the hard ridge of his jaw line looked as if they could have been cut from the same stone upon which we stood.

"Nate, I didn't make this world. I didn't conjure up DeLong, Miss'ssippi. I surely didn't ask to be born into the family I was born into," he said quietly, his voice mixing with the murmur of the river below. "But things are what they are. Until I sign a scholarship, and some big booster with a fat wallet slips me the money to get my momma and sister out of DeLong, I'm going to give them what they expect. What they want. A dumb jock with nothing on his mind except the next game."

I tried to think of something to say, but my thoughts were foggy with alcohol and knocked a little off kilter by the way Cutter had opened up to me. We were friends. He was my best friend. But mostly he kept his own counsel. Now he kept his eyes on the house across the dark fields, a sad place wrapped in a chain of shadows.

"Football is all I've got," he said. "Without it, I'm just the son of a crazy woman and a drunk, mean, dago cripple."

Chapter 6

❧

The early light poured onto the yellow brick of the Cattahatchie County Courthouse as Holly and Eve – and Charlie, too – turned the old beat-up Lincoln onto the town square in DeLong.

"My goodness," sighed Holly, "it hasn't changed a bit. If it weren't for the cars, I'd think it was 1959."

Indeed, DeLong, Mississippi had changed little since the last big surge of civic pride when the majority of the plank storefronts were replaced by mostly two-story brick structures in the 1920s. Wood sidewalks were replaced with cement. The town square was paved in the '30s but even into the '50s many of the town's residential streets were hard-packed red clay. Drugstores, clothing stores, appliance stores, hardware stores, grocers, barbers, beauticians, jewelers and an ice cream parlor faced the courthouse. The President Jefferson Davis (CSA) Hotel was the only three-story building on the square, and though the rooms had mostly gone to seed, the lobby and dining room hung on to a worn elegance. The Rebel Theater occupied all of one corner, the marquee announcing Paul Newman in *Cool Hand Luke*, which had debuted in L.A. two years earlier.

Eve laughed, and smiled the same TV-star perfect smile as her mother, actress Carol Howard.

"What's so funny?"

"You know that TV show *Time Tunnel*?"

"Yes."

"I think we're in it," said Eve. "Or maybe *Lost in Space*."

"I'm glad you didn't say *The Beverly Hillbillies*," said Holly, smiling.

"Ohhh, I was headed that way."

"Once you're here a while, you'll find out it's just another soap opera. Like most small towns."

"I hope I'm not here that long," said Eve, almost to herself, an undertone of anger imbued in every word as it had been since Sunday. Then to Holly, "I hope neither one of us is."

Holly forced a smile but said nothing. She made a second trip around the square, waving as she passed the truck farmers who dropped their tailgates beside the courthouse each morning. Fresh from the fields were vegetables and fruit of every kind – sweet corn, okra, snap beans, peaches and strawberries, and tomatoes so big, firm and delicious they could be sliced up and served on a plate like red steak. What wasn't locally grown, the men bought off the railroad dock, queuing up by four a.m. to determine who got first crack at the crates as they were unloaded from Tennessee & Gulf boxcars.

Cattahatchie Current-Leader was painted at the top of the red brick building that squarely faced the front doors of the courthouse. That was no accident. When Holly's grandfather erected the building there in the 1890s, he wrote that it would be "the eyes of the community watching its government at work." And so it had been. A fair, consistent, even progressive voice, at least for the white community, through depressions and wars and good times. There were so many old hurts and hates between Holly and her father, and many of their battles had been fought inside those walls, but she could not look at the building now without feeling a powerful sense of pride in what *The Current-Leader* had meant to Cattahatchie County for more than a century.

Holly turned off the square and down the steep hill that led to the river and the newspaper's parking lot. "The carpenters weren't able to widen the hall from the front lobby," she told Eve. "Those walls help support the second floor, so we'll have to use the back door and take the freight elevator up."

"Now you're getting a taste of how my people feel," Eve quipped.

"Touché," agreed Holly as she stopped the car beside the zigzag ramp. The air was fragrant with the clean scent of fresh-cut pine. Holly looked at her watch. "Six-twenty. Good. Miss Frances opens the front door at 7 a.m. This first day, I just want to get in the building and make sure I can get around without any embarrassing hassles."

"Understood, Madam Publisher. So, let's do it," said Eve, stepping out. "That means you too, Charlie."

The Current-Leader building really was three stories, though only two were visible on the square. The first, more like a basement, was set deep into the hill upon which the square and courthouse sat. Past the loading dock and metal doors, a big room held the press, the five-hundred-pound rolls of paper that the machine devoured and the fifty-five-gallon drums of ink that made the stories and pictures come to life.

Using a set of keys Tom reluctantly had sent her, Holly unlocked the door and pushed through ... into her newspaper. The sweet, woodsy scent of paper mixed with machine oil and ink filled her nostrils. She had not been in a newspaper office in more than three years, and almost had forgotten how much she loved the smell. It smelled like *now!* Like energy about to be unleashed, like history caught in that moment before it slipped away into the past.

Without even looking, she reached for the switch and turned on the long rack of overhead lights.

"There they are," she said, motioning to the set of Goss presses that T.L. Carter had mortgaged *The Current-Leader* to purchase in 1966, converting the paper from an out-of-date Linotype system to offset, just like the big boys. "They're what's killing us," she told Eve. "The paper isn't getting enough use out of them to make them pay for themselves. That's got to change."

The freight elevator clanged and rattled and groaned. It automatically stopped at the first floor where the advertising and circulation departments were located. At the front desk, Mrs. Frances Ragland, who had been with *The Current-Leader* for over fifty years, controlled access to the interior of the building with the tenacity of a centurion guarding the gates of Rome. Miss Frances took in classified ads, birth announcements and death notices, and wrote one of the paper's most popular community news/gossip columns.

On the second floor were the composing room and the newsroom. There was plenty of clearance between the tall angled tables where strips of film were pasted onto white, news-page-sized cardboard to create the image that later would be photographed by a giant camera, transferred to a metal plate and finally stretched onto one of the press's steel cylinders. The newsroom, however, was like a maze thrown together by a madman. Piled high with papers, open phone books and eight-by-ten photos, desks were pushed into corners and into any cubbyhole where there was room for a telephone and a typewriter.

Several spots were a tight squeeze for Holly's wheels, but she loved it. Even empty, the room felt busy. The walls seeming to hold within them the echoes of ringing phones and clattering typewriters. As she passed Ridge Bellafont's darkroom she smelled the developing chemicals. They were more intoxicating to her than the best weed she'd ever smoked.

The newspaper had only four full-time reporters and a sports editor, but several of the community correspondents and part-timers had desks in the office, a jealously guarded perk. They all reported to C. Michael Morton, the newspaper's eager, young managing editor.

It had been quite a show yesterday in the newsroom, Holly's chief source had told her. Tom packing up his possessions from the publisher's office, carrying them to a small windowless room down the hall. He'd declined to return to the general manager's office downstairs.

"Oh, my, it was like a movie, *The Good Son Wronged*," photographer Ridge Bellafont told Holly and Eve over a delicious dinner of chicken piccata he prepared in the kitchen at Wolf's Run. "It was absolutely dramatic. He was carrying this small cardboard box and his chin was a'quaverin'.

"You'd have thought he was walking to the gallows. I was dying to make a photographic record of the tragedy, but feared for my life should I go to clickin'."

Holly nearly fell from her chair laughing, not at Tom but at Ridge's way of telling a story. In conversation, he could make the folding of a dishcloth sound interesting, turn it into an event. He never had been able to translate that wonderful humor into words on paper, but in the crystal dew on a single cotton stalk, the rolling hillscape of northern Cattahatchie County or the deep sun-blistered ruts at the corner of a farmer's eye, Ridge could see a photo. First in his mind's eye, then through the lens of his camera and finally onto paper in the darkroom.

"Magic!" Holly had enthused the first time Ridge let her watch him dip a piece of photographic paper into the developing bath and coax an image into being. She had been only four then, but Holly never had lost the sense of alchemy she'd felt that first time with Ridge, or the sense of peace and accomplishment that came to her when working alone in the dim red light of a darkroom.

What wasn't funny, however, was Tom's attitude or that of his wife, Mary Nell.

When the phone finally had been answered late Sunday afternoon at Tom's house in town, Mary Nell had said, "Ohhh, honey, don't be angry with Tommy about Wolf's Run. He asked me to oversee the renovations, but it's such a beautiful old place I just couldn't bear to see it torn asunder."

"'Torn asunder?' What are you talking about? All I asked for was a ramp up to the exterior porch by the kitchen door and one from the interior porch to the courtyard. And a wooden sidewalk out to the garage."

"Yes, well, even though Wolf's Run is more a cottage than a classical antebellum manse – such as Wilmont Place, where my people reside – it does have some wonderful architectural lines. I said to Tommy, 'Why, Holly, has been through *sooo* much, she just isn't thinking straight. There is simply no way she'll want to distract from the country elegance of Wolf's Run with … *ramps.*'"

Holly had felt the heat in her face and had forced herself to take a deep breath. "Mary Nell, Wolf's Run has been changed many times over the years," she had reminded her as calmly as she could manage. "At one time, the kitchen was in the building that now is the garage. There was no indoor plumbing or electricity, and there certainly was no swimming pool. Which, by the way, no one cleaned."

"Darling, I called several swimming pool services in Memphis. To come down to DeLong? My goodness! You'd have thought I asked them to travel to the back side of the moon. Their fees were simply exorbitant, and I told them so."

Holly had been so angry that she was afraid to speak.

"Sweetie, are you there? Are you all right?"

"Mary Nell, may I please talk to Tom?"

"Why of course you may," she'd practically bubbled with artificial sweetness like the foam at the top of a shaken diet soda. "He's ever so eager to talk to you. But, honey, I trust you're not going to alter Wolf's Run very much. I mean, surely there must be places where someone in your – well, condition – would be more comfortable."

"Mary Nell, Wolf's Run is my home, and I intend to be perfectly comfortable right here for as long as I remain in DeLong," she'd said from the desk phone in the library. "But don't worry. I don't intend to replace all the furniture with hospital beds. When I go back to California, the house will still be livable for normal people."

"Oh, good! I'm so glad. ... Tommy, dear! Your sister is on the line."

As Holly waited, she absently ran her finger over the outside of the envelope containing the glass she'd crushed under the hard rubber of her wheel. She could hear the voices of her niece and nephew, playing perhaps in the back yard of the two-story Victorian on Jackson Street where Holly had spent her early years. Finally, Tom had picked up the phone. Pleasantries were brief. Like most of the town, by now he probably knew about the incident on the highway – even if he hadn't planned it, but he didn't ask and she didn't give him the satisfaction of telling him how close she'd come to the bridge abutment at Yancy Creek.

"None of the changes I asked for at Wolf's Run were done," she had said. "But I assume you took care of things at the paper."

"Well, actually, you see, we had some questions about the specifications –"

"Damn it, Tom!" she had cursed, then closed her eyes as she fought to rein in her exasperation. "I don't intend to have to crawl or be carried into my own place of business." She'd heard one of Tom's sarcastic snorts at the other end of the line. "I'm sorry, Tom, I didn't mean that like it sounded. Daddy left the paper to both of us."

"A little more to you than me," he'd reminded coldly. "And that makes all the difference. Doesn't it?"

Now as Holly sat outside the double doors leading to the publisher's office, she knew that Tom was right. Whether she wanted it that way or not. It was all going to be on her. She was going to have to try to stabilize the paper financially while walking the fine line between practicality and the social and political issues that were boiling just beneath the surface of the town. Tom was going to be of no help. In fact, he likely would hinder her in whatever small, mean ways that he could. After what happened Sunday, Holly knew he might even be dangerous, but without absolute proof it was something she wouldn't allow herself to dwell on.

On the exhale of a deep breath, Holly opened the big doors and pushed into what had been T.L. Carter's office for thirty-five years. She stopped in the middle of the big room and took it in as Eve spotted the coffeemaker on a table by the door to the office's private bathroom.

"Thank goodness! I need more caffeine," said Eve. "I'll make a pot."

Charlie crossed the worn Oriental rug, hurried past the conference table and leaped onto the leather sofa pressed against a wall of glazed brick. She marched up and down twice to get the lay of the piece then settled into a corner by a large window.

"Glad to see you're making yourself at home," Holly told the little dog, which gave her a quick yap in response.

The first thing Holly noticed was that the hardwood floor tilted toward the four eight-foot-high windows in the front of the room. Not much, but a little. On her feet, in high heels and hose or tennis shoes and dungarees, she'd never felt the small angle in the heart pine. Now she had to hold onto the steel grab-rims on the outside of her tires to keep her chair from rolling toward the balcony that overhung the sidewalk and looked onto the town square. Ornate wrought iron rails guarded the porch's edge, as they did on many such second-floor sitting areas around the square, a nod to the French influence that once rode the river north, up from Louisiana. On election nights and when a jury was out on a big trial, the lawyers, accountants and doctors who occupied most of the upstairs offices moved chairs outside to take the breeze and wait for news while discreetly sipping their after-work highballs.

Holly rolled over next to one of the windows and looked out.

Always it was this balcony where the loud speakers were set up. Her father and his father before him took microphone in hand to read election returns to the farmers and townsmen gathered on the square to spit tobacco, speculate and barter with the hill people for quilts, firewood and moonshine. Wives spread blankets beneath the big oaks that shaded the courthouse and unpacked picnic basket suppers of fried chicken, cornbread and sweet potatoes while black fiddlers, guitar pickers and vendors passed among them. Holly's earliest memory of her father was not a toy he'd bought her or a playtime moment at the house on Jackson Street. No, she was four and T.L. Carter was standing on that porch, his seersucker suit pants braced by red suspenders over a white shirt, the back wet with sweat, the sleeves rolled above his elbows. He was holding up a paper and crying and smiling at the same time. The headline read:

JAPS SURRENDER; WWII ENDS
Fathers, husbands, sons coming home

Holly felt her eyes welling and pushed away from the window. The last thing she wanted was for her makeup to start running before she saw Tom or the staff. She knew the day, and several to follow, likely would be emotional. She had grown up in this building as much as at the Jackson Street house or Wolf's Run. Many of the longtime employees had treated her as a surrogate daughter, especially after her mother disappeared and her father changed, hardened by anger and disappointment. On top of the homecoming would be the wheelchair. It would not be easy on Miss Becky in classifieds, Miss Frances at the front desk, "Shorty" Rodgers in composing or Frank Hodges, the paper's advertising director, to see her in the chair. It wasn't going to be easy on Holly either. In all their eyes she would have to watch their image of the girl she'd been disintegrate into the truth of the woman she was now. It was a truth that with God's help Holly had mostly come to accept. But that didn't mean her heart wouldn't ache, if only for a moment, each time the sadness and pity in their eyes forced her to relive that moment in the Honolulu hospital when the doctors told her she'd never walk again.

Chapter 7

༄

G ospel music was something Holly Lee Carter remembered fondly about her upbringing at First Denomination Church. Even if it was just about the only thing. She loved the omnipresent four-part harmonies, the raucous rattling of the soprano piano keys and the uncomplicated spirituality of the music played there – and by WHCI, DeLong's only radio station.

"The sweet gospel sounds of WHCI" were interrupted hourly by local news, farm price reports and sports – mostly taken right out of the pages of *The Current-Leader*, and editorials by the station's owner, former Governor Cecil Weathers. The station carried Brother MacAllister's sermons live on Sunday mornings and replayed them daily at 10 a.m. and 10 p.m.

It was early Friday afternoon and Holly had heard Weathers' latest editorial about ten times since returning from California. It urged all "morally upright" citizens of Cattahatchie County to support the new private school that was to open in September on a piece of property donated by Weathers. He walked a fine line when it came to inciting violence – "It would be better if God utterly destroyed the public school system of this nation than have it turned over to *Nee*-groes and those who seek to create a mongrelized mud race. ..."

She wheeled around the publisher's desk, turned off the radio and put on the turntable one of the record albums she'd brought with her. Bob Dylan's *Sitting on a Barbed Wire Fence* sing-songed through the speakers. Holly smiled at the appropriateness of the tune as she pushed over to the conference room table. She again flipped through a copy of the most recent edition of *The Current-Leader* – July 11, 1969. At the bottom of page one was a story announcing that she was back and would assume the title of editor-in-chief, and that Tom Carter would remain as the paper's general manager. It didn't mention the publishership.

Holly looked at the plaque behind her father's desk – *A newspaper is the conscience of a community*. And as far as she had run, the truth was, DeLong still was her community, her home. She pivoted her chair and rolled next to one of the four big windows, all open to catch what little air was moving outside. Her roots went as deep in the Mississippi soil as the oaks on the courthouse lawn. In fact, deeper, since her ancestors had helped plant some of the very trees that now were thick and mighty.

Outside on the busy square women with hair as solid as combat helmets leaned over tailgates in their high heels, purses on their arms, squeezing huge, red, ripe tomatoes. Some actually wore white gloves. It was like looking at a postcard mailed from DeLong in 1959. So little had changed since she'd left, especially compared to California. Holly scanned over the men in overalls and work khakis and off-the-rack suits, studied the women walking in and out of the courthouse, the bank, and the drug store. Not one of them in pants. Heaven forbid, jeans! Walking, stopping in front of the big window at Handley's Department Store, in two's and three's, and walking on. No tennis shoes, not even sandals. Pumps or high heels. Some laughing as they walked into the lobby of The Jeff Davis Hotel or walked under the marquee of the Rebel Theater.

Holly ran her hands over her skirt, over legs sheathed in pantyhose that her thighs and hips couldn't feel. Her calves were thinning and there was nothing she could do about it. If she didn't take care to keep her feet positioned correctly on the chair's pedals, they flopped at odd angles. Her feet remained pretty, maybe prettier than ever since they suffered almost no daily scuffing. She studied the pale coral nail polish on toes peeking from the brown, open-front pumps. All of those women on the square walking … some carrying babies … walking … some girls she'd gone to high school with leading children ready for first grade or more … walking … others buying dinner or running errands or going to work or planning for the hour when the kids are put to bed and the lights are off … Holly drew in her breath … all of them *walking!*

In her throat, Holly felt a sob or a scream welling up but she choked it down, whatever it was, and pivoted hard away from the window – fighting not to focus on what she'd lost. On what her headlong rush toward some illusion of absolute independence had cost her before it came to a halt with the suddenness of a .762-millimeter slug traveling at 2,346 feet per second. Her legs had gone out from under her as if severed by some great scythe. Even as she hit the ground hard, she was rolling trying to tear off her green army T-shirt – her back on fire, sure she must have been smoked with a blast of napalm that she'd neither heard nor seen. But when she got the shirt over her head she saw only blood and the holes ... the holes.

Holly shook off the memory and pushed behind her father's desk – her desk, at least for now – and locked the chair's brakes. With a shaking hand she slipped her reading glasses onto her nose and picked up her pen. She had work to do. Thank God.

A few minutes later through the open doors to the hall and nearby stairs, Holly heard Tom's voice.

"Yep, it's small but it'll do for me," she heard him say, no doubt referring to the nearby office he'd wedged himself into. "Bein' in that chair and all, Holly needs the space and the privacy," he went on, as if she required almost continuous medical treatment. "It's really amazing that she's held up as well as she has considering the *severity* of her condition."

Tom knew nothing about Holly's "condition." He had returned few of her calls from Los Angeles, and during Thursday's cold fifteen-minute meeting, he'd asked nothing about her health or Vietnam, her time in California or what her life was like in a wheelchair. Holly had tried to draw him out with talk of his children – Georgette, thirteen, and Thomas Lanier Carter V, ten – and even with polite questions about Mary Nell, clubs and church, but his response had been negligible. In the end, she'd gotten down to business, wanting to lay out her preliminary plans for the paper, get his ideas and meld them with hers, if possible. But, "No, thanks," he'd told her. "I'd just as soon find out with the rest of the employees."

Only thirty-five, Tom looked at least ten years older. His firm, athletic frame was gone; his brown eyes were flat and lifeless. The spare tire around his middle was somewhere between truck and tractor size, a double chin hung from beneath his jaw and the capillaries of his cheeks and nose broke red across his face like the fissures of a smashed windshield. They provided the only color to his otherwise pallid skin. If anyone looked in need of continuous medical care, it was Tom.

"Let's see if she's up to talking with you," she heard Tom say. "Holly?"

"Yes!" she replied, more sharply than she intended.

"There are some folks here who'd like to see you," he said, stepping into the office.

The words, "Do they have an appointment?" formed in her mind but not on her lips. She knew that wasn't how things were done in DeLong, for the most part. People often simply stopped by, and her father somehow found the time to chat about kids, fishing or farming before letting them share, in their own time, what they'd come about. Holly never had that gift of small talk, and it was one of the reasons she'd become a photographer and not a reporter. She preferred letting her pictures do the talking, but, "All right, Tom," she said. "Please show them in."

As Holly wheeled around the desk, she did her best to disguise her shock and dismay as Charlie hopped down from the sofa and began to greet them. There were eleven mostly middle-aged businessmen who represented the newspaper's largest advertisers – Handley's Department Store, Grisham Supermarket, Kamp Motorcars and The Rebel Theater among them. Brother C.E. MacAllister was next. The last through the door was Cecil Weathers, who owned the Cattahatchie Valley Bank, among other things. He was flanked by his Mississippi Highway Patrol body guard, Sgt. J.D. Benoit, and state Senator Haughton Wellingham.

"Oh, Miss Holly," Wellingham sang as he extended his hand. "It's so good to see you up and on your – err, well, up and around. When I saw you in that terrible contraption in Los Angeles, I feared so for your health."

"Thank you for your concern, Mr. Wellingham. It took a couple of months of hard work in rehab, but I have my strength back now and I feel great. The surgery relieved much of the pain I'd been dealing with since – uhm, since Vietnam," she said. "Charlie, *le silence de ve et règle*."

The little dog went to a corner of the room and lay down under a side table where Holly had placed her food and water dishes. "Well, gentlemen, I have to confess that you've caught me a bit off guard," said Holly. "I wasn't expecting this august delegation."

"Nonsense," said Weathers, a round-faced man, five-ten or so, of medium build in his sixties with thinning hair dyed shoe-polish black above a long forehead. His critics described him as "the bulldog of segregation," and that was apt both physically and philosophically. He had full lips below a puggish nose that separated large dark eyes. His ears were small and lay flat against the side of his head. When on the political stump, he favored off-the-rack suits in various shades of white, from bone to cream. Today he was wearing a gray, vested suit, probably tailored for him in New Orleans, or maybe Dallas. Below hand-sewn French shirt cuffs his nails were manicured but his hands remained the beefy mitts of a pig-farmer's son. "We're all family here. You dig deep enough, and all our roots are intertwined. Common blood.

"We just wanted to come by and welcome you back to the community and hear *all* your plans to rejuvenate this grand ol' newspaper," he went on, and without invitation settled into a chair at one end of the conference table. Haughton Wellingham sat at the governor's right hand and Charles MacAllister at his left. The others found positions at the table or around the room. Sgt. Benoit closed the office doors and stationed himself in front of them. Holly was becoming more furious by the moment at the high-handed gall of Cecil Weathers and with Tom, who likely set up this ambush. She forced herself to remain calm.

"Well, I appreciate your concern about my health, and *The Currrent-Leader* family appreciates, as always, your continued advertising support," she said. "But as far as my – as *our* plans for the newspaper, I'm afraid there is very little I can tell you. But I can say that Tom and I are going to be looking at ways to improve the appearance of the paper and increase circulation to give you the best possible return on your advertising dollar."

"Do you plan to increase your ad rates?" asked Walter Kamp, owner of the county's largest automobile dealership.

"We haven't increased our rates in almost three years," she said, having spent the last two months studying the paper's recent history.

"Some small increase probably is warranted, but our rates will remain far below those of the Tupelo and Memphis dailies."

There was some grumbling but Milton Handley spoke up. "*The Current-Leader* always has been a valuable advertising tool. But it can only remain so if it continues to reflect our community values."

"Our white community," added Walter Kamp.

"The talk is you've already hired a colored reporter," said Clifton Reese, who owned the Rebel Theater.

Holly drew her hands together, giving herself a moment to find a diplomatic response. She knew she had to be careful. "If that's 'the talk,' I hope you all will help me set it straight. There's no truth to it."

"What about the Negro girl you've been seen with?" asked Handley.

"Eve Howard is a talented photography student who is working on a book while assisting me with my personal – while working with me as my personal assistant."

"Like a nurse, you mean?" asked Wilbur Grisham.

Holly drew in her breath and her pride as she thought again of all the women walking … walking around the square below. "Yes, sir. That's what I mean," she said, without further explanation. Negro nurses caring for elderly or infeebled white folk was a tradition. It was acceptable, and no threat to DeLong's tightly woven social fabric. Holly felt ashamed of relegating Eve, her friend, to the role of body servant in the eyes of these men, but the answer was truthful as far as it went. This was no political science class or Philosophy 101, she told herself. These men could keep the paper afloat or sink it.

"What about the paper's whites-only news policy?" asked Governor Weathers. "Will you keep it in place?"

Holly knew she had to carefully choose her words. "Gentlemen, I've been in this office less than two days. Before I make any changes, I intend to carefully study the needs of this community."

"Then let us be blunt, Miss Carter," said Milton Handley, meeting her eyes. "What this community does not need, and will not tolerate is a rag carryin' nigg'ah news and advocatin' for race-mixers. Is that understood?"

Holly held his fierce gaze for a long moment. "You've made your position quite clear," she said, flattening her hands on the table and pushing away from it. "Gentlemen, thank you for coming. Tom and I certainly will take your feelings into consideration when making our decisions about *The Current-Leader*'s future. But at the moment, we're on deadline for our weekend edition. So, if you'll excuse me."

"Very well," said Governor Weathers, standing. "Tom, thank you for your kind invitation to share our thoughts with you and your sister."

Tom Carter smiled and nodded. Holly was almost surprised he didn't bow.

Chapter 8

᷒

From my desk next to that of Sports Editor Clete Rainy, I saw the doors open to the publisher's office and watched the men file out and down the stairs. Brother Daddy and I made eye contact but he kept his thoughts focused on a higher plane and did not acknowledge me. The newsroom, which had been buzzing about the meeting, fell silent. Just as a few fingers were beginning to fall again on typewriter keys, Miss Carter pushed into the hall, her purse in her lap and her little dog trailing behind.

She wheeled into the tiny office Tom Carter was using. With her chair inside, the door could not be shut, but she was so angry she didn't care.

"Tom, you're my brother, and I love you," those nearby heard her say. "But don't you ever pull a stunt like that on me again."

"Why, sister, I don't have a clue what you mean. But whatever you say, Holly. You're the boss."

It took Miss Carter three attempts to back her wheelchair out into the narrow hall and get it pointed toward the freight elevator in the composing room. By that time Ridge Bellafont and Eve Howard were out of the darkroom. Eve hurried after her boss, stepping into the elevator just before the big doors rattled shut.

"What happened? What did those men want?"

"I don't want to talk about it right now," Holly told her. "I'll fill you in later. I just need to go for a drive and clear my head."

"Do you want me to go with you?"

"No. I mean, no thanks."

The elevator doors opened in the pressroom where the two-man crew was preparing the big machines to print the weekend edition starting at ten o'clcock. Eve followed Holly onto the loading dock.

"Girl, are you sure it's smart for you to be out on the road by yourself?"

"Despite what people around here may think, I'm not an invalid."

"Hey, come on! You know that's not what I meant."

Holly stopped at the bottom of the new ramp. "I know. I'm sorry. But I doubt the Klan would try anything in broad daylight, and I *really* need to be alone for a little while," she said. "Besides, they've already delivered their message for today. And I sat there and took it."

Eight miles east of DeLong on the Dumas Road, the Continental convertible dropped over a steep hill and into a long bottom. Cotton fields, cut by three creeks, spread away from the pavement. The air was whipping through Holly's auburn hair and a Rolling Stones eight-track was roaring in her ears. The louder the better. The less able she was to hear Milton Handley's words … and her weak response to them.

She was barely aware of the dark blue Mercury coming toward her, but even before it went by, the red lights on the dash and behind the grill were flashing. "*Ohhh, shhh-oot!*" Holly groaned as she looked down at the speedometer. Eighty-four.

The last time she'd been on the Dumas Road, she might have floored it and kept going. Her '56 Corvette had outrun more than one police car in its day. But that 'Vette was gone and so was the girl who drove it. Holly looked for a place to pull over on the narrow shoulder and watched in the rearview mirror as the unmarked cruiser turned around.

Two minutes later an older gentleman in a white short-sleeved shirt and khaki pants stepped from the Mercury and set a fedora on his head. He left the red lights flashing as he approached, giving the bruised convertible and woman behind the wheel a long once-over. He studied the wheelchair folded behind the front seat.

Holly held out her California driver's license and the registration. He motioned it away and rested his hand casually on the hilt of his revolver. "I don't know how fast you were going, Miss Carter, but I know it was too danged fast for this stretch of road," he said. "If you don't care if you kill yourself, that's between you and your maker. But if you plow into a family pullin' out of one of these side roads, that's something different. And I assure you, if you live, it'll be between you and me and the state of Miss'ssippi. I don't care whether you're in a wheelchair or not."

Holly held up her hands in surrender. "I'm sorry. You're absolutely right. I guess I was letting off steam but –" she shook her head. The excuse sounded weak even to her.

The man studied Holly with neither pity nor lust. It felt to Holly more like fatherly interest, perhaps even amusement. "I don't think we've met. I'm Sheriff Johnson," he said, extending his hand. "I moved back to DeLong in the fall of '59. I believe you'd already escaped to the West Coast."

Holly smiled, instantly liking the man. "Escaped? That's a very – uhm? – perceptive way to put it."

"You're not the first teenager ever to want to spread your wings and fly the coop. I did it myself back in the twenties. I did six years in the Navy before hooking up with the Memphis police. But ol' Cattahatchie County? I guess it called us both home," he said, taking a step back to look at the scrapes and green paint still evident on the Lincoln. "From what I hear, you had a pretty rough welcome last Sunday. You should have come by and filed a complaint."

"And said what?" she asked. "That two hooded men driving a Ford sedan that's as common as dirt ran us off the road? And, by the way, it didn't have a tag."

"We weren't hurt, thank the Lord. It had been a long drive from L.A., and all I wanted to do was get out to Wolf's Run."

The sheriff nodded but said, "You still should have put it on the record. You never can tell, I might run across a green Ford with a strip of baby blue across the doors."

"No you won't. I'll guarantee you that car was rolled into some river or lake, or torched at the end of some dirt road before noon on Sunday," she said as Sheriff Johnson gave her a look of quizzical respect. "I rode with the night cops writers at the *L.A. Chronicle* for three years while I was working part-time and going to college," she explained. "I kept my ears open when the detectives talked."

He changed the subject. "Is everything out at Wolf's Run aw'right?"

"Pretty much," she said, not sure how far Johnson could be trusted. But the fact that he'd run against Weathers' hand-picked candidate for sheriff and won spoke well of the man. So, she cracked the door open. "The only thing – well, my mother's portrait was missing from the library. It was there right before Daddy died. He mentioned it in a letter. Now nobody knows where it is."

"By nobody you mean Tom?"

"Yes."

"And nothing else appears to be missing?"

"No. Not that I can tell."

The sheriff drew air into his cheeks and slowly let it out. "Well, your father left Wolf's Run and all its contents to you. If anyone removed anything without your permission, it's theft. If you want to come by the office and file a report, I'll go over to Tom's place and have a talk with him."

"No, no. Of course not," Holly quickly told him. "It's just strange. I suppose I'm more curious than anything else."

"Is there anything else you're curious about?" asked Sheriff Johnson.

Holly tilted her head to one side as if trying to hear him better. Was Floyd Johnson inviting her to question him about her father's death? Holly thought again of her mother's missing portrait and of the piece of glass she'd run over in the library. She wasn't certain what it was, but over the last five days, she developed a good and perhaps troubling guess. But that's all it was, a guess, and she didn't intend to share it until she was sure. Still, there was something else that had bothered her since the first time she'd heard about her father's accident.

"It was a bad, rainy night, the night Daddy died, right?"

"Yes'um. And cold."

"Well, where was Daddy going?" she asked. "It seems like if he had a meeting in town or even a card game out at the country club, he'd have stayed at the office." Sheriff Johnson adjusted the thick black gun belt on his hips. "He kept a change of clothes at the paper. He had his own bathroom and shower.

"Of course, he could have gone home with no intention of coming back out, and gotten a phone call that –"

"Nope. We checked that," he told her. "Your father left the office early that Tuesday the 25th. Just after three o'clock. He was afraid he was coming down with a cold. He wanted to get home and get some of the chicken soup in him that Miss Frances had brought him. There were no calls into or out of Wolf's Run."

Holly thought about that for a long moment. "Then that makes even less sense. Daddy must have been sick as a dog if he left the office early on a night when the paper is put out."

"No. According to Miss Frances, T.L. only had the sniffles," the sheriff told her. "But he was already nervous about flying. So, he wanted to make sure he wasn't down with a cold."

"Flying?" asked Holly. "What are you talking about? My father was never on an airplane in his life."

Floyd Johnson started to speak then reassessed his words. The mysteries within families never ceased to amaze him. "So, no one told you?" he asked gently.

"Told me what?"

"Miss Carter, your father was scheduled to be on a 10:25 flight out of Memphis on Thursday morning. He was going to Los Angeles. He intended to be at your bedside when you woke up from your operation. He wanted to surprise you."

Holly twisted her hands on the steering wheel as an old truck roared past loaded with pine logs. She stared off into the long cotton-filled hollow between two sets of low hills. Twice she started to speak, but couldn't manage it. Patience was one of Floyd Johnson's virtues and Holly was grateful he let her take her time.

Finally, "No. No one told me," she said, clearing her throat. Then, "Sheriff, would you mind if we got together and went over the accident report, autopsy and such?"

"No, ma'am, I wouldn't mind that at all," he said. "I'll have those files pulled from the county records office. My wife and I are going down to the coast this weekend to attend our granddaughter's wedding. We won't be back until late Monday. How does Tuesday, nine a.m. sharp sound to you?"

"That'll be fine. In fact, it'll give me time to check on something I've been curious about."

"What's that?"

"I'd rather not say until I'm sure."

"You know, Miss Carter, if your father's death wasn't an accident, there'll be someone out there who won't appreciate you askin' questions."

"Don't worry, Sheriff. I'll be discreet."

Floyd Johnson chuckled. "Miss Carter, you *have* been away a long time. If either one of us start pickin' at your father's case, it'll be like tossin' a brick in a very small pond."

"Maybe you're right. Maybe we shouldn't meet at the paper."

"And if you come to my office, it'll be the talk of the town before noon."

"How about I buy you a cup of coffee out at Wolf's Run?"

"Aw'right, that sounds good," he said, touching the brim of his fedora. "In the meantime, young woman, slow it down. Please!"

Chapter 9

❧

"What are you so blue about this early in the morning?" Cutter asked over a plate of biscuits smothered in white gravy speckled with spicy brown sausage. Miss Winona St. Julian's sawmill gravy was famous, and the only place to get it was at The Cotton Café.

It was just past first light on Sunday and low river fog hung among the warehouses across the Cattahatchie River. The mist made them look like movie sets painted on soft canvas rather than the tough plank-and-nail reality of commerce in our little corner of the world.

Cutter was just off work at The Gin.

"You and Patti on the outs?"

"No, not really," I told him between mouthfuls of pancakes. "Not exactly, that is."

"That clarifies it."

"The thing is, I went over to the MacAllisters' last night to watch TV with Patti – you know, just hang out, eat some of her momma's chicken. Well, Brother Mac wouldn't let up about Miss Carter and the paper. He wanted to know everything I saw, everything I heard. He grilled me like a murder suspect," I explained, putting down my fork. "Ever since it got out that Miss Carter was coming back to run the paper, he's been hinting that 'the righteous should have no truck with a woman of such questionable morality.' Meaning I should quit the paper."

"Well, you do have more than enough farm work to do," Cutter said reasonably.

"The farm? Screw the farm!" I said more loudly than I meant to – loud enough that several regulars glanced up from their plates. I lowered my voice. "If Daddy wants to be a farmer, he can sober up and be one. Or at least help. But I was born to write. It's like I have this whole huge reservoir of words and thoughts built up inside me. The paper is like my spillway to let them out. If that gets cut off – well, I, I –"

"Might get all green and slimy inside?"

"Cutter, this is no joke."

Paula Simpson came over and cleared our plates, her body pressed as snuggly against the seams of her pink-and-white uniform as the coffee against the walls of the glass pot. "More coffee?"

"None for me," I told her.

"Could I get a cup to go?"

"Sure thing, Cutter. You know you can have all you want, any time you want."

Cutter let a smile play at the right corner of his mouth. "I'll keep it in mind."

Paula filled a Styrofoam cup and smiled at Cutter as we paid for our breakfasts. We went outside and propped against his jeep. I went on – "I'm not like you, Cutter. I'm not gonna have women fallin' all over me wherever I go. Patti is a knockout. She's even a cheerleader! And I love her and I'm lucky to have her. If I lose her ...." I shook my head, the fog cool and damp on my neck and bare arms.

Cutter blew on the black surface of his coffee. "Nate, you sell yourself way too short. You always have. PattiWac is the one who's lucky to have you. You're the only thing keepin' the cork in her bottle."

It was then that the baby-blue Lincoln turned onto River Street.

"Speak of the devil," said Cutter. I groaned.

Holly Lee Carter pulled into the only available parking place ... next to where Cutter and I were standing. She was wearing those Tuff-Nutt overalls again. And doing it very well. Her auburn hair hung loose on the shoulders of a green Army jacket bearing the blue-and-yellow insignia of the U.S. 7th Cavalry. She pulled Janis Joplin's *Cheap Thrills* from the tape player and dropped it on the seat as Charlie perched on the passenger door and sniffed at us.

"Good morn —" Miss Carter started but her words were overtaken by a long yawn. She covered her mouth then said, "Pardon me." She stretched her arms over her head, her hands balled into fists. "Good morning."

"Mornin'," I said, patting Charlie's curly hair. Cutter nodded, but said nothing.

"It seems like the three of us meeting at dawn on Sunday mornings is turning into a habit. We'll have to be careful or people will talk," she teased.

"People are talking already," said Cutter.

"Really? What are they saying?"

Cutter looked off toward the river. "This'n'that."

"Wow! That's a big subject," she said. Then to me, "Nate, I called in a takeout order. Would you mind running in and checking on it? Just tell them to put it on my tab."

I glanced at Cutter, dipped my head. "Sure," I said and went through the glass doors, leaving Cutter and Miss Carter alone on the misty street. Inside, people were, indeed, talking and craning their necks to get a better look.

"That was one of the first things I did when I got back – set up a tab at The Cotton," Miss Carter was saying by way of conversation. "No one can fry up a chicken or make a pan of cornbread like Miss Winona. She's a bona fide culinary legend."

Cutter was someone who felt no need to fill even the most awkward silences with the sound of his own voice. He could stare a frog off a flat rock and never utter a word.

"You know, out in L.A. they call this kind of cooking 'soul food.' I think that's true. I know it feeds my soul. Unfortunately, it also feeds my hips and thighs," she went on, smiling, but Cutter only sipped his coffee. Then, more seriously – "Cutter, I can understand why you might have a, well, distaste for people with disabilities. For people who use it as an excuse to –"

"Look, Miss Carter, the way I hear it, you've got a lot bigger problems than worryin' about what I think," he interrupted. "If I were you, I'd keep my mind steady focused on dealin' with those things." Cutter climbed into his jeep and turned the key. "But since you sent Nate to step-and-fetch your breakfast, if it's not too much trouble, would you tell him I'll be at The Well after four? In case he cares to drop by."

"The Well, huh? That's a beautiful spot. I made a lot of memories there. And a few of them are even good," she told him, smiling. Cutter did his best to look past her. "Did you know I held the record for two straight years? Two-minutes-eighteen-seconds."

He dropped the shifter into reverse. "Good day to you, Miss Carter."

Two sausage-biscuit meals were in a paper sack on the back floorboard when Holly Lee Carter turned west onto Blue Mountain Road, crossing the railroad tracks. The gravel cut twisted through fields of cotton, soybeans and some corn, and past the Old Ambrose Place, where Cutter had grown up. Ahead, the fog curled above the

river like a thick, white snake keeping close to the hills before exposing itself on the open floor of the Cattahatchie Valley. Holly eased
back on the hand control and stopped the car on the heavy plank floor-
ing of the Old Iron Bridge. In the early morning dew, the rust stains
leaking from the rivets looked like blood. Sunlight was yet to dip
into the fissure cut next to the limestone face of Blue Mountain, and
under Holly the river ran black and deep. This was the spot where her
father's car had gone in.

It was easy to see how it could happen. Just past the bridge and the
rutted lane leading to The Well, the gravel road rose sharply and curved.
Coming at night from Wolf's Run, in the rain, T.L. Carter's Oldsmobile
quickly would pick up momentum and with only a little too much speed
it would overshoot the turn, miss the bridge and go right off into the
river – swollen then by spring rains and spiked with debris.

T.L. Carter did not know how to swim. More than once he'd told
his water-loving daughter that he had no use for it as "I do not intend
to make a spectacle of myself by bathing in public."

There was no sense brooding now. Still, Holly wished there had
been a little more time. Through letters and phone calls, for the first
time in their lives, she and T.L. were getting to know each other – starting to accept each other's flaws, fears, hopes and regrets. Filled with
drugs and sandwiched tight in the Stryker-like frame, it had been a
struggle even to cry when Tom called with the news. But cry she had,
and longer and deeper than she would have supposed she might in
that situation. Crying not for the father she'd lost, but the father Holly
hoped T.L. might finally become – and the daughter she wanted to be.

Now here she was back in DeLong, at the very spot where he'd
died. Or was it?

Holly couldn't shake what Sheriff Johnson had told her about
T.L. resting up for a trip to California. "To be at my bedside when I
woke up," she whispered, exhaling a long sigh as she stared at the soft
shoulder at the west end of the bridge.

The new will … the increase in Klan violence … the trip to
L.A. … the accident … the missing painting of her mother.

It all was probably only coincidence, Holly told herself, but it's a
lot of coincidence. And it sounded as if Sheriff Johnson thought the
same thing.

Chapter 10

❦

One of Wolf's Run's most favorable features was that the limestone bluffs rising on either side of the plateau kept the house and courtyard mostly in shade except for a couple of hours on either side of noon. That meant that even without air-conditioning, the house stayed reasonably cool even on the hottest days. And now that the pool had been scrubbed, acid-washed and refilled, the wrought-iron patio table at the edge of the bluff was a beautiful spot for breakfast or dinner.

Eve put a silver coffee service on the table and Holly placed a tray of cookies, doughnuts and fresh fruit beside it. Sheriff Johnson probably had eaten breakfast several hours earlier, but they could snack. Holly was both eager for and anxious about the conversation.

"Okay, you're set," said Eve, looking at her watch. It was almost nine a.m. Tuesday morning. "I'm going to take a shower."

Holly watched her friend walk away, up the steps to the west wing and disappear into the house.

Eve had borrowed the car Sunday afternoon to go to a voting rights rally at Pickens' Ferry A.M.E. Church, where Reverend Clemmer and the National Coalition for Justice volunteers were making their headquarters. She returned with the news that Roy Hayes' little girl, Cynthia, had indeed lost her eyesight in the Klan attack a week earlier.

"That would be front-page news in a lot of papers," Eve had pointed out. Holly could only respond with silence, and the tension between them had been growing since.

Shaking off those thoughts, Holly sipped her coffee, glad to have a few minutes to review the notes in her steno pad from two calls she'd made on Monday, and a meeting with Dr. Martin Dale, DeLong's only optometrist and one of her father's oldest friends.

The first call had been to the attorney in Greenwood, down in Leflore County at the edge of the flat, fertile alluvial plain known simply as The Delta. His name was James J. Emmerich.

"Your father came to me as a referral from Gilroy Baddin, whom, as I'm sure you know, owns the newspaper here," Emmerich told her. "The other witness to the will was Conrad Whittington, a local planter and circuit judge."

"Now you say Daddy was emphatic about keeping the will a secret?"

"Absolutely," said Emmerich. "Until he chose to reveal it, or his death."

"And why was that?"

"I couldn't tell you. But he was very clear on that point."

"Is it possible either Mr. Baddin or Mr. Whittington violated my father's confidence?"

"Miss Carter, when you've been an attorney for thirty-five years, you come to realize that very few things are *im*-possible when it comes to relationships among members of our species. But in this case, I'd find it very difficult to imagine," he said. "These are men of excellent reputation. And from what I could surmise, they and your father were old and dear friends. Fraternity brothers at Tulane, I think."

"Yes, that sounds right," Holly agreed. "Did my father tell you why he came a hundred and fifty miles to execute a new will?"

James J. Emmerich was silent for a moment. Then, "Not in so many words. But I would postulate that he feared that the legal community in Cattahatchie County and nearby environs has been – shall we say, compromised? – by political influence. I think he was concerned that many of the attorneys there might not take their oath of confidentiality seriously enough."

"Last question," she'd said, "Did he tell you why he was changing the will? Why he was leaving controlling interest to me?"

"No. I'm sorry, Miss Carter. He did not."

So, she thought as she speared a piece of cantaloupe, *if someone wanted Daddy out of the way, he surely would have assumed that the newspaper would fall into Tom's hands.*

Holly flipped to the next page.

"**O**ld Man" John Pierce, who had run the DeLong Funeral Home for more than half a century, was not so affable or forthcoming. When she asked about the disposition of her father's effects, he took immediate umbrage. "If you're implying some impropriety on our part, young woman, I won't have it."

"No, sir. Not at all. I'm simply trying to do due diligence as the executor of my father's estate," Holly had assured him.

"I don't see why you're pestering me," he said. "Why don't you ask your brother? I turned everything over to him and Miss Mary Nell."

"No, sir. I need an official inventory of my father's effects as they were delivered to you."

"Hold, please," he said and the line had gone silent. Several minutes later he spoke again. "Very well. I have it. But it's rather short."

"That's all right, could you –?"

"Young woman, you realize, of course, that Mr. Carter's body was not recovered until five days after the accident," he interrupted. "It was discovered by two fishermen over in the edge of Lafayette County. The autopsy was performed there, so DeLong Funeral Home workers were not the first to handle the remains or Mr. Carter's effects. If there are any items missing, I suggest you call Dr. Phelps in Oxford."

"Thank you, I –"

"I'll have a copy made and left for you at the front desk. Goodbye, Miss –"

"One more question, please, Mr. Pierce. Was my father buried with his glasses on?"

Holly heard Mr. Pierce draw in a ragged breath. "Ahh, how could I have forgotten? You were not present for your father's funeral," he said, twisting the blade of guilt in her side. "So, you would not know that it was a closed-casket ceremony."

"Be that as it may, Mr. Pierce ..."

"I was present when my staff sealed the casket. The answer is no, he was not."

Holly opened the file folder next to her plate. There was a DeLong Funeral Home letterhead at the top followed by a brief list of all the items recovered with her father's body – or at least those delivered to DeLong Funeral Home. She read it again and it was about what anyone would expect under such circumstances. Two socks (one black, one brown), but only one brown leather wingtip shoe; brown suit pants and a white shirt; one brown belt; one pair of red suspenders; the remnants of one suit vest, brown; one pair boxer shorts; one white T-shirt; one black tri-fold wallet containing six dollars and various photographs.

More notable in Holly's eyes was what was not listed.

In many ways, T.L. Carter was quite old fashioned. He practically put on a tie to get up in the middle of the night and go to the bathroom. The gold watch he'd been given when he retired as president of the Mississippi Newspaper Association also was absent. But more glaring than anything else was that no raincoat, not even a suit coat, was recovered.

If he went home early that afternoon trying to hold off a cold, Holly reasoned, *it made no sense for him to go out in a cold rain that night in nothing but a vest and shirt sleeves.*

The final set of notes regarded her visit to Dr. Martin Dale's office. Three generations of Dales had been taking care of the eyes of Cattahatchie County for almost eighty years, including Holly's. Though she saw perfectly at long and medium distances, she had worn reading glasses since childhood.

After the usual formalities of re-acquaintance following a decade of absence, and the perfunctory compliments about how good she looked, how young and healthy, came the all-too-typical moment of silence when the person took in the wheelchair – really took it in – and let their eyes drift down her legs. Holly had come to think of it as "the broken-china moment." But Dr. Dale quickly freed himself from the familiar spell of compassion and pity, saying, "I'm sorry I couldn't see you this morning. I was simply jammed. I do believe this whole county is going blind. It's good for business, but – well, Holly, what can I do for you? Do you need new glasses?"

"No. I need to speak to you about a private matter," she said. Dr. Dale's receptionist, Susan Hodges, shuffled papers and worked hard at pretending disinterest. Susan had graduated from CHS two years ahead of Holly.

"Of course, come on back to my office," he said, and Holly followed the tall, stork-framed doctor down the narrow hall, barely able to make the sharp turn into his cramped quarters. He pushed a chair older than Holly out of the way and made room in front of his desk, then sat down.

"Dr. Dale, when was the last time you talked to my father?"

"T.L. and I had lunch together a week to the day before the accident – across the street at The Jeff Davis. His death was a terrible shock."

"Did he seem particularly worried about anything?"

"Other than your upcoming back surgery, no."

"He mentioned that? And his plans to fly to Los Angeles?"

"Yes. He was nervous about flying, but he was quite excited about seeing you. Such a shame," said Dr. Dale, his eyes losing focus for a moment, then settling again on Holly. "Did the surgery go well?"

"Yes, very. Thank you."

"Is there any chance it will allow you to, to uh –?"

"Walk? No, sir. I'm afraid this is – well, quite permanent. But the surgery did alleviate a lot of pain, and I'm grateful for that," she told him. "Now, beyond any concerns about me, did he seem particularly worried or upset?"

The optometrist studied the woman in front of him and his own recollection. "Well … T.L. was agitated about Weathers and his bunch, but then he always was. Still, he was beside himself at the notion that DeLong's place in history might be as 'the last battleground of segregation.' Which at this point seems a wholly valid concern."

Holly reached behind her and freed the purse straps that were wrapped around one handle of her chair. She took out a white business-size envelope and handed it to the doctor. "What's this?" he asked.

"That's what I want you to tell me." Martin Dale felt the exterior of the envelope. "Careful," she said. "You might cut yourself."

He put down the envelope in the center of his desk calendar, and leaned back in his chair. "Where did you get this? This whatever it is?"

"Again, doctor, for the moment I'd rather not say. But I'd like for you to examine the contents and tell whatever you can about it."

A slender finger played at the corner of Dr. Dale's narrow lips. "All right, Holly. I'll help, if I can."

"Thank you, doctor. Also, how many pairs of glasses did you make for my father in his most recent prescription and frame style?"

"As always, two. One to wear and a spare."

"Did he still keep the spare in the glove compartment of his car?"

"To the best of my knowledge," said Martin Dale. "As you know, your father's eyesight was quite poor. He was always fearful of being off somewhere and losing or breaking his glasses. He knew he couldn't drive without them."

"Certainly not on a pitch-black, rainy night," Holly added.

"Certainly not," agreed Dr. Dale. "Holly, where are you going with this?"

"Probably nowhere. But before I say anything more, I'd appreciate it if you could help me satisfy my curiosity."

"Very well. I'll get back to you as soon as possible."

"Thank you, Dr. Dale," she'd said.

The optometrist had stood and come around the desk. As he reached for the door knob, he and Holly had heard low-healed pumps clicking away on the tile. They looked at each other. "Welcome home," he said.

Holly bit deep into a large, delicious strawberry purchased from one of the county's many roadside vendors selling from their tailgates. The area was famous for them. She looked at her watch – 9:08. Sheriff Johnson probably was simply running late.

At 9:20, Holly dabbed a napkin at the corner of her mouth and pushed up the new ramp into the house. From the living room windows, she could see the circle in front of the house and all the way up to the road. She pushed back to the kitchen and took hold of the phone, but decided against calling. After all, Floyd Johnson was the sheriff. Any number of emergencies could have come up; and if she called looking for him, it would only rev up the talk her Monday inquiries probably already had generated.

Holly placed the receiver back on the hook and startled when it instantly rang. It sounded as loud as a siren in the quiet house.

The voice on the other end of the line was excited, almost gleeful. "Miss Carter, it looks like we've got our lead story for tomorrow. And it's a big one! It sure is," enthused C. Michael Morton, *The Current-*

Leader's young managing editor. "I sent two reporters and Ridge Bellafont out there."

"Calm down, Michael," said Holly. "Sent them out where?"

"Out to Sheriff Johnson's house on Buena Vista Road," he said. "Haven't you heard?"

Holly suddenly felt the pit of her stomach drop out. "No. Tell me."

"It looks like somebody planted a bomb in the sheriff's car. He got in it this morning to come to work and *ka-boom!* "

"Is he –?"

"Oh, yeah. Very," said Morton. "Ridge called from down the road at Kyle Renfro's house. He says the car was blown to bits, along with half the house."

"Mrs. Johnson?" Holly managed.

"She was in the back bedroom. She's all right."

Holly thought of the nice, steady, likable man she'd met on the Dumas Road less than four days ago. "At least you got to see your granddaughter get married," Holly said to herself.

"What's that, Miss Carter?" asked Morton. "I didn't catch that. Something about a granddaughter?"

Holly forced herself to don the hat of editor-in-chief. "Nothing. It was nothing," she said. "I'll be there in twenty minutes."

Chapter 11

❦

Eve Howard stood in the door to the publisher's office holding a page proof. It was just after sunset Friday night and the mid-July heat was stifling, even with the ceiling fans turning overhead and the big windows open onto the balcony and the square. And open, too, at the back of the building to catch whatever breeze was stirring along with the river's current.

Holly looked up from her desk "Which page is that?"

"Five."

"How many pages do we still have left?"

Eve was staring at the page in her hands. "Six. No, Mr. Rodgers said seven. I think. I'll have to check."

"May I see that proof?"

Eve crossed the room and laid the page in front of Holly. Most of Wednesday's paper had been about the murder of Sheriff Johnson. Most of Saturday's paper would be about the investigation and funeral arrangements. The headline at the top of the page read:

Ex-Gov. blames 'outside agitators' for sheriff's death

By Randall Murphy

Staff Writer

Flanked by four state legislators and three of five county supervisors, former Mississippi Governor Cecil Weathers rose before a crowd of more than three hundred gathered at the site for the new Riverview Academy and accused "outside agitators" of orchestrating the Tuesday car-bomb murder of Sheriff Floyd Johnson.

"We've all heard of them. Seen them on our televisions. In their black leather jackets and funny little foreign caps. Some people are afraid to name them because it is no longer fashionable to call a spade a spade," Weathers told the crowd at the Thursday night. "But I'm not afraid. I'll name them! They call themselves

The Black Panthers, and these Negro thugs will stop at nothing to see that the social and moral fabric of this nation is torn to shreds.

"We know that they have killed police officers in Oakland, California, and Chicago, Illinois. And now they've brought their murderous ways here by killing one of the best and most decent lawmen in Mississippi, my dear friend, Floyd Johnson," continued the former governor.

"Holly, I just can't believe you're running this crap," said Eve.

"I'm burying this 'crap', as you call it, on page five," she said.

"Well, la-de-dah, page five? I guess that makes you a candidate for some sort of social justice award?"

Holly straightened in her wheelchair and took off her reading glasses. Her shoulders ached from hours at that desk reading stories and checking pages. She rubbed her eyes and ran her hand down her neck where a sheen of perspiration glowed. The editor of *The Current-Leader* said, "Whether I like it or not, when the ex-governor of this state, flanked by members of the county board of supervisors and the state legislature, speaks to three hundred people, it's news. By all rights, front-page news."

"What about the two hundred people who came to Pickens' Ferry Church last Sunday for that voting rights rally?" asked Eve. "I have pictures. Mr. Rodgers says there's a hole we need to fill on page three."

"Stop it, Eve."

"Why? You don't think it's news? Or maybe you don't think black folks qualify as people?"

Holly felt a bolt of heat rush up her neck and into her cheeks as she pushed around her desk, intending to face young Eve Howard. Instead, she forced herself to turn away, stopping beside one of the large open windows. She stared out at the courthouse, letting the flash of anger cool. After a moment, "Eve, when you agreed to come to DeLong with me – practically begged to come here with me, I told you that I want to make changes in this newspaper," she said. "Especially in the way news from our black community is handled. But I warned you, that I was *not* returning to DeLong as some sort of political crusader. My first responsibility is to stabilize this newspaper financially, so that I *can* keep it out of the hands of people like Weathers. And if that means that I have to hold off for a time integrating the pages of this paper, then that's just the way it is."

Holly felt her friend's eyes fixing her. "Then tell me, when is the time going to be right? How many more black families are going to have to have their homes or businesses shot up? How many more black churches have to burn? How many more little black children have to be blinded? Or worse?" she demanded. "What's it going to take?"

"If you'll read my editorial, it calls for calm and a cooling off of the rhetoric by–"

"That's not enough," said Eve.

Holly pushed away from the window and returned to her desk. "I'm sorry, Eve," she said as she reset the glasses on her nose and picked up the page proof. "I guess I'm no Martin Luther King."

"No," said Eve. "I guess you're not."

Less than a minute later the editor's private line rang – "Holly Lee Carter."

"I'm not much of a hunter, but with the shutters open and your office lit up like that, I could put a deer slug right in your ear," said the voice.

Holly felt her heart suddenly thump in her chest as she looked out the second-floor window onto the quiet square. Those going to The Rebel Theater already were inside, chuckling at Michelle Lee and Dean Jones in *Herbie The Love Bug*. Then the soft Carolina drawl registered. She hoped her relieved sigh wasn't audible.

"Nice to hear from you, Mr. Burke," she said. "Where are you?"

"Third floor. Corner room. The Jefferson Davis Hotel," he told her. "With a 30.06 and a scope, I could take the side of your head off."

She took off her glasses and squinted across the square, but the third floor room was dark. "Do you have a scope or a 30.06 with you?"

"No."

"Good."

"Seriously, Miss Carter, you should be more careful. At least close the shades."

"It's hot in here. Daddy never bothered to have this place air-conditioned," she said feeling the dampness under her arms and along her collarbone. "Besides, don't you think you're being a little paranoid?"

"Being a little paranoid is a lot better than being a little dead. Just ask Sheriff Johnson."

"That's not funny."

"It's not meant to be."

The editor of *The Current-Leader* and the U.S. Attorney had talked several times before her return to DeLong, and a couple of times since. It was part of a pact they'd made. If Holly came back and ran the paper to keep it away from Weathers, Burke agreed to keep her abreast of things as best he could without endangering any ongoing investigations or prosecutions. Burke worked closely with the FBI and controlled his own force of federal marshals. Next to U.S. District Judge Oren Mulberry, who had ordered the desegregation of Cattahatchie schools and public offices by September 2, J.L. Burke probably was the most powerful and most hated man in north Mississippi.

"Seriously, Holly, if the Klan is willing to take out a county sheriff," he went on, "then they won't think twice about a newspaper editor."

"The Klan? Haven't you heard? It was the Black Panthers."

"Yeah, right."

"Besides, why should they come after me? I'm toeing the Ku Klux line. I'm running a segregated newspaper," she said, resting her elbow on her desk and holding her forehead in her hand.

"Is that what that exchange with Miss Howard was about?"

"I don't appreciate having a Peeping Tom."

"You look tired."

Holly sat back and ran her fingers through her hair. "I am. And I still have a newspaper to finish putting out tonight. So, if this is a social call –"

"It's not," said Burke. "I've got a scoop for you, though you can't attribute it to me."

"Sources close to the investigation?"

"That'll do."

"All right," said Holly, opening a steno pad. "What've you got?"

The U.S. Attorney told her that on the previous Thursday an informant spotted a man buying gas at a country store in eastern Cattahatchie County whom the FBI believes to be Robert Bedford McBride of Jasper, Alabama. McBride was a former Army Ranger and demolitions expert who served in Europe during World War II and later Korea.

"He's known in Klan circles as Dynamite Bob and is one of the main reasons why Birmingham, Alabama got its nickname – Bombingham," Burke went on. "In fact, we've always liked him for that 1963 church bombing there."

"The one that killed the four little black girls?"

"That's the one," said Burke. "We think he's responsible for at least sixteen bombings from Richmond, Virginia to Houston, Texas, since 1955, resulting in more than fourteen deaths and dozens of injuries. More recently, we think he engineered a series of break-ins at four military amories. Everything from M-16s and ammunition to hand grenades and C-4 plastic explosives were taken.

"McBride is smart and mean and Klan to the core. We've arrested him four times but never been able to make anything stick. We do our best to keep track of him, but when he wants to be, he's a ghost. About six weeks ago, he dropped completely off the radar."

"And you think he killed Sheriff Johnson?"

"We can place him in Cattahatchie County within a few days of the murder and he certainly has the requisite skills and mind-set," said Burke. "So, yes, Bob McBride certainly would be our leading candidate. We also think he's helped plan and carry out the recent string of church arsons and attacks in black communities in the county."

"And the motive for killing Sheriff Johnson?"

"Multiple motives. The sheriff had refused to break up the voting rights rallies or the NCJ encampment up at Pickens' Ferry. He'd also made it clear that unless it was overturned on appeal, he would enforce Judge Mulberry's integration order," Burke told her. "And just two weeks ago he had a run-in with Weathers and his cronies at The Cotton Café."

"Yes. I heard about that," said Holly absently, wondering if another motive should be added to the list? That the sheriff had pulled her father's file from county records. Was someone worried that Floyd Johnson was about to start asking new questions about T.L. Carter's death? Maybe, maybe not. It wasn't time to talk about that. Not yet. After all, what did she have? Nothing but an empty spot on the library wall where her mother's portrait had hung, and a feeling. Holly refocused on the moment, asked, "How much of this can I use? Can I call McBride 'the prime suspect'?"

"No. But you certainly can say he's wanted by multiple law enforcement agencies for questioning in the matter," said Burke. "As for the rest of it – well, you can use all the background. And I'm sending a marshal over right now with mug shots and a tag number. The tag probably was stolen, but who knows?

"We think he's moving from one Klan safe house to another along the Tennessee-Mississippi line. Hopefully someone has seen him in transit. Maybe we'll get lucky."

"Aren't you afraid this will spook him?"

"Spooking McBride is the best thing that could happen. That he'll bolt, and we'll run him down two or three months from now on some empty stretch of highway in Utah or Montana," said the U.S. Attorney. "But Bob McBride operated behind German lines for nearly fourteen months during World War II. Spook? No, Bob McBride won't spook. He's a true believer in The Cause, as they call it. He'll stay here until we catch him or his mission is completed, however he defines it."

"You almost sound as if you admire him."

Burke grunted. "Admire him? I despise him and all he stands for. But I don't underestimate him."

Holly sat back in her chair, saying nothing, letting that thought settle in. "Then I wish you luck, Mr. Burke, and I'll keep you and your efforts in my prayers," she said. "I think you'll need it with J.D. Benoit in the sheriff's office. I doubt you're going to get a lot of cooperation from the locals.

"You heard, I'm sure, that the county board of supervisors voted this morning to recommend to Governor Broderick that Benoit be appointed to fill the position until the November elections. In fact, Benoit's already bragging that Broderick is coming here Wednesday to personally administer the oath of office and get an update on the investigation into the bombing."

"Yes, I heard. Weathers controls the supervisors. It was a forgone conclusion."

Holly laughed sarcastically. "Under the circumstances, you sound pretty nonchalant about having Cecil Weathers' bodyguard as sheriff.

That's like having not just the fox, but a wolf guarding the henhouse, isn't it?"

Now it was Burke's turn to be silent, to measure his words. "Miss Carter, it's a long time from now until Wednesday," he told her.

Holly thought about that for a beat. "Would you care to elaborate?"

"No. But a word to the wise is sufficient," he said. "If I were you, I wouldn't put my Tuesday night paper to bed until you've heard from me."

Burke stared through his binoculars as a smile spread across Holly Lee Carter's face. Even from all the way across the square, it was like sunlight.

PART II

Chapter 1

❧

On Saturday I awoke to a golden blade of sunshine cutting across the bookcases that my brother Steve had built for me before Vietnam. From the depth of my pillow, the worn spines of books by Twain, Fitzgerald, Steinbeck and Eudora Welty glowed in the shelves like jewels touched by morning light ... morning light!

I bolted up in the bed and looked at my clock – 7:34. I should have been up two hours ago.

Quickly I hurried into the bathroom to relieve my bladder, brush my teeth and wash up. It wasn't until I was back in my room and was dressing that I noticed the curious smell of coffee laced with the scent of bacon frying. It had been a month of Sundays and then some since anyone made breakfast at my house except me.

Daddy was lifting strips of bacon from a black iron skillet when I entered the kitchen. He poured some of the bacon grease into a Mason jar and put the skillet back on the stove, then began cracking eggs into the pan.

"Sit down," he said. "Eggs'll be ready in a minute."

"I must have forgotten to set the alarm. I'm sorry," I said, though why I was apologizing to Billy Wallace I wasn't sure. He hadn't seen more than a dozen sunrises in the last two years.

"I shut it off," he said as he scrambled the eggs. "I figured you could use a break."

The man at the stove looked like my father – barefoot, worn jeans, a white T-shirt and denim work shirt open down the front. His whiskers were thick and mostly white, and his sandy blonde hair was disheveled. But all I could think about was that 1950s movie, *Invasion of the Body Snatchers*. In it, aliens kidnap humans and put them in giant pea pods, and when they emerge they're compliant zombies.

I poured myself a cup of coffee as Daddy said, "In fact, I dropped by Elmo Washington's place yesterday. He and his boys are lookin' to pick up some extra work. I told 'em you could use some help startin' Monday mornin'."

"So, I can't handle the farm? Is that what you're sayin'?"

I'd been angry for months that I had next to no help on the place, and now when Daddy was providing with me with three willing bodies, I took it as an insult. It was stupid, but there it was.

"I'm sayin' that this farm is too big for any one person to handle. Even if that person loved farmin', and you don't," he said, dumping a big yellow pile of eggs onto a plate. "Sit down and eat."

He fixed himself a plate and sat down with me. His right hand trembled when he lifted his coffee cup, so he steadied it with the other. "Nate, I know I've been pretty sorry the last couple of years. Pretty worthless," he said. "You've done a good job under rough circumstances. I'm proud of you."

The words tugged at something inside me and caused the corners of my mouth to twitch.

"The truth is, I hate farmin' too," he told me. "When I got back from fightin' in the Pacific, I swore I'd never put my butt on another tractor seat. And wouldn't have if it wasn't for your Grandpa Vernon gettin' sick and your momma missin' her people as much as she did. Then Steve took to plowin' and plantin' like a duck to water and I suppose I felt like I was buildin' a legacy for him. And for you, in a different way. So we could afford to send you off to college wherever you wanted to go. It made it tolerable.

"But when Steve was killed and Neesie grieved herself to death –" Billy Wallace shook his head. "There just didn't seem to be any point. To keepin' up the farm or anything else."

I dropped my fork and it clattered on the plate. "Then why the hell have you made me work like a dog the last two years?"

Billy Wallace swallowed a mouthful of eggs. "I don't have a good answer for that, Nate. Except that when you own a piece of land like this, that's what you do. And I supposed you might come to like it."

"Well, I don't."

"I know that. It wasn't fair to you."

The words my father was speaking should have sounded sweet to my ears, but I had so much resentment built up inside me that they simply sizzled on my eardrums like water on a hot griddle. I studied him suspiciously.

"If you don't mind me askin', what's the cause of this miraculous turnaround?"

Billy Wallace rubbed his whiskers, sighed. "I can't tell you the number of times over the last two years I said to myself things like, 'Come the first of the month I'll sober up. ... Come plantin' time I'll put the bottle away. ... Come Monday, I'm gonna turn over a new leaf. ... Tomorrow I'm pourin' it out.'

"Then, finally, I'd say, 'Just one more drink, then I'll be done with it.' But there was always just one more drink."

"So, what changed?"

Daddy stood and poured himself another cup of stout black coffee. "You know that Floyd Johnson was my boss, my teacher – my best friend when I was on Memphis P.D.," he said. I nodded. Of course, I knew. "I'm sure Floyd thought he'd have another day or another hour – another minute to deal with worldly affairs. Then he turned the key in his patrol car and time ran out.

"We just don't know, Nate, how many days or minutes, or even seconds, God has allotted for us on this earth. I've wasted most of the last two years swimmin' in self-pity, and that's a sin," he said. "Floyd was as good a man as I've ever known. I wish I could give him a little of that time I wasted. But, of course, I can't. At least not in that way. All I can do is pull myself out of this cesspool I've been in, and not waste any more of the time the good Lord gave me."

I suppose some sons would have jumped to their feet, shouted *hallelujah, praise God!* and hugged their daddy's neck. I did none of that. It wasn't so much that I didn't believe him, it was simply that my father had separated himself so completely from me over the last twenty-four or so months that it just didn't seem to matter. It was like having a conversation with a stranger.

After several long, awkward moments, I managed, "That's good, Daddy. I'm glad for you."

"The funeral is at eleven. I better get cleaned up. Myrtle Johnson asked me to be a pallbearer."

My brows arched, surprised. "I didn't know."

"Thought maybe we could ride out to New Hope together."

I wasn't ready to go anywhere with Billy Wallace, besides –
"Brother Mac has a carload of ministers riding with him. So, I'm picking Patti up."

"How are things with you and her?" Daddy asked as if he'd only
this morning returned from a long trip that afforded him no mail or
phone calls.

"They're good. Real good," I told him. "We can't wait to get away
together to college."

Even as he was trying to make peace with me and himself, I knew
I was sticking the knife in his side and twisting it. Saying, in essence,
that I could hardly wait to get out from under his roof and away from
him and this farm. But if he was wounded by my response, he didn't
show it.

"Aw'right, son. I guess I'll just see you out there," he said and
headed down the hall to the bathroom for his first shave in two weeks.

Chapter 2

୧

Had Sheriff Johnson's funeral been held in DeLong in the sanctuary of First Denomination Church, as Brother Mac and other county officials had wanted, it might have been the biggest in years. Maybe even bigger than T.L. Carter's service back in April. But Mrs. Johnson was adamant that she wanted no part of a show funeral at First Denomination.

Though she and the sheriff had not been regular church-goers over the last several years, mostly due to her emphysema, he had grown up in New Hope Community. If he had a church home, New Hope was it.

The church's floor and beams and joists pre-dated the Civil War. A new clapboard shell had been put on around the turn of the century and a new tin roof sometime in the 1940s. But the building seated only about ninety people and air-conditioning had never been installed. The massive oaks that surrounded New Hope Church and stood sentinel in the adjoining cemetery provided good shade, but with the temperature at ninety-three it didn't help much.

Highway patrolmen directed most mourners into a nearby pasture that had its share of dips and chuck holes. We were at the far end of one of the last rows since we were near the tail of the mourner caravan. Patti had insisted we slip off down a side road, park and smoke a joint before we got to the church.

"Funerals are so depressing," she said and took the baggie from her purse and rolled a fatty. She licked the edge of the Top paper like a pro and fired it up. I didn't like pot and I didn't like her smoking it, but whenever I tried to talk to her about it she said it was the only thing that calmed her nerves.

"All the MacAllister women are high-strung. We can't help it," she'd say. "Momma has her nerve pills, and I have this."

As usual, she insisted I join her, and I coughed my way through a couple of hits to keep the peace. I admit that Patti's blonde hair, gray eyes, hefty chest and motor-driven hips blinded me to a lot of her faults, but this wasn't one of them. I knew she couldn't care less if I smoked, except that by her calculations if she involved me in her crime, I was less likely to tell. I thought the pot was a phase she'd grow out of, and that as she matured in college away from Brother Daddy her sharp tongue and prickly attitudes would soften.

"Sometimes, Nate, you're such a wimp," she said, exhaling the last of the smoke out the truck window and applying fresh dabs of perfume behind her ears and at her wrists. "Let's go."

The walk up the gravel road to the small dirt churchyard where only family members and dignitaries were allowed to park was long, hot and particularly perilous for women in their Sunday go-to-meetin' heels. Pot was supposed to make a person mellow, but sometimes it had the opposite effect on Patti. Under her breath she cursed the gravel, her hose, her shoes, the heat and Mrs. Johnson for refusing Brother Mac's "most generous invitation" to hold the sheriff's funeral at First Denomination.

When we reached the churchyard and Patti saw that we'd have to stand at the back of the circle of mourners ten deep around the outside of the sanctuary, she cursed me for getting us there so late, but I let it roll off, knowing it was only the pot talking.

"We'll be able to hear," I said. "See, they've got loudspeakers set up."

"Hear? What do I care about hearing some barely literate redneck stumble through a sermon that my father could deliver twice as well in his sleep?" she asked. "But they've got ceiling fans inside. I'm melting like a popsicle on a car hood."

Then she spotted Miss Carter, sitting in her scraped-up Lincoln convertible next to the cemetery fence. She was wearing a sleevelss black dress, black lace scarf and Wayfarers.

"What do you suppose she wants here?"

"To pay her respects, I imagine. Like everyone else."

"Huh," Patti snorted. "That woman shouldn't be allowed anywhere near a church until she repents. The way she stole the paper from Mr. Tom and Miss Mary Nell. After all the years of hard work he put in. It's a shame and it ought to be a crime.

"She's no good. She's never been any good. My brother-in-law went to high school with her. He says she'd spread her legs for any man who could get it up. Now look at her. Got what she deserves, if you ask me."

There was a part of me that wanted to inform Patti that no one had asked her. But those would have been fightin' words, for sure. I let it pass and two minutes later the black DeLong Funeral Home hearse stopped in front of the old church.

Holly Lee Carter pulled a handkerchief from her black purse and patted the perspiration shining along her collarbone as she watched Mrs. Johnson make her way inside with one of her sons at her elbow. Old Man Pierce took his time organizing the pallbearers who had arrived in two sheriff's cars. Daddy was wearing his black suit, one of only two he owned. He'd lost so much weight it looked as if he'd borrowed it from the closet of a much bigger man. I saw he had his tie tight to his collar, but the shirt was still loose around his neck and already discolored with perspiration. As he passed close with the casket he smelled of the Aqua Velva on his face and the grain alcohol seeping out of his pores.

In my ear Patti whispered, "I hope your daddy doesn't have the shakes so bad he drops the por' ol' sheriff." Then she giggled. The muscles in my arm twitched and wanted to slap her. Instead I tightened my fist so hard that my nails cut into my palm, releasing the anger through my own pain. *It's the pot*, I reminded myself. *The pot*.

To the side of Holly Lee Carter and slightly behind her, a man cleared his throat. She twisted in the car seat. A young sheriff's deputy was standing there.

"Hi! Can I help you?" she asked. When he hesitated, she said, "I have permission to park here. I talked to –"

"Oh, I know!" he said stepping forward a bit so that she didn't have to crane around. "That's fine. You're fine." The young officer's hair was so blonde that it was almost white; his eyes were the blue of soft denim and he still seemed to be hanging onto a layer of baby fat at – what? – twenty-three or twenty-four. "Hon-, Honestly, I came to ask if I could help you?"

"Help me?" she asked, pulling off her sunglasses. "Help me how, Officer – ?"

"Deputy. Deputy John-Thomas Hinton," he said, pointing to the gold nametag above his badge. "My sister, Shirley, graduated with you in '59."

"Of course! How is Shirley?"

"Doin' pretty good. She's got two little'uns. Me'n the rest of the family spoil 'em like crazy, but – well, her husband, Charlie Jumper from over Booneville way, he got killed in Vietnam."

"Oh, I am sorry."

Deputy Hinton looked away then back. "I tried to enlist, but I tore up my knee playin' high school ball, and they wouldn't take me."

"Count yourself lucky."

"We all heard about what happened to you over there. You were in some of the worst of it. Ia Drang back in'65." When Holly said nothing, he went on, his eyes moving between her and the wheelchair folded behind the front seat. "Anyway, I just wanted to say I'm sorry how it turned out. I mean, about, uh –"

"Don't be," said Holly, launching into her standard answer. "I'm one of the lucky ones. I came back alive." And even as she said it, thought the same thing she always thought but never uttered ... *At least half of me did ...*

"Shirley took me with her to the fair the night you won the Miss Cattahatchie County Pageant," Deputy Hinton continued. "I was only in the eighth grade, but I won't ever forget. When you sang, *Faded Love*. Wow! I get chills just thinkin' about it."

Holly felt a warm flush at the base of her neck. "It was a lot of fun," she said as he continued to look her over as if she were some exotic cat. "So...?"

"Oh! So, I thought maybe you needed some help. I mean, getting in your wheelchair or whatever. I could put you in it."

Holly finally was recognizing the signs of a crush, apparently long held – and hung onto now despite the wheelchair. "That's very sweet of you, John-Thomas, but I've gotten pretty good at that over the last four years."

"I could even carry you inside if you want," he said, a little too enthusiastically. "I'm plenty stout."

"I'm sure you are. But really, I'm fine right here. Thank you."

John-Thomas Hinton's soft blue eyes looked crestfallen. "Well, aw'right, then. maybe I'll see you around town."

Suddenly, something crossed Holly's mind – "Oh, John-Thomas, you might be able to help me with one thing."

"Sure!" he enthused. "Whatcha need?"

"I was supposed to meet with Sheriff Johnson when he got back from the coast regarding my father's accident. Just to tie up some loose ends."

"For insurance? That sort of thing?"

"Something like that, yes," she told him. "Anyway, he was going to have the file pulled from county records. I was wondering –?"

Deputy Hinton already was shaking his head. "Holly, I think you may be outta luck there. I was in the office when Sheriff Johnson came by Saturday morning. He picked up some files from his desk and took them with him. I imagine he planned to study them over the weekend.

"I'll look around, but if I had to guess about it, I'd say they were in his car on Tuesday morning."

Holly bit her lip. "That's what I was afraid of."

"But I was there that night. At the bridge. I helped with the investigation."

The family and pallbearers still were arranging themselves inside the church. Holly hadn't expected this opportunity and she didn't want to let it pass. "Well, then, I was wondering, was there any indication that the brakes failed? Or that Daddy was going too fast?"

"After the car was pulled out of the river, we had a mechanic go over it. As far as he could tell, there was nothing wrong with the car," the deputy told her. "And speed wasn't a real factor from what we could see. It appeared that your dad just kinda of lost track of where he was. He went directly off the bank. There were no skid marks at all."

"And Cutter Carlucci's sister, Rose, saw the whole thing?"

"Yes."

"What, exactly, did she see?"

"I'm sorry, Holly. I wasn't there when Sheriff Johnson interviewed her. She was pretty upset. Besides, she's a little slow in the head," said the young deputy, tapping his temple. "She has trouble gettin' her words out. It's no wonder, livin' in that crazy house."

That certainly was true enough – it was no wonder, that is – thought Holly, as she tried to think of anything else she needed to ask while she had the chance. "John-Thomas, you didn't find a raincoat or a suit coat in the car or the river, did you?"

"No. But if Mr. Carter had one on, he probably threw it off getting out of the car. Or it could have been swept out of the car by the river. The windshield was smashed and the driver's side window was open. The current in that bend was as fierce as I've ever seen it."

Holly thought about that for a moment. "The driver's window was open? On a cold, rainy night like that? Not broken out?"

"That's right. In a situation like that, it's almost impossible to open a car door until the vehicle is full of water. We figure your dad rolled down the window to try to equalize the pressure and open the door. Or to try to get out through the window."

"Makes sense," said Holly. "Thanks, John-Thomas. You've been a big help."

The service lasted an hour and a half, and by the end of it we all looked and felt as wilted as the white gladioluses beside the pulpit. The fans stirred the air in the church but it had to be at least a hundred degrees inside that tin-roofed sweatbox. I was glad to be outside but Patti kept complaining about her feet and how hot it was. Finally, the family marched down the steps behind a nearly empty casket draped in a Mississippi state flag, the stars-and-bars of the Confederacy prominent in the upper left-hand corner. About fifty mourners went down to the gravesite, but most of us headed to our cars. The lucky ones had air-conditioning.

Dr. Martin Dale got his wife situated in their gold Chrysler Imperial, started the engine, put the air on high and excused himself. He crossed under the oaks shading the small parking area to where Holly was watching the graveside service.

"Am I intruding?" he asked, mopping his face with a linen handkerchief.

"No, doctor. Not at all," she said, removing her sunglasses. "I was just waiting for the traffic to thin a bit so that the car doesn't fill up with dust."

"I'm sorry I haven't gotten back to you this week on that matter we discussed, but it's – well, it's been a difficult few days for everyone," he told her. "Floyd was my wife's second cousin. She wanted to go down to the graveside, but it's far too hot for her."

"Oh, I didn't know they were related. I'm sorry."

"In any case, yesterday I got around to piecing together those shards of glass you brought to me," he said. Holly held her breath for a quick moment as she waited, not sure what she wanted to hear. "As I'm sure you suspected, it was a lens from your father's most recent glasses." He paused, considering. "I want to ask, where did you find it?"

"For now, I'd rather not say. And I'd prefer that you not share this information with anyone else."

"All right, Holly," he agreed, straightening. "But promise me, you'll be careful."

"I promise, doctor," she assured him, even as both knew careful might not be good enough. "Thank you. You've been a big help."

Chapter 3

∽

Blue Mountain Road dropped suddenly down the face of the hill in a long, steep S. Near the bottom, Holly had to dramatically slow the big convertible to make the turn onto the bridge. That on a clear, bright summer afternoon. On a wet, slick night, T.L. Carter would have had to slow his four-door Oldsmobile to a crawl. It would have been easy for her father to overshoot the turn in the darkness.

"So, why don't I believe it?" Holly asked herself again as she finished driving the route for the third time and parked beside the bridge on the narrow cut of road that led to The Well. Fish jumped in the brown, gentle current and a breeze fanned stalks of cotton and soybeans that spread for miles to the east away from the river. The crops paused at the railroad tracks and Highway 27, then picked up again and ran all the way to the eastern hills.

The road beside the bridge was a familiar one to her. As a teenager, she and friends often had found refuge at The Well. They would dive deep into the spring's maw to retrieve beers and shiny flasks of whiskey then swim off the chill in the warm summer waters of the Cattahatchie. Even though there was a pool at Wolf's Run, there was more danger, more thrills and more privacy at The Well.

With Charlie next to her, Holly lay her head back on the seat piecing together the apparent sequence of events.

… T.L. Carter went home early that rainy Tuesday afternoon. … At some point, his glasses were damaged and he lost a lens. He would have had to go out to his car, probably parked in the garage, to get his spare pair; otherwise he wouldn't even have been able to function around the house. … There was nothing on his schedule and there were no phone calls in or out of Wolf's Run, but at about 8:30 he left the house, apparently without a raincoat or even a suit coat, even though he was trying to hold off a cold. … Not even a tie, which was very atypical of T.L. Carter III. … Wearing his spare glasses he would have negotiated the S of the hillside road as he had done hundreds of times and yet he failed to make the turn at the bridge – or even try.

... Could he have been distracted by something? Maybe a deer or raccoon running across the road? she wondered. *Or simply overconfident that he could handle the turn in the wet conditions?*

Holly stared up at the clouds sailing languidly in the July sky. To the west, from behind the mountain, there was a rumble of distant thunder. She tried to think like the detectives she'd ridden with in L.A.

... So, then the car goes into the river. ... The windshield probably was intact when the car went into the river, she figured. *But Daddy, who could not swim, has the presence of mind in the utter blackness of that freezing water to roll down his window to try to escape? ... He surely wouldn't have been driving on a night like that with the window down. ... And at that point, while fighting for his life in the raging current, he shed his top coat, lost his pocket watch and so on.*

Holly straightened in the seat. There was nothing in the scenario that was impossible, she told herself. "But there sure is a lot that's improbable," she said aloud.

Now, with Sheriff Johnson dead and her father's file probably destroyed, the events of that night would have to be reinvestigated from scratch. She took a small day planner from her purse and wrote a note in the square for Monday, July 21: "Call Dr. Phelps in Oxford. Get copy of autopsy report." But Holly knew that the first step in the process was right in front of her, about a mile across the bean fields at the Old Ambrose Place. She put the car in gear. She knew she needed to talk to Rose Carlucci.

As she approached the turnoff to the paint-faded, dog trot house that represented all that remained of Jennifer Carlucci's once considerable inheritance, she eyed the dilapidated structure. She'd seen Tony Carlucci driving around town in an old white pickup with a missing tailgate. It wasn't present, or at least it was not parked in the dirt yard in front of the house. She turned down the pocked lane that ran between two barbed wire fences, fighting the urge to jam on the the brakes and back out of there as quickly as she could. The eleven-year-old memory came rushing back more powerfully than she had expected it might, jangling her nerves and unsettling her stomach more with every turn of the Lincoln's big whitewalls.

It was 1958 and she'd just done a couple of songs with the house band at The Gin. She was alone in the backstage hallway when Tony stepped from the shadows and pulled her into a janitor's closet. Holly remembered thinking, with the unlimited confidence of a seventeen-year-old, that she knew how to handle men like Tony Carlucci. For an instant she was more angry than scared, and the slap she had delivered sounded like thunder in the small tin room, but it had barely slowed him. He slammed her into the wall, smiling with bloody teeth before he threw his weight against her and jammed his lips onto hers. She tasted his blood and beer-soured spittle in her mouth. She twisted her face away and tried to scream but he grabbed her breast so hard that it squeezed the air from her lungs. As he shoved his hand up her skirt, the stink of sweat and cigarettes and testosterone filled her nostrils.

If the band hadn't decided to take a break at that moment, there was no telling what might have happened. They pulled him off of her, but he beat the crap out of three of them before a Tennessee highway patrolman, who happened to be in the club, put a .357 to the back of Tony's head and cocked the hammer.

No charges were filed – the courts weren't interested in the goin's on at state-line roadhouses unless a corpse had to be explained – but Tony was banned forever from The Gin.

Now after spending many nights riding with L.A. cops, a summer smoke jumping with wilderness firefighters and many weeks in Vietnam, Holly knew she could handle herself better now than at seventeen – even without the use of her legs. Besides, she told herself, dragging a paralyzed woman out of her car and attacking her in the front yard of his house within sight of his daughter and a public road probably was a stretch even for a worthless bastard like Tony Carlucci.

At the end of the lane, a flower bed fitted into a massive tractor tire created a circular driveway in front of the old house. Behind a nicked and rusted screen, the former Jennifer Ambrose Cutter was bent over a quilting frame on the side porch. She had been Holly's homeroom teacher at CHS until one February morning in 1958. She came to school as usual, chatted amiably with fellow teachers at the front desk, went to her classroom, removed her top coat and began writing algebra equations on the blackboard in nothing but her high heels.

Holly had been sitting in the third seat in the second row. Every place that normally would have been covered by a teacher's modest clothing was crisscrossed with scars, bruises and burn marks. Some old, some new. Some very new. Holly remembered the tears of pity and outrage that had scorched her cheeks as the girl beside her lost her breakfast on the black-and-white tile floor. Holly remembered how shaky her knees were when she pushed up from her desk. No one else moved as she walked to the coat rack, then to Jennifer Carlucci. She placed the coat around her teacher's bruised, boney shoulders and then drew her into a long, long embrace.

Mrs. Carlucci never had been heard to speak in a derogatory fashion about the father of her children. Whatever the problems of their marriage, she'd kept them all inside that house and inside herself – until she just couldn't do it any longer. Though she could not bear to speak it, she exposed it in a wordless cry for help. In the end, it made little difference. The Cutter and Ambrose clans had long since disowned Miss Jenny for marrying and then staying with Tony Carlucci; and Tony's war buddy and employer, Cecil Weathers, had made what little investigation there was go away. School officials were more shocked and concerned about the impact of Jennifer Carlucci's nudity on the children than on what caused it. After six months in the state mental hospital, one of Weathers' cronies on the bench placed Miss Jenny back in Tony's hands as her legal guardian.

To the best of Holly's knowledge, the bright, talented, big-hearted teacher with the amazing blue eyes had not spoken or written a word aside from mathematical formulas since that morning of Holly's junior year. Through winter and summer she sat on that porch making quilts with the geometric precision of rag-box Einstein. Quilts Tony sold as fast as his wife could make them.

Still, Holly stopped the Lincoln as close to the porch as she could. She put it in park and called, "Miss Jenny! Hello, Miss Jenny. It's Holly Lee Carter. I recently moved back. I'm living just up the road at Wolf's Run." But Jennifer Carlucci continued her rocking and stitching, as her lips calculated and figured and recalculated numbers that had meaning only for her.

At that moment, Rose Carlucci emerged from the house and came down the foot-worn, swayback steps of the front porch carrying a large tin bucket. She looked for a moment at the big car, then began watering the colorful rose bushes that grew inside the planter.

"Sh-Sh-She don't talk," said Rose.

"I know. But I thought I'd try."

"Tr-try all you want. But sh-she don't talk."

"Okay. Rose, do you know who I am?"

"Y-Y-Yes'um. Y-Y-You own the n-newspaper," she said. "I-I can r-read. I r-read it every-everytime somebody br-brings me one."

Holly had to fight a sudden quivering in her lips and a hot, dampness in her eyes. The last time she had seen Rose Carlucci, the girl had been a big-eyed eight-year-old carrying a stuffed panda bear doll down the sawdust midway at the county fair. If memory served, her brother had won it for her, throwing baseballs at milk jugs. Miss Jenny was sharing a swirl of pink-and-white cotton candy with her children when Holly stopped to say hello. Rose was shy with huge brown eyes, long brown hair and large, dark features – bearing no resemblance to the Cutter side of the family. She'd had a slight stutter even then. Now her eyes were just as huge in her face, but she had grown tall for a girl and broad-shouldered like her brother. Holly could see that Rose was shapely and full-figured, but the teenager was doing everything she could to hide it under baggy overalls, a loose T-shirt and work boots. Her hair was tied up and stuffed under an old straw sunhat. And her stutter was worse, so much worse.

"Your roses are beautiful," said Holly, wanting to say something nice. There were pink, red, white and yellow roses growing in a bright, healthy profusion at the center of the otherwise tired and ill-cared-for property. "You must take wonderful care of them."

"Th-Th … Thank … you," Rose managed. "Cu-Cu-Cutter br-brought me a, a book."

"A book on roses? About caring for them?"

The teenager nodded, smiling at the rainbow blossoming amid the decay of the surroundings. "'R-Roses for a, a Rose,' he-he said."

There was no sense in putting it off, thought Holly, knowing it might be difficult to get another chance. "Rose, I came to ask you about the night my father died." The girl's smile faded. "You saw it? You saw what happened? Yes?"

Rose nodded but offered nothing more.

"Y-Y-You *shhhh*-ould go."

"Rose, I'm just trying to understand what happened that night," Holly persisted. "I understand you saw the whole thing. I was –"

"Y-You should g-go!"

From the long open hall of the house, Holly saw a screen door swing open. Tony Carlucci let it slam behind him as he leaned on a nicked and scarred set of under-the-arm crutches. He swung his one leg forward followed by his crutches until he was propped at the edge of the porch in a strap T-shirt and his boxer shorts, the gnarled remainder of his thigh poking from the left leg opening. *His truck must have been parked around back,* thought Holly.

"Well, if it's not the high-and-mighty Miss Cattahatchie County herself, come to call in her big, fancy car," he said. "Welcome to our humble dwelling. It's no Wolf's Run, but we call it home."

For all his meanness of spirit and ugliness of soul, Tony Carlucci had been a handsome man a decade ago. Six-foot tall with coal black hair and an olive complexion paired with a chest as broad and hard as a keg of nails. He still had the short, thick, tattooed arms of a boxer who enjoyed working in close, but now his middle was much broader than his chest, and the whiskers on this chin and cheeks were the color of dirty dishwater. His hair still was black, though there was less of it except what was sprouting from his ears and nostrils.

Holly fought to keep her disgust and revulsion, and a twinge of fear, in check. "Mr. Carlucci, I came to ask Rose about the night my father died."

"Well, well. So Holly Lee Carter finally wants something from the lowly Carluccis. How does it feel to have people stare at you with nothing but pity and disgust in their eyes? The same as I saw in your eyes plenty of nights at The Gin."

Holly knew she should bite her tongue, but such had never been her nature. "If I looked at you that way, it had nothing to do with your leg."

"Kiss my ass," he snarled. "Rose had to answer the sheriff's questions, but you ain't no kind of law. She's weak in the head and she don't have to talk to you.

"Rose, get in the house!" he barked.

The girl gripped the watering can in her arms like a tin shield. "T-T-Talk to C-C-Cutter," said Rose.

"Shut up, girl! Get in the house like I told you."

Rose turned and hurried up the steps and past her father into the deep shadows of the hall.

From his vantage point on the porch, Tony Carlucci looked down into the convertible. Holly felt his eyes fix on her wheelchair, then on her. It felt like someone was rolling dirty marbles over her skin.

"Thought you were too good for me, didn't you? A one-legged dago mechanic," he said and spit into the dirt yard. He wiped his mouth with the back of his huge hand. "Well, just look at you now. Draggin' that *fine* backside of yours around and loading in and out of a rollin' chair, as dead as a sack of flour in a wheelbarrow." Holly gripped the car's wheel. "I bet you *wish* you could feel my hand between your legs now, don't you?"

Slowly she met the man's angry, lustful gaze. "Honestly, Tony, I'd rather be paralyzed."

A red rage suddenly boiled up under the olive skin on the broad surfaces of Tony Carlucci's unshaven face, and he began to curse. Holly pushed her Wayfarers onto her nose and Charlie stood in the seat and yapped a feisty reply. As she pulled away, Holly heard a crutch clatter off the car's trunk.

"*Bitch!*"

Chapter 4

☙

The Gin was an intersection of sorts – geographically and culturally – in our small part of the world.

Just across the Tennessee line at the northern terminus of Two-Mile Bridge, it was within a rock's throw of the Cattahatchie River and on the banks of Moccasin Slough, which sprawled westward across twenty swampy miles. Before the Cattahatchie, and its mother, the Tennessee River, were dammed in the 1930s for flood control and electrical power, it was one of the biggest cotton gins in the South. From September through November, Moccasin Gin #1 ran twenty-four hours a day, seven days a week. For decades, barges and mule-drawn cotton wagons brought the bright, white fiber there by the tens of tons to be cleaned and separated. Flatbed trucks and rail cars waited at the other end to haul away the burlap-wrapped bales. But the damming of the rivers and the construction of low-slung bridges for car and truck traffic eliminated the barges and small riverboats that had worked the Cattahatchie. Smaller gins sprang up and massive Moccasin #1 was no longer practical to operate.

By the time Gilbert Clanton, whose family owned the property, returned from four years in Europe during World War II, it was nothing but a huge, barn-like tin shell. But Gil Clanton saw the possibility for a supper club and music hall like he'd seen in England. For years The Gin struggled, until he heard a sound that was being called "rockabilly" and fell in love with it. Before long, unknowns such as Carl Perkins, Johnny Cash, Jerry Lee Lewis, Ray Charles and even Elvis Presley were playing The Gin and singing what came to be called "rock'n'roll" – and everyone wanted to hear it. Blacks and whites, and all shades in between. All of their money was green, and Gil Clanton expanded and improved the restaurant until it was famous from Memphis to Birmingham for its steaks and ribs and Cattahatchie catfish. Added were a dock and a screened deck that hung over the slough, and a "colored balcony" that wrapped around a dance floor the size of a basketball court. To the side was a big room with eight pool tables, and through a semi-secret door was a room where poker and blackjack were dealt every day but Sunday.

With so many black singers and bands regularly performing at The Gin, the color barrier inside the building pretty quickly broke down even in the early 1950s. By the last night Holly spent there in May of '59, The Gin was as integrated as any club in the South. That's not to say there wasn't tension, especially as the Civil Rights Movement began to make headlines, but that was where a bulky staff of no-nonsense bouncers came in handy.

Still, it created a stir when a young white woman in a wheelchair and an attractive black woman in jeans, sandals and a rainbow-colored dashiki came in. The place was packed and cigarette smoke as thick as L.A. smog hung in the high wooden rafters.

"I think I see a table," said Eve.

They worked their way to it, a row off the dance floor, as peanut shells crunched under Holly's wheels. The band was on a break.

"How's this?"

"It's ... It's fine," said Holly as if she'd heard the question from a distance across the din of voices and a kaleidoscope of memories inside the large tin room. The stage she'd often stood on looked the same, as did the dance floor scattered with sawdust. How many times had her high heels tapped on that hardwood? How many times had her tennis shoes left their mark? How many times had she felt the fine warm tingle of sawdust under her bare feet?

She looked toward the balcony and saw a mix of black and white faces, and smiled when she saw that a hoop was still in position at one end of the dance floor. On Sunday afternoons when the club was closed, employees and their friends often played pickup basketball games on the freshly swept hardwood. Holly had loved those games, and developed a reputation for being unafraid to take it to the hoop even against the biggest guys from the kitchen or the roadies just passing through.

"Do you see him?" asked Eve.

"No," said Holly.

"How do you know Mr. Mean-and-Gorgeous is even working?"

"It's Saturday night."

At six-three, Cutter Carlucci would be a hard guy to miss, but in the moving, shifting crowd of hundreds he could be anywhere – working the outdoor deck or the balcony. When the waitress came to the table, Holly asked for him.

"He's around here somewhere," she said.

"If you see him, could you send him over?"

The young waitress eyed Holly and then Eve with a mix of suspicion and curiosity. "I haven't seen you around here before. Are you a friend of his?"

Eve and Holly shared a glance. "I wouldn't go quite that far. Acquaintance might be a better word. Just tell him that Holly Lee Carter would like to speak to him, if he can spare a couple of minutes."

The band was pure rock with a Southern fried, bluesy edge. They were a bunch of unknowns but they really knew how to jam. When the waitress brought a second round and another basket of parched peanuts, Eve asked, "What's the name of the band?"

"The Alton Brothers," she said. "No, more like nuts. The Almond Brothers. No! The *All*man Brothers. That's it! I think they're from Georgia."

"Did you bump into Cutter?" asked Holly.

The waitress, who was all of twenty, hesitated. "Yes, Ma'am. I saw him. I told him."

"And?"

"And … well, a lot of women ask to talk to Cutter. You know?"

Holly felt a warm glow at the base of her neck. "I don't doubt it. But it's nothing like that," Holly assured the young woman. "I just need some information."

The waitress ran her eyes over Holly and the wheelchair. "Okay, look – he was going on break. He's probably over in the pool hall. That's –"

"I know where it is. Thank you," said Holly and handed her a ten.

Eve had to pull Holly backwards up two small steps to get her into the long side room where colorful lights hung from the ceiling and low over the tables, perfectly illuminating the green felt surfaces.

The rest of the room was deep in shadow except for the bar at the end. Behind the bar was a hidden stairway that led to a poker room.

Cutter was leaning against a wall next to a rack of sticks three tables down. Holly pushed toward him as Eve followed and a number of eyes followed them. Cutter held his cue and pretended not to notice.

"I thought if you didn't have time to come to my table, I'd come to yours," Holly said without preamble.

"My break's just about over," he said. "I'm workin' the upstairs. I'll have to get back to it."

"I won't keep you long," she continued as Cutter's opponent paused to check out both women and the conversation.

"Miss Carter, if you haven't noticed, I'm a little busy at the moment," he told her. "Jake, are you gonna shoot or –?"

"Sure," said the man in the John Deere cap. "I'm just linin' up my shot so I put you away."

"Look, Cutter, I only a need a few minutes," she persisted as one ball clicked against the other and moved silently off a cushion near a side pocket. The man straightened and sighed, almost groaned. With cat-like smoothness, Cutter moved around the table. He sank the nine and the fourteen together. A tough shot. The eight was a gimme.

Cutter lifted a small blue cube of chalk and pocketed the ten that had been beneath it. "Thank you, Jake. Come again."

At first the man looked angry as Cutter chalked the tip of his cue, then he laughed. "You just wait till next week. I'm gonna nail your cocky –"

"I'll be here," Cutter told him as the man shook his head and waddled toward the bar.

"So, you hustle," said Holly, reaching into a pocket on her brown skirt.

"I wouldn't call it that."

"Why not?"

"Because hustlers take advantage of people they know they can beat. I only play people who can compete with me. And if I happen to win a little something on the side, then I do."

"But you win a lot more than you lose?"

"Mostly."

Holly lay a twenty on the end of the table. "You rack 'em," she said.

Cutter didn't move but he could feel all the eyes in the room turning toward him and the woman in the chair. Eve was trying to melt into a wall. The room was quiet as Holly laid another twenty on the rail. "Forty dollars against ten minutes of your time," she said.

"Go ahead, Cutter!" someone called.

"Teach her a lesson," said someone else.

"I told you, Miss Carter. I play for the competition. I don't hustle people."

Holly put two more twenties on the end of the table. "There's eighty dollars that says you can't beat a ... a cripple in a wheelchair."

Now a circle was forming around the table. "Do it, Cutter!" urged one voice, then another. Someone grabbed the rack and began arranging the balls. "There you go," said the man. "You two're all set."

Holly dug in her pocket one more time. She found a five, two ones, a quarter, a nickel and two pennies. "All right, that's it," she said. "That's all I've got. Are we going to shoot or not?"

"Against ten minutes of my time?"

"Yes."

"Find yourself a cue."

Cutter won the break and slammed the cue ball hard just right of center as Holly rubbed white chalk onto her hands from a round next to the wall. He sank the eleven and the four giving him his choice of stripes or solids. He surveyed the table and took stripes, sinking the ten and the fifteen, bang-bang; then gently dropped the thirteen into a side pocket off two rails. He called the twelve in the corner pocket but it hung on the lip.

It was Holly's turn. The crowd, now two and three deep in places, had to back up as she wheeled around the table, checking the angles. She started to shoot the six but then backed off and took the one long down the rail, before putting away an easy three and a hard five-seven combination. She called the two in the side and squeezed it past Cutter's nine ball, leaving her only the six and the eight. But the six was at a tough angle from her chair. If only she could sit on the edge of the table and stretch for it, keeping a foot at the end of one long leg on the floor as the rules required.

"Excuse me, could you pass me that bridge, please?" she asked a man near the cue rack. He handed it over.

Holly placed the tip of her cue into a slot on the bridge and studied the angle. She could hear a murmur among the men surrounding her. Cutter watched her, his face and deep-set blue eyes showing nothing. Holly knew if she missed, Cutter was set up. She adjusted the bridge one last time and called the corner, but she could only stab at the ball. Without smooth follow-though, it kissed the rail just before it got the pocket and spun away.

Cutter dropped the nine and twelve in the same shot, then put the fourteen in past Holly's six in the corner. That left only an easy eight, straight in. Instead, he crossed to the opposite side of the table and called it off the rail and into the side pocket. His eyes met Holly's for an instant as he took aim. Then, with a perfect, gentle touch, banked it off the rail and in.

A shout went up around the table. Cutter picked up the money from the end of the table, folded it and shoved it into the pocket of his jeans.

He laid the cue on the table. "Break time's over. I've got to get back to work," he said and walked away.

Chapter 5

෴

Late Sunday afternoon I was returning to the house from a church softball game. I never was a big guy, but I had good speed and covered a lot of ground in center field. The First Denomination Crusaders had won 12-9 and Patti had been there to cheer us on, so I was feeling good as my truck rattled east on Pleasant Ridge Road. I had time for a good shower and a sandwich before heading back to First Denomination for choir practice. I already was thinking about how good Patti would smell standing in front of me in the big choir loft – the fine blonde hairs on the back of her neck shining like a golden pathway leading down the neck of her blouse.

I was maybe a quarter of a mile away when I saw two black four-door sedans pull out of our driveway and turn right, toward the eastern hills and away from me. I parked by the barn and walked up to the house.

Daddy was sitting on the porch swing in a pair of freshly washed khaki work britches and a clean white shirt. His hair was neatly combed, his chin clean-shaven and he appeared to be sober for the fourth or maybe fifth straight day. A modern record.

"Who were those men?" I asked.

"Government men. Federal men."

"What did they want? Are you in some kind of trouble?"

Billy Wallace chuckled. "Trouble? Yeah, you could say that."

I was starting to get nervous. Maybe Daddy had been so drunk the last couple of years he hadn't paid his taxes. That was the only reason I could imagine for the feds wanting my father. But on Sunday afternoon?

Billy Wallace extended his arm, a glass in his hand. It was steady or near about. "Son, why don't you get us both some tea and we'll talk."

I was hot and tired and wanted a shower; and I wanted to get back to Patti … and the fine blonde hairs on her neck. "I'm in kind of a rush."

My father sighed. "Nate, I know I haven't done a lot lately to deserve your respect, but don't take that tone with me again," he said firmly. "I've got something to say that you need to hear, because it's gonna affect you, too.

"Now go on, boy. Get us some tea."

I took the jelly glass from my father's big hand. His voice and eyes, and the set of his jaw left no room for discussion.

* * *

It was 8:30 that night when the doorbell rang at Wolf's Run.

Holly was in the library working at the desk and watching the latest on the Apollo 11 mission. The Eagle lander had settled onto the lunar surface a few minutes after three o'clock our time. Now two American astronauts were getting ready to leave the module. Holly already had changed for bed, into an extra-long Doors T-shirt that was faded from so many washings and soft from so many nights between her skin and the sheets. Eve was taking a bath, so Holly pushed up the long hall and into the foyer as Charlie skittered behind her.

Through the windows framing the door, Holly saw Cutter Carlucci leaning against a porch post – his shoulders broad, his waist narrow and his hips cocked under the tight fit of his Levis. No one else seemed to be around. Holly looked at herself. She surely wasn't dressed for company – braless in a T-shirt barely long enough to cover the catheter bag strapped to her thigh. The memory of the way Tony Carlucci had pawed her backstage at The Gin welled up again and caught in her throat, but she did not want to pass up a chance that Cutter might be willing to talk about her father's accident. Holly swallowed the memory as she tried to pull the hem of the T-shirt a bit lower on her thighs, telling herself that Cutter was not Tony. She opened the door.

"Hey," he said.

"Hey, yourself," she said as Charlie peeked out from behind Holly's chair, sniffing the air.

Except for the sing-song of crickets, there was a long silence as Cutter worked hard at not letting his eyes settle on the ... obvious. Holly crossed her arms across her chest, waiting him out. Finally Cutter said, "I know it's late to be visitin', but Mr. Gil sent me to Memphis first thing this morning to pick up some supplies down at the rail yard. The train was late. Then there was a hassle about – well, you don't want to hear all that." Holly decided to simply let him talk. "The point is, I didn't get back until a couple of hours ago, and then had to unload the truck. So, this is the first chance I've had to come by." She said nothing. Cutter dug into the front pocket of his jeans. "Eighty-seven dollars. And thirty-two cents. I told you, I don't hustle people."

Holly backed up, her green eyes suddenly flaring. *This is why he came?* "I don't want the money or your pity," she told him.

"I didn't mean –"

"You beat me. Period."

"Yeah, but I wouldn't have if you hadn't had to use that bridge. You're good. You'd have made that shot."

"Maybe. But I put my money down and took my chances. You don't owe me anything," she said, her temper cooling. "Except perhaps a rematch one of these days."

"You got it," he said, but made no move to pick the money up from the porch railing where he'd placed it. "Well, then I better take off."

"Wait. It sounds like you've had a long day," said Holly, thinking she still might get her ten minutes with Cutter. "Would you like something to eat?"

"Thanks, but I stopped at a barbecue place in Memphis. Besides, it's late. And the truth is, the astronauts – Apollo 11, you know? – they're about to step out on the moon. It's kind of exciting. I was listening to it on the radio."

"Then you have to come in," said Holly, backing into the foyer. "I'm watching it on television. Wouldn't you rather see it than just hear it?"

"Well, I –," he considered as Holly held her breath. "Sure, that would be good."

Cutter followed Holly around to the library. He stepped through the doors, took in the room and whistled. "Nice."

"Thank you," was all she could think to say to a young man whose worldly possessions were all out front in a rebuilt Army jeep. "Come on in."

The grainy black-and-white image of the lunar surface glowed from a 24-inch set fitted into one of the floor-to-ceiling book cases. CBS News anchor Walter Cronkite was talking with experts from NASA as they waited for the hatch to open.

"Make yourself comfortable," said Holly indicating a long, leather sofa.

Cutter sat and stretched an arm across the sofa back. "This could be a bed."

"It has been, quite a few times. I used to lay there and look out at the lights of the valley and up at the stars. I never imagined a short ten years later men would be about to walk on the moon." She smiled a wistful smile and felt Cutter's eyes settling on her. She couldn't blame him. "Look, I'm going to go change into something a little more – uhm, presentable. There's some lemon ice-box pie in the 'fridge. Straight from The Cotton. Let me get you a piece. And how about some coffee? Or milk?"

"Milk would be good. But only if you're eatin', too."

"You're on."

When Holly returned ten minutes later there was a tray resting on the lap of a colorful peasant skirt that hung almost to her ankles. She was wearing a sleeveless white linen blouse that buttoned up the front. Cutter was so engrossed in a section of glass-encased books on the back wall that he barely noticed.

"Find something that you like?" asked Holly as she placed the tray on the massive coffee table in front of the sofa.

"Twain. Poe. Dickens," he said as Holly wheeled over. "Some of these look like they could be first editions."

"Some of them are," said Holly.

"Wow."

"You're familiar with –"

Cutter grunted. "Even jocks can read, Miss Carter."

"I didn't mean it that way," she said. "It's just that when I was in high school, Mrs. Gadwell practically had to poke me with a pitchfork to get me to read the classics."

Cutter made no comment. Instead he nodded toward the TV. "Sounds like they're about to do it."

By 9:17 the pie plates were set aside and astronaut Neil Armstrong was on the steps of the lunar lander. Then as the whole world listened, Armstrong spoke: "This is one small step for a man, one giant leap for mankind." An instant later, he was standing on the surface of the moon. Holly applauded as Cutter smiled. For a few moments his face was open and unguarded, she noticed. His long arms and legs were relaxed and all the icy walls behind his blue eyes seemed to melt away.

They continued to watch in amazement for ten minutes or so until Holly pivoted and pushed toward the big window. The stars were bright in a clear night sky tinted yellow by the quarter moon. She bowed her head and clasped her hands. When she opened her eyes Cutter was standing on the other side of the chess table, watching her more than the night sky.

"'The heavens proclaim the glory of God. The skies declare the work of his hands,'" she said. "From Psalms. I can't remember which one. Nineteen, I think. It's just amazing when you look up and see the infinite universe that God spoke into existence. And yet, all these millions of years later, He still can call each of us by name and hear our prayers."

"Do you really believe that?"

"Yes, Cutter, I do."

"I wouldn't have taken you for the prayin', scripture quotin' type."

"And I wouldn't have taken you for a guy who reads Poe and Dickens," she said, smiling up at him. "People are full of surprises."

"Then I guess we've surprised each other tonight, haven't we?" asked Cutter as he moved a pawn on the chessboard. "You said you needed ten minutes of my time. What do you want to know?"

This was what Holly had been hoping for, but now she had to decide how much she wanted to reveal – and the answer was not much. She told him that as executor of T.L. Carter's estate, she was trying to "wrap up some loose ends," but with Sheriff Johnson dead and her father's file probably destroyed, she had to reconstruct the events herself. In attempting to do so, she'd tried to talk to Rose, she told Cutter. "But Tony was there. She got pretty upset. She told me I should talk to you."

With each word Cutter stiffened a bit more and another layer of ice formed at the back of his blue eyes. "My sister is carrying enough weight on her shoulders. I'd appreciate it if you'd not bring any more into her life."

Holly cleared her throat in the face of Cutter's sudden hardness. "All right. But I do need to get a better understanding of what happened that night. Can you tell me what you saw?"

"Honestly, Miss Carter, by the time I got to the bridge, there was nothing to see," he told her, staring out the window. He seemed to be looking beyond the valley and the sky, back through time to that March night. "Rose was worried about a history test the next day. She knew I'd likely be camped under the overhang at The Well. Daddy was off someplace. After she got Momma to bed, she started walking over so I could help her study for it.

"People think Rose is stupid, but she's not. She just tangles up her words."

"I understand," said Holly.

"Anyway … a light rain was falling. It was cold. The clouds were thick so there was no moonlight. Suddenly Rose came runnin' up, all excited. After a few tries, she managed to to get out the words 'car' and 'river.'

"I pulled my boots on and grabbed my slicker, and we hopped in the jeep. By the time we got back to the bridge, there was no sign of a car, but I could see where it had gone over the edge."

Holly considered all Cutter was telling her. "How much time was there between when Rose saw the car go into the river and you two got back to the bridge?"

"Well, let's see. Now you know, Rose wasn't right at the bridge when it happened?"

"No. I didn't know. Everyone made it sound like she was right there."

"I don't know who you've been talking to, but – no, Rose was probably seventy-five yards east of the bridge. All she really saw was a set of headlights go over the bank and into the river."

"Then she didn't recognize it as my father's car?"

"No. We had no idea it was Mr. Carter."

"So, how long …?"

Cutter calculated. "Between five and seven or eight minutes, I'd say. I took my flashlight and a length of rope from my jeep and went as far south along the bank as I could – maybe two hundred yards – before I hit Wilbur Creek. It was way too deep and wide to cross. So, I worked my way back, checkin' the banks as best I could."

"Did you see anything unusual?"

"Unusual?"

"Like a raincoat or a suit coat caught up on a limb?"

"Nope. Sorry."

"All right. Then what?"

"When I got back to the Jeep, we high-tailed it to the Landry house at the intersection of Highway 27. It was the closest phone."

"And from the time Daddy's car went in until then, how long was it?"

"Twenty to twenty-five minutes, I'd say. Maybe a little longer," he told Holly as she bit her lip, deep in thought. "Look, Miss Carter, if you're thinkin' I should have gone for help first thing – well, I've wondered that myself since –"

"No!" said Holly, snapping out of her thoughts and settling her eyes on his. "No, Cutter, I wasn't thinking that at all. You did every-thing any daughter could ask someone to do in that circumstance. And more.

"Just one more question. Did you see any other cars on the road from the time Daddy's car went in until the sheriff's cars showed up?"

"No. Not a one."

"You sound pretty sure."

"I am. I was hoping someone would come along to help. Someone with a stronger light. But no one did."

"What about while you were still at The Well?"

"No. No vehicle could have crossed the bottom between the bridge and the railroad tracks without us seeing it," he told her. Then, "Miss Carter, what's this really about?"

Holly considered her response. "Cutter, you've been a big help. And I appreciate it. I appreciate you coming here tonight. But I'm not comfortable saying anything else just yet. It's probably nothing."

He studied her for a moment. "All right. Then I guess I'll be going. Thanks for the pie. It was good."

"Thank Miss Winona," said Holly as she pushed beside Cutter up the hall and to the front door. "Do you suppose you could do me one more favor?" Cutter didn't do anything automatically except run for touchdowns, so he waited to hear the request. "Could you talk to Rose and see if there is anything else she remembers? Even something small could be important."

Under the yellow porch light, Cutter turned. "I'll try, but if I see it's upsetting her, then that's it."

"I understand. That's all I can ask," she said, knowing she should leave it at that, but couldn't. Holly wheeled onto the porch as Cutter started down the brick steps. She held the screened door open. When he got to the bottom he turned. "Cutter, I can only imagine what you and Rose and Miss Jenny have gone through under Tony Carlucci's roof. And I –"

"Don't," Cutter interrupted. "Don't try to imagine. Don't think about it. Don't –" He kicked at the pea gravel in the turnaround. "Don't try to crawl inside somebody's else nightmare."

"Cutter, I –"

"Look, Miss Carter, I appreciate whatever you're trying to say. But we've all got our struggles. I've got mine. And … And you've got yours," he said. "Let's leave it at that."

"All right, Cutter," agreed Holly as he climbed into his jeep. To her surprise, he didn't instantly turn the key. Instead, he rested his arms on the steering wheel and looked up through the walnut and pecan trees and past the crest of the house. "Do you remember where you were when President Kennedy was killed?" he asked.

"Yes. I remember exactly."

"Me, too. I'm guessin' this moon landing is going to be the same way. Thirty years from now when someone asks, people will remember exactly where they were and who they were with when Armstrong stepped off that ladder."

Strange, she'd had the same thought earlier, but hadn't voiced it. Now, "Yes, I think you're right," she said.

"Thanks for lettin' me watch it with you. Good-night, Miss Carter."

"You're welcome, Cutter. Good-night."

* * *

"Where have you been?" I demanded as Cutter stepped out of his jeep at The Well. "I've been waiting here since the end of choir practice." He tugged at the front of my shirt. "What are you doing?" I asked, my voice sounding shrill, as if it was coming from somewhere outside myself.

"I was checkin' to see if you'd grown a set of boobs. 'Cause otherwise you don't look like my mamma."

"You think this is a joke?"

"Nate, I don't know what it is," he said, starting to take some of his gear out of the Jeep. "You're not makin' any sense."

Cutter was right, and I knew it, but I was so shaken I could barely steady myself. "I left the house, and Daddy. All my gear is in my truck. I, I, I want to rough it with you until we get out of school, and me and Patti can get away to college."

That stopped him. He propped his shotgun against a boulder and dropped his sleeping bag next to the blackened fire pit. He lit a kerosene lantern and put if off to the side so only a light, yellow glow touched us. "All right, Nate. Sit down and tell me what's happened."

I wanted to tell him but I didn't want to sit. I felt like a cat in a cage with griddle for a floor. "It's Daddy. He's gone crazy. He's lost his mind!"

"What? Did he go back on the 'shine?"

"No! He's sober as a judge," I said, pacing. "But that's not a bad idea. I swear I'd buy him a year's supply if he'd crawl back in his bottle. I mean, havin' a drunk for a daddy is an embarrassment, but at least people kinda understood. With Steve and Momma and everything. Even Brother Mac cut him slack. But this? Nobody is gonna understand *this*."

"Nate, stop prowling. Stand still and tell me what happened."

"Daddy swore me to secrecy."

Cutter looked at me as he wanted to toss me in The Well. I couldn't blame him. "Then you ought to honor your word to your daddy," he said and began unrolling his sleeping bag.

"Daddy's gonna be the new sheriff," I blurted. Cutter said nothing but he stopped what he was doing. I had his full attention. "It's true!

I came home this afternoon and that Burke guy – the U.S. attorney – and a bunch of FBI men were leavin'. The governor is gonna appoint Daddy sheriff to fill out Mr. Johnson's term."

"I thought the county board of supervisors already appointed Tony's runnin' buddy, Benoit."

"According to Daddy, the supervisors can't appoint, they can only recommend. It's all up to the governor."

Cutter laughed as big and long as I'd ever heard him laugh. It made me want to punch him, but even at that high level of agitation, I had better sense than to try. "I'd give a week's wages to see Tony's face when word gets out. Him and Benoit and Weathers! They'll be kickin' and cussin' and spittin' brimstone."

"This may be funny to you, but it's not to me. Not even a little bit."

"Your daddy used to be a Memphis police detective, right? So, it's not so far-fetched. A lot of people would be proud for their daddy to be appointed sheriff."

"Proud?" I gasped. "Don't you understand what this means? Everybody will know Daddy's sidin' with the race-mixers. Brother Mac could split me and Patti up over this. That's why I knew I had to move out. To show I'm not part of this."

Cutter's smile was gone now. He knelt by The Well and splashed cold water on his face, then around the back of his neck and shook the remaining droplets off his hands. "It could be, Nate, your daddy needs you more than ever now. You're all he's got. You're his son."

"Yeah, well, he should have thought of that before he went into the bottle the last two years. And before he got mixed up with integrationists."

"Dad-gum-it, Nate! Would you stop talking like Preacher MacAllister? Integrationists? Race-mixers? I never heard you use those words in your life until you started datin' Patti."

"That don't make it wrong."

"It don't make it right either," he said, then considered. "Look, my advice is you sleep here under the stars for a few nights until things cool off. Then go on home."

"And what if I don't want to? What if I want to stay here?"

Cutter blew out his breath and walked to the ledge overhanging the river.

"It's a free country, Nate. My people don't own this land. Not anymore. I've got no right to run you off. But just so you understand – I go my own way and keep my own schedule. This ain't Boy Scouts. This ain't 'Camp Cutter,' either, with three hots and a cot, and a counselor to tuck you in. This is a hard, rough way to live for more than a few days," he told me as we stared across the bean and cotton stalks to the Old Ambrose Place. The light was on, as always, in Rose's room at the northwest corner of the house. "I know if I could go home and trust that Tony wouldn't blow my brains out in the middle of the night, I wouldn't be sleepin' here."

I didn't know what to say to that, so after a moment I just said, "I guess I better unload my truck."

I thought maybe Cutter would help, but he didn't. Instead, he simply stood there on the ledge, looking up at the moon.

Chapter 6

∾

As it turned out, I didn't have to find a way to tell Patti and her father about my daddy's new job. On Tuesday morning, someone in Governor Broderick's office leaked it in time for the noon news on the Memphis TV stations. To say that the information sent Weathers, Benoit, Mr. Wellingham, Milton Handley, Walter Kamp, Tom Carter and three of the five county commissioners – and, of course, Brother Mac – scurrying about like decapitated chickens would be a tremendous understatement. They were more like rabid dogs with their tails on fire as they climbed into a trio of big cars and headed for Jackson to confront the current head of state before the reported Wednesday swearing-in. But U.S. Attorney J.L. Burke outflanked them.

"Governor Broderick is in the air now," Burke told Holly Lee Carter in a late afternoon phone call. "He'll be landing at Cattahatchie International Airport at about five o'clock."

"You mean that cow pasture west of town that the crop dusters use?"

"That would be the one," he said. "The governor will swear Billy Wallace in right there, then fly on to St. Louis. His daughter is about to have a baby. So, he has a family emergency and probably will be unavailable to the press, and everyone else, for several days."

"Ahhh," sighed Holly. "The all-purpose family emergency."

"Yes. But if you hustle a photographer out to that airstrip, you'll be the only paper with pictures of the swearing in," he said. "I'd hoped to give you another exclusive, like the McBride thing, but Weathers still has a lot of friends in the state capital."

"Yes. And Broderick is supposed to be one of them," said Holly. "You must have something pretty nasty on him to get him to publicly embarrass his mentor this way."

"Let's just say, we do our homework."

"Uh-huh. Speaking of McBride, is there anything new?"

Burke paused, then, "Off the record?"

"If that's how it has to be."

"It is."

"All right, off the record."

"He's definitely in Cattahatchie County," Burke told her. "We had a confirmed sighting on Sunday."

"Where?"

"Sorry, Holly. I can't say. But it gets worse. A sergeant at Fort Hood, Texas, went AWOL last week. When he left, he took fifty pounds of military grade C-4 plastic explosive with him."

"I saw that stuff work in Vietnam," said Holly. "With fifty pounds of it, he could – he could –?"

"Level most of city block, I'm told."

"My God," she sighed. "But what makes you think this has any connection to McBride."

"The sergeant is McBride's nephew, but on his sister's side and by her second marriage. No one ever made the connection," explained Burke. "The FBI and Army CID now think Sergeant Rudolph has been buying or stealing weapons, ammunition and explosives for years – maybe more than a decade, and passing them on to Uncle Bob and his buddies with the pointy hats. We're fairly certain he was involved in two of the four recent armory break-ins."

"Why did Rudolph take off now?"

"With our, shall we say, reinvigorated interest in McBride, we were turning over rocks we'd never looked under before. I think he was feeling the heat."

"What makes you think the guy is coming here?"

"In the first place, he's not a demolition man," said Burke. "So, he has no real use for C-4 himself. And you can't just set up a roadside stand and sell the stuff. Second, McBride's nickname is Dynamite Bob, but C-4 is his weapon of choice when he can lay his hands on it.

"And also, well –" he started then reconsidered.

"And also what?"

"This is way off the record."

Holly paused a beat. "Okay."

"A young police officer in Eudora, Arkansas – not far from the Mississippi River bridge at Greenville – stopped an eastbound car

Saturday night with Texas plates stolen from near Fort Hood. The driver came out of the car with two .45 semi-autos. He emptied both of them. The officer told his chief that he's pretty sure he wounded the shooter before he got away."

"And the officer?"

"He died on the operating table."

* * *

A s soon as the news broke on TV about my father's appointment, I made myself scarce from *The Current-Leader* office. I was afraid Miss Carter would be mad that I hadn't told her, and either way, I didn't want to answer questions or be quoted for the story. I read about Daddy's swearing-in like everyone else in the Wednesday morning edition of the paper. Even as angry with him as I was, I had to admit that in the front page picture of the governor pinning the badge on his shirt, William Tice Wallace looked handsome and steady, and more full of spirit than I'd seen in two years or more. But for me, I had narrowly avoided a personal disaster.

When I rang the bell at the parsonage Tuesday afternoon, Brother Mac was in his study filled with what he called "righteous wrath" as he prepared a radio editorial condemning the "demons of deceit who have corrupted the godly decisions of Cattahatchie County's duly elected public officials."

It would have been the end for me and Patti had I not been able to tell him that my father had made me give him my word not to tell *anyone*. There wasn't a lot of "righteous wrath" he could lay on me for honoring my word to my father. And when I told him I'd moved out in order to distance myself from Billy Wallace's misguided deeds, C.E. MacAllister was appeased, or at least stymied.

Chapter 7

෧

Wednesday afternoon was rainy as Holly drove through the wet streets of New Albany, twenty miles south of DeLong, and headed west on Highway 30 toward Lafayette County. She had a 3 p.m. appointment in Oxford with Dr. Ferguson Phelps, the county medical examiner.

The rain was drumming on the convertible's canvas roof and Otis Redding was on the eight-track player singing about *Sittin' on the Dock of the Bay*. Charlie was curled next to Holly's hip, sleeping. Eve Howard stared out the window at the rolling hills covered in thick pine woods and the long fertile bottoms alive with cotton, soybeans and corn. Cattle stood in pastures on the low hillsides, chewing their cud, oblivious to the rain. Holly had stopped trying to make casual small talk with Eve; it only seemed to make her angrier. Had Holly not feared she would need Eve to get her over curbs or up a step here or there, she would have left her in DeLong.

Eve lifted her camera and focused out the rain-streaked window. She pushed the shutter release and the motor-drive click-click-clicked.

"I told you my grandparents grew up near some little hole-in-the-road called Skuna, Mississippi, didn't I?" Eve asked without looking at Holly. "Before they scraped together the money for train tickets to Chicago. I guess that was in the 1920s."

"Yes. You told me," Holly said carefully.

"Where is that from here? Skuna?"

"About fifty miles to the southwest. Down in Calhoun County, I think."

"When they came to visit out in California, they'd get to cooking their ribs and collard greens and cornbread, and talking about old times 'down home in Mississippi,'" Eve remembered. "They'd laugh, and Grandpa DeRitter would slap his knee over some crazy story about a mule. He'd reminisce about sleeping in a cotton wagon or guarding their watermelon patch with a piece of wood cut and painted to look like a shotgun.

"Then Grandma would talk about how beautiful the hills were and how magical the winter's first frost always seemed. 'Like a white satin wedding dress,' she'd say.

"And I'd think, 'This can't be the same Mississippi where they lynch black teenagers for just looking at a white woman ... where they burn black churches with no more thought than lighting a campfire ... where the Klan kills civil rights workers and buries them in the woods.'"

The wet black pavement rolled on across the Cattahatchie River bottom ten miles east of Oxford then rose back into the hills. "Eve, we all have a choice about what we carry forward with us in this life," Holly finally said. "Your grandparents chose to leave the ugliness behind and carry in their hearts only the good times. It doesn't mean they've forgotten, but it sounds like they've forgiven."

The windshield wipers churned back and forth. "I suppose," said Eve. "But I don't have that kind of forgiveness in my heart right now. I don't know that I ever will. I feel more angry by the day. Angry at myself, too.

"Holly, I don't know how much longer I can justify to myself living in a slave-built mansion while lots of my people are still using outhouses. Living in the bubble of protection and privilege that your name and family history here creates while regular black folks are being harassed and threatened every day. Simply for wanting to vote and to send their kids to a decent school."

Eve stared out the window as they passed a sign reading: Welcome to the Town of Oxford: Home of THE University of Mississippi Rebels.

"You need to do what your heart tells you, Eve. I just hope you won't make a choice based on anger," said Holly as they stopped at the light where North Lamar ran into the town square. The red brick courthouse with its tall, white cupola made famous in William Faulkner's novels, stood in front of them. "All I ask is that you give me enough notice that I can find someone else before you leave."

"Okay."

* * *

The clinic was housed in a three-story Victorian on Tyler Avenue. Fortunately, there was a ramp up to the porch for wheelchair-using patients. But Dr. Phelps' office was upstairs. so they met in an examination room on the first floor.

Dr. Ferguson Phelps was bent and balding and leaned heavily on a black cane with a silver handle in the shape of an eagle with its wings folded back. He dropped onto a stool and dismissed Eve with a glance of his milky eyes then carefully looked Holly over. She guessed the man to be close to eighty.

"You're a paraplegic," he said without introduction.

Surprised, Holly responded automatically – "Yes."

"Do you have any use of your legs?"

She hesitated, then, "No. None."

"Can you stand at all?"

"With leg braces and crutches."

"What about bladder function? And your womanly functions?"

Holly and Eve shared a look. "Doctor, I'm not here for an examination. I called about my father's autopsy. You are the Lafayette County medical examiner?"

"Oh, yes. Have been for forty-three years."

"T.L. Carter?" Holly prodded. "He was found in the Cattahatchie. Back in March you ruled his death an accidental drowning."

Dr. Phelps slapped his forehead. "Oh, my goodness! Of course. You're Mr. Carter's daughter. I've read about you. You were a reporter. Got yourself shot in Vietnam."

"I was … I am a photographer."

"A woman has no business in a place like that," he went on. "Perhaps that's the lesson God wants others to learn through your suffering."

Holly bit her lip then let go of it and her irritation. He was an old man born in another and very different century, and she needed his help. "Doctor, what can you tell me about my father's death?"

"Nothing without the report."

"Is that it there in your lap?" asked Eve.

The old doctor looked down and grumbled something. He opened the file without response. "Let's see," he sighed as he studied the file. "Yes. ... Uh-hum. ... Yes. ... Yes. ... Well, Mr. Carter drowned."

"May I see the report."

Dr. Phelps gave Holly the folder and she quickly read through it, forcing herself not to react to detailed descriptions of numerous injuries to her father's body. There were no photographs. At the back of the file was an inventory of the items found with the body. No suit coat or rain coat was mentioned, nor was there anything about glasses or a gold pocket watch.

"Doctor, how did you determine that my father drowned?"

"Young lady, your father is not the first drowning victim I've autopsied by a long shot. I've seen more –"

"Doctor, I'm not questioning your competence," Holly assured him. "I'm merely asking a question."

"Well, as long as that's understood. Some people around here think it's time for me to be put out to pasture. But I've still got it up here," he said, tapping his skull with a boney finger. "I examined your father's nasal passages, sinuses and lungs. We took slides and looked at them under the microscope. They contained water, grit and microbes consistent with those found in the Cattahatchie. I've seen it many times."

"So, he was breathing when he went into the river?"

"Obviously. Else he could not have drowned."

"Right," agreed Holly, taking a moment to think. "What about all the injuries to my father's body. Broken ribs? A broken leg? A separated shoulder?"

"As you're probably aware, during the spring rains the Cattahatchie flows hard and fast. Those injuries were sustained by being struck with debris, pummeled against rocks, bridge pilings, that sort of thing."

"What about the large gash on his forehead? And the skull fracture?" she asked, handing him the report.

Dr. Phelps glanced at his notes. "Oh, yes. That's consistent with someone striking their head on the steering wheel during an automobile crash."

Holly nodded, but said nothing as she considered. "Doctor, did you go to DeLong and examine my father's car? Specifically the steering wheel? To see if it matched the wound to my father's forehead."

"My dear, there was no need," he told her. "DeLong is a long way to haul these old bones. Besides, there was an eyewitness to the accident. A girl walking on the road, I believe. And, sadly, I've seen this sort of impact head injury dozens of times in the last forty years."

"Impact head injury?" asked Holly, having trouble now holding her temper. "Doctor, there was no impact. My father's car could not have been going more than twenty miles an hour. It slid over a soft, earthen bank and into the river."

Dr. Phelps straightened himself as best his bent old spine would allow. "Young woman, I've seen people suffer similar catastrophic head injuries during five-mile-an-hour automobile mishaps in a grocery store parking lot."

The doctor's hand was gripping the head of his cane so tightly that his knuckles were growing pale. Holly said, "Just one more question, doctor. Did you know that witness saw my father's car go into the river before or after you issued your report?"

Dr. Phelps huffed and pushed himself up. "I don't see what possible difference that could make."

"Maybe none, maybe a lot," said Eve.

The old doctor stared at the tall young black woman leaning against his examining table. His face colored and his hand clenched the head of the cane. Then he wheeled with surprising spryness and opened the door. "I believe I've said all I have to say," he told them as he stepped into the hall. "I'm not sure what your purpose is in coming here and attempting to impugn my professional abilities, or who sent you, but I won't have it." Patients and staff paused at the check-in window and necks craned in the nearby waiting room. "Miss Carter, your father succumbed to an accidental drowning. Period. I'd stake my professional reputation on it."

Holly pushed toward him. "Dr. Phelps, I'm sorry if I —"

"You and your girl can leave now," he told them, pointing. "The door is that way. Please show yourselves out."

Chapter 8

❧

It didn't take long for the Klan to react to Billy Wallace becoming sheriff, or for my father to flex his muscle as the county's chief law enforcement officer.

On Wednesday night in a community east of town known as Chester, the devout of a congregation of a small African-Methodist-Episcopal church were meeting for mid-week services at Clement Turner's Country Grocery. Their church had been burned two months earlier.

Twenty minutes into the services and just on the back side of a misty twilight, hooded men in the back of a pickup opened fire with automatic weapons on a nearby transformer, casting the gravel crossroads into darkness. A moment later another truckload of men pulled up in front of the grocery and unleashed a fusillade of lead that tore the store apart as the little congregation hugged the floor or crawled out the back door and ran for the woods, where slugs were snapping off limbs and smacking into tree trunks. Inside, cans of beans and peaches exploded and twenty-pound sacks of flour were eviscerated, their contents filling the air with a white fog. Display cases shattered and the antique cash register rang and chimed as it was hit again and again.

The attack lasted less than a minute, but next morning Sheriff Wallace, his deputies and the feds found more than two hundred 5.56 millimeter shell casings of the type used by M16s – the same weapons our military was using in Vietnam. There also were more than a dozen spent shotgun shells, and that didn't count what they found down the road near the electrical transformer.

Swinging from a hangman's noose hooked to the power pole was a scarecrow with a sign around its neck. The name Billy Wallace was written, then struck through with red paint. Under it was the word "Judas," in black.

"I want every shell casing dusted for fingerprints," Sheriff Wallace told Deputy Leonard Young.

"Mr. Wallace – err, I mean, Sheriff Wallace, we've done that in the other shootings and never got anything. It takes forever to –"

"I don't care how long it takes," the sheriff told him. "Maybe we'll get lucky."

Then to Ridge Bellafont, who was the department's semi-official photographer during major investigations, such as they were in Cattahatchie County – "Ridge, I want a picture of that scarecrow and ten prints. We'll hit the farmers' co-ops and country stores. Maybe somebody'll recognize it."

"It's probably stolen," said Hugh McGregor, the FBI agent overseeing operations in the county. "Surely, no one would be so stupid as to use a scarecrow from their own field."

"With the arrogance of these people, who knows?" said the sheriff, shaking his head. "But what I do know is that this little display was planned. They didn't just happen across a scarecrow and decide to do this. That means that at least one of them probably was familiar with our well-stuffed friend."

"Meaning that at least one of the perps probably lives nearby to wherever the scarecrow came from," said McGregor. "It's thin."

"Yep, but we have to start somewhere," said the sheriff.

The only good thing about Wednesday night's attack was that no one was seriously injured. Four of the people in the store received cuts from flying glass or minor flesh wounds to the thigh or buttocks, probably from ricochets off the black iron skillets hanging from pegs above the counter. One woman who ran off into the woods went into premature labor and gave birth beside a quick-flowing stream as the moon broke through the clouds. She and the baby were fine.

When Reverend Clemmer arrived to comfort the folks in Chester, he shook his head. One side of the store had collapsed. "God must have been with them," he said to the sheriff.

Billy Wallace worked his jaw, adjusted his fedora. "That's as good an explanation as any," he agreed.

At *The Current-Leader*, the tension between Miss Carter and her brother was as palpable as hickory – no, coal smoke. There was nothing sweet or woodsy about it. It was just hot and nasty, and loaded with a long-buried history and the promise of flaring at any moment.

Meanwhile, the angry flame between Miss Carter and Eve Howard was as open and obvious as a torch in a midnight hayloft.

Miss Howard and Ridge Bellafont were pressing Miss Carter to at least run some of the photos they'd taken at the Turner's Grocery. Ridge's urgings were subtle; Miss Howard's were loud and angry. At the same time, Miss Carter was getting phone calls from Milton Handley, Walter Kamp and several other major advertisers over the large front-page photo and story about my father's swearing-in.

"We may be just plain ol' country folk," Milton Handley told her, "but we're not fools. First, frightening everyone with that ridiculous McBride story, and now you're the only one who knew where and when Broderick was swearing in that washed-up drunk, Billy Wallace.

"Miss Carter, we were willing to give you a chance, but it is becoming increasingly clear that you have returned here with ulterior and pernicious motives. That you may well be in cahoots with Burke, Mulberry and the race-mixers.

"You've got two strikes against you now," he said. "One more and your newspaper is out. Handley's Department Store will pull all of its advertising. Others, I'm sure, will follow."

By the time I left the newspaper late Friday afternoon, the decision had been made not to run anything regarding the attack out in Chester. Miss Howard was so upset that she stormed out of the building with tears streaming down her cheeks. When I was leaving, I saw her striding across the Theodore J. Bilbo Bridge that connected DeLong to all the bright petals and painful thorns of Roseville. I braked my truck at the stop sign beside the jail and watched her turn left next to a cotton warehouse and disappear down a dirt street into the town's only black neighborhood, squeezed as it was between the river and the steep hills that rose around it like high green walls.

Five minutes later, I was picking up Patti for supper and a movie. We were going to New Albany to see the new John Wayne picture, *True Grit*, playing there at the Cine'. Patti told Brother Daddy that we probably were going to eat at Nicholls, a family steakhouse on Gandy Lake south of DeLong. Words like "probably," and phrases like

"I think," "I believe," "I suppose" and "we plan to," were always the operative parts of Patti's speech. No matter what statement of dubious truth she delivered to her parents, teachers or anyone else, she always left herself enough wiggle room within her sentence structure so that she could never be caught in an out-and-out lie.

Before we'd backed out of the driveway, she pecked me on the cheek and said, "I've changed my mind. I don't want to go to Nicholls. I'm in the mood for catfish. I want to go to Ripples."

So off we went, south on Highway 27, past the fairgrounds and the cutoff to Nicholls Steakhouse while Patti rolled a joint in the lap of her pleated skirt and sang along with Jerry Garcia and the Grateful Dead. Had Patti told Brother Daddy that we "probably," or even "possibly" were going to Ripples, he'd have never let her out of the parsonage. Ripples did, indeed, have some of the best fried catfish around and hush puppies loaded with onion and spiced to perfection, but it also was a backwoods hangout for fishermen, roughnecks, loose women, errant husbands and reprobates of all sorts. Though illegal, there was plenty of cold beer to be had, and in the off-season rooms in the motel across the gravel parking lot could be rented by the half day or even the hour.

From my perspective, the most uncomfortable aspect was that it was owned by J.D. Benoit's kin. All the Benoits, Hugheses and Gabbersons were from the swampy low country at the south end of the county where the Cattahatchie overflowed its banks most every spring. The unpredictability of the big river tended to make their lives and personalities hard-bitten and chancy, at best.

As we sat on a narrow, sandy cut beside an algae-streaked backwater smoking Patti's joint, I started to mention the fact that Billy Wallace's son might not be all that welcome in Ripples right now. I even wondered for a moment if Patti was trying to instigate something, just to see the sparks fly. But I forced myself to dismiss the notion, blaming it on pot-inspired paranoia. Besides, any mention of such concerns would only draw Patti's ridicule. She could use words like "wimp," and worse, with the cold, quick brutality of a fencing master.

By the time we went up steep steps to Ripples' front door, I had convinced myself that I could be as tough as any of the regulars. In any case, all I could think about was Patti's bare legs scissoring up-down, up-down, up-down as she climbed the wooden stairs in front of me.

We got some hard looks when we came through the door and found our way to one of the picnic tables inside the big hall of a room. A Confederate flag the size of a bed sheet hung amid the open rafters. It was still early and the crowd was thin for a Friday night. That was fine by me.

The waiter took so long coming over for our order that I wondered if they would serve us at all. I recognized him behind a dirty apron as one of J.D. Benoit's young cousins, Ronnie Gabberson. He had a pinch of tobacco between his cheek and gum, and his sparse brown mustache squirmed on his upper lip like a night-crawler exposed to the light.

Ten minutes later, we didn't have our food. "You should complain," Patti told me, but I sat tight. Finally, the waiter returned with our food sandwiched between the thick paper plates Ripples served everything on. He dropped them in front of us and walked away. When we flipped the top plate, there were our meals with several thick streams of tobacco juice spit across them.

Patti pushed the plate away as if it held live snakes. I thought she was going to be sick, and I didn't blame her. Once her stomach settled a tad, she looked at me. "Nate Wallace, you march right up there to that counter and tell them we want fresh meals!" she told me.

"Patti, let's just get out of here," I said reasonably. "I've kind of lost my appetite anyway."

She cursed me and them. "I don't care if we throw it in the garbage!" she growled through tight lips and clenched teeth. "If you're any kind of a man, you'll make them give us fresh meals. And apologize!"

"Patti, I don't think that's —"

"Nate, I swear! Sometimes I think you should be the one wearing the skirt," she snarled. "Now get up there!"

I rose on knees that felt soft from the inside out.

"And take those disgusting plates with you."

I picked up the defiled meals and walked toward the counter. Ronnie was wiping his hands on the apron, his worm of a mustache twitching. One of his uncles was at the register and another was monitoring a row of deep fryers. Several other employees, mostly consisting of inbred cousins, stopped what they were doing. The stillness and quiet were contagious. Other diners grew quiet. The only sound I was aware of was a jukebox playing in the back room and men sitting on the outdoor deck telling fish stories over cold beers.

Ronnie Gabberson stared at me across the counter as I put the plates down, then withdrew my hands so the men would not see that they were trembling. He was at least two or three inches taller and thirty or so pounds heavier. He'd played linebacker for New Albany High before he'd been expelled for something or other.

"Excuse me," I said, clearing my throat. "It looks like someone – someone spilled something on our food."

Ronnie leaned on the counter and grinned at me, the same tobacco juice staining his crooked teeth as colored our meals. The tune on the jukebox had ended and the room was silent except for the hiss of the deep fryers and the turning of ceiling fans. My fists tightened at my sides.

The groan of the rusty spring on the screen door was as attention-grabbing as fingernails on a blackboard. The squeal seemed to go on for minutes, but in the time it took to cross a threshold, my father was standing in the doorway – his silver badge shining nearly as brightly as the black leather of his gun belt. He had a stack of fliers in one hand and he crossed the silence to the counter.

Daddy surely had noticed my truck in the parking lot and thus was not surprised to see me there. I, on the other hand, could not have been more surprised if he'd dropped out of the rafters. But I did my best to hide it, along with the strange mix of relief and anger that was sizzling through my bloodstream. Daddy looked at the ruined meals in front of me. Ronnie stepped back from the counter.

"Nate," he said, by way of acknowledgement.

"Daddy," was all I said.

"Looks like we're infested with Wallaces tonight," said Ricky Hughes, who owned the place and ran the cash register. "What do you want?"

My father was calm and made no mention of the plates. "Ricky, I'd like to put up a couple of these fliers in the restaurant and a few more at the dock and around the lodge."

Hughes studied a sheet that bore mug shots and a description of Robert Bedford "Dynamite Bob" McBride of Jasper, Alabama. State Trooper Sergeant J.B. Benoit chose that moment to emerge from the deep shadows of Ripples' back room. Ricky Hughes handed the flier to his cousin.

"The only R.B. McBride I know of was a decorated Army Ranger and demolitions expert during World War II," Benoit said loudly enough to be heard throughout the quiet room. "He's a hero and a patriot, as far as I'm concerned."

"He's a murderer who does his work in the middle of the night like the coward he is," Sheriff Wallace told Benoit in an equally firm voice. "He probably killed Floyd Johnson, and I intend to see him in Parchman Prison or in hell for it. Which one is up to him. Now where can I put these up?"

Benoit told my father exactly where he could put them.

"That's right!" said Ricky Hughes, laughing. "You tell him, J.D."

The silence was long. I felt like I was in a movie and wanted to turn around and look at the room to see how the scene was playing out, but I couldn't move.

All Daddy said was "Excuse me" as he stepped around the younger, bulkier man and went behind the counter. "I'm feelin' a tad dry."

The sheriff's coolness only seemed to make Benoit hotter. "I heard you've already had three out of your fifteen deputies quit on you," he prodded. "And there's more resignation's comin'. You'll see!"

The sheriff reached into a long cooler and set aside some sodas. He lifted a case of longneck beers onto the counter. "Well now, I've always said nothing washes down a mess of catfish and hush puppies like a cold brew.

"That's a big fine cooler you've got there, Ricky," he was saying. "How many cases will that thing hold?" Ricky Hughes stared at cousin J.D. "Don't look at him," said the sheriff. "I asked you a question, Ricky."

Ripples' owner swallowed, answered – "Forty-two."

"Well, let's see, according to Cattahatchie County Code, each bottle carries with it a twenty-five dollar fine." Daddy did some figuring on his fingers. "That's $150 a six-pack or $600 a case. Times that by forty-two, and you're talking about $25,000 – give or take.

"Add on however many more cases you've got in your storage rooms, and you're lookin' at bootleggin' charges. And if I find one person to testify that your underage nephew there served them a beer, then you can count on state time."

"J.D.?" whimpered Ricky Hughes.

"He's bluffin'," said Benoit.

"Do you want to bet your livelihood? Maybe prison time?" said the sheriff. "How about if I station a deputy out there on the road to write down the tags of everybody who drops by your motel to enjoy the businessman's special?"

Ricky Hughes eyes went back and forth between his cousin and the sheriff. He and I could see that my father wasn't bluffing. "Now, Ricky, this is your place of business. So, I'll just leave you a stack of these flyers, and let you put 'em up where you see fit. Me or a deputy will be around every day to make sure you don't run out. Do you understand?"

"Yeah," grunted Hughes.

"Good. The Cattahatchie County Sheriff's Office appreciates your cooperation," he said. Then to me, "Nate, I think it's time for you and Patti to be leavin'."

Chapter 9

❦

O n Saturdays, the offices of *The Current-Leader* were open only to receive classified ads and allow people to step in from the hustle and bustle of the town square and pay for their subscriptions or purchase a copy of the weekend edition. Vendors hawked their fresh vegetables, fruit, corn and watermelons from their trucks parked around the courthouse. Children were running and laughing along the sidewalks.

Through the big open windows of her office, Holly could smell the salty-butter-rich scent of popcorn being sold in front of The Rebel Theater. She looked at her watch. The kids' matinee of *Chitty-Chitty Bang-Bang* and *Heidi* was about to start. She hadn't left the office until nearly midnight when Eve Howard returned from Roseville more than a little stoned. The tension between Holly and Eve was like heat lightning. It burned between them in an ever-widening chasm of silence and allowed Holly to sleep little. There was no point in simply laying there, and over breakfast she didn't want to deal with Eve or her own guilt about continuing the newspaper's segregated news policy. So she dressed and returned to town. She'd been at the newspaper's account ledgers for almost four hours as the busy weekend of local commerce built outside her window.

The phone on Holly's desk buzzed. Christine Wright, who worked the front desk on the weekends, said, "Cutter Carlucci is here. He'd like to see you."

This is a surprise, thought Holly, and chided herself when she realized how pleasant the surprise felt. "Send him up," she said.

There was a pause. "Uhm, Miss Carter, he asked if you could meet him around back on the loading dock?"

"Well … all right. Tell him I'll be down in five minutes."

Cutter was at an old picnic table where the pressmen and other employees sometimes sat for lunch. Charlie came scampering over. Cutter extended his hand and let the little dog sniff it. "Do you remember me, girl?" he asked. "I was at your house the night when men landed on the moon."

Charlie yapped and pranced as Holly pushed onto the dock. "And praise God, our astronauts are safely home."

"Yep. Pretty amazing," said Cutter, standing as Charlie sniffed around his work boots. Holly liked that Cutter wasn't muscle-bound like most football players she'd known. He was stout and sturdy, but he was strong in the way a coiled spring is strong. On this day his boots, his hands and big forearms were speckled with green paint. His gray T-shirt was dark with sweat from neck to waist and he smelled like turpentine. "I apologize for showing up looking like this. Smelling like this. That's why I didn't want to come upstairs. I figure I'm better in the open air right now."

"I needed the break anyway," said Holly. "It looks like you have yourself a painting job."

"I'm helping Scotty Thompson and his boys paint a couple of the warehouses they're converting for classroom buildings for the new academy."

"Is that where you're going this fall? To Riverview?"

She was not the first to ask. Cutter offered his standard response – "I'm going wherever they're playing football. Just mark off the field and turn on the lights and I'll be there."

"A diplomat in the making," said Holly. Then, "You look hot. There's a Coke box inside the door."

"No thanks. I'm about to head up to The Well and get cleaned up before I go to The Gin. But I was passing by and saw your car and thought you'd want to know, I talked to Rose."

"Oh, good. What did she say?"

"Mostly what you already know. She said Mr. Carter wasn't going very fast. That he just seemed to never even try to make the turn onto the bridge."

Holly nodded, listening.

"I asked Rose if she recalled seeing brake lights. She said she couldn't remember one way or the other. But she did remember the dome light coming on just as it was going over the bank. Like your dad opened the door trying to get out."

"Really? Did she actually see him trying to get out?"

"No. It was only a flash, for a couple of seconds."

"Did she recognize the man as my father?"

"No. Like I said, we had no idea who the car belonged to until it was pulled out of the river."

Holly reconstructed the scene in her mind. "How long did it take Rose to run to the bridge from where she was when she saw the car go in?"

Cutter calculated. "Well, my sister isn't a world-class sprinter. Especially on a night like that, wearing a raincoat. Maybe a minute, give or take."

Holly was doing her own figuring now. One minute. Sixty seconds. That would be plenty of time for someone to drive her father's Oldsmobile off the road, roll out onto the bank and hide himself among the brush and debris and pilings under the bridge before Rose got to the railing. It would be risky with the river flowing high and hard, but then murder always is a risky proposition.

"Miss Carter, if there's something you're concerned about in connection to your daddy's death, Mr. Wallace is a good man. Even if he has had his troubles with the bottle the last couple of years," Cutter told her. "I'm sure he'd look into it."

Holly blinked as if coming out of a light sleep. "Yes. Yes, Cutter, I'm sure he would, but with all he has to deal with right now – Sheriff Johnson's murder, this McBride lunatic running around and the local Klan crazies – I don't want to add to it unless I'm sure."

Holly watched Cutter drive away, then sat staring past the parking lot and the street at the green-brown summer river.

The next step would be locating her father's 1965 Oldsmobile Ninety-Eight. If his spare glasses were in the glove compartment, then T.L. Carter could not possibly have driven himself from Wolf's Run, down the curving mountainside road to the Old Iron Bridge. Either way, Holly knew she needed to get her hands on the steering wheel of that Olds to see if it matched the wound to her father's forehead. That would mean an exhumation and another autopsy. The thought made her queasy, but there probably was no way around it – eventually. And that likely would draw her into still more conflict with Tom and Mary Nell. They would see it as her questioning the management of her father's death, and probably some sort of sacrilege as well. It was one of the reasons Holly had spent all morning going over the company books, looking for the sale of the Olds, which had been an asset of DeLong Newspapers Inc. She had not wanted to ask Tom about it, but there was no notation in the company ledgers that she could find.

"Conflict? That's all my life seems to be about anymore," Holly said to herself as she drove the short distance across town. "Conflict with Tom and Mary Nell. Conflict with Eve. Conflict with the newspaper staff. Conflict with the advertisers. Conflict with white folks who think I'm a traitor, and conflict with the black folks who think I'm a racist.

"And conflict with … with? … with myself."

Holly stopped at the corner before she turned down the street she'd played on as a child. She bowed her head.

"Lord, please guide me in fighting only the battles I must fight, and in letting go of all the other anger and frustration and anxiety that I have," she prayed. "Please, Lord, help me to stay calm with Mary Nell, my brother's wife, so that maybe we can come together again as a real family someday.

"It's in Jesus name I pray …."

The yard at the corner of Jackson and Hood streets was large and shaded by elms and magnolias. They looked larger than she remembered as a child and yet the three-story Victorian seemed so much smaller. Holly turned down Hood Street then into the long driveway that wound between the trees and led behind the house. There a boy who looked like a younger, more innocent version of Tom was winding up and throwing baseballs at a target painted on the side of the clapboard garage.

Thomas Lanier Carter V stopped his pitching and stared at Holly, his red St. Louis Cardinals baseball cap twisted slightly on his sandy brown hair. The sight of him caused Holly to choke up. It reminded her of how much of her life had passed by since the last time she was in this yard. The last time she'd seen her nephew, he was only toddling around, taking unsure steps. Now he was at least five-eight with the long, limber limbs of the Carter clan and his mother's sharp nose and jaw.

"Hi, Lanny."

The boy stared, uncertain what to do or say as he picked up another baseball from the bucket and worked it into his glove. "I'm not supposed to talk to strangers," he finally said.

"Lanny, honey, I've been away a long time, but I'm not really a stranger. I'm your Aunt Holly. Your father's sister."

"I'm not supposed to talk to you either."

The response stung Holly as surely as a slap and she felt her cheeks redden, not with anger but with frustration and sadness that what little family she had left was in such a state.

"Lanny!" Mary Nell called as she came through the screen door from the back porch. "Go change into your swimming suit. We're going out to meet your father at the country club and have dinner there."

"Awww, Momma, can't I stay here. I'd rather try to get up a baseball game."

Mary Nell was wearing a white tennis outfit. She tossed her racket into the back seat of a big Buick before approaching Holly's Lincoln. "Don't argue with me, young man," she told him. "I have a two o'clock doubles match and I need to warm up."

The boy took a long last look at his aunt then headed for the back door.

"He's a handsome boy," said Holly.

"That's what everyone says."

"Where's Georgette? I'd love to see her. She's what now? Almost fourteen?"

"Yes, but she's not here. She rode out to the club with Tommy earlier. She's quite a little golfer."

Holly looked around at the yard she'd played in as a girl, the trees she'd climbed.

Mary Nell cleared her throat. "As I was telling Lanny, I have a tennis date. Does your visit have some purpose?"

Holly fought to remember her prayer. "A purpose? Yes. It does. I've been going over the company books covering the last year or so and I have a question."

Mary Nell Carter's mouth drew itself into a small knot.

"Daddy's Oldsmobile was an asset of DeLong Newspapers. I'm wondering how it was disposed of. I can't find anything on the books about it."

Mary Nell's gray eyes were hard and Holly could see the color rising in her slender neck. "What are you accusing us of?"

"I'm not accusing you of anything," Holly told her sister-in-law, who also was the company's treasurer. "Daddy's car was worth several thousand dollars and I want to make sure that it's properly written off our books."

"Several thousand dollars?" grunted Mary Nell. "Maybe before it went in the river. Afterwards, it wasn't worth a dollar. In fact, we were going to have to pay to have it towed out of the sheriff's impound lot once the investigation was completed."

"So ... ?"

"So, the Kamps, who are personal friends of Tommy and I, offered to haul the vehicle away at cost."

"The Kamps?"

"That's what I said."

"And what were they going to do with it?"

"Sell it for scrap, I assume. I didn't ask and I didn't care. I just wanted it out of the sight of my husband and T.L.'s grandchildren."

Holly thought about that for a moment. "All right. What about insurance?"

"Tommy decided to wave an insurance claim," she said. "The car was nearly five years old. It wasn't worth it."

"Still, there should be some paperwork. A bill of sale or a transfer of title? Something?"

Mary Nell's jaw shifted under her pale skin. Holly could see blue veins throbbing beside her sister-in-law's ear. "I suppose that is how they do things in California where everyone's a stranger," said Mary Nell. "But here, a person's word and a handshake among friends remain sufficient. The Kamps have an impeccable family line. Colonel Kamp served gallantly under General Nathan Bedford Forrest. They can trace their lineage all the way back to Charleston."

Holly wanted to ask what that had to with anything, but resisted. Instead, she said, "Whose hand did Tom shake on the deal?"

"Actually, I was the one who made the arrangements. Tommy was far too distraught to deal with such matters."

"All right, then who –?"

"Levon? No, LeRoy. He's Ann Burton Kamp's son. He runs some sort of scrap metal business. And I believe he's around your age. Perhaps you remember him?"

"LeRoy Kamp? Yes. I remember him. Unfortunately."

Burton LeRoy Kamp was one of Holly's mistakes. One of many she made between fifteen and twenty-five. But LeRoy stood out. Three years older than Holly, he came home on leave from Germany in the winter of '57. She was only sixteen but already had a Corvette and a reputation, and he looked good in and out of his Army uniform.

Initially, they'd gotten along fine – lots of laughter, dancing and hot, sweaty fun –even though LeRoy had a rough streak in and out of the bedroom. But as he became more possessive of Holly, the streak went from rough to mean and she saw him for what he was, a bully – especially when it came to women and black people. When he was ordered back to Germany, she said good-bye and good riddance. Not long after, Corporal Kamp was sentenced to four years in the stockade for the attempted murder of a sergeant, who was black. He had written to Holly a few times from prison and, feeling sorry for him, she even responded until the letters became too lurid and venomous to open.

"Impeccable family line …?" she thought as she turned into the Kamp Motors lot and drove around to the service bays in back.

Holly tapped her horn and a man in greasy blue coveralls came out. He glanced at the Lincoln with its missing chrome and scab of green paint down the driver's side. "Our body shop closes at noon on Saturdays," he said. "But if you bring this'un back on Monday, Gilbert and his boys can fix her up good as new."

"Thanks, but I'm not here for body work. Is LeRoy Kamp around?"

The man looked across the lot. "That's his red Firebird over there, so I 'spect he's somewheres on the place."

"Could you track him down for me?"

"I'll have Mary in the office make a P.A. announcement."

Three minutes later a man in work boots, jeans and a T-shirt came around the corner of the building. Holly recognized the walk – the strut. But that was all she recognized. LeRoy's straight brown hair was almost longer than hers. He had a mustache and beard that was haphazardly trimmed. His eyes were shot full of blood and bitterness.

"Holly Lee Carter. Miss Cattahatchie County," he said. "Where's your 'Vette?"

"I traded it in for this big ol' boat, and that," she told him, casting a thumb over her shoulder in the direction of her wheelchair.

"I heard about that. Playin' soldier over in 'Nam. I don't feel sorry for you. You had no business over there."

"I didn't come here for your sympathy, LeRoy. Or to chat about old times," she said. "I'm here as the owner of DeLong Newspapers Incorporated. My father's car was an asset of the company. I need the paperwork on it to clear it from our books."

"Paperwork? There ain't no paperwork. I did your family a favor, hauling that waterlogged piece of junk away."

Charlie stirred on the seat and sniffed the air. She growled in LeRoy's direction.

"I know. And I appreciate it, but to clear it from our books I need a bill of sale. Maybe a picture of it to get the insurance people off my back," she lied in service of the larger question.

LeRoy stared at Holly, his gaze a mixture of resentment and curiosity and remembered lust. "Insurance, huh? Well, I'm afraid you're out of luck. I sold that wreck to a wholesale scrap man a few days after we drug it onto the lot."

"Then you have a bill of sale, right?"

LeRoy grunted and stepped closer to the car. Charlie climbed into Holly's lap and yapped up at the big man. "It was a cash-and-carry deal. Neither one of us had any interest in tithing to Uncle Sambo concerning the transaction."

"Okay, then just give me the name of the wholesaler."

LeRoy leaned on the car door and Holly had to hook her hand in Charlie's collar to restrain sixteen pounds of angry bichon. Kamp ignored the dog's tirade. Finally Holly snapped, "*Arrêtez-vous, Charlie. Installez-vous!*"

Charlie grumbled but settled in Holly's lap so that she could think.

"Those guys are like gypsies," LeRoy told her. "They pull in with a long flatbed. If you've got something they want, they load it up and head on down the road."

Holly thought LeRoy might be lying, but why? Maybe to spite her, if nothing else. "And you've never done business with this guy before?"

"I never laid eyes on him until that day," he told her as he straightened beside the car. "But as best I recall, the trailer had Oklahoma plates."

Chapter 10

༄

Cattahatchie County's only black school for grades eight through twelve, Roseville High, didn't have a football program, so its best athletes played basketball and baseball and ran track. Moccasin teams typically were lean, tough and blindingly fast, and Tommy Ray Banks was the finest point guard in the school's history. Barely six-feet tall, he could dunk a basketball with both hands or pull up and can a fifteen-foot jumper with the grace and quickness of an ebony hummingbird.

Cutter liked to compete against the best, and on many a winter Sunday afternoon, his jeep could be found parked behind the time-worn Roseville gym. For hours, Cutter, Dodge McDowell and Jimmy Garner would play pickup games with the Banks brothers, the Prathers, Gathers and Storeys – all legendary names in Moccasin sports. Four, six, even eight or ten hours of basketball was not unusual on gray January days that settled into black wind-bitten nights.

After the games were done, Cutter, Dodge, Jimmy and the others would walk around the corner to a squat, lopsided brick building with a flat roof. In the spitting snow, a man in a long apron and short over-coat stood under an open-sided tin shed tending barbecue smoking over coals glowing red in a brick trough. Inside, Luther Banks' Good Eatin' House, the air was warm from the heat of the griddle and big oven and deep fryer, and the number of bodies packed together. At a big table at the back of the room, the competitors laughed and recalled and critiqued over ribs and beer, ice tea, dirty rice, collard greens, corn and chicken fried St. Julianne style.

Had Marine Lance Corporal Tommy Ray Banks been a little luck-ier while on patrol in the Mekong Delta of South Vietnam, my plan to put some distance between me and Daddy, and thus appease Brother MacAllister while continuing to write for *The Current-Leader* might have worked – for a time, at least. So might Miss Carter's plan to institute incremental integration of the newspapers' pages. But on that final Tuesday of July 1969, time ran out.

The newsroom was in the midst of a busy production morning when Miss Winona St. Julianne walked with short, stiff steps past my desk hugging to her chest a large, framed photo of a handsome young Marine. The way her arms crisscrossed the portrait, I could not recognize the face, though I was sure it must be one of her many great-grandchildren. Miss St. Julianne's descendants and their cousins were so numerous that they populated one entire section of Roseville.

Small and frail, and slightly stoop-shouldered, Miss St. Julianne was sandwiched between U.S. Attorney J.L. Burke and his bodyguard, Reverend Clemmer of the National Coalition for Justice, Roseville High Principal Harriett Houston, and, to my surprise, Ron Simpson – Paula Simpson's father and owner of The Cotton Café. Jean Baptiste, the preacher at Roseville African-Methodist-Episcopal Church, walked with a Bible in one hand and the other resting on Miss Winona's shoulder.

Tom Carter stood at the door to his small office and watched the group pass without acknowledgement, except for Ron Simpson, who was a frequent advertiser. Miss Carter met them at the door to her office, and when the group had filed in she asked, "Tom, would you like to join us?"

"I have *work* to do," he said, and stepped back into the tiny office he'd chosen, but did not shut the door.

Charlie got up from the spot on the sofa where she'd been sleeping and scampered over to stand beside Holly's wheelchair. The pooch yapped a time or two, but her master said, "Quiet, baby. These people are our friends. I hope."

"More importantly," said Harriett Houston, "I hope you are prepared to be a friend to the black community."

"A community that will be sending its children to Cattahatchie High School this fall and voting," said Reverend Clemmer.

"*If* the federal Court of Appeals lifts the stay on Judge Mulberry's integration plan," reminded Holly.

"Oh, it'll be lifted," said J.L. Burke. "The injunction was issued on only the flimsiest legal grounds. A super-technicality."

"Weathers and his bunch are only trying to buy time," said Clemmer.

"Time to garner more funding and support for an all-white private school," said Mrs. Houston, who had been at RHS for nearly 28 years.

"So, Mrs. Houston, is that why you requested this meeting?" asked Holly. "To talk politics?"

"No, Miss Carter," offered Reverend Baptiste. "We're here on a matter of the spirit, a matter of fairness for a son of DeLong."

Looking at Miss Winona holding fast to the young Marine's portrait, Holly felt what was coming as surely as if her wheelchair was chained to railroad tracks at the end of a long tunnel. The vibration rumbled through her, but there was nothing she could do about it except try to keep her breakfast down.

"Why don't you all sit," she said, indicating the big conference table.

A s if on cue, Miss Winona unwrapped her bony arms from the picture, laid it on the table and edged it close to Holly. The old woman used brown fingers twisted by tens of thousands of biscuits made, years of knuckle-pressed pie crusts and the weight of one black iron skillet after another lifted for six decades in the kitchen of The Cotton Café. She stroked the edge of the cheap, faux wood frame as if it was something alive, as if it was a little boy's head resting on great-grandma's lap. From a drawn face scarred pink across one cheek by a long-ago splash of cooking grease, she looked up at Holly with eyes bloodshot with age and remorse and too many years in sweat-box kitchens.

"That's my great-grandson, Tommy Ray Banks," she said with a ragged, aged voice. "He's on his way home now, from Veet-nam. He'll be home Sunday."

Reverend Baptiste covered Miss Winona's hand. "Tommy Ray was killed a few days ago. The patrol boat he was on was ambushed."

Holly nodded. "I am sorry."

Mrs. Houston told Holly about Roseville High salutatorian Tommy Ray Banks, about his exploits on the basketball court and baseball diamond, and about the athletic and academic scholarships he'd earned to Alcorn A&M University. "He was planning to come back to DeLong and teach," she said.

Reverend Baptiste called him a role model for the youth in his church. "Tommy was engaged to another A&M student."

"The daughter of one of Reverend Baptiste's deacons," offered Clemmer.

"She was too broken up to come to this meeting," said Mrs. Houston. "They've kept steady company since eleventh grade."

Holly knew where this was headed, and she could feel her stomach writhing inside her. There was nothing to do but face it.

"I truly am sorry for your loss," she said, "but what can I do for you?"

Mrs. Houston reached into her purse and withdrew from it a folded newspaper page. It was *The Current-Leader* front page from Jan. 8, 1969. She unfolded it and laid it on the table in front of the newspaper's new editor-in-chief. The entire top half of the page was framed in black and dedicated to the memory of redheaded, freckle-faced Staff Sgt. Wesley Palmer, who was killed when a mortar shell landed on his barracks at the giant Da Nang Air Force Base. There was a large picture of Sgt. Palmer in uniform and a photo of him from a Cattahatchie High yearbook, a story about his life and family, and funeral information.

This was the traditional way in which *The Current-Leader* had handled the death of local servicemen since the Spanish American War. White servicemen.

Holly stared at the page. Since returning to DeLong, Holly had felt like she was trying to keep her balance on a tightrope while sitting in a wheelchair. Now it was as if the rope was soaked in kerosene – *or is it napalm?* Holly thought – and Clemmer and Burke were encouraging these nice, sincere, hurting people to light a match that could burn it down under her.

Reverend Baptiste must have sensed a bit of what Holly Lee Carter was feeling. "It doesn't have to be as much as – "

"No!" Miss Winona St. Julianne said firmly. "It should be just like that. Just like the one they gave that Palmer boy."

"I have to agree, Reverend," said Principal Houston. "Tommy Ray deserves to be treated with the same respect."

For a moment there was silence around the table. Ron Simpson offered, "I'm prepared to buy a full-page, so you can run it as an advertisement if it gives you some cover to –"

"No. No, thank you, Mr. Simpson," said the editor-in-chief of *The Current-Leader.* She bit her lip in a little-girl habit she'd never been able to lose, then – "Miss Winona is right. It should run at the top of 1A. Story. Funeral arrangements. Pictures. Just like the Palmer story."

* * *

"**Y**ou've ruined us!" Mary Nell Carter screamed at her sister-in-law.

Everyone in the newsroom froze – everyone who remained – as the general manager's wife shrieked. Down on the sidewalk and even across the street on the courthouse lawn passersby stopped to listen. Mary Nell Carter's voice sliced through the sticky Tuesday afternoon air like a scythe, and she was using it to cut and wound Holly Lee Carter as deeply as she could. Charlie yapped and growled. Miss Carter tried to quiet her but the feisty little dog wouldn't quit.

On her eighty-nine-year-old legs, Miss Frances covered the steps from the first floor to the second in what seemed like four long strides once Mary Nell Carter began her shouting and cursing.

"Nate, run get Tom," she said to me. "He's probably over at The Jeff Davis, gettin' lunch and gettin' drunk. Now run! And don't take no for an answer."

"Yes, Ma'am," I said and galloped down the stairs, through the front door and right out onto the street as tires squealed and I cut between honking cars and pickups.

Once Miss Carter made the decision to handle Tommy Ray Banks' death notice the same way *The Current-Leader* handled the death of white soldiers, word spread fast. Tammy Gilroy, who covered county government, and Clete Rainy, the sports editor, resigned on the spot. Several of our country correspondents who were in the office typing their columns, stopped virtually in mid-sentence – mid-word – and left the building. Circulation Manager "Hap" Medlin and Tom Carter had left together at 11:30 and by the time Mrs. Carter stormed in at 2:45, they had not returned. Neither had Andy Wilbanks, who ran the big camera that created the page-sized negatives that were used to burn the tin plates that went on the press. Randy Sparks, one of the pressmen, had stopped his preparation for the Tuesday night run, rubbed degreaser onto his hands and washed them over a sink stained nearly black with printer's ink.

"No, sir," he said to production manager Shorty Rodgers. "I ain't puttin' out no nigger news."

Advertising Director Frank Hodges had been sitting in his downstairs office for several hours, staring at a wall covered in certificates, commendations and photos. He looked as if he'd been hit by the train that Miss Carter had felt coming down the tracks.

Only Eve Howard expressed enthusiasm for the decision, as I guess we all might have expected. She let out a cheerleader whoop in the middle of the newsroom and hugged Ridge Bellafont's neck with a naive effervescence that demonstrated how little she knew about DeLong, Mississippi. Ridge hugged her back, but the tight seam of his full lips and the worry in his soft brown eyes told the rest of the newsroom how concerned he really was. Mister Ridge made it clear that he thought Miss Carter's decision was morally and ethically correct, but he was not naive enough to believe that being right was always enough; or that it would save the newspaper and its new editor from an avalanche of repercussions.

After the initial whirlwind of resignations passed, C. Michael Morton rallied the newsroom troops and Shorty Rodgers reorganized the production shop so that he could run the page camera. Two pressmen could run the big Goss unit in the printing bay, but preparation would take twice as long, so deadlines were adjusted.

Through it all, Miss Carter had been steady and decisive even as she wrote the Banks story and an editorial explaining her decision. If she had any doubts, she didn't let them show in the newsroom.

This would wring out of Governor Weathers and, far more important to me, Brother MacAllister whatever little sanity they had remaining. And Patti would go right along with them. I knew I would have to resign from the paper, and the thought made me sick. But for this one historic afternoon in the annals of our little town, I was determined to stay where the action was – at the center of the storm.

By the time I returned with our well-buzzed general manager, several members of the staff had gathered at the door to the editor's office, and more than one had tried to calm Mary Nell Carter, but she'd have none of it – breaking away from their touch and cursing them, too. C. Michael Morton had threatened to call the police, but his boss shook him off even as she absorbed the ongoing tirade. From what I could see, and by all accounts afterwards, Miss Carter's expression never gave way to anger or fear, only surprise at the level of coarse and vile invective her private-school-raised, Sunday school teacher sister-in-law was able to muster and maintain, pointing her finger and pounding sometimes on T.L. Carter's desk and sometimes on her own thigh.

When a winded, sweating Tom Carter dragged his overweight frame up the stairs to the newsroom, his wife still was thundering at his sister.

"Go back to California! *Get out of our lives!* There's no place here for a race-mixin' fornicator!" yelled Mary Nell Carter, her face, ears and upper neck bright red, her lips pale even under the heavy shellacking of make-up she wore.

"If you think I'm going to let you roll in here and destroy my home, my life, all the plans I've made, you're crazier than your daddy! You're not even a *woman* anymore! If Tom was any kind of a man, he'd have the Klan run you right out of town," she ranted. "You've never been any good. You've never been anything but trouble. A tramp! I wish you'd *died* in Vietnam!"

Tom touched his wife's rigid shoulders as if he were trying to maneuver a hot stove. She wheeled on him and looked up into his wet, jowly face. Then her hand came up, the big diamond on her finger flashing like a comet. The sound of her palm striking Tom Carter's face made us all wince.

"Get rid of her," Mary Nell Carter growled through clenched teeth.

Chapter 11

꩜

The sun was setting on the last day of my part-time career at *The Current-Leader*. As I stood on the fire escape outside the big windows at the back of the production room, I hoped it wasn't setting on the newspaper itself – though whatever feelings I had were mixed with anger, frustration, disappointment, confusion, uncertainty, and an underlying swell of apprehension that bordered on the restless edge of dread. For Miss Carter, for the paper, for our town. Though I felt terribly hemmed in by Cattahatchie County's narrow, stiff-necked attitudes and its inability to see the future beyond next year's crops, everything else was just words in books, pictures on a page or on the TV set. I had been on one four-day vacation with my parents to Panama City, Florida, twice to the Grand Old Opry in Nashville and to Memphis a handful of times to shop for school clothes. Otherwise, DeLong was the only reality I knew, and it felt as if it were shifting out from under me.

Beyond the parking lot and River Street, the Cattahatchie was flowing from dusk into darkness, the day's last light making the river molten with color, as if someone had melted an enormous box of Crayolas and sent the rainbow mix flowing through town. Over in Roseville, a juke near the river had Jimi Hendrix cranked up. Night fishermen were lighting their lanterns and hanging them from poles affixed to the prows of their small boats. Several were casting lines into eddies south of the bridge while black children splashed and laughed and swam near a big sandbar.

Holly Lee Carter sat on a small, grassy plateau above the river where an old willow tree held fast purchase to the narrow slip of earth, and thus to life itself. The tips of its long, corded tendrils shifted slightly in what little breeze was stirring.

Eve Howard stepped out onto the fire escape. She had been in the sweltering production shop helping its depleted crew put together pages – pasting strips of type onto cardboard dummies. Her blouse was damp with perspiration down her back, and under her arms and breasts. She stretched her neck and drew in a deep breath as she took in the pink twilight.

"How's she holding up?" I asked cocking my chin toward Miss Carter.

"Holly is the strongest woman – the strongest *person* I've ever known," responded Eve Howard. "She'll do whatever she has to do."

There was a part of me that hoped Eve Howard was right, that Holly Lee Carter would be able to successfully face down Governor Weathers, Brother MacAllister and the Klan – not to mention the many Mary Nell Carters in DeLong. But it was clear to me that I couldn't, and if I tried, I'd lose Patti. I went back inside, through the production room and to my desk and began typing out my resignation.

It was nearly dark when Scotty Thompson turned his paint truck down River Street, the aluminum ladders rattling in their racks. Scotty, his sons and Cutter had spent twelve long, hot hours on those ladders, rolling green paint onto the big warehouses at the edge of Governor Weathers' Chalmette Plantation. Cutter climbed out of the truck cab across from The Cotton. He'd left his jeep there after eating one of Miss Winona's ham steaks for breakfast.

Holly was studying the river and didn't notice the paint truck go by or Cutter's approach. She rested her hand on the Bible closed on her lap as she watched the river changing colors below her.

"You've never been any good. ... You've never been anything but trouble. ...I wish you'd died in Vietnam ...You're not even a woman anymore ..."

Her sister-in-law's voice echoed in her ears and tumbled down inside her with the weight of rocks sheathed in ice. She tried to make herself focus on the here and the now, but the here and the now felt so much like the then and back when. Back before Ia Drang. Children splashing in a warm, twilit river – laughing, unaware, or pretending for the length of a sunset unawareness of the danger looming around them. Vine-covered, shadow-filled banks and a soldier with his transistor radio cranked up to the naive harmonies of *California Girls.*

Now, in the near distance, Jimi Hendrix was wailing the chords of Dylan's painfully beautiful harbinger *All Along the Watchtower.*

"What was it the joker said to the thief?" Holly asked herself. "'There must be some kind of way out of here ...?'" But if there was any way out of the fix she'd gotten herself into – and worse, gotten the paper into – Holly couldn't see it.

How could she – *especially she?* – deny equal treatment to Lance Corporal Tommy Ray Banks? In the turmoil of battle, as surely as she had given her legs attempting to help boys who were wounded, others – white *and black* – gave their lives to cover and hide her and their injured comrades. As mortar shells exploded and hundreds of Russian-made rifles crackled through the bamboo, there was no black or white, male or female, soldier or journalist – there was only watching each other's backs through the long night of hunger and pain, of blood, thirst and terror ... and prayer.

Holly had told Eve she would pray about how to handle coverage of the black community in the pages of *The Current-Leader*, and she had prayed. Now she searched the river and the sky and her own heart, and knew that this was God's answer. All she could do was turn her fears and worries over to Him.

Easy to say, but hard to do, she thought. The presses would start turning soon, spitting out thousands of newspapers that quickly would pile up on the loading dock without enough carriers to stuff the advertising inserts inside and deliver them. Nine of twenty five carriers had called to say they wouldn't deliver "colored news," and many others simply wouldn't show up.

"Rough day?"

Holly startled, her hand jumping to her chest. "Oh, Cutter! You nearly scared me right into the river. Although that might not be the worst thing that could happen."

"I guess you're already catchin' hell about the Tommy Ray Banks story," he said.

Holly laughed softly. "This town doesn't need a newspaper. The clothesline telegraph is faster than anything we can put out. How did you hear about it?"

"Scotty Thompson talked to his oldest girl on the phone at lunch. She worked in your classified ad department. Until about noon," Cutter explained. "She was pretty upset."

As soon as Holly wheeled into the newsroom and informed the staff of her decision, she knew it would travel throughout DeLong and the county as quickly as shoe leather, Firestone tires and telephone lines could carry it. That accounted for the eighteen subscription cancellations Miss Frances already had received, and some two dozen businesses attempting to cancel their ads – including the paper's biggest client, Handley's Department Store. At four o'clock, Advertising Director Frank Hodges came into her office, sat down on the sofa, put his face in his hands and cried.

"Are you going to stick with the story?" Cutter asked.

Holly hesitated for a beat, not knowing where he stood on the issues that were coming to a head in Cattahatchie County. Then, "Yes, I am," she said. "Corporal Banks gave his life for his country – for us – just like any white soldier. He deserves no less."

Cutter squatted so that they were level with each other. He caught her eyes, and in them saw gold flecks sparkling on green satin. His eyes were so blue-white that they were hard to read, but Holly detected no anger in them. Only … concern?

"Are you okay?" he asked.

Holly arched her spine, relaxed it then rolled her shoulders. "Other than a terrible backache, I think so. I just had to get out of the office for a few minutes."

"You know, don't you, that you're kickin' a hornets' nest?"

Holly sighed, a tired, nervous sigh. "I can't help that. This isn't how I wanted to do it. It isn't my timing," she said, patting the black leather cover of the Bible Grandma Carter had given her as a teenager. "But I was reading in Daniel. Chapter 11, Verse 32. '… Those who know God will display strength and take action.'"

Cutter let his eyes drift across the river and then back to Holly. "Isn't that the same Bible that Brother Mac and his bunch use to justify the way they treat black folks and poor whites and anybody else who doesn't agree with them?"

The corners of Holly's mouth formed a quick, sad smile. "Same one."

"I've heard tell you can find a verse in the Bible to justify near'about anything."

How many times had she heard similar words come out of her mouth? Holly wondered.

"Cutter, people use and misuse the Bible in all sorts of ways. They always have. Sometimes intentionally. Sometimes out of ignorance. Sometimes because their heart is so filled with selfishness and darkness that no light can get in," she told him. "But that doesn't change the fact that the Bible is God's Word. And once His Word really is in your heart, you don't need anyone to interpret it for you. You just need to listen to your heart and trust God.

"Ever since I got the news about my father's will, but especially since I've been back in DeLong, I've been in conflict. With Tom and my sister-in-law and some other people in town, yes. Sometimes with my friend, Eve Howard. But mostly with myself, because I've been listening to my head and not my heart.

"For the first time in almost five months, I don't feel that conflict in here," she said, tapping her chest. "When I saw the picture of Corporal Banks in Miss Winona's hands, I knew why God protected me at Ia Drang while men died around me by the hundreds. Why he brought me back here."

The street lights flickered on with a hum and the voices of *The Current-Leader*'s two remaining pressmen cut through the thick air as they prepared the big machine for the printing run. Cutter picked up a stone from the bluff and stood. He tossed it out into the water. They watched as the ripples moved downstream with the current and disappeared before they could reach the bank.

"I better be going," said Holly, releasing the brakes on her chair. "I've got a newspaper to put out. Sooo, I'll see you around."

"Yep. See yuh 'round," he said as Holly pushed from the grass and into the street. She could feel his eyes on her. "Miss Carter?" he said.

Holly pivoted at the edge of the newspaper's parking lot. "Yes"

Cutter's hands where shoved deep into the front pockets of his jeans. "For what it's worth, I think you're doin' the right thing."

Holly started to speak but emotion choked off her voice. *Why did Cutter's opinion matter to her? Even a little? He'd been helpful at times and downright unfriendly at others. Even cruel.* She had no answer, but when she tried to speak again, it was the same. Finally, "Thank you," she mouthed.

Cutter nodded. It was enough.

* * *

By the time I got to The Well, Cutter had spread his sleeping bag, washed himself and had three big hamburgers cooking over the fire. There were two baking potatoes down in the coals. While I got my gear out of my truck, Cutter walked over to his ice chest. "How many hamburgers do you want?" he asked.

"I'm not too hungry. One'll do."

He tore a good-sized chunk of meat off a big pack of ground beef, patted it out in his hand and dropped it on the grill, then washed his hands in the stream from The Well.

"What are you down in the dumps about now?"

"I resigned from the paper this afternoon."

Cutter stared at me across the fire pit.

"I had to! I told you, Brother Mac was already making noises about not working for a Jezebel like Miss Carter. Now with her stickin' this colored news in the paper, I didn't have a choice."

The irritation in Cutter's gaze was as hot and easy to discern as the sizzle of grease on the fire pit coals. But I was wound up from the events of the day and eager for an ear to spill my story into.

"What a mess," I groaned as I spread my sleeping bag and began recounting in detail the day's events – from the time Miss Winona walked in to Miss Carter's announcement to the staff; from people resigning to just plain walking out; from Mary Nell Carter screaming her lungs out to overhearing Mr. Hodges crying in the editor's office; from subscription and advertising cancellations that already had come in to finding out that the circulation director was urging the route drivers to stay home.

"Some of the carriers called in saying they're not gonna deliver a paper with colored news in it. Others wanted to be paid in advance. Apparently, Mr. Medlin was also telling them that the paper is so broke Miss Carter might not be able to make another payroll."

"So, is Miss Carter going to be able to get the paper delivered?"

"Who knows? I'm out of it. I don't care anymore," I told him. "You know, I'm starting to think Miss Mary Nell is right. Holly Lee Carter ain't nothin' but trouble. Everything was fine until she showed up."

"Fine for who?" asked Cutter.

I pulled a net bag from The Well, took out a cold beer, cracked open the top and pretended not to hear the question.

* * *

We ate the hamburgers and baked potatoes in near silence, listening to the song of the crickets and of the river and watching the full moon on the rise. I was worn out and angry with Miss Carter, my daddy, Miss Winona, Clemmer, Baptiste, Burke and their whole bunch. Everyone who was conspiring to screw things up and derail the wonderful life I envisioned with Patti away from this place of contradictions and confrontation.

After recovering from the shock of a cold, quick shower in the waterfall issuing from The Well, I put up my tent. When I finished, Cutter was sitting on the rock ledge above the river.

"Well, there's no TV, so I guess I'll hit the sack."

"Good night, Nate," was all he said.

Deep after midnight I awoke needing to pee, and I crawled out of my tent. Clouds covered the moon, and the campsite was near pitch black except for the last glow of the cooking fire. Across the dark, mist-tinged fields, the light in Rose Carlucci's room glowed grimy white as usual. As I stepped to the edge of the campsite, I noticed Cutter's jeep was gone. I walked over and checked his sleeping bag. Empty. After relieving myself against the base of a chinaberry tree, I went back to my tent and pulled my watch out of the cigar box where I stashed it at night with my wallet. I held the watch close to the campfire's coals and tilted it so the pink light caught the face of the Timex – 3:18 a.m.

Chapter 12

❦

Annabelle Watson had a morbid fear of tornadoes, and for good reason. While plowing a twelve-acre field with a two-mule team along a Tishomingo County ridge line, her brother, Elijah, was snatched into a swirling sky by a sudden twister in the spring of 1845. She saw it all from the front porch, and would have died standing there – her arms wrapped around a post – had her father not grabbed her and her younger brother and dived into a ditch as the thunderous cyclone devoured their farmhouse.

The house and virtually all of the family's possessions were gone in the heartbeat of time it took the tornado to race through. Only the stubby brick piers upon which the small house rested remained. They found one mule on a rocky outcrop beside the nearby Tombigbee River. Like an egg dropped from a great height, the animal's body was more than broken, it was shattered. One eye was open – wide and wild with terror, a fear so deep that not even death could mask or dilute it.

About a week later, someone discovered their plow embedded deep into the trunk of an ancient oak two miles away. No trace of the other mule or Elijah ever was found.

So when Annabelle Watson married well-to-do planter John Henry Kamp in 1851 and he moved her back to his nine-thousand acres in northeastern Cattahatchie County, her only demand was that the home he promised her have a deep basement to serve as a storm cellar. Kamp did her one better. He had carpenters and masons, and more than two dozen slaves, construct their two-story Greek revival mansion next to a large, pine-covered hill. A door from the kitchen led down to a sprawling basement/root cellar that was dug beneath the hill. Floored in brick and walled in fieldstone, it was more bunker than basement, and from it a web of tunnels extended. One opened on the hillside, another beside the nearby Cattahatchie River, another beneath the family's cotton gin.

Mrs. Annabelle Kamp spent hundreds of stormy nights under its twelve-by-twelve heart pine beams until she died in 1926.

In the Great Depression of the 1930s the farm became unprofitable and the Kamps moved to DeLong and started a successful automobile dealership. Though most of the land had been sold to raise money to pay taxes and start the car lot, the Kamps had held onto the old home place and a hundred or so acres around it. Now nearly swallowed in kudzu vines, honeysuckle and wild roses, it was almost invisible by day, and at night melted so completely into the moonlit woods that one would almost have to stumble over the carcass of the house, trip over the bones of the front steps to know that a structure existed.

But the Kamp heirs knew, and so the Klan knew.

Thus it was on that late July midnight in 1969 that the Klarogo, Furies, Terrors and Grand Wizard of the Kattahatchie Klavern of the Imperial White Knights of the Ku Klux Klan met by lantern light amid the stone and shadow of the Old Kamp Place basement. There would be no loud speeches or cross burnings. Such spectacles mostly were for public consumption, cameras and reporters welcome, to a point, as long as they were white. The marching and chanting theatrics were staged to reassure "decent white folks" that the Klan still was on guard, to scare "uppity niggahs" and to intimidate any Jews or Catholics who might, like "stray dogs," be wandering through the county. This was a business meeting, and their business was death.

Overhead and along the rarely used dirt road members of the klavern's outer guard, known as Klexters, patrolled in black coveralls or camouflage hunting gear. Some carried shotguns, others deer rifles, and eight of the most trusted held M-16s. As Kommander of the Klexters and Kaptain of the Klarogo – the klavern's inner guard – Tony Carlucci was well-pleased with the arrangement of his troops. He always had known he possessed excellent military skills, even if the Army officers over him had been too stupid and prejudiced against "*I*-talians" to see it.

The Kludd, or klavern chaplain, leaned forward in his chair and opened the box at his feet. There was a buzz like the noise made by a cheap doorbell. Tony hated this part and had to fight the urge to reach for the Luger on his black utility belt. "Idiot," Tony whispered to himself as the man bare-handed a three-foot rattlesnake from the box and held it over his head like a scepter. All rose.

"Dear Lord," began the Kludd. "We ask your blessing and protection for this gathering, and these defenders of the ancient laws ...."

Tony wondered if Olin Farber – the preacher from a backwoods snake-handling church out from Challabeate Crossroads – milked his babies before sticking his hand in that vented wooden box he carried. Or maybe they were defanged. Whatever the case, watching the serpent slither between the Kludd's bare hands made Tony's skin crawl.

As Kaptain of the Klarogo, Tony wore black gloves and boots, and a police-style Sam Brown belt on the outside of his black satin robe. A red cross on a white field inside a crimson circle was the only color on his uniform. His dark eyes floated white in the holes cut for them in the black veil. In his meaty fist, Tony held the traditional whip – a cat-o-nine-tails. A Confederate officer's saber that had belonged to Jennifer's great-grandfather, General Manfred Ambrose, hung from one side of the cargo belt while a holster containing the Luger was on the other side. Tony always claimed to have taken the pistol off a Nazi officer after heroically piloting his B-17 bomber to a belly-landing in occupied France. Through his derring-do and with a little help from the French Resistance, he got his entire crew safely back to Britain – though the lack of immediate medical attention cost him his leg. Of course, all of that was a lie, like the rest of Tony Carlucci's military record. He had swapped two bottles of Scotch for the gun while serving as an Army Air Corps mechanic in the south of England. The pilot's wings, lieutenant's bar and bronze star, which he flashed with regularity in the decade after World War II, were stolen from a casket bound for Weema, Iowa while Tony was assigned to graves detail during a stretch in the brig. Several months later when he lost his leg during a German air raid on his base, the zipper-like stitching at the terminus of his thigh and his own Purple Heart made him a hero in his own mind. That's when Tony was shipped back to the States – to a military hospital in Gulfport, Mississippi – and his favorite role was born, that of Wounded Flying Ace.

While the war continued, the nurses and the younger and even more naive aides at the military hospital remained easy picking – like firm fruit hanging pink from a giant peach tree planted beside the Gulf.

Their skin covered in the fuzz that passes for hair on a woman's body and a salty dew of perspiration; their juice ready to burst free, warm and tangy. Those hailing from little crossroads like Plainville, Kansas, Iron River, Wisconsin and DeLong, Mississippi – four hundred miles to the north – seemed particularly susceptible to his dusky charm and sometimes rough-around-the-edges ways. Away from home, most of them for the first time – away from papa, preachers and prying neighbors – they were ready to taste something different, something with a little spice to it and the exotic tang of garlic.

Much to Tony's surprise, being one-legged didn't slow his amorous efforts at all. In fact, with most of his eventual conquests his wooden leg gave him instant credibility as a war hero and a sympathy card that he could use to trump almost any fault or flaw they found in him. Just pull off his prosthesis, hop around a little and rub the scarred stump. Moan about phantom pain – which sometimes was real, but most often not – and talk about how it was all worth it for God, country and momma. Before he knew it, pretty, compassion-filled nurses and innocent young aides were asking to rub the stump for him. *And one rub usually led to another,* he smiled – thinking of how patriotic and sincere they had been, while his only allegiance was to the Nation of Tony, the Continent of Carlucci, which sat fortified above a sea of fools.

Tony's acting skills were somewhat overwrought, however, having been learned from his showgirl mother backstage at vaudeville houses from Philly to Buffalo, New York to Carbondale, Illinois, to Scranton, Pennsylvania. They couldn't fool men for long, especially those who had seen a con or two before the war or real air combat during it. That insight, and some checking with the military, had cost Tony Carlucci a sales job at a Gulfport car lot and a teller position at a small bank in Bay St. Louis. Even these years later Tony's thick neck burned when he remembered how the bank manager had humiliated him in front of the rest of the staff – fired him, called him a liar and a disgrace. Four nights later, Tony and a tire iron made sure the banker would never talk that way to anyone else, at least not through his own teeth. And the banker's plump little wife? Behind his veil Tony's smile changed and he felt another kind of warmth, remembering how she had begged then screamed. But a quick right hook, just like his father had taught him, turned her cries into an indecipherable whimper as her jaw separated from the rest of her face and she crumbled into the corner, spilling blood and slobber down the front of her torn nightgown. That's when he put the steel to her. When he was done, he knew she'd be lucky if she could ever conceive.

Now, despite the cool stones and damp air of the hidden basement, Tony felt himself sweating under his dark robes. *Nobody embarrasses Anthony Joseph Carlucci and gets away with it,* he told himself with a hidden smile, forcing himself to slow his breathing.

After the Kludd finished his prayer and put away the snake, the Grand Wizard ordered the Kaptain of the Klargo to escort forward the "honored Klavaliers, travelers by night, guardians of the light." The Wizard instructed Robert Bedford McBride and Tony Carlucci to kneel at the stone altar in the center of the room. Tony made a show of the effort. Open there was the Klan's holy book, the Kloran, and both men placed their right hand on the book and raised their left. The Wizard drew his sword and held it in front of his face and told them to repeat again their blood oath allegiance to the Klan and the white race.

Tony spoke the words with his full lips, his distinctly Mediterranean features hidden beneath his black veil. There had been a time in the early part of the 20th Century when no one with his features or a last name that ended in a vowel would have been welcome in the Klan. As it was, he'd had to renounce the "Papist church and all its evil minions." That was fine with Tony, since he hated the nuns and detested the priests who'd tried to rein him in as a willful child and later as a teenage street tough. In any case, the post-World War II Ku Klux was interested in only one thing – controlling or eliminating the Civil Rights Movement. Nearly anyone who shared that goal was welcome to wear the robes, and the handful who were willing to go beyond rhetoric to direct, and if necessary, deadly action could rise quickly in the post-war Klan. Even a well-known liar, womanizer, wife-beater and hard-drinking barroom brawler with a name that ended in *i*.

The Grand Wizard touched each man on the shoulder with the flat of his sword. "Arise brave Klavalier Knights," said Wizard Milton Handley. "And know that we all are here to serve you in your gallant quest for the salvation of the white race."

Chapter 13

❦

Cutter's painting job ran out at the end of the day Thursday. Since I'd left Daddy's farm and quit the paper, we both found ourselves temporarily out of work. The start of two-a-day football practices still was a couple of weeks away and the start of school two weeks past that. If it started on time. And who knew what would happen with Cattahatchie High? Governor Weathers' lawyers still were battling Mr. Burke in court.

So, Cutter and I were awakened by the sun in the unusual position of having no place we had to be on a Friday morning.

I crawled out of my sleeping bag and staggered to The Well. The rocky surface was hard on even young joints when it came to sleeping. I stretched out and dipped my face into the cold, clear water, then splashed some in my hair and onto my back.

"Mornin'," I said to Cutter as he rolled over next to the fire pit.

"Mornin'."

Cutter and I had talked little since Tuesday night when I told him I'd resigned from the job I loved at *The Current-Leader*. He thought I gave way too much control of my life to the MacAllisters, and I was sure that the movie-star handsome Cutter Carlucci – a collegiate All-America in waiting – could not possibly understand what it meant for a scrawny, third-team wide receiver and clipboard carrier to land a girl like Patti. Every time we tried to talk the conversation seemed to circle back to some form of that discussion. We both were tired of it.

"You want to go get some breakfast at The Cotton?" I asked.

"Brother Daddy hasn't put The Cotton off limits as a den of race-mixers?"

As a matter of fact, the Reverend Dr. C.E. MacAllister had suggested at Wednesday night's prayer meeting that those who want to "walk in the way of righteousness" should not frequent businesses that continued to advertise in *The Current-Leader*; but I didn't want to get into that with Cutter.

"You think Brother Mac owns me? Well, he don't," I told him.

Cutter sat up and rolled his neck atop his powerful shoulders. "Aw'right then. Let's go eat."

It was 8:20 when the tires of Cutter's jeep rolled onto the square. *The Thomas Crown Affair* was on the marquee at The Rebel Theater. As we circled toward Commerce Street, we saw the crowd gathered between the front entrance of the courthouse and *The Current-Leader* building. Several sheriff's cars were sitting on the street, their lights flashing, as a work crew finished bolting plywood over the front windows. Another sheet covered the front door. Broken glass glistened at the curb and black soot stained the bricks where the windows and doors had been.

Cutter wheeled into a parking space. I followed him over to one of the patrol cars where Deputy John-Thomas Hinton was propped.

"Hey, Cutter, Nate."

"Hey, John-Thomas," said Cutter. "What happened?"

"Fire bomb through the front window. About four this mornin'."

"How bad?" asked Cutter.

"Pretty bad in the front offices there on the first floor," he said as Cutter studied the men working while Miss Carter sat to the side. Eve Howard was behind the wheel of the beat-up Lincoln and Ridge Bellafont was shooting pictures. Miss Carter was wearing a Van Morrison T-shirt and the jeans she'd quickly pulled on when she was called in the middle of the night. "It could have been a lot worse, though," Deputy Hinton was saying. "Deputy Belle was workin' the night radio shift at the jail. He was standin' out front smokin' when he heard glass break and tires squeal. So, he jumped in a patrol car and came up here. He called in the fire alarm and did some good with a couple of fire extinguishers from the car before the smoke got him."

"Roy's my third cousin on my momma's side," I said. "Is he aw'right?"

"He swallowed some smoke and got some burns on his right arm and hand," said the young deputy. "They admitted him to the hospital but they ain't sendin' him on to Memphis. So it cain't be too bad."

I nodded, relieved.

About that time, my father walked around the corner with two men in dark suits and sunglasses. They might as well have had FBI stenciled on their foreheads. A knot of men standing on the courthouse square booed, and a few loudly cursed Billy Wallace and the agents. Not far away, Sgt. J.B. Benoit stood on the sidewalk in front of the Cattahatchie Valley Bank building. Behind the front window, Governor Weathers looked like a ghost in the sun glare shining on the glass.

Sheriff Wallace and the FBI agents spoke briefly to Miss Carter, then she wheeled over to one of the workmen loading up their truck. The man dug around in a tool box and handed her a can of something. She shook it and pushed next to one of the plywood panels and began writing there in large orange letters – then on the panel covering the front door and finally the other window.

OPEN! ... 4 ... BUSINESS!

* * *

That night I rode with Patti and her folks to a revival Brother MacAllister was preaching in Bolivar, Tennessee, about fifty miles northeast of DeLong. By then, anyone who cared knew the names of each and every carrier who had delivered *The Current-Leader* on Tuesday night, and the names of a handful of others who had simply shown up at the loading the dock and pitched in. Several – including Dr. Martin Dale, Mr. and Mrs. George Ragland, C.B. Davis and Ruth-Louise Melbourne – were longtime members of First Denomination. Mr. Davis, who owned a garage east of town, and Doctor Dale were deacons.

Remembering what Cutter told me the night I left our farmhouse – about him going his own way and keeping his own schedule, I had resisted asking him directly about where he'd gone in the wee hours of Wednesday morning. But word was out on the clothesline telegraph that he'd been among the volunteers. I wasn't surprised. I knew he and Tommy Ray had played a lot of basketball together at the Roseville High gym, and hoped that was all that had caused him to leave the peace and safety of The Well. Someone told Mrs. MacAllister that their cousin's best friend had seen Cutter having lunch with "that woman" at the picnic table on the loading dock the previous Saturday afternoon. But that seemed to be only a rumor. Still, there was something in the way he looked at Miss Carter as she sprayed those defiant words – OPEN! ... 4 ... BUSINESS! – across the front of her charred storefront. I had seen Cutter turn desirous eyes on other women at The Gin, some older than Miss Carter. But what I saw in his eyes at that moment? It was something different. And it worried me for his sake, and the sake of our friendship.

When we got back to DeLong, I kissed Patti good night in the driveway and climbed into my truck. I started north toward Blue Mountain Road and The Well, but turned around in front of Kamp Motors.

Why? I'm not sure.

Curiosity? Concern? Guilt?

It was 11:25 as I drove onto the courthouse square. A deputy sat in a patrol car in front of the K.L. Eustis Insurance Agency. He was writing in a notebook. I waved to him but couldn't make out his face in the shadows. At the foot of Commerce Street and next to the Bilbo Bridge, the front of the jail was lit up but the cells were all dark. A man's arms protruded from one second-floor window, his hands clasped outside the bars.

I turned south on A Street, past Weathers-McLemore Trucking and into the lot between the tall metal silos of the Emerson Grain Storage Company and the Randleman Cotton Warehouse. Turning out my lights, I parked next to the rail above the river and almost directly across from the back of *The Current-Leader* building. From beneath the seat, I pulled a pair of binoculars and focused on the open bay doors. In the large, brightly lit room, I could see the press still was turning while Miss Carter was leading a line of people inserting advertising flyers into stacks of newspapers. Eve Howard was bundling stacks of thirty papers and Ridge Bellafont was carrying them out to the edge of the loading dock. C.B. Davis was loading several stacks into his truck.

It was then that Cutter's jeep turned into the parking lot. He shook hands with Mr. Davis and climbed the steps up to the dock.

"You need some help?"

"Oh, Cutter!" said Miss Carter without missing a beat in the inserting line. "Hi! I think we have it covered tonight. But I do want to talk to you.

"Shorty, could you take over my spot for a minutes?" she called to her production manager over the clatter of the press. He was catching a breather on a bench beside the massive rolls of paper.

"Sure thing, Miss Holly."

"Let's go out in the parking lot so we can hear ourselves think," she said.

I watched from a distance as Cutter followed Miss Carter down the ramp. "Where's Charlie tonight?"

"She's up in my office. Charlie is a little too small and curious to be turned loose in the pressroom during a run."

Miss Carter pushed nearly to the edge of River Street where the rattle of the presses was a rumble and not a roar. "What's she trying to do?" I asked myself as I watched them. "Get Cutter in trouble on purpose?"

She turned to face the breeze that was moving south above the river, then shook her mane of auburn hair before running her fingers through it. Pulling her blouse out from her chest to let in a bit of the air, she said, "This time I'm the one who smells too rancid to be indoors."

"I doubt that," he said, propping against the fender of someone's GMC pickup.

"Well, you shouldn't. Everything in that building, including me, smells like a campfire somebody put out with sour water."

"But you are open *four* business," he said slowly, drawing the number in the air.

Holly Lee Carter smiled. "Yes, we are. For the time being. And part of that is thanks to you," she said. "We kept missing each other Tuesday night. Every time I came in for another load of papers, you were out running another route.

"You ran three whole routes on the south end of the county. It made a huge difference. I just wanted to tell you how grateful I am."

Cutter looked at the river and then back at the woman in front of him. "I couldn't sleep. I figured I might as well make myself useful."

"You are lousy at taking a compliment. Do you know that?" she said. Cutter shrugged. "Anyway, DeLong Newspapers Incorporated is happy to pay you for your work. If you'll come in and see Miss Frances on Monday, she'll write you a check."

"I didn't do it for the money."

"I know. You did it for Tommy Ray. But there's no reason you shouldn't be paid. At least enough to cover your gas."

"What about tonight?" he asked. "You have enough carriers?"

"Enough to do what we're going to do," Miss Carter told him. "We're only going to deliver the in-town routes tonight and to the racks at businesses right on Highway 27. We're not going to run the rural routes until in the morning."

"Miss Carter, if you'll give me a load of papers I'll go anywhere you need –"

She shook her head. "I know you would, Cutter. So would some other folks. But it's too dangerous. We caught the Klan off-guard the other night. Tonight, they're out there waiting," she said, hugging her arms across her chest. "I can feel it."

Holly was ready for Cutter to argue with all the vehemence of a testosterone-stoked teenager who is sure he is as indestructible as the limestone shelf holding The Well. But there was none of that.

"I think that's a good decision," he said, demonstrating a level of a maturity that surprised her. Cutter understood his own mortality, she saw. It was a lesson it had taken a shattered spinal cord to teach her.

"There might be something you can help me with, though," she said. "I hear from Mr. Davis that you're a pretty good shade-tree mechanic. That you rebuilt that jeep of yours just about from the ground up when you were only fourteen."

"I had some help," he said. "But I'm not a body man, if that's what you're lookin' for."

"It's not. I'm looking for someone who knows all the backyard, behind-the-barn junkyards around here. I need to find my father's car," she said. He looked at her curiously then listened patiently as she told him about her conversation with LeRoy Kamp. "I spent Monday and a good bit of yesterday calling every junkyard the phone company has listed between here and Tulsa, Oklahoma. Nothing."

Cutter squatted next to the pickup. "So, you think LeRoy is lying to you? Why?"

"LeRoy and I have some history," she said. "Back when I was running wild at The Gin, and before LeRoy went to prison."

"It didn't end well?"

"It ended just fine for me. He was in jail and I was free of him. But his perception may be somewhat different."

"I'll bet," said Cutter. "I've seen him get rough with women at The Gin. We've had to escort him out a couple of times. He fancies himself a big-time dope dealer, but I think it's mostly to impress the girls who like that stuff. Still, there's not much I'd put past him."

"Neither would I."

"So, you think he's just jerkin' you around as payback?"

"Maybe."

"Or?"

"Or … I don't know," she said, not completely trusting Cutter and still not completely sold on her own guesswork "But I do know I need to find that Oldsmobile."

He stood but kept his eyes on hers. "You'll be lucky if it hasn't already been crushed up for scrap or eaten up for parts. That is, if we can find it at all."

"I know. Will you help me?"

Cutter drew in a breath. "Sure. Why not? I can ask around."

Miss Carter pushed her chair forward and took Cutter's hand. She squeezed it. "Thank you."

I couldn't hear anything they said, but through my binoculars I saw clearly the smile they shared. It was warm and as intimate as any I'd ever seen cross Cutter's face. Seeing it made me so angry that I tossed the field glasses on the seat and ground the gears as I shoved my old truck into reverse and gunned it away from the railing. Gravel rattled under my fenders as I whipped the truck around and I caught a glimpse of Cutter and Miss Carter looking my way. I didn't care if they saw me, or if they knew I'd been spying on them.

My best friend was betraying the town, the people who had loved and lauded him. And he was betraying me. For that – that? – that woman, that *cripple!*

* * *

For the next couple of days, I kept my distance from Cutter. I was angry and hurt. Besides, who knew how many more people saw him and Holly Lee Carter holding hands right there next to River Street? I didn't want to be caught in the fallout if their relationship – whatever that meant – was exposed and Brother Mac went off like an atom bomb.

On Friday night, I drove south and turned down Pleasant Ridge Road toward our house but I knew I couldn't go back under that roof. A quarter-mile from the driveway, I hung a right down a field road and parked near Asher Creek under a large oak – the only tree amid one-hundred and twenty-five acres of cotton. On one side of the tree's massive trunk was the rusted, wrought-iron fence that surrounded the Wallace family cemetery. My mother and brother were buried there, and Wallaces all the way back to the 1850s.

I didn't know where I'd be laid to take my final rest, and was too young and naive to care. That night, I slept in the cab of my truck.

Cutter worked his usual all-nighter at The Gin from Saturday into Sunday, so we didn't run across each other again until Sunday night after choir practice when I went back to The Well. He was propped against a rock with a lantern on one side and his shotgun on the other, reading a book about architecture – *Modernist Interpretations of the Roman Arch.*

"Hey," I said, walking up to the pit where a small, low fire burned.

"Hey."

"Am I still welcome here?"

"I told you, Nate. It's not for me to say who's welcome here and who's not. But there's plenty of room."

It irritated me that he didn't ask where I'd been or what I'd been up to the last couple of days. He didn't even mention my tire-spinning, gravel-throwing exit from the riverside parking lot on Friday night. More by way of trying to stimulate conversation than anything else, I said, "Klansmen have been thick as fleas in DeLong this weekend. Comin' in from all over. Did you see 'em?"

"I haven't been in town much the last couple of days."

"They've been marchin' around the square in their robes, carryin' signs, makin' speeches. Handin' out flyers, too," I said, pulling a piece of folded green paper from my hip pocket. It was announcing what was being billed as a "historic" Klan rally on the Oscar Campbell farm northwest of town at 7:30 Monday night. There was a map to the location deep in the countryside northwest of DeLong and a drawing of a hooded Klansman carrying an automatic rifle. The U.S. stars-and-stripes and the Confederate stars-and-bars were crossed behind him. I unfolded it and handed it to Cutter. He looked it over and gave it back. "It's supposed to be the biggest rally the Klux have held in years. I've never been to one, have you?"

Cutter looked at me like a parent might look at child, or maybe more accurately, like an older brother might look at his much younger and more sheltered sibling. "A few," he said, and I thought he was going to leave it at that, but he didn't. "Tony used to take me to them before I got smart enough to run for the woods or old enough to look him in the eye and say no."

"Then I guess you're not goin' to the rally?"

"No. I guess not."

"You're gonna be lonesome then, 'cause everybody is going," I told him. "I ran into Dodge this afternoon. He's goin'. So is Jimmy Garner. There's gonna be music and everything. I'm takin' Patti. It's supposed to be a heckuva show, if nothin' else."

For a long moment he looked at me. "I'll pass," he said and went back to reading the textbook in his lap.

Chapter 14

❦

A trickle of sweat slid down the back of Ridge Bellafont's neck and beneath the collar of one of the French-cut shirts he had shipped to him from a shop on Magazine Street in New Orleans. Nothing surprising about that, since the old Chevrolet station wagon driven by *The Current-Leader*'s longtime photographer didn't have the best air-conditioning. Especially when moving slowly down a dirt road baking in the late afternoon light of a Monday in early August. At 6:30, the temperature was still in the low 90s. What surprised Ridge was that the droplets moving from his perfectly groomed hair and sliding onto his back felt cold.

Cold like winter raindrops. Cold like fear. Cold like, "Eve, I think this was a big mistake. I can't believe I let you talk me into this."

"Calm down, Ridge," Eve said from beneath a tarp spread over her and a gamut of photographic equipment in the back of the station wagon. "I'm the one who's about to melt. Can't we go any faster?"

"No," said Ridge, testy. "We can't. I just hope we don't run out of gas. This old needle is pointing at E-*eeek!*"

After fifteen minutes of winding northwest of DeLong through dirt lanes and low hills, Ridge was locked into a line of vehicles a quarter of a mile long – cars, pickups, a couple of logging trucks and even a mule-drawn hay wagon were waiting to turn across a cattle guard gate into a large up-sloping pasture. In the distance, a long flatbed truck sat atop a hill in the shadow of an enormous cross, wrapped in burlap. A four-piece country band sounded tinny in the distance.

"I can't believe this," said Eve. "It's like a concert or a fair."

"One put on by the devil," said Ridge. "If Holly ever finds out I did this –"

"Stop worrying about it. She's not going to find out. I told you, this is strictly for my personal portfolio. Besides, what could happen?"

she asked. "You said yourself there would be cops and FBI agents all over the place – observing."

"That's what I'm afraid of," he said, "that if something happens, they'll observe and not intervene."

"Ridge, don't be such a ninny. You have as much talent as any photographer I've ever met, but you're still shooting for a small-town paper. What's missing about you is a spirit of adventure," Eve said with all of the certainty of a twenty-four-old raised in the arms of privilege. "Nothing is going to happen, except that I may die of heat-stroke under here."

"If some of these old cobs get hold of yo' black bootie, you'll wish you had died of heatstroke."

"Oh, Ridge, you are such a worrier. But I love you."

"Then show your love by shutting up and lying still," he said. "We're getting close to the gate."

Eve Howard ducked her head, her blouse already soaked in the thick, dark air beneath the tarp. After Holly told her that Ridge would be shooting the rally and that, "There is absolutely no way in this world you can be anywhere near that place," Eve had told Holly she was going to stay at the newspaper and develop film. But this was a once-in-a-lifetime opportunity, a chance to photograph the actual KKK in action at what was being billed as the "largest Klan rally in the history of North Mississippi" – *which might make it the largest in the history of the universe*, thought Eve. Her mouth went into over-drive as she reasoned with, pleaded with and cajoled Ridge into taking her with him. Now her mind raced with possibilities and anticipation. After all, Holly, her mentor, had honed her chops as a photographer by jumping out of airplanes, riding with cops and finally going into battle with the 7th Air-Cav. What a coup it would be for a black female photographer to have shots of a Mississippi Klan rally in her portfolio.

This could be a career-maker, thought Eve, breathing in the heavy air under the tarp. *This is why I came to this god-awful place.*

"We're at the gate, and they've got guards," said Ridge. "So be very still and very quiet."

As Ridge made the turn he felt some reassurance, some com-fort seeing Sheriff Wallace leaning against a patrol car a few yards down the road. A man in a dark suit was standing with them and photographing every car entering the rally. Less reassuring – in fact, downright unnerving considering his cargo – were the robed and hooded Klansmen checking cars as they entered. Two Klexters in white robes with red sashes wore pistol belts and sabers in plain view, and a black-robed member of the Klargo sat horseback with a shotgun propped on his thigh like prison gun bulls.

The Klexter looked in. "I'm Ridge –"

"We know who you are. The Klan knows all," said the man behind the veil. His breath smelled of peppermint and gin. "And we know the rag you work for, too. We're gonna put it out of business, one way or another."

"Well," Ridge sighed nervously, "maybe so. But for now we're still printing. And I'm here to take pictures."

"Wasn't this yo' momma's car?" asked the other guard.

"Yes."

"It looks like a growed man could do better than drivin' his dead momma's car. But you always was a momma's boy, weren't you, Ridge-y?" The man waited but Ridge kept his eyes forward and didn't respond. Eve clenched her fists, showing the anger that Ridge couldn't. Then, "What all you got under that tarp?" the Klexter asked, and Eve's breath caught in her throat.

Ridge cleared his throat. "Photographic equipment. Lights, tri-pods, cameras. That sort of thing."

"Why don't you drop the tailgate and let us take a look?"

Ridge felt his heart skip a beat.

As Eve readied her legs to kick and her hands to scratch, one car horn in the line went off, then another. And another.

"Forget it, Rob," said the first guard. "Sister Ridge is harmless. Go on."

Before the second Klexter could object, Ridge accelerated under the stars-and-bars of a Confederate flag that hung from the top of the gate.

They were in Klan territory now.

* * *

Holly pushed down the ramp from the side porch at Wolf's Run and headed for the car and the Klan rally. If she had to cover this – *this? disgrace!* – she at least wanted to be comfortable. A loose denim skirt, a blousy peasant top with embroidery in front and white sandals fit the bill. During ten years on the West Coast, Holly had become very much a casual California girl. She was tired of tight-fitting heels that made her feet swell, hose, lipstick and made-up eyes – all of the expected trappings of a "proper small-town businesswoman."

She loaded her hips onto the bench seat of the Lincoln. Lifting one leg into the car and then the other, she noted that the polish on her toes was faded and smiled at her own vanity, even when it came to limbs paralyzed for nearly four years. But she'd had little time to deal with such superficial details, even if she'd wanted to. She, Eve, Ridge, Shorty Rodgers and a couple of others had slept in *The Current-Leader* building Friday night, both as cursory watchmen and so they could begin delivering papers to the rural routes at first light, which they did. Despite receiving hundreds of cancellation requests in the wake of Wednesday's integrated edition – particularly from the county's most rural areas – Holly had made the decision that she would drop no subscribers. At least for the time being they would continue to deliver to everyone who'd been a subscriber prior to Wednesday, hoping they'd eventually change their mind. Running those long, dusty routes had taken most of Saturday; and she had spent all day Sunday and into that night at the office working on stories to fill the gaps left by her decimated staff. Eve had worked right alongside her, *bless her heart*, thought Holly. Some wounds between them were still there but they're healing, she thought, thankful that Eve hadn't put up a big fight about not going to the Klan rally.

As she drove, Holly realized how exhausted she was – not merely from the events of the last few days, but from everything since she'd returned to DeLong. She had tried to "let go and let God," as the old saying went, but she couldn't quite manage it. Instead, she had played her guitar deep into Monday's early hours, and run the numbers again and again in her mind. Unless things turned around in a hurry, she could keep the paper going for about four more weeks, six at the outside.

At the foot of Blue Mountain, Holly had to slow the big car to a crawl as she prepared to make the turn onto the bridge. Just as her father should have done that rainy night. Suddenly, Holly's right arm flew forward on the hand control, jamming on the brakes. Cutter dropped his left foot hard onto the jeep's brake. The two vehicles stopped nose to nose, inches apart. Once an instant of surprise washed out of Holly's face, she laughed. Cutter smiled, chuckled, then backed the jeep onto the narrow cut of road that led to The Well. Holly stopped the Lincoln on the bridge and Cutter walked over as Charlie sniffed the air and wagged.

"Sorry about that. It's a blind turn," Cutter said from behind his aviator shades.

"I know, I made it many times when I was your age," said Holly, lifting Charlie out of her lap. "*Tais-toi, mon amour*." The little dog settled on the seat.

"I was headed up to Wolf's Run to see if you were home."

"Don't tell me you've already found Daddy's car."

"Maybe. At least, I think I know where to look."

"How'd you do it so fast?"

"It's a matter of knowing the right back doors to knock on. And knowing which Kamp Motors employees have an axe to grind with LeRoy."

"Ahhh, I see. So, where's the car?"

"The fellow I talked to told me he saw it hauled away by an old, beat-up wrecker with the words 'Conway Tow & Salvage, Moore's Bridge, Alabama' on the door. The driver seemed to know LeRoy pretty well."

"Looks like LeRoy's still the same old liar he always was."

"That's not news to anybody around here."

"I guess not," said Holly, giving herself a moment for a flash of temper to cool. She wanted to stick a cattle prod down the front of LeRoy's jeans. Then she refocused on Cutter. "Does this Conway guy still have Daddy's car?"

"I think so. I called over there this afternoon and told him I was lookin' for parts for a '63 Dodge, a '61 Ford and '65 Olds. I didn't want him to get suspicious about the Olds."

"Smart."

"Anyway, he said he had several Fords but only one '65 Olds."

"*Fan*-tastic!" Holly enthused.

Cutter smiled. "I'm glad I was able to find it. But look, I told the guy I wanted the steering column and some other stuff from the Olds, for sure. I asked him to hold 'em for me. But he said he runs a first-come-first-served business."

"So when can we go?"

"We?" Cutter asked, surprised.

"I don't know how to take a steering column apart. You do. I'll be happy to pay you for your time," said Holly.

Cutter propped against the iron bridge railing and said nothing. His shoulders were flat, his chest was carved and his jeans were tight. He reminded her of a young Paul Newman, but a much bigger man.

"Aw'right," he finally said. "I don't have any for-sure work lined up until next week. But I wouldn't wait too long."

"How about Wednesday?"

"That'll work."

"I'd go tomorrow, but with our staff down to the bone as it is, I can't afford to be away from the paper," she told him, looking at her watch. "And speaking of the paper, I've got to go. I don't want to miss any of the *speechifyin'* out at the Campbell place."

Cutter grunted. "You're coverin' the Klan rally? The same people who tried to torch your building?"

"I know. It makes me mad, too," she said, putting the convertible into gear. "But I don't have anyone else to send. And, no matter how repulsive I find it, whenever two thousand people gather in Catta-hatchie County for anything, it's news."

Cutter studied Holly Lee Carter for a moment. "You're not exactly Miss Popularity with the Klux."

She laughed and Cutter found himself liking the sound of it. "I appreciate your concern. But the Klan has been very public about this rally. There are going to be reporters and TV cameras, deputies and FBI men all over that hill tonight. Even by Klan standards, it would be bad P.R. to pull a paralyzed woman out of her car and tar-and-feather her while the cameras roll."

"Yes, ma'am. But there's a lot of empty road between here and the Campbell farm."

That thought had crossed Holly's mind as well, but she'd put it aside because she needed to. Now she shifted the car back into park. "So, were you going out to the big event?"

"I hadn't planned to."

"You might as well. The rest of the town is going to be deserted," Holly told him. "If you're not worried about being seen with me, you're welcome to ride along."

Chapter 15

❧

Ridge Bellafont pulled the station wagon into a long row of cars halfway up the green hill. The sun had slipped down behind a stand of maples, but Ridge and Eve still were sweating as if it were noon.

"That was a little closer than I would have liked," said Ridge.

"Do you think they'd have really hurt us?"

"This isn't a movie, Malibu girl. It's not your momma's TV show. People don't get killed one week and show up again on the next episode," he said, staring up the hill where a large crowd was gathering. "When they shoot you here, you stay dead."

Cecil Weathers was among those already seated on the long flatbed truck. An old man was walking between the rows of cars carrying a wooden box containing straw and mason jars filled with white lightning. Klexters directed traffic into semi-orderly rows like volunteers at a high school football game. Around the edges of the field, the black-clad members of the Klargo sat on black saddles on horses covered in their own shiny black robes. Most of the Klargo propped shotguns or deer rifles on their thighs.

"I've got to admit, those guys in black are a little spooky," said Eve, peeking out from under the tarp.

"They're more than a little spooky. They're the real hard cases. The Klan's version of the Gestapo," he told her. "Now stay down."

Holly turned the Lincoln under the Confederate flag. The Klexter on the driver's side looked into the car. He stared at Cutter then propped on the door frame so he could get a better angle on the opening in Holly's blouse.

"You don't belong here," said the man by her door.

"Thank God for that," said Holly. "But I have a job to do, so I don't have any choice."

"You always did have a smart mouth. Thought you were too good for all of the boys in high school."

"Wrong, Toby," she said, recognizing the voice of Toby McLemore, whose family partnered with Weathers in a trucking firm. The same voice that asked her for dates throughout her junior year, and had gotten very ugly when she'd declined. "I just thought I was too good for you."

Cutter pushed his sunglasses up the bridge of his nose and fought a smile. "What are you laughin' at?" asked the Klexter by the passenger door.

"Not a thing," said Cutter, recognizing the voice of Noble Russell, a farmer and CHS booster. His son would be a sophomore linebacker in the fall. "I'm just enjoyin' a late ride in the country."

"Yeah, well, you ought to be more choosey about who you ride around with," Russell told him. "You don't want people to start worderin'?"

"Wonderin' what?"

"Wonderin' if you know which side your bread is buttered on," said McLemore. "This town's done a lot for you."

Cutter looked at McLemore but said nothing. Holly wondered what was going on behind Cutter's Ray-Bans.

"Can we go?" she asked.

"Yeah, go ahead. Your *fag*-tographer is already here."

Holly did a double take. "You know, Toby, it's good that I know you're only joking since it's impossible to take seriously a man who wears a bed sheet and a dunce cap in broad daylight."

"You're going to take us seriously before we're done," he snarled. "We got somethin' for you."

"Oh, yeah?" said Holly. "I've got something for you, too."

Holly rested her elbow on the door frame and gave the Klexter a one-fingered salute.

"You bit –"

Holly gunned the big convertible out into the field, letting it fishtail, a spray of grass and dirt showering the men. The horse under the Klargo guard reared. Billy Wallace and the FBI agent who'd been watching the exchange from across the road, looked at each other trying to surpress smiles. When the horse settled under the black-robed

Klansman, he started to go after Holly. Then, remembering the proximity of the sheriff, he glanced at the lawman through the cutouts in his veil. The sheriff's face was serious now as he shook his head. The Klargo seethed beneath his robes but calmed the horse and stayed put.

As they bounced along the hillside, Holly could feel Cutter staring at her. "What?"

"Which book of the Bible did that come from?" he asked, amused.

Holly swung the car into a parking spot as directed. "Cutter, I'm a believer, not a saint," she said, turning off the ignition. "I struggle with sin every day. And my temper is part of it. But Jesus is the God of sinners and second chances. I learned that in Vietnam."

Cutter considered. "I've heard the story. You were photographing a battle and got shot. You lived, and a lot soldiers didn't. So what – you cut a deal with God? Let me live and I'll be a good girl from now on?"

"No, it was nothing like that," said Holly, taking off her Wayfarers and laying them on the seat next to Charlie and her camera. "It was ... It was Sergeant Gary Watson."

"Who's that? A chaplain?"

"Definitely not a chaplain," said Holly with a soft laugh before her smile faded into memory. "No, Sergeant Gary Watson was a big, handsome, blonde guy from Waco, Texas. Confident on the edge of cocky. We were on the same chopper on the way into the Ia Drang. He was flirting with me. Telling me about a special place he knew on the beach near Da Nang. The locals called it *thiên đường của cửa khẩu.* Heaven's Gate." Holly looked at Cutter, but he showed no reaction. She went on. "Late that morning, we started taking fire from North Vietnamese Army regulars. The sergeant winked and said, 'Stick with me, honey. You'll be all right.'

"And I stuck with him. A few hours later in a clearing on a low ridge, he took two in the chest. Me and a couple of privates ran for him, tried to pull him out of the line of fire, but ...'"

Holly's voice trailed off.

"Is that when you were hit?" Cutter asked.

Holly nodded but said no more about that. "The sergeant died not six feet from me. His eyes open, looking right at me. They were filled with ... surprise. Like, 'Oh, you mean this is really the last day of my life?'"

Cutter took off his Ray-Bans as if to see Holly better.

"I lay there next to him, and the two dead privates, from four in the afternoon until seven-fifteen the next morning before the 7th Cav was able to fight its way back up that hill to get me and three others out alive. During the night, I was losing blood, going in and out of consciousness. But every time I woke up, Sergeant Gary Watson was right there, the look of surprise frozen on his face. He was only twenty-four. Like me."

Holly paused a moment to see if Cutter would interrupt with a question. She almost wished he would. This was not a memory she enjoyed reliving and why she was allowing herself to revisit it now, she wasn't sure, except that it provided the only honest answer to Cutter's question. When he said nothing, she continued. "I'd given my heart to Jesus when I was fourteen. Partly because I truly believe Jesus touched me that night, and partly because I thought that might make Daddy love me. When it didn't, I felt betrayed and me and Jesus parted ways. But I never forgot the sense of peace and joy I had the night I walked the aisle. I just always thought there'd be plenty of time to come back to Jesus when I was older, married, had kids. But laying there in that clearing next to the sergeant ... laying there through that *endless* night with the NVA prowling around, it just came clear how fast our chances can run out. And I saw how emptyt my life was. Empty vodka bottles. Empty pill bottles. Empty ... empty sex.

"Sometime in the darkest moment of that night, I looked up into a billion stars, into the universe spread out above the jungle and me, and said, 'God, if there's a better way to live, then I pray you'll let me make it out of here, and you'll show it to me. If not, then take me now, because I don't want to go back to the life I've been living.'"

Holly forced a shaky smile. "And here I am," she said, the memory of that long, long night in the jungle still raw and painful.

Cutter moved his eyes from Holly's face to her long legs and back to her face. She didn't shy away from his gaze. "You're not mad at God about the wheelchair?"

"Every day. Until I think of Sergeant Watson," said Holly, sniffling. She took a tissue from her purse and dabbed her nose. Then, "That's the simple answer, and it's true," she said. "Not a day goes by that I don't think of Sergeant Watson, and that I'm not grateful that November 14, 1965 wasn't the last day of my life. But if I'm being one-hundred percent honest with you, and with myself – well, if they'd flown me back to Da Nang and the docs had been able to fix me up as good as new, if I'd been able to *walk* out of the hospital, would I have really changed my life? I don't know.

"So God changed it for me," she said, running her hand along her thigh and patting her knee. "I've come to accept it as God's way of keeping my attention. But that doesn't mean I have to like it."

Behind the towering cross and the flatbed, above the ridgeline and the maples, the sky was lavender and cream. A sweet concoction melting in the dusk. In the sweltering twilight, Ridge Bellafont checked his camera bag.

"Ridge," said Eve from beneath the tarp. "I'm sorry about the way they talked to you back there."

"It's not your fault, sweetie. Besides, I'm used to it. I've lived with it all my life."

"Test … test." Some bozo in a hood was checking the microphone on the flatbed. "Test … one, two."

"Ridge, can I ask you something – personal?"

"Why, sure, sweetie. Like most ever'one else in DeLong, my life's an open book. Sometimes you have to read between the lines to get it, that's all."

Eve felt awkward but – "The Klan hates black people. But I always thought they also hated, well – "

"Ho-mo-sexuals?"

"Yes."

"Well, here's how it is," said Ridge. "The Bellafonts and DeLongs, the Kamps, Carters, Cutters and Wellinghams have roots in this county deeper than all but the oldest oaks. I'm probably kin in one way or another to nearly everyone on this hill. I know where the line is with these people, and I don't cross it."

"What does that mean?"

"It means, I don't hang my lace undies out on the line in DeLong. If I want to do that, I go to Naw'lins or to take the waters down in Florida's lovely, warm Keys," he told her. "Get down! Here comes one of them."

Naturally most eyes were focused on the flatbed as the bluegrass band wrapped up. But Holly also was aware of the number of looks and glances and even fingers being pointed in the direction of the Lincoln. She'd been a head-turner since she first became a teen, so she was used to people – particularly men – looking her way wherever she went. Now with the wheelchair, she was used to being stared at for another reason. But this was different. There was a heat in the eyes of many of the people on that hill that made her uneasy, like coals being passed too close to her skin. If Cutter felt it, he said nothing.

Holly swallowed. "Cutter, I think I may have done something very ... selfish." He looked at her, but didn't ask the question, so she continued. "You were right. I was nervous about coming out here. Especially about driving back in the dark. But I shouldn't have asked you to ride with me." Still he said nothing. "You don't make it easy do you?"

Still nothing except his steady gaze.

"Cutter, there are a lot of people out here who will see this as you taking sides with me – if they haven't decided that already," she told him. "I shouldn't have –"

"Shouldn't have what?" he finally asked.

"Shouldn't have gotten you involved in such a public way."

"You think people don't already know I helped deliver the paper the other night?"

"Yes. They know. But that was on backroads in the middle of the night," she reminded him. "This is poking them in the eye with a stick – in public."

"Miss Carter, I may not be as old as you or been as many places, but I'm not stupid. I knew exactly what some people would say if I rode out here with you," he told her. "But whether it was tonight or tomorrow afternoon, the Klux weren't gonna be happy with me."

"Corporal Banks' funeral?" asked Holly, a new level of respect for Cutter rising. "You know, that could cost you –"

"It costs what it costs," he interrupted, almost angrily. "Tommy Ray was my friend. I don't intend for him to go to his grave without payin' my respects." Cutter grunted and looked away. "Besides, when I score four or five touchdowns in the first game in September, nobody on this hill is gonna care who I rode out here with. Or whose funeral I went to. That's just how it is."

"**L**ookee there!" Patti said to me, pointing down the hill. "Cutter and Miss Carter. She's been back less than a month and she already has her hooks in him. Has she been coming 'round The Well?"

"No," I told her. "Not that I know of."

"When I heard Cutter was having lunch with her behind the paper and then helping her deliver that rag, I knew something was going on between them," Patti went on. "Of course, I don't know why I'm surprised. A whore and the son of an *I*-talian drunkard."

Before I could throw my brain and mouth into neutral, I blurted, "It's funny you don't call Cutter that to his face. In fact, you're the first one on the field after a game to hug his neck."

"I'm a cheerleader. It's my duty to support the team," said Patti, her back stiffening, her perfect little chin jutting out.

"Is that why you climb all over him in every picture you can for the newspaper? Is that why you signed his yearbook 'someone who admires you more than you know'? Yeah, I saw it!"

"Nate Wallace, I don't like your tone or insinuation," she told me and reached for the door handle. She slid out and I knew I'd gone too far, pricking a nerve of hypocrisy that always was just below the surface with Patti, but also dangerously close to the bone. I hopped out on my side and ran around to catch her.

"Honey, stop!" I said, getting in front of her. "I'm sorry."

"You should be," she snapped.

I reached to take her hand but she stepped back as if I were on fire. She whirled and started down the hill to where Brother Mac and several First Denomination deacons were leaning against his car. Though C.E. MacAllister's sympathies ran the same as those of the men on the flatbed, even he wouldn't allow himself to be photographed with Klansmen in their robes. I didn't follow Patti because I didn't want a fight in front of her father. Besides, while Patti's temper often burned white hot, it usually burned fast. I knew it was better to leave her be for a few minutes than try to argue with her.

On cue, all the cars along the front row by the flatbed turned on their headlights, illuminating the politicians and Klan leaders seated on the long trailer. From the microphone, the Kludd of the Cattahatchie Klavern intoned, "Let us pray."

"It's almost dark," said Ridge Bellafont. "I'm going to work the crowd for some photos. You can peek out and shoot some stuff, but stay under that tarp. And promise me you'll stay in the car."

"Will do," said Eve.

"Say it."

"Say what?"

"Say you promise you won't leave this car."

"Okay, Okay, Ridge. I promise."

In the mirror, Ridge Bellafont looked at Eve's smooth ebony face framed in the blackness under the tarp. "I wish I hadn't brought you here," he said and stepped out with his camera bag. "*Please*, stay down."

On the other side of the field, Holly made notes on a steno pad in her lap. Though for the most part Cutter stared straight ahead without comment, it was as if the air pressure on her right was different than in the surrounding atmosphere. She could feel it against her arm and the side of her face, and it had become more intense after what Cutter said about attending Corporal Banks' Tuesday afternoon funeral. ... *It costs what it costs.* ... He already had a maturity, a simple morality and sense of loyalty that some men work all their lives to achieve and never manage. Women, too. More than it should – much more then it should! – Cutter's presence on the other side of the bench seat made concentration difficult, but Holly forced herself to focus even though she almost could have written the story from memory. Other than J.B. Benoit's announcement that he was running for sheriff and his promise to maintain "the safe, orderly, traditional way of life dear to all real Cattahatchie Countians," the speeches by politicians and the harangues by a rainbow of robed Klansmen were right out of the 1940s.

Twenty years later, as she looked over the long blue hood of the Continental, she could see herself sitting straddle of the hood on her father's '37 Buick. On one side her dad stood, scribbling into a notebook, nearly grinding his pipe stem in two; on the other, Tom, a handsome teenager, stared, transfixed by the ghostly parade and the hate-scalded rhetoric.

Two decades had passed but as in '49, Cecil Weathers' speech was the climax of the evening. Love his *speechifying* or despise it,

Mississippi's former governor was an arm-waving, foot-stomping spellbinder in the mold of Bilbo, Huey Long or, some would say, Adolf Hitler. Weathers himself credited the tent revival preachers on whom he was weaned – a barefoot, overall-clad, pig farmer's son in northeast Cattahatchie County. But by the time he was twenty-one he had a cheap seersucker suit and a following for his toxic mix of white populism, race-baiting and Old Testament us-against-the-heathens religion. He learned to use the modulation of his voice to hammer home his points and became a protégé of longtime U.S. Senator Julius DeLong; and he used his corn-fed charm to marry the senator's simple-minded daughter. When the late senator's son died in the crash of his private plane in 1947, Weathers effectively took control of the massive wealth of sprawling Chalmette Plantation. After his wife died four years later in a riding accident, Weathers had complete control – making him one of the wealthiest men in the state, even the whole South.

Sadly, thought Holly, Weathers was still using the steel in his powerful voice to pound rusty nails about "segregation ... mud people ... the decline of American morality ... state's rights ... nullification ... (and) the natural order of God's universe."

"**I**diot," whispered Eve as Weathers went on and she slipped out through the back window of the station wagon. Getting any decent shots laying on her belly in the car was going to be impossible. The angle was bad, and besides, the drive in on the dirt road had left the car glass thick with dust. This was a once-in-a-lifetime chance, and Eve Howard was determined not to let it slip away. Besides, it was dark now and the only real light was focused on the flatbed. So was everyone's attention.

Eve crouched beside Ridge's station wagon, cradling her Nikon and the long lens. She happened to be wearing dark clothing and, for once in Mississippi, her skin tone was an asset as she kept to the deep shadow between cars – popping up for a quick click-click, click-click-click of the camera's rapid-fire shutter. And she wasn't even breaking her promise to Ridge she told herself. She hadn't left the car. She was right there, close enough to touch it. She smiled thinking about Holly's outright refusal to allow her "anywhere near that rally" and

Ridge's Nervous Nelly attitude. Well, she was near it now, inside it, in fact. And it hadn't been that difficult.

"The Invisible Empire, my ass," she whispered – marveling that anyone could take seriously these … these? … *Rednecks in drag,* she thought, and had to stifle a laugh.

Yet, Eve reminded herself to stay aware of her surroundings. The moon was on the rise behind her, but by the time it ate into her sanctuary of shadows, she'd be back in the car, back under the tarp. Hot and sweaty, but safe and sound, and in possession of the sort of pictures that could launch a serious career in photo-journalism.

Suddenly, Eve heard someone walking behind the row of cars. She hit the deck beside the station wagon, her heart suddenly pounding. Her survival instinct knew more than her intellect would let her deal with. If it was one of those guys in black, the Klargo, she sensed she could be in real trouble. But when she glanced over her shoulder she saw it was only some blonde girl passing by smoking a cigarette. The girl paused near the back of the station wagon, looking around – *probably looking for her boyfriend's car*, thought Eve – but thankfully the girl really didn't look into the deep shadow where Eve had pressed herself. After a moment, the girl walked on and Eve breathed a long sigh of relief.

Eve refocused her camera and her attention to the flatbed truck at the top of the hill and the huge cross beside it.

Sheriff Wallace turned slowly through the rows of cars in his cruiser. He was looking at everything and nothing. Did he expect to spot Dynamite Bob McBride or his nephew leaning against some old Ford. He had no evidence, nothing solid, but he was as sure as sunrise that the sociopath still was in Cattahatchie County. Making his plans. Maybe making his bombs. Billy Wallace had passed out fliers to practically every business in the county where a man like that was likely to show up. Nothing. But McBride was here. The sheriff could feel it. Maybe right on this same hilltop. The truth was, McBride could be five feet away, under his Klan robes, grinning at him. The thought made the sheriff's hand clench on the steering wheel as he kept one ear to the speeches and one to the low buzz of chatter on the police radio.

Cecil Weathers pulled a checkered, five-and-dime handkerchief from the jacket of an off-the-rack suit and mopped his shining face. Now he was saying, "I tell you folks, I've got an ol' coon dog that I dearly love. He's lazy and slow, and he can be a little snarly at times, but I love him nonetheless. I swear before God, I do," Weathers went on, his baritone rising and falling like that of a singer. "But I don't pull up a chair and have him eat at my dinner table!"

"Amen!"

Laughter.

"No, sir!"

Laughter.

" 'Course not!"

"I don't have my ol' coon dog dine with me at The Jeff Davis Hotel. I don't expect him to use public restroom facilities next to me. Drink from the same water fountain. *Or vote!* And sure as kingdom come, I do not expect him to sit next to my two little grandbabies in a public school classroom," Weathers roared. "It would merely distract my grandchildren and bore my dog!"

The crowd whooped and hollered, even though many had heard the string of ugly analogies numerous times. Ridge worked the row of Klansmen in front of the truck, finding the perfect angle to frame Weathers among a sea of pointy hats. Eve fired away from a distance with her motor drive ... click/click/click/click ....

Sheriff Wallace stopped his car behind the Lincoln convertible and got out.

"Miss Carter," he said, tipping his hat. "Cutter."

They nodded – "Sheriff."

"Is Nate behavin' himself?" asked my father. "I've only caught glimpses of him since he moved out."

"As best I can tell," said Cutter. "We don't check in with each other. I've told him he ought to go on home, but he's bein' pretty stubborn."

"Until we catch that McBride character, it's probably just as well," said Billy Wallace. "We live a good ways out in the country, and I can't afford to station a deputy at my house twenty-four hours a day.

If McBride set his mind to it, it'd be easy pickin's." Then to Holly – "Same thing goes for Wolf's Run. You might consider moving into town until we get through this patch."

"The governor is in fine form tonight," she said.

"He should be. He's been givin' this same speech since 1932. That coon dog he keeps talking about should be six times dead by now. Don't change the subject. I'm serious, Miss Carter. I can't guarantee your safety out at Wolf's Run."

"No one is asking you to," she told him. "I appreciate your concern, but I'm a grown woman. Any luck with the mason jar fragments you found at the paper?"

"No. No prints. But it was strictly amateur hour. Probably some ol' boys who were mad about you running the Banks story. They got liquored up and decided to waste a couple of jars of moonshine."

"Mr. Wallace, how do you know McBride wasn't in on it?" asked Cutter.

"That's easy, son. Because the *Current-Leader* building is still standing."

Cutter and the sheriff held each other's gaze. It was the answer Cutter expected; he merely wanted Miss Carter to hear it. Billy Wallace understood. But if the paper's editor-in-chief heard, she gave no acknowledgement of it, and continued to focus on Weathers and her notes.

"**N**ow folks, as much as I love my ol' coon dog, if he turned up rabid tomorrow, you know what I'd have to do," Weathers asked the crowd.

"Put him down!" someone hollered.

"I'd shoot him!" yelled someone else.

"Now then, there is a terrible disease movin' amongst our colored folks these days. It's carried by Jews, common'nists, our own federal gov'ment people and impure hippies come back from Cali-*fornicate*. It's worse than rabies. It's called in-*tee*-gration!

"Taking up the sword should always be the last resort. And while I would never encourage violence by one human being against another, I am saying you must search your heart for the strength to defend the sanctity of your white, Christian home, your community and the way of life our forefathers fought and bled and died to keep.

"His will be done!"

That was the signal to touch a torch to the cross. A *whooooooosh* roared up into the night sky as a volcano of flame erupted from the ground and leaped up the kerosene-soaked burlap. The Klansman who ignited it had to dive to the ground to keep from being caught up in the flames. Then there it stood, the most sacred symbol of the church, the Christ – a symbol most have been raised to worship and revere, twisted into a symbol of fear and subjugation.

A single bagpiper in Klan robes stepped to the microphone and the instrument's mournful wail sent a long shudder of disgust through Holly. Behind her heart, she felt a tremble of fear, but there was no way she would let it out. Not here, not now anyway. Not for any of these robed monsters to see.

Click/Click/Click/Click/Click … Eve snapped away as the burning cross cast long yellow light down the hill. It was a fire that made her cold inside, and she noticed her hands were shaking. Things had turned spookier than she expected. Then a horse's bray startled her so badly that she nearly jumped to her feet. She caught herself, but peeked over the car hood and saw one of the black-robed horsemen shining in the fire glow. He was coming up the row in front of her.

The Klargo ... they're the Klan's version of the Gestapo ... the real hard cases ... Eve gasped. She peeked again. Another guard was walking his horse up the row behind her. *Did they see me? No. No! They couldn't have ...* Eve told herself. But there was nowhere to run and no way to get back into the car.

They were coming closer and she was boxed in. Every story about the Klan she had ever heard from her grandparents, mother, on television or read in the newspaper rushed into her mind. As did Ridge's warning, *This isn't a movie, Malibu girl. ... When they shoot you here, you stay dead. ...* There was only one thing to do. Eve flattened herself on the grass and rolled onto her back. It was a tight fit – her breasts brushing against the car's undercarriage – but she managed to squeeze beneath it.

As the Klargo reached the back of the Chevy, she pulled her camera bag under the car with her.

Over the piper's wail, Holly, Cutter, my father – all of us really – heard shouts from the road and engines cranking. FBI agents in dark suits and white shirts were running out of the nearby woods carrying big cameras, directional microphone dishes and sniper rifles as if a platoon of bears or tigers had been turned loose up in the pines. Police radios suddenly were alive with chatter. In the background of the urgent radio call Billy Wallace could hear the town's fire alarm going off. Some of the members of DeLong's volunteer fire department already were running to their cars.

Sheriff Wallace reached into his cruiser snatched up his microphone. "Ten-four, Base. John-Thomas, don't wait. Call in the fire departments from New Albany and Booneville. I'm on my way."

Holly twisted in her seat. "Sheriff, what's happened?" she called over her shoulder as my father got into his car and hit the red lights.

"Sounds like Dynamite Bob just hit the funeral home in Roseville. Most of a block of houses and stores is on fire."

"Ohhh, no!" gasped Holly as the police cruiser sped away.

Cars were spinning their tires as they swung out of the rows and headed down the hill toward the one small gate. But none of the Klansmen broke their Nazi-like salute. As the pine beneath the burlap crackled and hissed, the piper continued to play – the Kluxers making a fine show of ignoring the news vans racing away on the gravel road.

"They knew this was going to happen," said Cutter, disgusted. "They timed it."

"Yes, I suspect you're right," said Holly, trying to rein in her own anger and revulsion … and fear. "There's Ridge!"

She flashed her lights at him, bumped her horn. He jogged over, his shirt and round face slick with perspiration.

"You heard what happened?" she asked.

"Yes. It's awful. I've got to stop at Peterson's Grocery for gas, but I'll be right behind you," he told her. "I got good stuff tonight, Honey Girl. I did us proud."

"You always do, Ridge. I'll see you in town."

"Right-oh," he replied and hurried toward his car on the far side of the pasture.

In the confusion and noise, no one noticed the pops from the .22 caliber automatic in the hand of a Klargo guard. The little pistol made less noise than a car backfire, hardly as much of a – *crack!* – as a decent firecracker.

Even Eve didn't realize what was happening until she heard the sudden hiss of air from the left rear tire and felt the big station wagon settling onto her foot. She squirmed and twisted the leg away. But then came another pop. When the right rear tire deflated she tried to push herself toward the front of the car and out from under but the tire collapsed almost instantly, trapping her leg – trapping her!

Panic rose in Eve's chest like a red tide. They knew she was there. They had caught her. The Klan!

Another small slug penetrated the left front tire and the weight of the engine came toward her chest, her face. They were going to crush her under the car. "Please!" she begged as best her constricted chest would let her, trying to wedge herself away from the two tons of metal.

"Don't!" she cried but the sound was buried in the hiss of the final tire deflating. "*Noooooo!*"

PART III

Chapter 1

෴

A t dawn a haze of smoke hung as thick as winter fog above the Cattahatchie as it bent through DeLong. In the still summer air, smoke clung to the dirt lanes of Roseville and along River Street behind *The Current-Leader* building.

As Cutter walked across the Gov. Theodore J. Bilbo Memorial Bridge, the sun was rising red and bloody above the town. A number of black families were streaming back into Roseville carrying suitcases and belongings tied with rope, like refugees from a war zone on the other side of the world. Some nodded or whispered their thanks to Cutter and others who had crossed the river to help the firemen. Behind Cutter were nine burned homes, another seven or eight that were badly damaged, an incinerated beauty shop, dress shop and funeral parlor – the one where Tommy Ray Banks' services were scheduled to be held later that day. Two people who had been in the funeral home were dead, for sure – a funeral home employee and one of Tommy Ray's cousins, who had volunteered to sit with the body through the night, as was tradition. There might be more dead in there or in some of the houses. There probably were, but no one would know until there was good light and time to dig through the charred, smoldering remains.

At the east foot of the bridge, deputies were keeping television crews and reporters at bay. As Cutter slipped though the gaggle – women and men studying their hair and makeup with equal degrees of obsession – Sheriff Wallace stepped off a Corinth Fire Department ladder truck as it slowed. Like Cutter, his face and arms were streaked with soot and his clothes stained with sweat. They both reeked of smoke. Someone in the reporting pool recognized Billy Wallace and the covey surged toward him.

"Keep those people back!" he barked as he caught up with Cutter. They'd both been breathing smoke and oven-like air much of the night and the sheriff had to fight through a coughing spasm before he could speak again. Finally, he wiped his mouth with a sooty handkerchief and said, "Thanks for helpin' out."

"I didn't do much. Dragged some hoses around. That's about it."

"You did a lot more than that," the sheriff said, but said no more. There was nothing more that needed to be said. "I don't guess you saw Nate anywhere durin' the night?"

Cutter rubbed his eyes, then his face, thinking. "No, sir. Not that I can recall. Last time I saw him was out at the Klan rally with Patti MacAllister."

Billy Wallace nodded. "When you see him, would you ask him to come by the sheriff's office or give me a call? If I'm not handy, ask him to leave a message with whoever answers the phone.

"There was a lot of meanness afoot last night," he told Cutter. "While we were all focused here, the Klan shot up a church and several houses out in the Knox Community. No one was seriously hurt, thank God, but – well – I'd just like to know he's okay. Bein' my son and all –"

"Yes, sir. I understand. I'll tell him, for sure," promised Cutter. Both men stood in silence as reporters shouted questions from where they'd been corralled across the street. Their voices were like echoes in the heads of both men. Finally, Cutter added his own gravelly voice to the chorus. "Mr. Wallace, what is going to happen? Here, I mean. With all this?"

One side of Billy Wallace's face felt sunburned. He hadn't been asleep in nearly twenty-four hours and his eyes stung with smoke, exhaustion, sweat … and frustration.

"Honestly, Cutter, I don't know," he said, letting his tired eyes survey the column of smoke still rising between the chimney of high, green hills to the west. "Me and my guys, and the FBI and U.S. Marshals, have been doin' all we know to do. Obviously, it's not enough.

"I talked to Mr. Burke about an hour ago. Governor Broderick is considering sending in the National Guard. If he doesn't, President Nixon probably will send in federal troops. Just like Eisenhower did in Little Rock in '57 and Kennedy in Oxford in '62. Right now, I'm hard-pressed to think of a reason why not."

* * *

Out Highway 8 for many miles on both sides of the road, the land and barns and storage sheds, grain elevators and gins mostly were the property of Chalmette Plantation, and thus Cecil Weathers. Holly disliked the feeling of Weathers' wealth and power, and hate, surrounding her, but the country morning was coming up beautiful and clear, and she was glad to be out of DeLong. The town – her town – reminded her of the burned-out villages of Vietnam. And the odor, the lack of food and depth of worry over the whereabouts of Ridge and Eve made Holly's stomach queasy as she turned north onto the weary pavement of County Road 214 – toward Peterson's Grocery and the Campbell farm, where the Klan rally had been held.

Nine hours had passed since she and Cutter pulled into her parking place behind *The Current-Leader* building. "I'm gonna go see if there's anything I can do to help," Cutter had said as soon as the car came to a stop. Then he'd noticed the shattered glass across the back of the building, across the back of nearly every building with windows facing the river. "Will you be okay?"

Holly had given a quick look to the damage, but wasn't worried about broken glass. In the shards, a red-orange light was dancing. Across the river, people's homes, businesses, their livelihoods were being destroyed. Lives probably were being lost.

"I'll be fine," she'd said. "But you be careful."

"Always," he said, but Holly knew better as she watched him hustle up the street, jogging behind a firetruck with Union County markings.

Amid the noise of sirens and confused voices and the distraction of flashing lights, Holly had transferred into her chair and pulled her camera onto her lap. She didn't bother to try to cross the bridge for pictures. She knew Eve had stayed at the office to develop film and print photos. So like any good photojournalist, Eve would have grabbed her Nikon, her lenses and as much hand-rolled 35 millimeter film as would fit in her bag, and run toward the fireball.

Holly knew Ridge would be back from the Klan rally any minute and would join Eve in Roseville. So she shot from the east side of the river, and later from the shattered windows of the newspaper building. Over the course of minutes and then during the long hours of the night, many of the remaining *Current-Leader* employees shuffled in –

both to get a jump on what would be a very special edition and to congregate on the roof and fire escape for a better view.

Refugees from Roseville began gathering in the parking lots along River Street, including the newspaper's space. About one a.m., Holly told production manager Shorty Rodgers to pass out the sodas, potato chips and other snacks stashed in a storage room off *The Current-Leader*'s small kitchen. He and Jim Boyd, one of the pressmen, and Miss Frances and her husband did so until everything was gone.

As the minutes passed into hours and the fires kept burning, Holly found herself more and more sitting by the third-floor windows at the back of the production room, using her 500 millimeter lens as a telescope to scour the wet, hose-strewn, fire-charred streets of Roseville. She kept looking for Eve and Ridge ... and Cutter. Though she never caught a glimpse of either employee, either friend, she was able to pick up Cutter's image now and then, and the amount of relief she felt each time created a strange sense of unease. She watched him take charge of a group of older men trying to wrestle a snaking firehose in the direction of a burning house. Cutter was eighteen, almost nineteen, Holly reminded herself, remembering his age from a story that had run in her newspaper. Clearly he had a presence and command about himself that belied his age. Besides younger men than Cutter were fighting and dying in Vietnam every day. Anyone who looked into the eyes of those young soldiers after two or three nights of jungle patrol would never call them "kids." Cutter's eyes had that same forged-in-the-fire maturity even though his battles all had been fought in Cattahatchie County.

Holly leaned the heavy camera away from her on its monopod. "Stop it!" she told herself, knowing that starting to care – really *care* – about Cutter would be a mistake. "This isn't Vietnam," she told herself. But when she looked up and saw Roseville burning across the river, she wasn't so sure.

By five a.m., when the pumpers finally had spread enough water onto the flames to settle most of one block and part of another into a soggy, smoldering quagmire, Holly was seriously concerned about Eve and Ridge. They had not returned to the office, not even for more film.

When first light began to brighten the smoky sky, Holly had wheeled downstairs and gotten into her car, fighting the nagging fear that was building inside her. She had driven around the square that was crowded with cars and emergency vehicles, and up and down nearby sidestreets where Ridge might have parked his station wagon. She went by the sagging old Bellafont mansion where Ridge lived on Hill Street. Nothing. And even if she found his car, that wouldn't account for Eve's whereabouts ... unless ... unless she had somehow talked Ridge into sneaking her into the Klan rally. Eve could be so persistent and persuasive, Holly knew, and Ridge was such a pleaser, never wanting to disappoint anyone.

Now Holly lifted her long hair off the back of her neck and let the fresh air blow through it as she drove through the rolling hills. "Dear Lord, Please protect them," she whispered as she turned down the narrow gravel road that led to the Campbell farm. "Please let me be wrong."

* * *

When Cutter got to the newspaper's lot, he saw the Continental was gone. Shorty Rodgers and some of the other employees already were nailing thick plastic sheeting above the building's shattered rear windows. Miss Frances was sitting at the picnic table on the loading dock. Her husband had his head down on the table, snoring.

"Oh, my goodness, son!" she gasped. "Are you hurt?"

"No, ma'am. Just dirty. Maybe a little scorched around the edges. Is Miss Carter here?"

Miss Frances twisted one arthritic hand over the other. "No, Cutter, she's not. And truth be told, I'm worried. She went to look for Ridge Bellafont and Miss Eve." Cutter felt his pulse quicken. "We haven't seen either one of them since last night."

"Do you know where she went?"

"She was going back out to the Campbell place. She thought maybe Ridge broke down on the side of the road. Or something."

"Thanks, Miss Frances," he said, heading down the ramp built for Miss Carter. At that moment, he looked up and saw me. "Nate!" he called as I eased my truck along River Street.

I heard Cutter's voice before I saw him jogging across the newspaper parking lot. I had spent the night at First Denomination with

Patti, her momma and Brother MacAllister and about twenty members of the congregation who had gathered for a prayer vigil for the
firefighters. I was getting my first look at the damage. I waved weakly,
shocked by what I was seeing.

"Hey, Cutter."

"I left my jeep up at The Well. I need to borrow your truck," he
said without preamble.

"Well, I –"

"Or I need you to drive me."

"To The Well?"

"No. Out to the Campbell farm."

I had been up all night, and was grumpy. "Why do you want to go
way out there? I haven't even had breakfast."

"Then get out and go eat at The Cotton, and let me have the truck."

Down the street, three of the café's four big front windows were
blown out but they were serving. Paula Simpson was pouring coffee
for worn-out men, black and white, propped against the front of the
building or sitting on the sidewalk.

"No!" I told him. "I mean, what are you –?"

"Nate, I don't have time to explain. Either get out or scoot over."

I threw the shifter into neutral and slid to the passenger side as
Cutter climbed in. He hit the clutch and ground the gears with unchar-
acteristic clumsiness.

We were headed west on Highway 8 before I took stock of my
best friend. He looked like he'd taken a bath in dirty water and rubbed
himself with charcoal. He reeked of smoke. Seeing him so haggard as
a result of his helping throughout the night made me ashamed of the
way I had spent the last ten hours. If I really had been earnestly praying for the safety of those fighting the blaze, it would have been one
thing. But I hadn't even been that much help. I only was there because
Patti was there, and again in a good mood.

My lips moved, starting to form the words to tell Cutter that but
the words felt like ashes in my mouth before I even said them. Instead,
I asked, "Can't you at least tell me what we're doing? What do you
expect to find out at the Campbell place?"

Cutter kept his gaze fixed straight ahead and took the curves as
fast as my old pickup would let him – "Nothing. I hope."

Chapter 2

❧

O ut at the Oscar Campbell farm, the burned cross stood black and charred and ugly against Tuesday morning's bright sky.

As Holly drove along the fence line, she saw nothing of Ridge's car, nor had she seen any sign of Ridge or Eve on the twenty-five-minute drive from DeLong. She was both relieved and increasingly fearful as she turned across the cattle-guard gate and maneuvered the Lincoln around a small herd of Black Angus grazing among discarded beer bottles and cigarette packs.

As she came over the curve of the hill – "Oh, no! No!" she gasped and shoved the hand control forward. The big car leaped and crossed the hundred yards in seconds, sliding to a stop next to the battered hulk of Ridge Bellafont's station wagon. All the glass was shattered and there were bullet holes in random locations in the sheet metal. The back of the long wagon was burned, as was a semicircle of grass behind it. The tires were flat.

She forced herself to look inside the car. "Thank God," she whispered as she saw only destroyed photographic equipment. *But if they aren't here?* Holly thought, and the realization of what that meant filled her with a nearly equal fear. Maybe they were hiding in the woods.

"Ridge! Eve!" she called and hit the car horn again and again. "Ridge! ... Eve!"

Nothing. Then she saw it. A hand almost hidden behind the right front wheel rim.

Holly slammed the Lincoln into park and threw open the door. "Eve!" she cried as she tumbled onto the grass. With her elbows, Holly dragged herself to the side of the station wagon. She grasped the bloody hand, held it to her cheek. "Eve, can you hear me?"

There was no response. Holly felt for a pulse. It was so shallow she couldn't count the beats.

"Eve, I've got to get this car off you," she said. In the three years and nine and a half months since Ia Drang, Holly had never felt so helpless, had never hated being paralyzed so much. She rolled onto her back, clenching shut her eyes and her fists, and said what would have to pass for a prayer. "You took my legs, damn it! If you're ever going to give me a hand, now's the time! Help me. Come on, God! Help me!"

When Holly opened her eyes and propped up on her arms, she looked around and knew what she had to do.

In the dew-slick grass, she scooted backwards to the open front door of the Lincoln and stretched her long arm in, snatching the keys from the ignition. She slid herself around the Lincoln and unlocked the trunk. Throwing one arm inside, Holly pulled herself up until she could see into the big space. The contents of the trunk were a jumble. If the jack was at the far side, she'd never reach it. She used her free arm to push a box out of the way and a raincoat and to throw a set of jumper cables aside.

There it was! The jack.

Holly's right arm felt as if it was about to tear from the socket, but she grabbed the jack with her left hand and tossed it onto the grass. Then the base. Then the tire iron. Then she let go and dropped to the grass as a sudden pain ripped up her side. Holly reached around and felt a long tear in her blouse and when she drew her hand back there was blood on her fingers. As she pushed up onto her hips, she glanced at the sharp edge of the car tag that bent out slightly from the bumper. However bad the cut, she didn't have time to think about it. Eve was dying! Every foot Holly slid with the heavy jack and tire iron across her thighs seemed to take hours.

"Hang on, Eve," she called. "Hang on!"

Finally Holly reached the front of the car. She secured the jack under the bumper. With all her remaining strength, Holly click-clacked, click-clacked up the jack, notch by notch, as high as she could get it – then fell back, spent.

There was no sound in the pasture except for birds in the nearby trees, and the occasional lowing of the cattle. Holly could see under the car now. The jack had relieved some of the pressure on

Eve's abdomen and pelvis. Holly stretched her arms under the unstable weight of the car and grasped Eve Howard beneath her arms. Holly pulled – once, then again – but Eve's legs were trapped. Holly lay with face in the grass.

"Eve, I'm so sorry," she told her. Then, "I don't know if you can hear me, but – I can't get you out on my own. I've got to go for help."

Holly pushed up. Pain burned her side, but she didn't let it stop her. She dragged herself to the convertible's door. Just as she grasped the steering wheel to pull herself up, she heard a vehicle coming fast on the gravel road. Hope jumped into her heart, but fell away as quickly. The driver wouldn't see the cars from the road. Holly stretched for the horn. She hit it – once, twice, three, four times – until she saw an old Chevy pickup bouncing across the pasture.

Cutter slid my truck so hard I was sure one of the retread tires would pop. He was out the door before it came to a good stop. When I came around the truck, he already was kneeling beside Holly Lee Carter lifting her blood-stained top. There was an ugly scratch from her waist to up under the side of her bra.

"It's long," said Cutter, "but it's not deep. How'd you –?"

Miss Carter pointed under the station wagon.

"Ohhh, shhh —" I started.

"I think she's been there since last night," Holly told us. "I got the front end up, but I couldn't –"

"This is bad," I said. "Real bad."

"What about Mr. Bellafont?" Cutter asked.

Miss Carter shook her head. "He's not in the car. I don't know."

"We need to go for help," I said.

"Cutter, she's dying," said Miss Carter, her green eyes locked onto his in a way that made me feel as if they were in one place, together, and I was somewhere else.

"I think we should go for help," I said again, the words like an echo in my head.

"She's not dead yet, is she?" Cutter asked softly, gently. It was a voice I'd heard only a time or two when he needed to calm his sister. *Why was he using it now on this ... this ... stranger?* I wondered angrily, my mind spinning.

Miss Carter shook her head, never taking her eyes off Cutter's. "No, but –"

"Then there's still a chance."

"I can go for help," I offered, but the noise I was making was of no more notice to Cutter and Miss Carter than the grumbling of the nearby cattle or the cry of a curious hawk.

Cutter stood. "Nate, get the jack out of your truck."

"Don't you think we should go for help?"

"I'm not a doctor but I've seen wounded people," said Miss Carter. "I don't think she can wait."

"But we could kill her by moving her," I warned.

"Yeah. We could. There's a good chance we will. But all we can do is the best we can do right this minute," said Cutter, discussion ended. "Nate, are you gonna get your jack? Or do I have to?"

Once we got one side of the big station wagon propped up precariously on the two jacks, Cutter reached under the front of the car and took an unconscious Eve Howard under her arms and drew her gently toward him. Cutter pulled her a little harder, and a little harder still, but it was no use. Her right foot was hung in the undercarriage toward the back of the car.

"Nate, come around here," Cutter said. "I'm going to slide under there and see if I can't get her foot loose."

I looked at the small space, narrowing as it did into what would be a black forever if the car slipped off the jacks. "Forget it, Cutter," I heard myself say. "You'll never fit. I'm the smallest. I should do it."

Cutter didn't try to talk me out of it; he knew I was right. Miss Carter started to say something, but I got on my belly and quickly slid under the engine block before I lost my nerve. With my right arm extended as far is it would go, I wedged myself under two thousand pounds of Chevy. I could smell blood and gasoline, sweat and urine and feces, and some sickeningly sweet odor like overcooked barbecue.

"Nate, you're doing great," Cutter encouraged. "Can you reach her foot?"

My chest felt tight and I could sense every ounce of the mountain of steel on top of me. "Yeah, I can –"

As I grasped Eve Howard's shoe, it crumbled in my hand and I felt the incinerated flesh of her foot slough off in my fingers. I gagged and choked, and would have thrown up had I eaten anything for breakfast. Instead, I spit bile into the scorched grass.

"Nate, are you okay?" Miss Carter asked.

I gagged again. "Yeah. Just another few seconds," I told her, and forced myself to take firm hold of Eve Howard's ruined foot. I twisted it hard, and heard something crack, but the foot turned. "Okay, Cutter. Go ahead!"

The woman's body slid past me as I scrambled backwards into the daylight.

Miss Carter quickly checked the artery in Eve Howard's neck. She shook her head. "I ... I don't know."

"She won't get any better layin' here," Cutter said and scooped my former boss into his arms with the ease a smaller man might use with a toddler. "Nate, open the back door."

I did as I was told and he placed Miss Carter on the seat. Then he knelt beside Eve Howard and slid his arms under her back and legs. She'd been bleeding from her nose and mouth, and one ear. Both legs were burned below the knee, but the right was much worse. Much! He lifted her and scraps of charred denim fell to the grass. I helped him arrange her as gently as we could on the back seat with her head resting in Miss Carter's lap. She showed no sign of life.

If she lives, it'll be a miracle, I thought as I closed the Linclon's trunk.

Cutter slid behind the wheel and fired up the big V-8. "Nate, stop at the first house you see with a phone. Call the hospital and tell 'em we're coming," he said. "Then call the sheriff's office and tell 'em what happened. Tell 'em they need to get out here in a hurry with some men to search. And maybe bloodhounds. Mr. Bellafont might be here someplace. He might still be alive."

All I could do was nod, glassy-eyed.

"Did you hear me?"

"Yeah," I managed. "I heard you."

"Nate, you did great," Miss Carter was saying, but it was as if she talking under water. "Thank you. Thank you so much!"

"Yeah, buddy, you did. You did great," he said, putting the car in gear and starting away. Over his shoulder, he yelled, "And call your daddy! He's worried about you."

As the convertible disappeared over the ridge of the pasture, I stood waving – stupidly, weakly – as if they were leaving for a vacation. I waved even after they were gone, until the first jack gave way with a snap and a pop, as loud as the crack of a rifle shot. Then the second. I watched as in an instant the big station wagon groaned and crashed down onto the hard ground, pieces of the second jack flying forty feet across the pasture.

I looked at the car and then my right hand. Eve Howard's blood and pus and blistered flesh still clung to my fingers. I fought to keep my bowels together and the bile in my stomach down, but I couldn't keep my knees from giving way. Suddenly I found myself on all fours beside my truck, rubbing my hand in the grass. I started to cry.

How long I stayed there like that with the morning sun rising hot on my back, I'm not sure. Long enough that I rubbed my hand raw and all my tears were gone.

Chapter 3

❦

Rose Marie Carlucci was crossing the Old Iron Bridge near the camp when I pulled out of the narrow road that led back to The Well. Wednesday's late afternoon shadows already were on the river.

"Hey, Rose," I said, idling the truck.

"Huh-Huh-Hi, N-Nate."

"If you're looking for Cutter, he's not at The Well."

"Wh-Where is he?"

I looked away and then back. Trying not to sound as agitated as I felt, I said, "Word has it, he's staying up at Wolf's Run. I was headed that way. Climb in."

She did and gave me a nervous smile as she closed the door and sat close to it. I supposed her edginess was natural, merely being in proximity to a boy in the cab of a truck. To the best of my knowledge, Rose Carlucci never had been on a date. Not surprising considering she wore what she always wore – men's work shoes and a loose shirt under baggy overalls. Still, the outfit did not entirely hide her ample figure, the strong, handsome features of her work-tanned face or the luster of the thick brown hair she pulled back into a ponytail tied with a rubber band. But other than for school, she never strayed farther than The Well from the Old Ambrose Place, except under the watchful and usually bloodshot eye of her father. She was allowed to participate in no after-school activities, no clubs and never had friends over or went to visit others. In fact, if Rose Carlucci had any friends, I didn't know it.

All she had was a mother who'd fallen into a nervous breakdown ten years earlier and never recovered, a father who was more jailer than daddy … and Cutter.

I put the truck in gear and headed up the steep S cut into the face of Blue Mountain.

Though I'd driven past Wolf's Run many times, never before had I turned through the opening in the faded white rail fence or been down the long driveway that sloped to the cleft in the mountainside that held the house. My first impression was that it wasn't as big as I expected. As I wheeled the truck around the pea gravel circle at the front of the house, Cutter emerged from the big garage, which stood separate from the main house. His clothes were clean and so was he, but he held in his hand a wet dish rag stained pink. Miss Carter's little white dog stood next to him.

Cutter looked so at ease, so at home in the moment that a sense of betrayal instantly boiled up in me anew. I made only a halfhearted effort to shove it down.

We got out.

"C-C-Cutter, are you o-okay?"

"I'm fine, Rose. You didn't have to come all the way up here."

"I-I-I w-was worried."

"I'm sorry. We didn't get back from Memphis until almost two o'clock. I stayed here last night."

"Everybody knows you stayed here last night," I told him sharply. "People are already talking about you and her."

Cutter turned around and walked back into the garage. The little dog followed and so did we.

"Cutter, are you listenin' to me?"

"I heard you, Nate," he said. "But there's no 'me and her.' If it's anybody's business, I slept on the porch. Miss Carter didn't need to be alone way out here."

"How come this is all of a sudden your problem?" I demanded. "A few weeks ago, you couldn't stand the woman. Now she's brought this on herself."

Cutter bent down and picked up the little dog and placed it on the work bench. He scratched the animal's back while he let me seethe. "Her name is Charlie."

Rose smiled and followed Cutter's example. "H-Hi, Ch-Charlie."

"Cutter?"

"How about the folks who lost their homes, their lives in Roseville? Did they bring it on themselves?" he asked. "What's the count now?"

"Four," I said. "Four dead. And that's a shame. But blacks and whites aren't meant to mix. Sometimes sacrifices have to be made to keep, to keep order in –"

"I guess Miss Howard and Mr. Bellafont brought all that on themselves?"

I felt my neck and face redden. "Of course, they did," I made myself say. "Showin' up at a Klan rally like that. Them!"

"And you think that gave the Klux the right to do what they did?"

"Brother Mac says –"

Cutter snapped his arm up and hurled the rag at me. I caught the damp cloth against my chest, and looked from it to Cutter, who was saying, "Good! You can finish cleaning Eve Howard's blood off the back seat of the car. That's what I was doing when you drove up."

Images of Eve Howard's burned and bloody flesh grabbed hold of me and wouldn't let go. I could see her crushed body lying under the station wagon and across the back seat of Miss Carter's Lincoln. According to the papers, the doctors amputated her right leg below the knee, but managed to save the other and stabilize her. Her mother, the actress Carol Howard, had flown in from Hollywood to be with her, but Eve remained in critical condition. By early Tuesday evening, word had spread throughout DeLong that Mr. Bellafont's chances had run out. He was found by a search party in an abandoned smokehouse about four miles from the station wagon. He was stripped, gagged and hung by his wrists from a rafter. He then had been whipped so brutally that he probably would have died from the beating. But to make sure, his torturers castrated him and left him to bleed out like a pig for slaughter.

"Nate, I've known you since junior high, and we've turned a lot a miles together," Cutter was saying. "I wouldn't do to a mad dog what the Klan did to Miss Howard and Mr. Bellafont. Neither would you. And that's not even counting the damage they did in Roseville."

I dropped the rag beside the car, my stomach queasy.

"Cutter, this is so much bigger than us," I told him, wiping my hands on my jeans. My right hand still was tender from the rubbing I'd given it in the dirt beside Mr. Bellafont's burned-out car. "We're just kids. We haven't even been to our senior prom. You're messin' with stuff that's none of your business. And I can't let you drag me into it any further. I took a room at Mrs. Fletcher's Boarding House. And I got hooked up with a job after school and weekends. A good job."

"Where at?"

"Handley's Department Store. I'll be working in the stock room on Saturdays and after school."

"Brother Mac fix you up with that?"

"He didn't fix me up. Mr. Handley is a deacon. He put in a good word. That's all."

"Mr. Handley is the head of the Klan. Everybody knows it."

"It's not like you think. The Cattahatchie Klavern doesn't sanction things like, like what happened the other day. Those are radicals. Outsiders, come in to make DeLong folks look bad. Heck, it may even have been the coloreds themselves or that NJC bunch, trying to discredit –"

"Shut up, Nate!" Cutter snapped, cutting me off in a way he'd never done before, not once. He scowled for a long hard moment but softened when he saw the surprise and hurt in my eyes. "Just shut up," he said, his voice a tired, smoky rasp as he turned his back to me. He coughed and cleared his throat, then – "I know that's not you talkin'. I know its Patti or Bother Mac or … some of that crowd. But I don't want to listen to you standin' there, making a fool of yourself."

I swallowed and ignored the insult. "Look, Mr. Handley – he's on the board of the new academy, too. Everybody we know is gonna leave Cattahatchie High and go there, as soon as all the particulars are ironed out. Come September, there won't be anybody at CHS but blacks and white trash. Mr. Handley says he can get me a scholarship to Riverview."

Cutter leaned on the workbench, his arms straight, his hands flat atop it, and said nothing.

"All I know is, I can't screw up again. If I do, Patti and I are done. Done for good."

"What do you mean screw up?" he asked.

"You know. What we did out at the Campbell farm. Interferin'!"

As was his nature, Cutter didn't rush to speak and with every passing second it was harder to keep my feet planted. I wanted to run from that place and from my own words. He turned. "Nate, you didn't screw up. You saved someone's life."

"The-The way the p-paper ha-had it," Rose struggled, "you, you, you're a hero, N-Nate."

"Then why doesn't it feel like it?" I said, my eyes roaming around the increasing darkness in the garage. "Why are people treatin' me like I pissed in the lemonade?"

"Maybe 'cause you're hangin' out with the wrong people."

"Maybe *you* are!" I told him, and felt tears of anger and loss – and fear – burning my eyes. Cutter was my best friend! *What had happened to us?* "You're the biggest thing to hit this county in a long time, but you're not bigger than this," I told him. "Why can't you just do what you said at The Well? Why can't you just give 'em what they want until you can get the hell out of here?"

Cutter simply looked at me as if I were speaking a language foreign to him. After a moment, I whirled, embarrassed, and trod off toward my truck, my jaw moving, my teeth grinding. I slammed the door. Charlie barked and I turned the key. *What could I say? How could I make him listen? Make him understand?* But there was nothing. Somehow we had stopped speaking the same language and it was all Holly Lee Carter's fault.

"Good luck, Nate," he called as I wheeled the truck around toward the road but I pretended not to hear him. I gunned it up the hill and left Cutter, Rose and Charlie in the twilight shadows already woven purple and deep around Wolf's Run.

* * *

Cutter stood in the bedroom door for a moment studying the womanly curve of Holly Lee Carter's body under the sheet. At some point after he'd laid her onto her pillows and positioned her wheelchair next to the bed, she'd gotten up and tossed off the skirt and blouse she'd been wearing for some thirty hours. They reeked of smoke and burned flesh and were stained by Eve's blood and her own. Sleeping on a blanket outside her open windows, Cutter roused for a moment when he heard movement from inside the room. He looked in through the screen and their eyes found each other in the darkness as Holly dropped her ruined blouse onto the floor. She was not surprised to see him there. Somehow she knew he would be nearby, that he would not abandon her to the shadows and her own fears. For his part, Cutter did not look away. He took in the fullness of her, the white bra she wore almost glowing in the deep shadows of the room and on her dusky skin. Holly knew she should cover herself, but for a long moment she did not want to and she did not. There was an appreciation and respect in Cutter's eyes that she had not seen from a man in a long time. Not curiosity or pity, and not even lust exactly – at least not the kind that had burned the eyes of Cutter's father those years ago at The Gin. It was something different, something deeper. *Appreciation? Approval? Comprehension?* Or was that only what she wanted his gaze to mean?

Cutter did not look away.

Holly drew a long breath over her teeth and forced herself to reach for the push-rims on her wheels. She made herself turn away and push into the bathroom, where she closed the door behind her.

Now Holly heard Charlie's claws clattering on the hardwood floor and saw her settle into her bed beneath the window. She sensed Cutter standing just inside the bedroom door. It wasn't that she heard him, really. He was a guy who, despite his size, had a light step. It was more like a change in the atmosphere, an increase in barometric pressure that she felt in her chest when he came near. She pretended to still be sleeping as Cutter placed a note on her bedside table. Just as she had pretended it often during the day as she allowed Cutter to head off the concerned and merely curious who called, and those who came by with casseroles, hams and platters of fried chicken. She was being treated like a family member of the deceased, and perhaps that was appropriate. The Carters and the other people at the newspaper had been the closest thing to real family he had. His aunts and uncles and his many cousins tolerated him, but few embraced him. Ridge had been her father's friend and confidante, and her most patient mentor and enthusiastic cheerleader. He had opened to her the universe of life within her reach and the reach of a 35mm lens. He had taught her how to make magic in the darkroom and helped her to believe she had a magic within herself, no matter how often T.L. Carter told his teenage daughter she was worthless and stupid, selfish and no good – *just like your mother.*

As Holly thought of Ridge, the tears started again on her cheeks and melted into the stains of the hundreds she'd already shed into her pillow. For Ridge, for Eve, for the Banks family and those others in Roseville dead or injured or homeless, for this place that she both loved and loathed, and that no matter what else was home.

Out her window she saw Cutter and Rose get into her car and head up the driveway. She listened to the tires crunching on the gravel until the sound disappeared and she was alone in the big, silent house. The voices returned. Holly still could hear Carol Howard screaming in the surgery waiting room – *This is all your fault! Get out! Away from my daughter! And don't you ever come near her again!* Then there was Sheriff Wallace's voice on the telephone late Tuesday afternoon. *Miss Carter, I hate to have to tell you this, but we found Mr. Bellafont …*

"Poor, sweet, gentle Ridge," Holly heard herself whisper now. "I'm so sorry."

The shadows in Meemaw Carter's bedroom seemed deeper, darker than Holly had ever known. They seemed to have a comfortable liquid weight to them that offered a dark, welcome hiding place; but they were filled, too, with the danger that they might crush her. That if she let herself remain too long in their cool arms that she might never emerge. She reached for the note on the bed stand. It was printed by a strong hand.

Miss Carter –

I borrowed your car to take Rose home and get some things at The Well. Will be back in less than an hour.

                                                               Cutter

Chapter 4

❧

"**H**ow's M-Miss Carter d-doing?" Rose Carlucci asked as Cutter drove her home.

"She's sick about what happened to Miz Howard. But the news about Mr. Bellafont. What the Klux did to him. It shook her pretty bad," he said. "But she's strong in ways I've never seen before."

"Wh-What do you mean?"

"She got that big station wagon up off Miz Howard. At least enough so she could keep breathing until me and Nate showed up. She did it by herself. Without legs." There was an inflection in her brother's voice that Rose had never heard. *Amazement mixed with admiration,* she thought, trying to place it. *And respect?* Respect – not just the per-functory yes, sirs and no, ma'ams of the South – but real respect was something Cutter granted to few people, she knew. In Cutter's book, they had to earn it; and with Cutter, it was hard earned. The fact that he seemed to have added Miss Carter to that short list surprised and somehow frightened Rose.

"But it's not just physical," Cutter went on. "Do you know she ran the newspaper from the waiting room of that Memphis hospital? She wrote her editorial right there, and dictated it back to the paper. She toughed it out during all the questioning from the cops, and even when Miz Howard's mother threw a fit, screaming at her."

A flicker of a smile crossed Cutter's face, though Rose had heard nothing funny in what her brother had said. "W-What's funny?"

"Not funny. Nothing's funny about any of this. Just that, like I say, she toughed it through everything until we got back in the car at the hospital, then she went out," he said, snapping his fingers, "like a light. She was stretched out on the seat, asleep, before we got to the first stoplight."

What Cutter didn't share even with his sister was that Miss Carter's eyes had fluttered, then closed and she'd slumped toward him there on Lamar Avenue, either in a faint or overcome by utter exhaustion. He had laid her head gently on his thigh and reached over and lifted her legs onto the seat. As they passed through the quiet early morning streets of Memphis then out onto the nearly empty two-lane darkness southeast of Collierville, she had slept there. Slept as they moved into the Mississippi night with the radio playing "sweet hits for lonely lovers," and he ran his fingers along Holly Lee Carter's firm right arm and over her strong shoulders, touched her cheek and long neck and stroked the luxuriant thickness of her auburn hair. Once back at Wolf's Run, he wasn't sure how long he stayed like that in the driveway, not wanting to move, not wanting to give up the closeness with her, no matter how one-sided.

Finally, he had scooped her up and carried her inside, her head on his shoulder, and put her to bed like a sleeping child.

They sat at the end of the rutted driveway leading to the Old Ambrose Place. Tony's truck wasn't in sight, but that didn't mean he wasn't around.

"How's Momma?" Cutter asked.

"S-Same as she's b-been for t-ten years. Good days, b-bad days," said Rose. "She stayed awake for al-almost f-four straight days finishing a qu-quilt. I think it's the pr-prettiest one she's ever d-done.

"D-D-Daddy took it with him wh-when he left this aftern-noon. I expect he'll get a good pr-price."

"Tony was at the house last night?"

Rose nodded. "Cutter, I'm sc-sc-scared for you. He came in l-last night. Drunk. H-He was so mad about you helpin' M-M-Miss C-Carter, and what happened out at the C-Campbell farm."

Cutter drew in a deep breath and slowly let it out as he thought about his sister's words. "He didn't hit you or Momma, did he?"

Rose shook her head. "N-No. But he s-s-says he's gonna f-f-fix you for good, and M-M-Miss Carter, too. I was coming to warn you."

Cutter stared into Rose's brown, gentle, fearful eyes. "Sister, don't worry about it. You know how Tony likes to talk big, talk tough. That's all it is." Rose grew quiet. "What?"

She looked at her brother, so unlike her in almost every way. Yet, there was no one in the world she felt closer to or loved more. "I know h-how m-mean Daddy is, but you d-don't think he could b-be the one who wh-whipped Mr. Bellafont, d-do you?"

Cutter fought to hold Rose's gaze. It wasn't fear he saw, but a strange mix of dread and of hope – that the blood that flowed through her did not derive from a man capable of such a thing. It was easy for Cutter to recognize because he had the same blood in his veins and the same worries troubling his thoughts.

"A lot of those creeps in the Klan carry bull whips," said Cutter. "Makes little men feel big."

"Th-Then you don't think it was D-Daddy?"

Cutter didn't answer quickly. He let his eyes move over the decaying corpse of the old house and at the circle of beautiful roses his sister maintained – hand-carrying the water and love they needed to survive. Then, "As much as I hate Tony, I don't want to believe it."

Rose swallowed and thought about that. "M-Me either."

It was nearly dark now and there were no lights on in the house. Rose got out and stood next to the Lincoln. She looked at Cutter in the driver's seat. "It l-looks g-good on you."

"It's not mine," he said.

"I know," she said, turning toward the weedy road, the sagging porch and the rusting roof. "I b-better go. Momma never sl-sleeps more than two hours at a t-time."

"I hate to let you go back in that place."

"It's ooo-kay."

"Tony hasn't –?"

Rose swallowed and shook her head. "N-n-no. He's t-too scared of you."

"Good," said Cutter. "He needs to be."

Lightning was glittering around the edges of Blue Mountain as he crossed the Old Iron Bridge and turned down the narrow road that led to The Well. He went only far enough so that the convertible could not be seen from the road, afraid he would drag off the muffler if he went farther. He turned off the lights and walked along the sandy road as the fireflies lit his way and the space above the river. Now and then a fish jumped and one small light flickered no more.

At The Well, Cutter built a fire in the pit – a big one that would take hours to burn out. He added kerosene to his lantern, lit it and placed it under the rock overhang where he often lay to read and sleep if he thought rain was in the air. Anyone passing on the road would think Cutter was encamped at his usual spot. But Cutter didn't care about anyone passing on the road. He only cared about Tony. Cared that if his father came staggering home drunk with thoughts of further meanness on his mind, he'd make it to the porch and look across the tops of bean plants and cotton stalks and believe that Cutter was at The Well – watching. Ready to do what he'd promised almost four years earlier when he slammed a .12 gauge shell into the chamber and blew Tony's wooden leg right out from under him – splinters spiking into the remainder of his father's thigh like hot, jagged needles as his heavy buttocks crashed hard onto the planks of the back porch. Cutter had jacked another round into the chamber and pressed the warm barrel to the side of Tony's face as the man whimpered and gripped his bloody thigh.

"Now you listen to me," Cutter had told him, his eyes ablaze, his breath smoking out of his nostrils into the January midnight. The moon was bright and the yard was white with frost. Tony Carlucci's blood poured black on the porch planks. "You've already killed my mother. If you ever lay a hand on my sister again, so help me God I'll blow your head completely off. Whatever happens to me later happens, but your brains'll still be scattered all over these walls.

"Don't you even think about it," he told his father, pressing the gun even harder into his cheek. "If you do, it'll be the last thought you ever have."

Doctors in DeLong sent Tony on to the Veteran's Administration hospital in Memphis where it took surgeons three hours to pick out the splinters. He was at the V.A. for almost three weeks and couldn't wear his new plastic prosthesis for almost five months. Of course, Tony swore revenge and Cutter had no doubt he'd try to exact it – which made remaining at the Old Ambrose Place untenable once Tony was released from the hospital. So, he installed deadbolts at the top, bottom and side of his sister's bedroom door, and they agreed on a signal. For a while, Rose had been sleeping with her bed pushed into one corner and the light on.

"If Tony ever – gets in, you turn off the light. Break it if you have to," Cutter told Rose. "Do whatever you have to to get it turned out. And I'll be there. I'll end it."

Now Cutter looked around the camp, satisfied with his ruse. Then he looked across the long fields to the old house where the light now glowed in Rose's window, worrying that the bare bulb might be as much a deception as his campfire. Worrying that Tony still was after Rose in the way that no father ever should be after his daughter. Worrying that Rose left the light on and never spoke of it not to protect Tony but protect *him* from carrying out his promise. The idea that his sister might be making that sacrifice, allowing that sacrilege of herself while he played at being a football star and all that meant in a little, pride-starved town like DeLong made Cutter want to kick something, or hit it or kill Tony right now. But Cutter knew, too, that he was Rose's ticket out, and his mother's – what was left of her.

Cutter knew that if he had killed Tony that bitter cold winter night, he would have his set of worries, but whether his father still was raping his sister would not be one of them. In the years since when he awoke in the night, usually several times, to rub his eyes and check that the light remained on in Rose's room, he hated himself each time for the spark of relief he felt when he saw the yellow-white glow.

The fire crackled, adding an even greater circle of heat to an already hot night.

Cutter threw on one more piece of wood from the remains of a cord stacked against the limestone wall and shielded by the overhang. He looked around and at his watch. It was the best he could do. He walked over to his jeep, unlocked the trunk attached to the bed and took out a small, elegant travel case. The hand-rubbed leather was tan in color, and it was one of the few items of athletic tribute, aside from food, that Cutter kept. He locked the metal trunk then tucked his tightly rolled sleeping bag under his arm left arm. With his right he took a box of .12 gauge shells from the compartment under the driver's seat and lifted his shotgun from its rack. Then he walked back down the dark road to the Lincoln.

Chapter 5

෨

When Cutter returned to Wolf's Run, only dim, flickering lights showed through the kitchen window and those of Holly's bedroom. Lightning glowed around the mountaintop, and the rumbling footfalls of thunder were close enough to be heard. Music was spilling softly onto the porch from a record player somewhere in the house. Cutter put down his gear outside the bedroom windows. Except for the shotgun. He quietly walked down the porch to the kitchen door and looked in through the glass. Two candles were burning between plates set out on the table.

Cutter knocked as he opened the door and stepped inside. From somewhere Charlie yapped and her paws began scrabbling on the heart pine. The ceiling fan stirred the candle flame on the table and thin shadows moved amid the yellow light cast on the cabinets. The music was full of violins, muted horns and a voice as smooth as good coffee.

"Miss Carter? It's Cutter."

Charlie came skittering into the kitchen and stood in front of Cutter, waiting to be petted. Cutter squatted like a hunter with the butt of the shotgun on the floor and stroked the curly white fur between the dog's ears. He smelled cornbread and saw a small red light glowing on the stove.

"Miss Carter?" he said again.

After several moments, Holly Lee Carter emerged from the hallway. She was wearing a green satin bathrobe that matched her eyes and stopped just below her knees. Her hair was still wet and the candlelight set aglow every copper strand in its dark red weave.

"Charlie likes you," she said, the stress and smoke and hours of tears adding to the natural huskiness of her voice. "She doesn't like many people."

"Neither do I," he said, standing. "But Charlie'll do."

Lightning painted the kitchen windows. "A storm is coming," Holly said as if she were observing the phenomenon from a long distance away. Removed from this place and time and the events of the last few days.

"Yes," said Cutter. "It's been so hot. It had to break."

There was a towel and a brush in Holly's lap, and she picked up the brush and began slowly drawing it through the remaining tangles in her hair. Cutter checked the safety and leaned the shotgun against a door frame, then propped himself on a kitchen chair. He watched in silence as Holly Lee Carter brushed her hair, stroke after smooth stroke, after long, slow stroke. She ignored the lightning and his gaze, and the passing of several minutes as if time had no hold on her or this night. When she finished she put the brush on the counter.

"Do you like Sinatra?" she asked.

Cutter's mouth was dry. He said, "I guess I'm more of a Johnny Cash kinda guy."

"Cash? Yes. He's quite a talent. But there's nothing like Sinatra when you're feeling low," said Holly. "That voice. The phrasing. He's the buddy you want sitting next to you at the bar when you find out everything has … has? … has gone to shit." She laughed softly but there was no humor in it. "Or maybe I'm just showing my age. *Ohhhh*, how I'm showing my age."

"No you're not. You look good."

Holly laughed, then coughed. "Cutter, you're a terrible liar. But I hope you never get good at it. A lot of people do," she told him, and placed the towel next to the brush. When she did, Cutter saw the snub-nosed .38 between her thigh and the arm of the wheelchair.

"Where did you get that?" he asked, eyeing the gun.

"The gun cabinet in the library," she said. "Most are antiques, but there's a veritable arsenal in there. Do you think I'm nuts for going around my own house with a loaded gun?"

"Considering what's happened the last few days, I'd think you were nuts if you didn't. One of the main reasons I went by the The Well was to get my shotgun out of the jeep. Just in case."

Holly looked at the window that alternately captured her image and Cutter's framed in black and the pulse of lightning growing more rapid by the minute. "Yes. Just in case," she said as if to the images in the window. Then to Cutter – "Are you hungry?"

"I could eat."

"Good. I put cornbread in the oven to warm," she said, wheeling to the refrigerator. "People brought enough food to feed a family of six for a week."

She opened the door as Cutter came over and squatted beside her. He began reaching for platters of meat and Pyrex dishes and casseroles filled with other treats. She grabbed his wrist, hard. "Stop it!" she told him with a sudden fearceness in eyes rimmed red by long hours of tears. "I'm not an invalid! I am *not* helpless!"

Slowly Holly released his wrist, realizing how panicked and desperate and angry she sounded. Cutter took his hands away from the dishes and looked at her. "I know," was all he said. She sat back, surprised. The two small words vibrated through her veins like a guitar chord, suddenly but gently touched. Her lips trembled then opened ready to speak in a language her body had all but forgotten, ready to –

Holly swallowed then forced words from her throat. "Then go sit down," she said, "before the cornbread burns."

Holly prepared plates of cold ham, potato salad and green-bean casserole. The storm rushed up out of the valley and broke across Blue Mountain as she lifted the pan of cornbread from the oven. The rain came in on a hard wind that rattled the French doors that led to the interior porch. It plunk, plunk, plunked onto the roof in big, wide-spaced drops then more, then more until it was an uninterrupted roar high in the rafters.

They slathered fresh cream butter from a dairy east of DeLong onto the hot cornbread that Ruth Wiggington had delivered at midafternoon. She had been Holly's English teacher through most of high school.

Holly held the cornbread and sweet butter in her mouth, savoring it with her eyes closed before swallowing. "Ummmm," she sighed. "That is so good."

"Yep. Miz Wiggington makes a good pan," Cutter said from across red-and-white checks of the vinyl tablecloth.

"Thank you for dealing with the people who came by today. And the phone calls."

"I was up. I wasn't sure if I should answer the phone, but I didn't want it to wake you."

"You did the right thing. Even when I was awake, I was in no shape to talk to anyone," she told him. "But you driving me to Memphis and taking care of things here today, it'll create a lot of talk. Me being in this – this? – 'condition' will ease it a little. But I'm afraid my reputation will precede us both."

"I'm not worried about it. You and I know the truth."

She smiled at him. "I wish it were that simple."

Cutter knew that Holly was right, but what was done was done. There was no point in worrying at it. He changed the subject. "Did you see my note about Miss Davis calling from Los Angeles? She said she was an old friend. That she'd be here tomorrow."

"She is. In fact, Julie was my best friend when I worked at *The Chronicle*. We shared an apartment a few blocks from the office. More of a crash pad, really, for anyone from the paper who needed someplace to sleep and didn't want to drive all the way home. L.A. is just so big! Now Julie is their star news features writer."

"I guess little ol' DeLong has turned into quite a story."

"Yes. I'm sure it has. They only send Julie to the big stuff."

"She said she'd like to stay with you while she's in town. That might be a good idea. I mean, with Miz Howard –"

Holly nodded. "Yes. You're right. I admit, I'm not eager to stay out here by myself right now."

"No one could blame you for that," he said. "I knew feelings ran deep around here about blacks going to Cattahatchie High and colored folks votin'. But these last few weeks? It's opened up a wide streak of meanness I didn't believe was here. Or I didn't want to believe it." He looked up at the ceiling fan for a moment as if he still couldn't bear to look at the truth square in the face, then – "Anyway, while you were sleeping Governor Broderick sent in the National Guard. But not local guys. He called up some units from the coast. There's a dusk-to-dawn curfew for the whole county. Maybe it'll help."

"Maybe," she said looking out the windows filled with rain and lightning and a darkness that was as deep as any she could remember. "I guess that means you have to stay here again."

"I'd already planned to. Curfew or no curfew."

In the candlelight, Cutter's eyes were like blue-white pearls. Holly felt blood warming her neck and a tingle sliding across her shoulders. "You know, you don't have to sleep on the porch," Holly heard herself say, and could hear her pulse thudding in her neck above the crash of the rain on the tin roof. She had spoken in the voice of another woman from another time, but she both liked and feared what she heard. *No, no!* she told herself as she broke her gaze with Cutter and busied her hands with more cornbread and butter. *This is wrong for all sorts of reasons.* She gathered her current voice. The voice of a twenty-eight-year-old woman bound to a wheelchair, a woman with responsibilities, with a newspaper to run. "I mean, there are, you know, six bedrooms in this house," she made herself say. "Four aren't occupied. Five now, I guess."

Holly wondered if in the candlelight Cutter could see the blush glowing on her cheeks. "Tomorrow night I'll be back to sleepin' on rocks. No sense in gettin' acquanted with a bed tonight. Thanks anyway."

Now Holly was happy to change the subject, even if by saying, "I guess you've had it pretty rough, especially since Miss Jenny –"

"Rougher than some, not near as bad as others," said Cutter, immediately deflecting that line of conversation. "This ham sure looks good. Tom-Ed Belle's wife brought it by. Nobody smokes a ham any better than Mr. Belle."

"You're right. Mr. Belle's famous for his hams," agreed Holly. "Do you mind if I ask the Lord's blessing on this food?"

"That'd be fine."

Holly clasped her hands in front of her at the edge of the table. "Dear Lord ..." she started but realized her mind was blank, as if the shelf where she kept the blessings in her life was suddenly empty, swept clean. She tried again. "Dear Lord ..." But there was only a hollow place where she looked to find the words. The moments stretched on and Holly felt tears rising at the rims of her eyes. She didn't want to cry anymore. She was exhausted with tears. More moments passed but no blessings jumped to her mind and no words came. Ridge was dead. So were Sheriff Johnson and four people in Roseville. Many others across the river were hurt or homeless. Eve's life would never be the same. The paper was on the verge of bankruptcy and the National

Guard was patrolling the streets of her hometown. And what of her father? Was T.L. Carter's death somehow tied into all of this misery? Holly thought of those things, and of her own fears, too. The past seventy-two hours had made her realize in more than a passing way that J.L. Burke was right. If the Klan was willing to murder a county sheriff, they wouldn't hesitate to kill her if they decided it suited their purposes.

Holly scanned her mind for words of praise, words of blessing but could not find them. She did not want to let her heart, her focus wander away from God, but when she thought of Ridge and Eve and her father and all the rest and it, she felt like God had wandered away from her. From DeLong.

Then Cutter's voice moved sturdy and sure through the roar of the rain and the vacant place in her spirit. "Lord, thank you for the good food in front of us," he said. "Thank you for a dry place to be tonight. And with all the meanness that's around, thank you for watching over Miss Carter.

"Amen," he said with finality. "Now let's eat."

They said little during the meal. Cutter was not given to small talk in the best of circumstances, and Holly was too worn out and hollowed out by all that had happened to provide the impetus for mealtime conversation. Instead, they listened to Sinatra and to the rain drum the roof and tatter at the windows, and they found a strange comfort in their ability to be silent with one another.

After dinner, Cutter washed the dishes and Holly dried them and stacked them on the blue and white tiles of the counter. It was only 8:30 but all she wanted was to be back, safe in Meemaw Carter's bed. She thanked Cutter and excused herself.

"You can stay up and watch TV in the library if you want to. Or read. Or work on your pool game."

"No thanks," he said, drying his big hands on a dish towel. "I'll just sack out. It's been a long couple of days."

"Yes. Yes it has. Good night, Cutter."

"Good night, Miss Carter. I'll be close."

"I know you will. And I appreciate it," she said and forced herself to pivot to her right, toward the hall, before she did something she would not be able to take back.

In the bathroom, Holly washed her face and throat with a cool wash-cloth. She lifted her hair and let the damp cloth rest on the back of her neck for a bit before slipping into one of her favorite sleeping T-shirts. She lay her battered Martin six-string on the big four-poster. She put Charlie up, too, and the little dog quickly found her usual spot and settled in. Holly blew out the candles on her bedside table and lifted herself onto the fresh sheets she'd put on while Cutter was at The Well. She moved her hips and then her long legs, as if they belonged to someone else. She slipped the Bible given to her by her grandmother under the pillow next to the .38, then propped on two pillows and picked up the guitar. The rain was only a soft purr now and the air from the open windows was cool and fresh and carried the vague scent of Old Spice. A small creek of water filled the gutters and ran down the drain-pipes to where it spewed onto a square of bricks fashioned by slaves more than one-hundred years earlier. Outside on the porch she could hear Cutter move from time to time as she strummed the guitar the way she often did when she was troubled or confused and needed to think.

How had the guy who had greeted her with such ugliness that first morning back in DeLong become her most valuable ally? How had be become even something more? Something she could not possibly –

And yet as Holly fingered the strings with unconscious eloquence, her thoughts returned to the previous night. She wasn't sure what had happened once she and Cutter were out of the parking lot. Had she fainted? Collapsed from exhaustion once she was out of the view of cops, news cameras and Eve Howard's hysterical mother? Whatever it was, when a bump in the highway jarred her eyes open, she had realized her head was in Cutter's lap. But she had given no sign even when his fingers began moving over her shoulders and neck. When they moved along the line of her jaw, she wanted to take them in her mouth but she continued her pretense of sleep as the miles clicked by. She had wished that they could drive forever through the warm summer air, his fingertips as soft as starlight on her skin, while the radio played "sweet sounds for lonely lovers." For the first time in a very long time, Holly had not felt lonely. She felt safe and comforted and appreciated, and even happy – as terrible as that sounded considering all that had happened.

On the porch, Cutter lay atop his sleeping bag. He could smell the gun oil on the .12 gauge next to him on the planks. The rain was nearly finished and the bright, loud part of the storm had moved off over the mountain to the northeast. He enjoyed the sound of Holly Lee Carter's fingers moving over the strings and sliding up along the frets. She was the most beautiful woman Cutter had ever seen, and he'd already seen quite a few in his eighteen years and eleven months. Standing by his jeep after football practice or a game. Dropping by his campsites unbidden. Especially at The Gin or sashaying through the pool halls and barbecue joints of Cotton Hill in south Memphis, where he sometimes went to escape not who he was, but who everyone in DeLong expected him to be – everybody's All-America. But none of those women ever had touched him the way Holly Lee Carter had on their way home from Memphis. *And she doesn't even know it,* he thought.

"Cutter? Am I keeping you awake?"

He cleared his throat and pulled himself out of the memory he was beginning to cherish in a way that surprised and confused him. If he chose, he could pull from the back pages of his thoughts images of women his eyes had fully seen, the feel of soft, compelling places his hands had been; but the recollection of Holly Lee Carter sleeping in his lap and the way her skin felt against his fingetips on the long ride back to Wolf's Run was the only place his memory wanted to rest.

"No. I like it," he said. "Play all night if you want to. I'll be here."

Holly smiled and began again moving her fingers over the strings as Cutter listened and the clouds finally cleared and the moon rose above Wolf's Run. Listened as a sheer white light filled the yard and painted shadows behind the pines, the old greenhouse and the garage. Listened while Holly held the guitar against her – in the darkness of her bed, like a lover – and played music that was sweet and Spanish and sad until her fingers were too sleepy to find the chords.

Chapter 6

❧

As the smell of smoke cleared from DeLong, things seemed to calm down a bit. Funerals were planned and bulldozers were brought in to clear debris in Roseville. Glass installers from Memphis and Tupelo made fast and plenty money plying their trade along River Street and at dozens of houses on the west side of the river. Payment plans were available, but even then some in Roseville could not afford the price. So they covered their broken windows with plywood, plastic sheeting or the cloth saved from twenty-five-pound Dixie Lily Flour sacks.

Really, Klansmen – whether local Kluxers or the unnamed "outside radicals" Brother MacAllister and Governor Weathers were so fond of blaming for the attacks – had little choice but to slip back into their spider holes, or into the supple anonymity of business suits, work khakis and overalls. FBI men were so thick on the roads that a fellow couldn't pull off into a stand of trees to take a leak for fear of exposing himself to a camera lens. Federal marshals, under the direction of U.S. Attorney J.L. Burke, staked out a handful of black churches that had been particularly active in registering congregants to vote.

A gaggle of reporters roamed the streets of town asking over and over the same questions of everyone from lawn men to doctors to dressmakers and mechanics and county officials. They came from as far away as Boston and New York, San Francisco, Miami, Los Angeles and even London. Most encamped at The Jeff Davis Hotel and ate dinner in the Gen. Nathan Bedford Forrest Dining Room or at The Cotton Café, the tragedy creating a strange and unexpected economic boon for local merchants. Several were known to be staying at Wolf's Run. To temporarily augment her staff, Miss Carter exchanged desk space and darkroom privileges at *The Current-Leader* for the right to use their material.

Meanwhile, the National Guardsmen parked jeeps with mounted machine guns on the town square and set up checkpoints on the main roads in and out of DeLong and at the Bilbo Bridge beside the jail. It was hard to drive more than a mile on Highway 27 without meeting a green National Guard troop transport or seeing a Highway Patrol car on the shoulder of the road.

Throughout the county it was common knowledge that Sheriff Wallace and a couple of deputies he trusted were shaking – sometimes violently – every tree in the county for information about the attacks. Plenty of Klan nuts were falling out but either the rank-and-file Kluxers weren't privy to the information or they really were the work of "outside radicals," I told myself, and did my best to believe it even as my father hauled Milton Handley out of his department store in handcuffs. They questioned him overnight but by Friday morning he was on the local airwaves along with Governor Weathers and Brother MacAllister praying for "the many lost and misled souls in Cattahatchie County doing Satan's work."

Standing in front of the crater that marked the spot where Bryant Funeral Home had been, a network newsman told the nation Thursday night that a "veneer of calm has settled over DeLong, Mississippi." And "veneer" was, indeed, the perfect word because the superficial tranquility was imposed by force and nothing else. Going into the Friday funerals, DeLong was like a fire that had been roughly but carelessly doused. Beneath the surface, the heart of the blaze remained – *hot enough to rend skin from bone,* I thought with a shudder as I rubbed my hand on the leg of my jeans.

The mirror above the chest of drawers in my room at Mrs. Fletcher's Boarding House vibrated against the flowered wallpaper as a Santa Fe freight picked up speed after slowing for crossings in DeLong. I walked through the screen door and onto the small balcony that came with my room in the sagging, paint-faded Victorian that sat in a wooded V between the railroad tracks and the river south of town. The rooms on the east side of the gabled dwelling were considered the least desirable due to their proximity to the tracks. So, I got a discount, but the truth was I didn't mind the four daily trains – not even the 2 a.m. express freight that squealed and whistled but slowed little and stopped for nothing – rattling, humming, keeping a hot, bluesy beat as it hurried through the cotton fields toward Oxford, then Vicksburg and all the way down to New Orleans. It reminded me that as sure as steel rails, there was something beyond DeLong. There were other places Patti and I could go, away from here and her daddy and this ugliness. We merely needed to find our train and ride.

With my new job at Handley's I normally would not have been in my room to feel the four p.m. train rumble up through my bones, but on that Friday DeLong was essentially shut down in terms of local commerce. Ridge Bellafont's funeral had been at 10 that morning at the old Episcopal Church at the top of Hill Street. Built in 1831, it was DeLong's first church, and even though it mostly had been abandoned over the decades for more charismatic denominations, it still held for the county's oldest families an emotional connection. They shut their businesses and left their big farms and turned out in their Cadillacs, Lincolns and Chrysler Imperials to honor one of their own.

At two p.m. five caskets were lined up in front of the pulpit in the brick sanctuary of Roseville A.M.E. Church. The church was packed and the small window air-conditioning units chugged and groaned and helped little. Outside, several hundred more mourners stood in the scalding August sun listening over loudspeakers as Reverend Baptiste spent two hours preaching the funerals. Holly Lee Carter sweltered across the street in her convertible along with her friend, Julie Davis, from the *L.A. Chronicle*. Cutter stood out in the crowd of mostly black faces.

Meanwhile, under the watchful eyes of the National Guard, the Klan was holding its own "Funeral for State's Rights" – parading around the town square while shouldering a mock coffin. FBI snipers were on the roofs of the courthouse and hotel, and with most of the businesses shut down, the rally drew only a couple of dozen Klux and a like number of observers. In fact, the local onlookers were almost outnumbered by reporters, photographers and cameramen shuttling between Roseville and the square as they looked for the best story.

According to the Memphis radio station that was covering the funeral, the five mule-drawn farm wagons that were hauling the caskets the three-quarters of a mile from the church to the Roseville Cemetery now were at the gates.

"It's ninety-six degrees and feels every bit of it," the radio reporter said, and he was right.

I went downstairs and poured myself a glass of tea from the large pitcher Mrs. Fletcher kept in the refrigerator. I drank a bit of it, held the glass to my forehead for a long minute, and drank some more. Then I crossed the back porch and went down the steps into the yard. A worn and uneven brick path led to the river.

Mrs. Fletcher – a big, white-haired woman with breasts that sagged to her waist and a spate of cancerous-looking freckles – and her sister, Mabel Richardson, were sitting in the shade on rusted metal lawn chairs near an old dock. The women had speckled porcelain bowls in their large laps and a bushel of purple-hull peas between them. Their thick fingers were stained blue-black from the dye in the pea shells, but their thumb nails cut through the dark husks of the legumes with the speed and skill of surgeons' scalpels.

"Young Mr. Wallace, you seem to be mighty partial to my ice tea," said Mrs. Fletcher.

"Yes, ma'am. It's as fine as I've ever had," I said, but my mind and eyes were across the river and hundred or so yards back toward town where Roseville Cemetery poked out into the Cattahatchie like a broken thumb. Because the people of color in DeLong always had been forced to live on the low, swampy land between the river and the Chalmette hills, they had adopted the burial traditions of their south Louisiana cousins – covering graves with slabs of poured concrete or bricking together above-ground crypts where generations of dead were stacked like cordwood. Most years the effort paid off, and did not allow the spring rise of the Cattahatchie to force loved ones from the grave. But every decade or two when the river topped its banks by several feet and temporarily reclaimed most of the soft land next to the hills, caskets could be seen floating downstream, driven by the cold current and spinning in the eddies like ships helmed by blind sailors.

I walked out on the rickety dock and with my hands shaded my eyes against the sun glinting off the water. I could see the caskets – one of them draped in our nation's flag – being borne by pallbearers through the maze of small crypts. They were carried though shafts of light filtering between the oak boughs and placed beside their final resting places as the crowd swelled within the graveyard. Soon a capella voices that were mournful, but hopeful and determined, too, rose in singing *Swing Low, Sweet Chariot,* and the sound swam downriver toward me as pure and beautiful as rose petals strewn in the current. The sound made my chin tremble with emotions I couldn't categorize at the time and I pursed my lips to get control.

From the end of the dock, I watched the brief graveside service. I saw my father and Miss Carter among the crowd. A petite blonde in a black dress stood beside Miss Carter taking notes. Occasionally, Miss Carter lifted a camera from her lap and snapped a few pictures. Knowing how Cutter felt about Tommy Ray Banks, I figured he was there, too, though I did not see him until the final hymn had been sung and the mourners began to shuffle away on the dusty road that twisted back into Roseville. He stepped from behind a crumbling brick vault and approached the women.

"Cutter Carlucci, this is my friend, Julie Davis, from the *Chronicle*," said Miss Carter.

The reporter extended her hand and Cutter covered it in his grip. "My goodness, you are quite the young Adonis, aren't you?"

"Down, girl," said Miss Carter. "I'm sure Cutter has plenty of local sweethearts without borrowing trouble from Los Angeles."

"Trouble? Me?" she asked, her impish brown eyes twinkling. Julie Davis' small frame, features and short haircut made her look like a thirty-year-old pixie.

"Yes, you. And with a capital T," teased her friend.

Cutter asked, "Miss Carter, do you have a minute?"

"Sure," she said. "But not a lot more than that. I've got to get back to the office and wrap up the weekend edition before dark. The curfew is still in effect. We're going to do all the deliveries tomorrow."

"Do you need help?"

"No. We've reorganized the routes and actually managed to hire a few new carriers. I think we'll be all right," she told him, purposefully trying to distance herself from Cutter and all she had felt lying in her own bed with him sleeping only a few feet away. The more she had thought about that and their candlelit dinner, the more embarrassed and awkward she felt. After all, she was twenty-eight and he was eighteen. *For goodness sake!* Well, almost nineteen. Still! Then there was the whole wheelchair thing, the paralysis. *What was I thinking?* But knowing that Cutter was little given to casual conversation, she asked, "Julie could you excuse us for a moment."

"Why, of course, Holly," said Julie Davis as she gave Cutter a long look. At six-three, he was at least a foot taller. "It was a pleasure to meet you."

"Yes, ma'am. You, too."

My jaw tensed and my lips tightened at the sight of Cutter and Miss Carter together in public. It made me angry and jealous, and filled me, too, with concern for my friend. My best friend! No matter the rough patch we were going through.

She lifted her hair off her sleeveless black dress and her neck. Even from a distance her shoulders looked beautifully strong. "It's sooo hot," she said. Then, "I'm sure the Banks family and Miss Winona appreciated you coming. I saw you at Ridge's funeral this morning, too."

"He took some of the best football pictures I've ever seen. And he gave me copies of a lot of them," explained Cutter. "I don't keep a scrapbook, but Rose does. He seemed like a nice man."

Miss Carter had to look away. "Yes. He was a very nice man," she said, clearing her throat. "But that's not why –"

"No. Look, I know a lot has happened in the last few days, and you've got an awful lot on your mind, but a '65 Olds is a popular car. Spare parts for them go pretty fast. Every day your daddy's car sits over there in Alabama –"

"The more likely it is we'll find it stripped or just plain gone," said Miss Carter. "I can't go tomorrow."

"And I start a week's worth of work Monday with a surveying crew."

"Do you think that junkyard would be open on Sunday?"

"From talking to the fella, I don't think it's a formal business," Cutter told her. "It's more of a backyard deal. I imagine he'd accommodate us. Especially if we called ahead."

"Do you have plans for Sunday?"

"Nothin' but a trip to Alabama," Cutter said and smiled, and whatever wall of separation Holly was trying to erect between them shook and shuddered.

Behind me and to my left I heard a splash in the river and I startled. A cottonmouth had dropped from a low limb into the water. I checked my watch. When I looked back toward the cemetery, Cutter and Miss Carter had disappeared among the tombs. I needed to go, too, if I was going to have dinner with the MacAllisters and get back to the boarding house before the sundown curfew.

"Ain't nothin' like a colored funeral to make you believe in God," said Mrs. Fletcher as I passed. She was stirring the air around her big face with a spade-shaped fan that depicted Jesus praying in the garden before his betrayal. It was provided by an insurance agency that sold burial policies for two-dollars a month. "If them po'r folks can keep the faith in the Almighty, then surely we can bow our heads to the Creator."

"I don't know, Sister," said Mabel Richardson, lowering a bucket into the river on a rope. She pulled it out, dipped a blue-and-white handkerchief in it and ran it around her wrinkled old neck. "Maybe it's easier for them than we think. All they got in this world is faith. They sho' ain't got nothin' else. Least not in these parts, wouldn't you say, young fella?"

"I guess," was the best I could manage as I watched the water moccasin swim with a poisonous ease across the brown-gold face of the river.

Chapter 7

༄

C utter rolled onto his back and rubbed his sleepy eyes.

"Puffy clouds ... blue sky ...birds chirpin' and a choir sing-ing," he said from the back seat of Miss Carter's Lincoln. "Am I in heaven?"

"No," she said from the front. "Just Alabama."

Cutter sat up and ran his fingers through his black hair as he looked around. They were parked in the shadow of a maple tree at the edge of a dirt parking lot of the small New Testament Baptist Church. The sanctuary windows were open and *What a Friend We Have in Jesus* filled the air. He stepped out of the car, stretching.

"I thought we were going to stop for breakfast in Tupelo," he said, yawning.

"We were, but you worked all night and this past week's been rough on you, too. I thought I'd let you sleep. We'll stop for a big lunch on the way back."

Cutter opened the ice chest Holly had put in the back floorboard across from her chair. He took out a plastic jug filled with water and unscrewed the lid. "If I was sleeping that good, I imagine I was snor-ing like a chainsaw," he said and took a long swig from the jug.

"For a mile or two I thought we'd lost a tire and we were riding on the rim," she told him. "When I realized it was you, I just turned the radio up. Loud."

Cutter finished washing the pasty taste out of his mouth and spit the water into the dirt. He half coughed, half laughed. Holly smiled and liked the sound but tried to keep her mind focused on the purpose of the trip. "Mr. Conway's house is about a mile on down this road," said Holly as Cutter poured water into his hand and ran it over his face and neck. "I drove by, but the gate to his driveway had a chain on it. They're probably at church. So, I thought this would be a good place to wait."

Cutter pulled out his black T-shirt, exposing the metal of his belly, and dried his face. Holly made herself look away, mostly. "Yep. This is a pretty place," he said, shoving his shirt back into his jeans. "But it doesn't look much different from Miss'ssippi."

"No, it doesn't."

Cutter came around and propped on the fender near Holly. "You want to hear something sad?"

She groaned. "Not really. I've had about all the sadness I can deal with for one week."

"Not that kind of sad. Just … ridiculous."

"In that case, sure."

"Other than riding the team bus down to Jackson for the state football playoffs the last couple of years, this is probably the farthest I've ever been from DeLong," he said, and took another sip of water. "What do you figure? About a hundred-and-forty miles down here."

"Something like that."

"That's farther than Memphis. Even West Memphis, Arkansas. One night I drove across the bridge and parked on the levee just to see what the city looked like from the other side of the mighty Mississippi. And so I could say I'd been to Arkansas, I guess. Now that *is* ridiculous," he said, and chuckled at himself. Holly simply added that to the list of things she liked about him – that despite his often stoic, even stern demeanor, he could laugh at himself. Countless older and supposedly more mature men she had known were not secure enough to manage such casual and unconscious humility. Certainly not Gerry Yards, her former boss at the *Chronicle*, long-ago lover and would-be husband. Yards was among the six out-of-state or international journalists encamped at Wolf's Run, covering the funerals, the Klan and the hunt for McBride. Though she considered Gerry a dear friend, she could do without his pitying eyes following her around the house and the newspaper office.

"I don't know about ridiculous," said Holly. "Everyone can use a change of perspective now and then. A look at things from the other side of the river."

"Now who's being the diplomat?" he asked. "Well, one of these days, I'm gonna get out and see a little of this ol' world. I'd like to see where my mother's people came from in England. And I guess I'd like to see Italy, too. Rome. The Vatican."

"Italy is beautiful," said Holly. "It's one of my favorite places."

"I guess you've been all over the world, haven't you?"

"The world is a big place. I wouldn't say I've been all over it, but I've hit some high spots."

"What's your favorite place?"

"Ireland is beautiful, especially by the sea," she told him. "Italy is lovely and filled with so much history and incredible art, but the Greek isles are ... breathtaking. Africa is like a storybook, or a *National Geographic* magazine come alive. Even Vietnam. It's very lush and green, and some of the beaches are just incredible. But, honestly, it's hard to beat the U.S.A. for variety and beauty, and the people.

"Where I live in the mountains north of Los Angeles, it's – well, it's almost indescribable. At the right time of the year, you can be swimming in the Pacific in the morning and snow skiing in the mountains in the afternoon. And be back in the city in time for a late dinner at the Beverly Hilton."

"It sounds nice."

"It is. And I'm incredibly blessed to have it. It's not a big place, but it's all mine. Mine and Charlie's," she said, stroking the side of the little dog who was curled beside her hip.

"Then you're not planning to stay in DeLong?"

"No, Cutter, I'm not," she told him. "I felt God called me to come back to Mississippi and do what I could to keep the paper out of the hands of people like Cecil Weathers.

"I had planned to stay for six months. A year at the most. But I've botched it so badly that I may get to go back to California a lot sooner than I expected."

Cutter took another sip from the water jug. "Just because things haven't worked out so far, doesn't mean it's your fault."

"Thanks. You're a good guy."

"I try to be. But don't let that get around."

The doors to the church opened and the sweat-dampened congregation began to pour out onto the steps and into the parking area. Cutter looked at his watch – 12:20. "If the Baptists are done, everybody ought to be let out by now," he said, getting in the front seat. "Let's go see how much of your daddy's car is left."

Holly pushed her Wayfarers onto her nose, turned the key and swung the convertible around.

"You know, one of these days when I shake the Miss'ssippi dust off my feet, maybe I'll come knockin' on your door in big ol' Los Angeles," said Cutter. "Maybe you could show me the view."

The words made a dozen images flash through Holly's mind – of dinner at the Malibu Inn, of driving high into the mountains, even laughing at Mickey and Minnie over in Anaheim. And all of them ended up back at her house with the deck and the ocean view and the distant thrumming of the surf mixed with the ever-present hum of vehicles on the Pacific Coast Highway.

What am I thinking? Stop it! Holly told herself and forced herself to keep her gaze on the gravel road. "Who knows where any of us will be a few years from now – even a few months from now," she managed evenly. "But I'm sure L.A. will still be there if you get out that way."

* * *

Back in DeLong, 12:20 passed, and 12:25, and Brother C.E. MacAllister still was preaching, though some of the most prominent members of the First Denomination congregation already had departed the sanctuary. But Mrs. MacAllister and her daughters watched, transfixed, as Brother Daddy marched around the dais, mopped his brow with a monogrammed handkerchief and slapped the leather cover of his large Bible.

I've often wondered if Brother Mac planned what he said that day or if he simply went off on a tangent and, like a train picking up too much speed on a steep grade, reached a point where the brakes failed – a point at which he was out of control, the momentum of his own horrendous rhetoric carrying him down. I've wondered, too, whether in their megalomaniacal arrogance Governor Weathers and/ or Milton Handley and Walter Kamp put him up to it. In the end, it doesn't matter except as a historical curiosity, because his "sermon" that day broke wide the fissures that separated not so much those who were for or against segregation, but between those who were willing to support brutality, intimidation and even murder to maintain what C.E. MacAllister described as "God's natural social order."

Without rehashing the hour-plus diatribe linking Old Testament battles and Dixiecrat politics, Brother MacAllister attempted to drill deep into unspoken white fear. It was a fear of the perversion and cruelty of our ancestors, and of the legalized social, economic and political repression of our own century. Fear that once freed of Jim Crow laws and the lawlessness of the Klan, blacks would rise up and retaliate with merciless bloodlust against generations of jailers, abusers and oppressors. It was a fear that gained its power from the instinctual knowledge that had the legal and physical leg irons been locked so long above our feet, once many of us were freed our vengeance would be pitiless and unquenchable. But when Brother MacAllister attempted to sanction the car-bomb murder of Sheriff Johnson and the deaths of four innocent Roseville residents as "regrettable but legitimate casualties in the war to protect white Christian society," a murmur such as I'd never heard passed under the chandeliers in the big sanctuary. It wasn't anything as dramatic as a thunderclap, but it was as clear as the sudden rise of a storm tide to push against a long-standing though ultimately rotten bulwark.

Had C.E. MacAllister stopped there and done his usual altar call and prayer for those listening on WHCI, that tide might well have slipped away in a grumbling retreat. At least for a time. But when he went on a harangue about "God's soldiers" rendering their "righteous judgment" in the whipping and mutilation of Ridge Bellafont, more than a few pews emptied. If First Denomination's pastor was perturbed by the sudden exodus, he gave no sign of it. In fact, it seemed to inspire him even more as he talked about God's wheat remaining while "the worthless chaff blows away."

It wasn't that those men and women who left their cushioned seats and guided their children up the long, carpeted aisles and out the doors supported "Sister Ridge's" assumed lifestyle. Most saw it for what the Bible calls it – an "abomination" – but they had the humility and social grace not to cast the first stone. And certainly not at one of their own. Ridge Bellafont was not an outsider, a radical or a black man. He was a cultured, soft-spoken, well-educated Cattahatchie County blue blood, known for the many beautiful and often hand-framed photographs he had gifted to moms, brides, businessmen and proud young athletes over more than thirty-five years.

In the hindsight of history, I wish I could say that the changes that began that day arrived on a surge of broader moral, racial and social enlightenment. But that simply was not the case. In fact, many of those same families continued to fund and enthusiastically support all-white Riverview Academy and pressured others to do the same. But what I can say from my limited Southern white-boy perspective is that the silent, tacit support that allowed the violent resistance of desegregation to flourish in DeLong began to crumble that day, soul by prayerful soul, when key members of several churches turned away from the ugly, twisted demagoguery of Brother MacAllister and his like.

He, and they, had gone too far; but, like the Pharisees, they didn't yet know it.

Chapter 8

⁊

A mile from the little Baptist church in Alabama, Holly and Cutter turned through the open cattle gate under a hand-painted sign that read: Conway Salvage & Towing + Cows. A number of beefs of ill-defined lineage grazed on the hillside leading up to the small yellow brick house, but Holly and Cutter saw no junked cars. To the left of the house, though, under a big oak tree was a small, paint-faded 1940s-era wrecker. A far cry from the eighteen-wheeler flatbed with Oklahoma plates that LeRoy Kamp had suggested.

A smallish blond man came out of the kitchen door wearing a white shirt that was whisker-worn around the neck and khakis that had wrinkled in the heat and humidity. Behind a glass door in the carport a pretty redheaded woman looked out, so pregnant she looked as if she might give birth at any moment. A young blond boy in overalls with no shirt stood beside her.

"I'm Ronnie Conway," he said. "Are you the fella who called about parts for the Fords and the '65 Olds?"

"Yes, sir. My name is Carlucci. This is my friend, Holly Lee," said Cutter, offering a handshake. He didn't want to tip their hand by using the Carter name in case there was something going on between Kamp and Conway that didn't meet the eye.

Ronnie Conway allowed himself a good long look at the woman in the driver's seat, at the hand-control mounted beside the steering wheel, and the wheelchair folded in the back floorboard. "Normally, I don't like to do business on the Lord's day," he told them, "but since y'all were comin' all the way from Miss'ssippi. Where'd you say you're from?"

"My goodness, it's so hot out here, I b'lieve I'm just gonna melt," Holly told the men, slathering on her best Southern belle accent. "Honey, can't we get on with this?"

Cutter looked at Mr. Conway. "Ma'am, you can wait inside with my wife and young'un, if you'd like."

"No, thank you," she said. "I'm the one paying for the parts. I want see what I'm buying."

"Aw'right. Come on," he said, and started walking along a field road beside the house. "My salvage yard is over the ridge in back, out of sight, so that the neighbors don't whine."

Holly idled the big V-8 beside the men as they walked. When they topped the ridge, below her on a gently sloping hillside was an old barn that served as a makeshift garage and fifty or so cars in various stages of salvage. Some were nearly new. Others were striped red with rust, and were without glass, upholstery, an engine or one body part or another.

"You want to look at the Fords first, or the Olds?" Conway asked Cutter as they walked.

"Let's see the Olds first."

They turned down a grassy alley between the cars as Holly followed. Cutter helped Ronnie Conway push on a grazing cow until it moved out of the way. They walked on another ten yards. "Here's the Olds," he said.

Holly stopped in front of the gold, four-door Oldsmobile Ninety-Eight as Cutter walked around the junked car. There were no wheels on it and it was sitting up on three cinderblocks and a metal milk crate. Holly had wondered what she would feel when she saw the car in which her father died. Really, though, the vehicle itself was purchased years after she left DeLong, so it held no emotional significance for her. No memories of T.L. Carter in the driver's seat. The only thing she felt was relief that it still was mostly intact. The windshield was gone, as were the left fender and the trunk lid. The interior looked moldy but otherwise together. Most importantly the steering wheel remained connected to its mount.

Holly pulled her Nikon out of her camera bag and began shooting, making sure to get Mr. Conway and the Olds in the same frame.

"What are you doing?" he asked.

"Shooting pictures."

"I see *that*."

"I'm a photographer. It's what I do," she said. "Cutter, would you please look in the glove box, and tell me what you find."

He opened the passenger door. "The glove compartment is open. It's full of dried mud."

"What is this?" asked Conway. "What are you looking for?"

Cutter opened the big blade of the Swiss Army Knife he carried, poking through the mud then digging it out. "Nothing left in here."

"Who are you people?" demanded Conway.

Holly put down her camera and didn't let her disappointment show. "We're the people who can send you to jail for a very long time."

"*Jail?*"

"That car belonged to my father's company, DeLong Newspapers Incorporated. He died in it. I inherited the company, and there's no bill of sale or title transfer anywhere," she told him as Cutter listened. "That means you're in possession of stolen property. Not only that, you transported it across state lines. That makes it a federal crime with federal time."

Holly was running a bluff. She knew the circumstances probably wouldn't sustain such a charge, but Ronnie Conway didn't know it. "Whoa! Whoa now! Wait just a dad-gum minute," he said. "I don't know nothin' about no stolen cars."

"Then you better have a good explanation of how this vehicle ended up here," said Cutter, picking up on Holly's rough-and-tough theme.

"An ol' Army buddy of mine, his family, the Kamps, they own a car lot over in DeLong," Conway told them. "He called me up and said he had a junker for me. Said a prominent local man died in it. People were comin' by to gawk at it. That the family just wanted it out of town and out of sight.

"LeRoy Kamp gave me two-hundred to come get it. That's all I know!"

Holly and Cutter shared a look. There was more to this and they both sensed it.

"What about paperwork?" asked Holly.

"Paperwork? Ma'am, look, lots of times with a wrecked car, especially one somebody died in, there's no paperwork," he told her. "People just want it gone."

"Then why did LeRoy lie to me about what he did with this car?" asked Holly.

Ronnie Conway swallowed hard and wet his lips.

"Mr. Conway, you seriously need to consider telling us what we want to know," said Cutter, propping one arm on the car's roof. "Miss Carter, here, owns a newspaper, and she's personal friends with the U.S. Attorney. One phone call from her and FBI men'll be swarmin' over this hill like red ants on a June bug."

"If your conscience is clear, then fine," said Holly. "But if not ..."

Ronnie Conway wiped his mouth. "Okay, Okay. Me'n LeRoy know each other from when we served together in Germany. In the Army. He was always braggin' about how his family owns a big car lot. I told him how I wanted to open my own garage and wrecker service. I did my tour and came back home to Moore's Bridge. I married and opened a shop, but it never took off. Now I do body work for the Ford place in town, and do a little towin' and shade-tree engine work on the side.

"Anyhow, a couple of years after LeRoy got out of the stockade, he called me. He heard I did some pullin' and salvage, and said he me might have some work for me."

The man's eyes darted back and forth from Holly to Cutter. "Is that it?" she asked. Conway stood silent but shifted from foot to foot. "All right. Come on, Cutter. Let's find a phone. We'll see if he has more to say to the FBI."

"No, wait!" pleaded Ronnie Conway. He wiped his sweating hands on his pants legs. "Just wait." He took a breath, then – "Three or four times a year, LeRoy calls me to pick up a car. Usually down some dirt road or out in a pasture," he told them. "All I have to do is haul it back here and leave it sit. Two or three days later, a couple of fellas come by and poke around in it. After they leave, I'm free to sell it off any way I want to."

"The same guys every time?" asked Cutter.

"One's always the same."

"And when they poke around in the cars, what do they find?" asked Holly.

"I don't know," he said and saw the incredulous looks from his visitors. "I swear! When they come around, all I do is point 'em to the car and make myself scarce. I don't know what they're fetchin', and I don't want to know."

Cutter propped against the Olds. "And you do all this for spare parts?"

Conway sighed. "LeRoy pays me five hundred up front."

Holly took a moment to think about all Ronnie Conway had told them, then – "Did those men you spoke of come around to get something out of my father's car?"

"No. No, they didn't." They looked at him. "Hey, you know the whole deal now. I got no reason to lie."

With Ronnie Conway's help, Cutter spent the next half hour tearing apart the interior of the Olds. They took out the seats, pulled the dash, tore out the buckled carpet and sliced into the cloth that hung from the interior of the roof looking for a set of glasses – which they did not find. They did, however, find T.L. Carter's gold pocket watch wedged in the crack of the back seat as Holly documented the process on film and Charlie watched. Her heart jumped when Cutter handed the watch to her. As a child she'd played with it many times. She opened the case. The hands were stopped at 8:38. She closed it, the hinges grinding with sand, and held it tight in her hand.

Cutter got his tool box out of the Lincoln's trunk and removed the steering wheel from the Olds. He placed the wheel in the convertible's trunk and shut it as Holly wrote a check for two hundred dollars. She handed it to Ronnie Conway as Cutter got in the passenger seat.

"What's this for?" he asked cautiously as she closed her purse and pushed her sunglasses onto her nose. "For your time and cooperation today, and for what I'll call a storage fee. No more parts get sold off that car. Understood?" He nodded, but Holly thought she saw the gears turning behind his eyes. "Mr. Conway, I believe this car was used in a crime, and I don't mean whatever piddling enterprise LeRoy Kamp is involved in.

"If we come back looking for it and it's gone, or if you tip LeRoy that we were here, so help me, I'll make it my business to see that the FBI turns your life inside out."

Chapter 9

∽

Holly and Cutter crossed the Sipsey River and turned north on Alabama 171. Just outside of Fayette they pulled into a burger and barbecue joint that had a paved parking lot. It also had four formidable steps but a sidewalk led around the side of the red clapboard building. In back, five picnic tables were situated on hardpack dirt beneath a large walnut tree. A small lake lay at the bottom of the hill.

Cutter placed their order at a window on the back deck and returned with two large glasses of tea and a basket of sweet potato chips. Holly was holding her father's watch in her hands, studying it.

"A sweet 'tater chip for your thoughts," he said.

Holly took it from Cutter's fingers and slipped it between her lips. "Those are good," she told him. Then, "I'm wondering how the watch my father carried during almost every waking moment of his life wound up lodged in the crack of the back seat."

"I could say it was because your father's car probably was tumbling in the current like a Matchbox toy in a washing machine. But you already know that," Cutter responded, watching Holly for a reaction. She kept her eyes on the timepiece. "We may never know. Just like we may never know whether your father removed those glasses from the glove box or if it was the work of the river."

Holly nodded as if she was hearing him from a distance. "Of course, you're right."

When it became clear she was going to say no more, Cutter said, "A person's family business is their business, and I try to stay clear of stuff that's none of my business. But it doesn't take a Sherlock Holmes to add up the questions you've been asking and see where you're going with them."

A bell rang beside the pick-up window. While Cutter went to get their food, Holly decided she was going to trust him with all she knew and suspected about her father's death. He'd earned it, more than once. When he returned, they ate and Holly shared everything – from facts to guesswork. Cutter listened and asked smart questions, Holly noted as she sipped her tea. Finally, he said, "When you add it all up? Yeah, I can see it bein' more than possible.

"Someone hit your father in the head with – well, we don't know with what yet. His glasses flew off and in the killer's panic he didn't notice the lens was missing," said Cutter, thinking out loud. "Then, Mr. Doe, let's call him, loads your father into the back of the Olds. Mr. Carter isn't dead, but since there's no sign that he was tied up – at least not according to the Oxford autopsy – he must have been unconscious. But Mr. Carter wasn't a small man. I'd say he went at least two-fifty. Maybe two-sixty or even seventy. That's a lot of weight to move from the library out to the car. Even if it was parked right in front."

"I've thought of that, too," said Holly.

"So, Mr. Doe would have to be a pretty big man or have help."

"Yes. How big would you say LeRoy Kamp is?" she asked.

"Six-one, two-thirty or so. He's big enough. But what was his motive?" wondered Cutter as he lifted a sweet potato chip to his mouth. "I suppose you've already ruled out plain ol' robbery?"

"Yes. My father never kept large amounts of cash at the house or in his wallet. And everything of real value is still there. There's noth-ing – well, nothing of real material value missing."

"But something is missing?"

Holly dropped her napkin into the plate and stared out at the lake. Two little boys were fishing with cane poles from a makeshift raft. "A painting," she said. "A painting of my mother that hung in the library."

"For all these years after your folks split up?"

"Yes. Daddy mentioned it in a letter just a few weeks before he died."

"That doesn't mean it had anything to do with your father's death. Or even that it was taken that night," he reasoned. "Maybe Mr. Tom took it for sentimental reasons. Especially after he found out you inherited Wolf's Run."

Holly smiled but there was no humor in it. "I wish I could lay it off on that. But if anyone loathed my mother more than Daddy, it was Tom. He never would have taken that painting."

Cutter considered all that he'd been told. "I heard Mr. Tom was out of town at a convention or somethin' when Mr. Carter died. I suppose you've confirmed that?"

"Yes. I talked to the deputy who reached him on the phone in Gulfport."

"So, he couldn't have done it himself."

"Himself?" asked Holly, looking deep into Cutter's eyes, trying to see if he had the audacity to be thinking the same thing she already was considering.

"Maybe Tom got tired of waiting for what he thought was going to be his inheritance," said Cutter. "Mr. Carter's will leaving the paper and the rest to you came as a shock to ever'body. Mr. Tom tried to play it off around town like he knew all about it. But –" he shrugged – "I don't know many people who believed it. And I heard Miss Mary Nell took to her bed for several days with one of her sick headaches."

When Holly didn't speak, Cutter went ahead and said it plain, "Tom could have paid LeRoy to do it and make it look like an accident. But in case there was any suspicion, Gulfport makes for a good alibi."

Holly finally blinked and heard herself swallow. She started to speak, but her mouth was dry. She ran her tongue over her lips. "Tom's my brother, but ... God help me, Cutter, I've thought the same thing."

"If you hadn't, you wouldn't be near as smart as I think you are."

"Sometimes smart's overrated," she said and pushed her plate away. "I think I've lost my appetite."

"I haven't," said Cutter, pulling the plate with the remaining half a cheeseburger to him.

Holly watched the kids fishing from the raft on the lake while Cutter finished. It made her ache to think Tom could somehow be a part of this – if there was any "this" to be a a part of. She still had no real proof a crime occurred.

Cutter stood and carried their empty paper plates and other scraps to a black, fifty-gallon drum mounted between two pine four-by-fours. When he returned to the table with his Ray-Bans on his nose and a toothpick at the corner of his mouth, Holly looked up at him. "Maybe I'm stacking one coincidence on another and creating a lot of melodrama over nothing," she said, squeezing T.L. Carter's watch in both hands in front for her. Cutter propped a work boot on the bench seat. "Knowing that Daddy was coming all the way to California to be with me after my back surgery, there are so many things I wish I'd had the chance to say to him. And so many I hope he might have said to me.

"Maybe I'm looking for somebody or something to blame because I never got that chance."

"What's your gut tell you?"

Holly didn't hesitate – "That my very fastidious father did not walk out of Wolf's Run on a cold, rainy night in his shirt sleeves headed for some unscheduled meeting, or whatever, then miss a turn he'd made at least five days a week for most of the last ten years in all kinds of weather," she told him, then drew in a long breath and let it out – "Ohhhh, but it breaks my heart to think Tom might have been … involved."

"Then prove he wasn't," said Cutter, picking up the keys from the table. "Come on. I'll drive and let you and your gut sort things out."

Chapter 10

෴

By the middle of the following week, the National Guard still was patrolling the streets of DeLong and major county roads. The word was that the curfew would be lifted for the weekend and the Guard would pull out on Sunday, but no one knew for sure. If any progress had been made on catching McBride or the Klansmen who killed Ridge Bellafont and maimed Eve Howard, no one knew about that either. On page three of *The Current-Leader* was a picture of a scarecrow depicting my father as a Judas. The caption asked for anyone who had seen the scarecrow in some farmer's field to call the sheriff's office. Ironically, the photo bore Mr. Bellafont's credit line.

On Wednesday afternoon Cutter pulled his jeep into a parking place in front of *The Current-Leader* building. A glazer was finishing the installation of a large piece of plate glass on one side of the new door while a painter was carefully lettering a sign onto the other window.

The Cattahatchie Current-Leader ... Since 1836 ... The Conscience of the Community ...

"Nice," he said to Miss Frances as he stepped into the rebuilt lobby. The smell of smoke was mixed with the fresh scent of just-cut pine. Most of the new work still needed painting.

"Yes," said Frances Ragland, who had worked behind the newspaper's counter for more than fifty years. "I'd been telling T.L. for years that this place needed to be renovated. I suppose I always knew it would take a fire or tornado it to get it done."

"Yes, ma'am. Is Miss Carter around?"

"No, son. She ran routes all morning, then she and her friend, Miss Julie, were going to Memphis to try to see Miss Eve before her mother takes her back to California. Of course, they'll have to be back in DeLong before dark."

"Yes, ma'am."

"Would you like to leave a message?"

"No thanks," he said and turned for the door. "I'll try to catch her out at Wolf's Run. Or drop by tomorrow."

"Before you go," said Miss Frances, "may I ask, are you a church-goer?"

Cutter paused a beat, then said, "My momma did her best to raise me and Rose in the church until, uhm –"

"Yes, honey, I understand."

"I haven't been much since, but I still like the music."

"We're starting a little Sunday morning prayer meeting," said Miss Frances. "I don't want to call it a church service. We don't have a pastor. At least not yet. We're just going to read the Bible and pray, and sing praises to the Lord.

"Miss Holly is letting us hold it here," she said. Cutter could hardly believe what he was hearing from one of the pillars of First Denomination. "Down in the pressroom. It's a big space. We can open the bay door for air and there's plenty of parking.

"You'd be welcome to come. Miss Holly is going to lead the music. She has an absolutely lovely voice, you know?"

"I know she can really play the guitar, but I've never heard her sing."

"When you do, you'll remember it. It has amazing strength, amazing depth. Like Miss Holly herself. And beauty, too, of course," said Miss Frances. "God blessed her with that voice and it does my old heart good to see her using it now to praise the Lord."

Cutter shifted on his feet. "Miss Frances, if you don't mind me asking – I mean, you and Mr. George have been members of First Denomination since … since?"

"My father was a brick mason and he helped lay the foundation for the original sanctuary at First Denomination in 1877," said Miss Frances. "My first date with George – though we didn't call them dates back then – he rented a buggy with the most beautiful bay mare I believe I've ever seen, and we went to services and an all-day singin' and dinner on the grounds." Cutter could see that her eyes were getting misty. "George and I were married there in 1898. And we were blessed to see five of our six children saved in that sanctuary. Along with scads of grandchildren and even great-grands."

Miss Frances wiped a tear from her eye. "I'm sorry," she said. "George and I love First Denomination, but somehow it's lost its way." Cutter nodded thoughtfully, assuming that was all Miss Frances would have to say, but she went on – "Mind you, I don't entirely blame Brother MacAllister. A flock can't be led someplace it doesn't want to go. But Brother Mac has given a lot of otherwise decent folks an excuse for their fear and hatred of nee'gras. And of plain ol' change. He's cloaked it in the robes of Jesus, and that's just wrong.

"George has tried to speak up within the leadership, but they dismiss him. Too old. Not in touch with today's world. But I think it's them that's not in touch with today's world. Jesus was all about people growin' in their spirit and changin', and learnin' to love each other. Not ... Not this," she said, opening her arms and looking around the room – its high corners still sooty with smoke. After a moment she dropped her arms tiredly to her sides and turned her milky eyes back on Cutter. "Anyways, after what Brother Mac said on Sunday about dear Mr. Ridge and the others, George and I spent a long time in prayer. We just can't be part of it anymore, as much as it pains us. And there are quite a few others who feel the same way."

Cutter wasn't sure what to say, so he said nothing.

"Well now, that's the end of my sermon," said Miss Frances, reaching for a tissue from a box by the cash register and dabbing her eyes. "So sorry. I started out merely wanting to extend an invitation. But ... But these are such fragile times."

"Yes, ma'am, I understand," said Cutter. "And I appreciate the invite."

* * *

When Holly turned her convertible into the driveway at Wolf's Run, the shadows were long and deep in the yard. The sun was down behind Blue Mountain and the sky glowed with a halo the color of a robin's egg tied with pink ribbons of cloud.

Cutter sat in his jeep next to the garage.

"My, my!" said Julie Davis. "This *is* a pleasant surprise."

"Hi," he said.

"Hi," said Holly, happier to see Cutter that she wanted to show. But Charlie didn't bother to hide her delight. Cutter squatted to pet her.

"How's Miss Howard?"

"How did you know we were in Memphis?" asked Holly as she transferred to her chair.

"I dropped by the newspaper this afternoon. Miss Frances told me."

"Eve's mother hired private security guards. We couldn't get in to see her," Holly explained. "But one of the nurses told me her condition had been upgraded from serious to good. But her life? It'll never be the same ... because she came here with me."

"No, Holly. It'll never be the same because she made a bad decision," said Julie Davis. "In the end, that decision is what got her hurt and got your Mr. Bellafont killed."

That hard truth hung in the twilight air before Holly broke the silence. "Cutter, what brings you here?"

"I've been giving some thought to what we talked about over in Alabama the other day." He hesitated. "About your dad."

Holly glanced at Julie Davis then back to Cutter. "You can talk in front of Julie," she said. "I've told her everything. She cut her journalism teeth as a night cops reporter in L.A. I thought she might be able to help."

"All right," said Cutter, propping on the front fender of the Lincoln – its paint job still scuffed from Holly's ugly welcome back to DeLong. "Here's what I've been thinking. I can personally vouch for the fact that no cars came down Blue Mountain Road headed to the highway in the two or three hours after Mr. Carter went into the river," he said. "That means that whoever did this had to go out the back way, around the mountain to Pickens' Ferry Road."

"Whoa!" said Holly. "You know that the road all but ends about two miles west of here in Lawler Bottom."

"All but ends," he said. "There's still a track through there. It can be done. I've done it."

"On a night like that?"

"No, but –"

"Wait a minute," said Julie. "Why not just hide in the woods until the coast is clear and then be on your way?"

"Whoever did this, didn't walk out here from town – or wherever he came from," said Cutter. "He had to have a vehicle. And between here and Lawler Bottom, there's no place to hide one – at least not on a night like that."

"They could have just sat and waited it out," said Julie. "Or abandoned the car and come back once things calmed down."

Holly was nodding more to herself than to something in particular that Cutter or Julie had said. She was beginning to see where Cutter wad going. "That's possible," he said. "But there are two more houses on this road, including one right at the edge of Lawler Bottom. He'd be takin' an awful big chance that someone wouldn't drive by, see the car and remember it."

"Or with all the excitement, that a sheriff's car wouldn't cruise down to the end of the road," offered Holly.

"Yep. That, too."

"Okay," said Julie. "How does that help us in terms of proving who killed Mr. Carter? Or even that he was killed?"

Cutter straightened and took his hands from the front pockets of his jeans. "We'd have to get lucky," he said, looking up the driveway toward the road, "but – well, Miss Carter is right. It'd be mighty tough getting across Lawler Bottom and around to Pickens' Ferry Road on a night like that. In fact, I'd say it would be nigh on to impossible without getting stuck at least once. So –"

"So!" said Holly. "He would've had to walk out to the other side of the bottom and knock on some ol' farmer's door."

"Yep. And hire him to pull the car out with his truck or tractor," said Cutter.

Julie had been listening carefully and Cutter and Holly could see the gears turning behind her reporter's eyes. "That's all good," she said after a moment. "And I hate to throw a monkey wrench in it, but –"

"Go ahead," said Holly. "We don't want to go down the wrong road."

"So to speak," said Julie, flashing a quick smile. Then – "Okay. If that bottom, as you call it, is as bad as you say in that kind of weather, if it got stuck, why not just leave it? At least for a few days. Then come back and get it pulled out. If questions came up later, you could claim you stuck the night before Mr. Carter's death, or the night after – or two nights after. With as little traffic as that bottom sounds like it gets that time of year, it would be hard to prove otherwise."

"That's a good question, Miss Davis," agreed Cutter, "if we were in a court of law. But we're not. We're just nosin' around, trying to see if there's anything the courts should be involved in. It wouldn't be iron-clad proof, but to my mind, it'd be mighty interestin' to know who got that vehicle pulled out."

"Yes, it would," said Holly, and they all were quiet for a time, turning over the possibilities in their minds. There was only the sound of cicadas and then the rustle of bat wings emerging from the ramshackle greenhouse as a string of them disappeared over the valley. Then, "There's something else, too," she said. "It's – what would you say Cutter? – twelve to fifteen miles back to Highway 27?"

"Closer to fifteen, I'd say."

"Unless you were dressed for it and used to it, that would be a very long, very cold walk in the middle of a rainy night," she said. "So, even if he left the vehicle, I'd say the odds are good he knocked on somebody's door and asked to use their telephone."

"Okay," said Julie. "Sold."

"Cutter, you're brilliant!" enthused Holly.

He laughed, saying, "Thanks, but it's only brilliant if I'm right," and Holly was reminded again how much she liked the sound of his laughter.

Julie caught the look between them. "I'm going to go on in and freshen up," she said, turning for the ramp by the kitchen door. "You two don't do anything I wouldn't."

In the late twilight Cutter's eyes glowed almost like cat's eyes, drawing to them whatever last light of the day remained.

"You said you came by the office today?" asked Holly, mostly to have something to say amid the sing-song cry of the cicadas. "I thought you were working a survey job."

"I went down to Hughestown Monday morning to meet up with them, but Mr. Scott said they had a full crew."

Holly considered that. "Did they? Or is it payback for helping me?"

Cutter shrugged. "All I know is what he told me."

"Either way, you're out a week's wages. Cutter, please, at least let me pay you for the time you put in on our trip to Alabama."

"Nope. No way," he told her. "But I was thinkin', if you have some chores that need doing at the paper or around here. Like, well – I see the grass has gotten pretty deep in the ditches along your fence line. I could sling blade 'em. And that fence could use a coat of paint. Of course, it'll need to be scraped first."

"And that old greenhouse," said Holly. "There are vines growing wild. No telling what's living in there. Besides bats. The tables and floors are covered with broken pots, broken glass." She tapped the right-side tire on her chair. "That's why I haven't been inside. I don't need a flat."

"Then how about it?" he asked. "I can take care of all that for you."

"All right, Cutter. You're on," she said. "But before you start those projects, how would you like a different job?"

"What's the job?"

"Reporter. Or private detective, if you prefer. Mostly it would mean shaking a few hands and chatting with some farmers."

"On the back side of this mountain?"

"Uh-huh. And I'll be glad to pay you for your time."

"The painting and cleanup around here, I'll be happy get paid for," he said. "The other? I'll put it on your tab."

Chapter 11

❧

Holly was shooting pool in the library with Gerry Yards on Saturday night when the phone rang. Mickey Dawton of the *London Telegraph*, Tim Holland of *The New York Times* and Julie Davis were playing gin rummy at the card table in the center of the room.

"If that's room service, tell them to send up another bottle of gin, if you please," said Mickey Dawton as Holly wheeled past on her way to the phone on the desk.

"Hello."

"Hello, Miss Carter?" she heard a voice ask over the twang of a country-rock band and the roar of raised voices and clacking glasses.

"Yes. Cutter? Is that you?"

Gerry Yards twisted his pool cue in his hands.

"Yes," he said from a pay phone beside the men's room at The Gin. "I wanted to fill you in on what I found out."

"Is it good news?" she asked, her voice raised.

"Maybe. But, hey, I can barely hear you."

"Same here."

"Look, with the curfew just bein' lifted, this place is crazy. How about I come by tomorrow?"

"I know Miss Frances told you about the little – well, prayer fellowship, whatever you want to call it – we're holding at the paper in the morning. Why don't you come?" she tried, nearly shouting into the phone. "We could go for a drive afterwards. I could pack a picnic lunch."

"Yeah, yeah. Okay," he said, holding a finger to the ear opposite the phone. "But I'll pick you up at Wolf's Run *after* your prayer meetin'. And this time, lunch is my treat. You paid over in Alabama."

"One o'clock?" he shouted.

"Yes. One is fine!" she told him. "I'll see you then!"

Holly turned, her lips revealing a small, optimistic smile that Julie immediately noticed. She cocked a brow and Holly did her best to wipe the smile from her face but couldn't get rid of it entirely.

"Your break," she said to Gerry Yards as she picked up her stick.

Without a word, he lined up the cue ball and sent it flying against the others so hard that it popped up and jumped off the table. "I'm tired of this game," he said, dropping his stick onto the table.

* * *

On Sunday afternoon, Cutter turned out of the driveway at Wolf's Run onto Blue Mountain Road, then north on Highway 27. It was hot but in his open jeep, the Sunday afternoon sun was comfortable on his face and on Holly Lee Carter's shoulders. She was wearing a yellow sundress. Her wheelchair was folded and tied down atop Cutter's steel footlocker.

"How did the prayer service go this morning?" he asked.

"Good, I suppose. There were about thirty-five people. And not just people from First Denomination. Miss Frances's husband, Mr. George, led us in reading from the tenth chapter of Matthew where Jesus talks about take up your cross and follow me."

"You don't seem too enthused about it," he commented as they met a trio of National Guard trucks heading south, out of the county.

"I don't have any doubt that Charles MacAllister and his pals are leading people down a wrong and ugly road," said Holly. "The kind of road that Jesus never intended for His people to go down. But I grew up in First Denomination, too. Before Charles MacAllister came along. Before the gospel according to Cecil Weathers was being preached. I hate to see First Denomination coming apart like it is. And some other churches around here, too.

"Before this is over, there'll be flocks that will never come back together," she said. "But that's really what Matthew Ten is about. It's about doing the right thing even when it's hard. Even when it's unpopular and painful. That's always been part of being a true Christ follower.

"But I don't take any satisfaction from what's happening. In the end, I have to believe it will all be for the best. Right now, though, it just feels very sad."

At the foot of Two-Mile Bridge, which terminated in Tennessee, they turned onto Pickens' Ferry Road. Ten minutes later, they passed the cutoff to Pickens' Ferry A.M.E. Church where Reverend Clemmer and his National Coalition for Justice volunteers had set up a tent city – or village, at least. Through a thick stand of cypress, they could only glimpse the clapboard church with its tin steeple, and the small circus-like tent that served as headquarters for the voter registration push. Several fire circles were visible and a row of outhouses had been built to one side, the plywood painted green. Two unarmed men sat on folding chairs at the end of the road, ready to check cars before they got close to the encampment. Some good that would do if push came to shove – or to gun shots.

Three miles beyond the church the road bent away from the water and began to wrap southwest around Blue Mountain.

Holly gripped the back of Cutter's seat, for balance, she told herself. But when her thumb slid between the vinyl and the dampness of Cutter's black T-shirt it raised the goose flesh on her arms and she had to fight to keep her breathing even. What in the world was she doing going out alone for a picnic with this *kid?* she asked herself. But in the sunshine and fresh air, and surrounded by the music beaming off of WHBQ's Memphis tower and through the radio in Cutter's jeep, she had to admit that at the moment she didn't care. Not even a little bit. But she was curious.

"You still haven't told me where we're going," said Holly. "You found someone who pulled a car out of Lawler Bottom that night, didn't you?" Cutter nodded. "*Who?*"

"A farmer name of Efram Cole."

"You're taking me to meet him?"

Cutter chuckled. "No. That probably wouldn't be the best idea. He's a pretty rough ol' cob. He doesn't care much for this integratin' stuff or people he thinks are pushing it."

"Like me?"

"Right. But he loves Cattahatchie High football. Listens to every game on the radio. Shoot, he remembered things about games I played in my freshman year that I don't even remember."

"Where we're going happens to be in the neighborhood, you might say, but it's a spot I came across several years ago on a Sunday afternoon kinda like this – just drivin' the backroads. Me and Nate enjoyin' a cold beer and God's own sunshine."

"Okay, okay. Come on, give!" she told him. "What'd this Mr. Cole say?"

Cutter smiled, the Ray-Bans hiding his eyes. "Take it easy. Let's enjoy lunch. That'll be dessert."

Holly wasn't smiling. "Come on, Cutter, this is serious business. We're talking about –"

"Easy there. I know what we're talking about," he said, not angrily but firmly. "The news ain't goin' no place in the next hour. Let's just relax. There'll be time enough to figure on what I found out after we eat."

"Do I have a choice?"

"No."

Holly took in a breath, her hand still on the back of Cutter's seat, but gripping it tight now with irritation. She was a woman not used to being told no. Her family's money and position, and her own beauty and considerable talent as a photographer and a singer, and as a lover, had insulated her from that word most of her life. Some had said it to her, but few had been able to stand by it or enforce it if they were denying her something she really wanted. The biggest no she had ever heard was in a Honolulu hospital room when she had asked her doctor, "Will I ever walk again?" And it appeared her own damaged spinal cord or nature or God Almighty was going to stand by that "no".

Holly let out her breath, took another and let it out, too. With it she let go of her impatience and let herself come back to the moment with Cutter. The afternoon was too beautiful to spoil.

"Okay then," she said. "What's for lunch?"

The gravel lane dipped and rose for another mile or so, then in the middle of a sharp curve was a steep cutback that twisted up the side of the mountain. Cutter rolled the steering wheel under his palm as he shifted into low. Suddenly, the jeep felt as if it were going straight up. Holly's fingers screwed into the back of Cutter's seat and gripped the frame of the windshield. They climbed on the road and made another sharp turn and emerged in front of the remnants of an old farmhouse surrounded by tall grass and shaded by old elms. Only the brick piers, part of the floor and a fieldstone chimney framed by the north wall remained.

They drove around to the back of the house to where the elms' high limbs met and tangled to create a frame for the black mirror that was Moccasin Slough, spreading below them for miles to the east and west.

Holly loosened her grip and sighed, "Oh, my goodness, Cutter. What a beautiful spot."

Cutter climbed out of the jeep and began unlatching his gear in back. He lifted out his ice chest and flipped open his foot locker. He pulled out one of the most ornately designed and perfectly executed quilts Holly had ever seen.

"One of Miss Jenny's?"

"Yes. I took it with me when I left. Otherwise Tony would have sold it like all the rest,"said Cutter, spreading it beneath the biggest of the elms. The pattern formed a brilliant orange, brown, gold and green sunflower. Cutter returned to the passenger side of the jeep. "Okay. I promised to take you to my favorite lunch place. You ready?"

Holly looked at him. "What about my wheelchair?" Holly made herself ask.

"I don't think you're going to need it."

In the blackness of Cutter's sunglasses Holly could see herself reflected. It was the image of a twenty-eight-year-old woman – healthy, whole, even beautiful. Thankfully the need and the fear didn't show. Without the wheelchair there was no sign of how much her life had changed since she last rode these gravel lanes with other handsome young football stars on other days, and on other nights. She looked like the Holly Lee Carter she had expected to be at twenty-eight. Not the one whose legs hung useless under the skirt of her dress; not the one who slept alone in Meemaw's bed.

"Put your arms around my neck," Cutter instructed. Holly was tired of demanding explanations, reasoning things out and giving orders. She did as she was told. "You ready?"

She swallowed and wet her lips. "I think so," she whispered. Cutter tilted his head. "I mean, yes," she said more firmly to his silent question. "I'm ready."

For an hour or more they relaxed on the sunflower quilt, eating cold fried chicken, potato salad and baked beans from the Cotton Café.

With the blade of his Swiss Army knife he sliced a block of sharp cheddar. He poured big glasses of sweet tea from a gallon jug. As they ate, squirrels performed acrobatics in the limbs overhead and in the clear middle of Moccasin Slough ski boats cut silver lines in the black glass surface. In the distance they looked like small, intricate models. The radio on Cutter's jeep remained tuned to the Best of The Beatles Weekend.

Having eaten their fill, they sat shoulder to shoulder against the big elm. Holly sighed, "Ohhh, that was delicious. Thank you."

"I didn't make it. I just bought it. Thank Miss Winona."

"Then thank you for bringing me here," she said, very aware of his nearness. "I'm sure there are any number of young women who would love to be here with you this afternoon."

"I don't bring people here," he said. "This is where I come when I don't want to be bothered. Sometimes I even pitch camp up here when The Well starts feelin' like a cheap motel. People showin' up, usually drunk, at all hours of the day and night wanting to talk about some game I played in two or three years ago." He shook his head. "Sometimes it amazes me how much those games mean to people." His lips tightened and he worked his jaw side to side as if chewing on something, then – "Like they're all livin' inside me."

Holly thought about that and how true that had been much of her life in DeLong. How many of her high school girlfriends had secretly wished they were her? Her looks, her independence. Her Corvette. Some even said so. Now there was the wheelchair folded at the back of the jeep and catheter bag strapped to her thigh. *Be careful what you wish for,* she thought, and more than supposed the same could apply to those who fawned over Cutter. How many would trade three hours of Friday night glory for the hell he'd lived through at the Old Ambrose Place? And, to a degree, still was caught up in.

"Anyway," he said, changing his tone, "I guess you could call this my thinkin' spot. I keep it to myself."

"In that case, I'm honored that you brought me here."

The muscles at the corners of his mouth twitched and his lips parted in a small, quick smile. "I'm honored that you came," he said and lay his hand atop hers. Not holding it really, simply resting it there atop her hand, on her leg. Holly straightened a bit. Imperceptably, she hoped. She knew she should move her hand, or his ... she knew she should ... *she knew!* ... but she didn't. They sat there for several minutes against the elm, listening to *Strawberry Fields Forever* – Holly feeling her heart beating harder in her chest than it should. She fought the urge to put her head on Cutter's shoulder, but if the subject didn't change quickly, she knew she'd lose that battle, too. She cleared her throat softly. "You told me that the news from Mr. Cole would be my dessert."

"I did. But the truth is I didn't tell you what I found out from Mr. Cole before we ate because I was afraid it would spoil your appetite," he said, and that changed the rhythm in Holly's chest again. She didn't look at him. She looked straight ahead at the lake –"Okay. So tell me now."

"All right," he said and began. "Efram Cole lives about another two miles or so farther around the mountain with his wife, three boys and a girl. He farms about two hundred acres. Corn mostly.

"One cold, rainy night in late March or early April, he says, a fella came to his door right about when the ten o'clock news was startin'. The fella said he was comin' back from a friend's house, hit a deer and slid off in the ditch. Mr. Cole didn't believe him because he knows everybody who lives between his house and Lawler Bottom, and just about all their friends, too. But the man offered him a hundred dollars cash money to pull him out. So, Mr. Cole got his clothes on and got his tractor."

"A hundred, huh? It sounds like he wanted out of that ditch pretty bad," said Holly. "What did he look like?"

"Hard to say, according to Mr. Cole. The fella was wearing a black rain slicker. The kind with the built-in hood and a piece that sort of snapped across the front. It hid most of his hair and the lower part of his face. Plus, the night was black as tar and this fella sort of shied away from the light. Stayed out on the porch, in the cold while Mr. Cole got dressed, even though Mrs. Cole tried to get him to come inside for some hot coffee," Cutter explained. "Mr. Cole said the man was about my size. Dark eyes. Dark hair and mustache."

"A big enough man to do what we think might have been done," said Holly. "He could have been LeRoy Kamp."

"He could have been anybody," Cutter cautioned.

"What about the car?"

"A white, late-model Ford station wagon."

"Huh," Holly grunted. "Not exactly the kind of ride LeRoy favors. Unless he's changed an awful lot, he's more the Camaro, four-wheel-drive pickup type. I don't suppose Mr. Cole remembered a tag number?"

"It didn't have one. But he did remember that the spot where the tag should have been wasn't covered in mud, like the rest of the bumper. Like it had been taken off right before the driver went to look for a farmhouse."

Holly sighed. "That's interesting. It confirms at least some of our speculation, *if* that was the same night Daddy died. Mr. Cole didn't remember? And what about the mystery man in the rain slicker? Could he identify him if saw him again?"

"He's not sure is the answer to both questions. And I didn't want to press him until I talked to you."

Cutter's hand still was atop Holly's and she still had made no effort to move it. That fact slowed down her thinking process as if every thought had to pass through that connection between them like a circuit. After a moment, she said, "It could all be a lot of coincidence. We don't even know if it was the same night. But something tells me – something tells me it was.

"But, hey, you misjudged me. It's not definitive but it certainly didn't ruin my digestion. I'm tougher than that," she said, smiling. "That was good work. I didn't expect you to come back with a signed confession from someone."

"I'm not finished," said Cutter and lifted his hand from hers. Holly nearly reached for it but made a fist and didn't as he twisted in the blanket so that he could look straight at her. "This could be a coin-cidence, too. So, I'm not accusing," he said. Holly's eyes settled on his now and he thought he saw the slightest flicker of fear in them regarding whatever it was he was about to say. "Up until right after Mr. Carter's passin', Miss Mary Nell drove a white, late-model Ford station wagon." Holly's eyes were fixed on Cutter's and her mouth parted slightly as if to speak or ask a question, but she didn't. "Miss Mary Nell is a cheerleader sponsor, you know. A lot of times, espe-cially durin' summer two-a-days, the cheerleaders come by after practice with cold drinks and stuff. I've drunk Kool-Aid from the tailgate of her station wagon many times."

The gold flecks in Holly's eyes sparkled as if the anger inside her was becoming molten.

"Here's the rest of it," he went on. "Mr. Cole told me there was damage to the right front fender. Broken headlight, a little crinkle in the sheet metal and a couple of cracks in the windshield. Like I said, the fella told Mr. Cole he hit a deer."

The pleasant buzz in Holly's chest had gone to a grinding of gears in her mind. "You're saying Mary Nell hit Daddy with her car? That doesn't make sense," said Holly. "We know, or think we know, something happened to Daddy in the library."

"I'm not saying she hit him with her car. I'm just telling you what Mr. Cole told me," said Cutter. "Everything could have gone down like we've talked about, and LeRoy or her – or whoever it was – hit a deer on the way out. There's plenty of 'em out this way to hit."

"But Mr. Cole didn't see a woman in the car?"

"He didn't see anyone else. But he didn't exactly search the car."

Holly nodded slightly as she thought. "You said Mary Nell drove the station wagon until right after Daddy died. How do you remember –?"

"There was a lot of talk about it," said Cutter. "You know, café talk. About how mean the world, in general, is gettin' and Memphis in particular.

"As best I recall, the story goes that Miss Mary Nell went up there a couple days after your daddy's car went in the river to shop for funeral clothes for her and the kids. I don't think they'd even found his body yet. Of course, everybody assumed. Anyway, how I heard it was a colored kid jumped her in the parking lot of some department store, beat her up, took her keys and stole the car."

"And you believed it?" asked Holly.

Cutter shrugged. "I didn't have any reason not to believe it at the time," he said. "And it wouldn't have made any difference if I didn't. In light of the supposin' we're doing, and what Mr. Cole told me, it's a *lot* of concidence. What I can say for a fact is that somebody beat Miss Mary Nell up pretty bad. By the time your daddy's funeral came around about a week later, they were faded, but you could tell she'd had a pair of deep purple shiners."

As was his nature, Cutter had said what he needed to say and didn't feel a need to keep on about it. Holly's eyes and thoughts had drifted away. He propped his forearm on his knee, his hand holding the ice tea glass. He sipped from it now and then. After a time, Holly's eyes came back to him.

"I hadn't considered Mary Nell. Mostly because she's about a size two. I can't imagine her overpowering my father," Holly said. "And she certainly could not have dragged him from the library and put him into his car. Not without help. But Miss Prim-and-Proper Sunday School Teacher, Cheerleader Sponsor, Country Club Queen Bee hooked up with a general scumbag, ex-con like LeRoy? It's hard to image."

"Work at The Gin for a few a months," said Cutter, "and no kind of hook-up surprises you."

"That's the truth," she said, remembering the many nights at The Gin when she'd hooked up with someone that would have shocked her friends – shocked anyone in DeLong who thought they knew her. Some of them even shocked her.

"Or it might not have been a hook up at all," said Cutter. "It could have been a straight cash deal."

"It could have been," Holly agreed. "Still, I'd have never thought LeRoy had the gumption for contract murder. But people do change."

Cutter nodded. "So what's next?"

Holly already had been thinking about that. She said, "To get a good picture of LeRoy for you to show to Mr. Cole."

"And how are we going to manage that?"

"Simple. I have a five-hundred millimeter telephoto lens, a dark room, and I know how to use both."

Except for the radio, the squirrels and an occasional bird song they sat in silence for a time. Finally, Cutter asked, "You okay?"

"I guess you'd have to define 'okay'," she said. "In spite of her snotty attitude, Daddy always treated Mary Nell very well. At least from what I know and have heard. He made her an officer in the corporation, gave her an office and a salary. Though from what I've learned since I got back, she did precious little except collect a check and attend press association conventions on the company dime."

Cutter thought about that for a moment. "A press convention? Is that where Mr. Tom was when your dad went in the river?"

"Yes," she said, thinking the same thought. "But Mary Nell didn't go. She stayed behind."

Cutter made a mark in the air with his finger. "Chalk up another coincidence."

Holly said nothing. Then, finally – "I need to get back. I have three or four hours of office work to do before I put my head on a pillow. And a lot to think about."

Cutter stood. "Sure," he said and began collecting the picnic gear and putting it back in the jeep. When everything was put away except the quilt, he returned and slipped his right arm under Holly's knees and his left around her back. She put her arms around his neck and inhaled his scent, which was salty and clean. He lifted her with ease, and held her not as if she was fragile or breakable, or perhaps already broken, but like she was precious.

"Thank you for not telling me about Mary Nell before we ate," she said, her face close enough that Cutter could feel her breath on his neck as he carried her the twenty feet to the jeep. "You were right. It would have spoiled my appetite."

He eased her into the seat. "I do have dessert for you, though."

"Cutter, I'm so full, I couldn't –"

"Just one bite," he said. "It won't take but a minute."

Cutter shook off the quilt and folded it with military precision, fit it into the footlocker on the jeep and closed it. Then he climbed into the driver's seat and wheeled the jeep around. But instead of heading for the steep road down from the plateau, he swung around what had been the front of the house and drove through a gap in the split-rail fence. He went over a small rise and down into a flat where an abandoned orchard spread out over several acres. Cutter stopped and walked around to the passenger side where a patch of strawberries had found its own wild ways. The fruit was ripe and ready – big and red and bright and plentiful.

"Those are amazing!" said Holly, the fragrance of the fresh berries permeating the air like sweet, red sunshine. "Look at the size of them."

Cutter pulled several massive berries the size of small apples. "Are they all right to eat?" Holly asked.

"I've eaten 'em by the dozen and they haven't killed me yet."

He held the fruit out to her and she reached for it but when she put her hand on it, Cutter didn't let go. She looked at him for a moment with large, questioning eyes, the buzzing in her chest returning with a roar. She pulled again, drawing the fruit toward her mouth along with Cutter's hand. She opened her lips, her teeth and took the fruit into her mouth as Cutter held it. Her first bite was tentative, but the next was deep, and by then the juice had hit her tongue and was streaming warm down her throat. She moaned with pure pleasure and her eyelids half closed and now she wanted it all. She took the third and largest bite and her lips, as full and ripe as the fruit, brushed Cutter's fingers. The juice swelled from the corner of her mouth and ran toward her chin but she never took her eyes off Cutter even as he pulled his black T-shirt from the front of his jeans and stepped closer so he could stretch it and wipe the juice from her chin. Suddenly her hand was on his bare belly. It felt like warm, evenly beveled metal, and she gasped.

It was then that Cutter bent to kiss her. For a split second it crossed Holly's mind that she should turn her face or say something or – but that thought never came to action and she didn't resist. She opened her lips, closed her eyes and eagerly took the fruit he offered and gave him the same. She tasted like warm strawberries and Cutter leaned in, wanting to taste all her juices. His hand cupped the back her neck and she rested into it as they kissed long and deep and again, and again. When her eyes finally fluttered open, she saw Cutter's hand on her left knee. Slightly above it really, on her thigh, and Holly's breath caught in her chest. She reached for his hand and grasped it firmly, and with all the strength she had left to resist him, she said, "No, Cutter! I – I can't!" And she turned her face away. In a flash all of the looks and smiles they'd shared came back to her, and the way she had allowed Cutter's hand to rest atop her hand, atop her leg as they talked. "I know I led you on. I know I did. And I'm sorry," she told him in a small, anguished voice, sniffling and not looking at him. "But I can't let this happen. I can't!

"Please take me home. Please take me home *now!*"

Chapter 12

꩜

Cutter and Holly said little on the drive back to Wolf's Run, only now the silence didn't seem easy or comfortable. Holly searched for the right words to explain why she had pushed him away, though she wanted him like nothing and no one she had wanted since Vietnam. Maybe long before Vietnam. But the words wouldn't come. Even small talk about two-a-day football practices and the annual county fair starting in a week felt strained.

When they got to the house Julie Davis was on the porch with Charlie and they both came out to greet them. "I thought you two had run off," she said.

Cutter untied Holly's wheelchair and placed the cushion in the seat. She'd been dreading this moment since they left the old farmhouse. The moment when he would take her into his arms again and her heart would start …and … "You know, if you put the chair right here, close, I think I can transfer myself down into it."

"Holly, are you sure?" asked Julie. "It's kind of a –"

"I'm sure."

Cutter positioned the chair as Holly instructed, and she managed the difficult shift, though her feet remained in the jeep. "Could you please get my legs?"

Julie Davis took Holly's legs by the ankles and placed them on the foot rests. They smoothed her skirt and Holly pivoted around and backed up at the same time, putting several feet between her and Cutter. He was nineteen – well, almost – and she had led him on in all sorts of small ways that had led up to the moment in the strawberry field. She expected hot-blooded anger, but when he spoke, there was none of it. At least not on the surface. "I'll clean out the ditches tomorrow. Then start on the greenhouse Tuesday. Maybe I can do it in a day. If not, I'll wrap that up Wednesday. Then strip and paint the fence on Thursday and Friday."

Holly was surprised he still planned to do the work. "That's fine, unless you have other –"

"No. Unless you'd rather I –"

"No. The work needs doing. I just thought –"

"Then I'll be here in the morning," he said, walking around the jeep. He got in and turned the key.

"Thank you," she managed. "It was a beautiful afternoon."

Cutter looked her over for a long moment, then backed the jeep up, swung it around and drove away. Julie Davis' eyes followed the jeep then came back to Holly. "What was that?"

"Don't ask."

"Seriously. There was enough tension between you two to break glass."

"Julie, please."

"And I'm not talking the good kind."

Holly pivoted away. "I don't want to talk about it."

When she turned to head for the ramp, Gerry Yards was leaning on the porch railing. "I've been waiting on you to go to the office," he told her. "If you're done playing in the sandbox with the local children, we grown-ups have actual work to do."

* * *

By the time Holly was ready for work after a mostly sleepless Sunday night she expected to – or was it hoped to? – look out her bedroom window and see Cutter's jeep next to the garage. But Cutter wasn't there, nor did she meet him on Blue Mountain Road. She supposed he'd probably changed his mind, and decided to wash his hands of anything to do with her. If so, she couldn't blame him. Oh, she hadn't been obvious, blatant or direct in the way she'd often been before Ia Drang – *"My room or yours?"* But there was no denying that she had opened doors and invited Cutter to step through them, one after another. Until he reached a door that was no longer hers to open.

As it turned out, Monday was too busy for Holly to give Cutter a lot of thought, though she found herself doing so anyway. Just before noon, the news came across that the 5th U.S. Circuit Court of Appeals, sitting in New Orleans, had lifted the stay of federal Judge

Oren Mulberry's integration order. Reorganization of the Cattahatchie County Public School System would take place without delay, as per the plan already approved by Mulberry. That sent county and school officials into a tizzy. Holly had to do much of the reporting herself because of her decimated staff. By three p.m., Cecil Weathers was on WHCI promising that if he had to bring in crews from Birmingham and St. Louis and work them twenty-four hours a day, "Riverview Academy will open on time for the education of any white student of good character."

So, it was almost nine o'clock when Holly passed the Old Ambrose Place on her way home. Though bone-tired, she found herself staring across the bean and cotton fields toward The Well. She saw the campfire glow, and wondered if Cutter was reading or listening to the radio? Was he laying there looking up at the stars, his body glistening with cold, pure droplets from a dive deep into The Well? Was he thinking of her? Or was he laying there, his body shining with feral sweat, some high school debutante or roadhouse waitress looking up at him with the stars in her eyes?

Holly crossed the Old Iron Bridge and followed the twisting road up the face of Blue Mountain, chiding herself for caring one way or the other. But when she rounded the curve near her house, and the headlights of the Lincoln illuminated a ditch cleared of brush and grass, a sob welled up in her throat and a wave of relief washed over her – *This is crazy!*

"Stop it!" she told herself and turned down the driveway. "Just stop it."

Tuesday was busier and even longer. Holly locked herself in her office for almost three hours in the afternoon writing a front page column that she knew would set the editorial direction of *The Current-Leader* for as long as it continued to publish.

"Which won't be long," she reminded herself, "unless something changes."

There was no ambiguity to it. No hedging. No gray areas. It was an impassioned plea for Cattahatchie Countians to accept the court ruling, "continue to support our public schools, and demand equal access to public facilities, especially the polling places, for all of our citizens." It called the actions of the Klan "heinous and cowardly" and said those who support them "overtly, covertly or through careful indifference are complicit in the brutality that the Klux continue to inflict upon those members of our community who are least able to defend themselves. It is repugnant and intolerable, and it goes to the core of what we are as a community."

When Holly got home Tuesday night at nearly one a.m., she saw the piles of junk Cutter had pulled out of the greenhouse. She had not seen him since Sunday afternoon, but just knowing he was still around, still nearby, felt almost as good as a hug.

On Wednesday, Holly wasn't ready to leave the house until almost nine, but Cutter still wasn't there. He probably was sitting down at The Well, waiting to see her car on Blue Mountain Road, headed to town. But she had prayed and read her Bible – especially the sixth chapter of First Corinthians where Paul wrote of our bodies being God's temple – and decided that no matter how difficult it might be, she had to find the words to tell Cutter why she'd pushed him away.

Holly finished a second cup of black coffee and the last of the Spanish omelet Gerry Yards had made. Julie Davis already had left for Oxford and an interview with Judge Mulberry. They were the only two left in the house.

"Thanks, Gerry. That was delicious."

"You know, I wouldn't mind making omelets for you every morning," he said from across the table, his eyes a dimmed by the years of alcohol that had made florid the capillaries of his nose and cheeks. Now that his long hair was nearly white, his face always looked sunburned.

"I know, Gerry," she said and tried to find other words. Kinder words. Better words. But she had turned him down so often that she had no new words for him. "I've got to go. I'm running late."

"What are you up to today?"

"Nothing special," he told her. "Just cruising the roads to see what my camera's eye can see."

"Be careful," she said, placing her dishes in the sink. "The Guard and the feds put a scare into the Klan. But they may not stay scared for long."

"After your editorial, I'd think you're in a lot more danger than I am," said Yards. "Do you want me to follow you to town?"

"No," she said, and patted her purse, the .38 inside. "If they want to try to run me off the road again, I'm ready for them."

Gerry Yards chuckled. "You never were scared of anything. That's one of the reasons I fell in love with you."

At the door Holly looked over her shoulder at him. She knew he'd mix a Bloody Mary as soon as she left. She wished she had the right words to say so that he would let her go, really let her go. Not for her sake, but for his. She wished he had someone else. "Be careful," she said again, and pushed down the ramp by the kitchen door with Charlie right behind her.

Yards crossed the kitchen and looked out the window as Holly wheeled to her car, then past it; and past the pile of stuff that Cutter kid had excavated from the old greenhouse, where Holly was headed. Holly opened her purse, took out what appeared to be a white, business-size envelope and taped it to a panel of dirty but unbroken glass where it could not be missed.

When Holly turned back toward her car and the house, Yards quickly stepped away from the window. He pulled a bottle of vodka from a lower kitchen cabinet, the tomato juice from the refrigerator and gathered up the rest of the fixings for his morning "steadier," as he called it. He heard the car door close and listened to the tires go up the long driveway as he worked. When there was no more sound of tires and the drink was ready he took a long swallow, and the heat filled his chest and cheeks and his belly. He drank the rest of it and made a second. Holding it cold in his hand, he walked down the ramp toward the greenhouse.

Two hours later, Gerry Yards stood in the kitchen window watching Cutter working shirtless in the noonday sun. Yards was sipping from a bottle of beer and eating a cold chicken leg and trying to tell himself that he once had had a body like Cutter's, but he wasn't yet buzzed enough to make himself believe it. There had been a time, however, when his hair wasn't receding and was more pepper than salt, and when the paunch around his middle was more like a bicycle tire than a truck spare. That hadn't been so long ago, had it? When he woke up next to Holly instead of two doors down from her?

Anyway, what he'd lost in physical attributes was more than made up by the knowledge he'd gained of the ways of the world and how to best manipulate any situation to his benefit, Yards told himself. He studied the handwritten note one last time …

> *Dear Cutter,*
>> *I'm terribly sorry about Sunday afternoon.*
>> *I'll be home by 5:30 and will bring dinner from The*
>> *Cotton. Afterwards, we can talk. I want to explain.*
>> *Please stay.*
>>> *Holly*

…then tore it into small pieces and dropped them in the kitchen garbage. Now he looked again at the one he'd typed at the desk in his room …

> Cutter,
>> As you can imagine, I'm extremely busy
>> this week and will be for the foreseeable future.
>> Please leave an itemized bill and I'll leave a
>> check for you at the newspaper's front desk.
>> If you have any questions, please inquire with
>> Mr. Yards, an old and very dear friend who will be
>> staying with me until this ordeal is over.
>> Thank you for your hard work.
>>> Holly Carter

… and slipped it into the envelope onto which Holly had written Cutter's name in her own strong script.

Yards finished the beer and chicken leg, washed his hands and dried them on a dish cloth, and headed out the back door. *This is going to be almost too easy,* he thought. "Hey, kid!" he called as he crossed the yard. "I have a note for you from Holly."

* * *

The picture had been there in Holly's *Current-Leader* office all along, but now, knowing what Cutter had told her about the white station wagon, it felt like something hot, always against her back, burning right through her blouse. It sat with a number of other framed photographs on a console behind what had been her father's desk. Now her desk and her office. There were multiple pictures of T.L. Carter's grandchildren, friends in the Mississippi newspaper industry, and a framed magazine cover bearing a picture of her in Marine fatigues, aiming her camera as a battle raged around her. It was the summer 1965 edition of National Journalism Quartley, which had printed a feature on her called: "On the Front Lines of Journalism".

But it was none of those photographs that now made Holly's skin crawl. Instead it was a five-by-seven of Tom, Mary Nell, Tommy and Georgette standing beside a white Ford station wagon during a 1967 trip to the Southwest – the vast gorge of the Grand Canyon open behind them.

Holly turned and looked at the photograph for the fiftieth time since Monday morning. She stared at it, as if she could read the intentions behind faces eighteen months in advance of events that transpired on a cold river in Mississippi. That, of course, was impossible but Holly intended to do whatever was possible now. *And what is possible now?* She asked herself. *Right this minute? At nearly noon on an August Wednesday in 1969?*

Turning from the photograph, Holly picked up her phone and dialed the sheriff's office. Five minutes later she was in her car, Charlie beside her and headed north on Highway 27.

* * *

When Deputy John-Thomas Hinton walked out of the Cream Cup café north of town holding a vanilla cone, Holly Lee Carter's Lincoln was parked beside his cruiser. His face lit up when he saw her but when the super cold ice cream hit the roof of his mouth it sent a shock of frozen pain into his forehead. He stopped and tilted his head back and held his nose, his mouth open, swallowing the hot August air. Trying to warm his sinuses.

"Ohhh, my goodness," he said, his head still tilted back. "Why do I do that to myself? It looks like I'd learn."

Holly laughed and that made the pain worth it to John Thomas.

"That hurts, doesn't it?" said Holly sympathetically.

"It does," said the deputy. "But I do love their ice cream. Ohh, my!"

"The dispatcher told me I could find you here," she said, stroking Charlie's stomach. The little dog was stretched out on the seat, enjoying Holly's touch and attention.

"Cute," said the young deputy.

"Thanks," said Holly, removing her Wayfarers.

"At least you didn't catch me eatin' donuts," he said and licked the cone. "What's goin' on?"

"I've got a question about the night my dad died."

"Okay."

"How long did it take you to figure out it was my father's car in the river?"

John-Thomas thought about it. "We didn't know for absolute sure until we recovered it the next morning," he said. "But we checked the houses there on Blue Mountain Road and no one reported a car missing or a friend who had visited and left around that time. When we checked at Wolf's Run, your father's car was missing and there was no answer at the door. No lights on. So we were just presumin'."

"All right, you were presuming. When did someone decide it was time to notify Tom and Mary Nell?"

"I'd say around ten o'clock," John-Thomas recalled. "Sheriff Johnson knew Mr. Tom was out of town at a newspaper convention – or meetin' or somethin'. Down on the coast. As you know, Miss Mary Nell can be a little, well, high strung. So we didn't want to upset her unless we had to.

"But about nine-forty-five the sheriff decided we had to let 'em know, even if we weren't one-hundred percent sure."

"Who –?"

"In fact, it was me," said John-Thomas, licking ice cream from the cone and his hand. "I stopped at the sheriff's office and called Miss Frances who gave me the name of the hotel in Biloxi that Mr. Tom was staying at. I tried his room but he didn't answer." John-Thomas grunted. "The truth is, I was hopin' if I told Tom I wouldn't have to visit with Mary Nell. But no such luck. So, I drove over to the house."

"Really?" said Holly. "What time was that?"

The deputy thought. "About ten-thirty, I'd say."

Holly calculated. "You're sure?" she asked.

"Give or take five minutes or so."

It couldn't be done. If the knock on the door of Efram Cole's farm-house came as the ten o'clock news was starting, there was no way the car could have been pulled out and Mary Nell have time to be back in DeLong to answer the deputy's knock. Impossible. Holly knew she should feel relieved that the time line, if correct, seemed to exonerate her sister-in-law – at least in terms of being physically involved in T.L. Carter's death. But there was still the white Ford station wagon. Holly refocused.

"Mary Nell answered the door?"

"After a bit. Yes."

"How did she look?"

"Look?" asked John-Thomas, obviously surprised by the question. He held the cone steady and clearly tried to picture the scene in his mind. He licked the fast-melting cone and said, "She had on a bathrobe. Her hair was wet. She said she'd just got out of the shower."

"And you told her?"

"Yep, I told her what we were presumin'."

"How did she react?"

"She was surprised, of course. Worried. She said she needed to call Tom. I asked if she wanted to come out to the scene, and she said no. That there was nothing she could do there and that she needed to go fetch Tommy and Georgette before they heard about this some other way."

"Fetch them?"

"They were spendin' the night with friends, she said, because she'd been having one of her sick headaches."

Holly thought about that, pictured it in her mind – John-Thomas stranding there under the porch light delivering the news to her sister-in-law. "So, Mary Nell was alone at the house?"

"As far as I know."

"What about her car?" asked Holly. "The white Ford station wagon. Did you see it?"

"No. But I was at the front door. The garage is at the back of the house."

"I know," said Holly. "I grew up in that house. I was just wondering." She paused, thinking. "But you did get in contact with Tom, right?"

"If you mean, did I talk to him personally? No I didn't. Mary Nell said she'd call and keep callin' till she got him. Which she did."

"How do you know that?"

"She must have. He was back in DeLong by eight-thirty the next morning when we recovered your father's car. To do that, he would've had to drive all night. Especially in the kind of weather we were havin' that week." The deputy bit into the cone and it crunched. "What's this about Holly?"

Holly dodged the question and asked her own. "Did anyone actually enter Wolf's Run and look around?"

"That's one of the reasons Sheriff Johnson wanted me to get in contact with Tom or Mary Nell. The house was locked up tight. We were gonna have to break in. The sheriff wanted their permission."

"And?"

"And Mary Nell gave it when I talked to her."

"She didn't object?"

"No. Why should she?"

"Did you go into Wolf's Run?"

"No. Sheriff Johnson went. And, I believe, Deputy Connelly."

"What did they find?"

"Nothing. Including Mr. Carter. Which was the point."

"But they didn't find anything out of place?"

"Not that I ever heard."

Holly nodded, thinking – *Unless someone was familiar with the house and library, they wouldn't have noticed my mother's portrait was missing.*

"Look, Holly, what's this about?"

"Just one more question, John-Thomas. I understand that a couple of days after Daddy's accident, Mary Nell was assaulted in Memphis and her car was stolen. The station wagon. Can you get me a copy of the police report?"

The deputy looked her over. "You're not gonna tell me what you're up to, are you?"

"No. Not now," she said without missing a beat. "If I'm wrong, it'll only add to the bad blood that's already like – like poison between me and Mary Nell. If I'm right, I'll be happy to tell you. And anyone else who'll listen."

John-Thomas Hinton put the last of the ice cream cone in his mouth and licked his fingers. "I guess I can do that for you," he said.

* * *

Holly drove home that afternoon feeling that at least she'd done *something*. Unfortunately, the *something* had revived the question of Tom's involvement. If no one from the sheriff's office actually talked to Tom in Biloxi, then they were only taking Mary Nell's word that she reached him there. Of course, there were other ways Tom's alibi might be verified, if it ever came to him needing one. It was a press convention, after all, populated by people who had known Tom Carter since he was old enough to walk into the lobby of the Edgewater Hotel on their mother's hand. Some of them even before then.

Still, Holly was looking forward to sharing what she'd learned with Cutter. But as soon as she turned down the driveway late that afternoon her heart sank. There was no jeep next to the house. Maybe he had gone down to The Well to clean up, she thought, stopping between the garage and the greenhouse. The old structure now was thoroughly cleaned out and the broken panes of glass removed, the frames made ready for a glazer to come in and fill them. Three piles of debris, about waist high, stood next to the driveway.

Gerry Yards emerged from the kitchen door as Holly turned off the ignition.

"Hey, Good-lookin'."

"Hi, Gerry," she said, swinging open the door and lifting her legs out. Charlie scampered onto the grass and began sniffing at the piles of detritus – broken pottery, rotted tables, vines cut and torn loose, an old bicycle and all sorts of odds and ends. "Julie isn't back yet from Oxford?" she asked, hiding her real disappointment.

"She called. She's got a shot at an interview tomorrow morning with J.L. Burke. So, she's staying down there tonight."

Gerry pulled Holly's wheelchair out of the back floorboard, opened it and positioned it for her. "By the way, that kid you've got doin' the clean-up around here –"

"Yes," she said more enthusiastically than she intended.

"I was talking to him. He said he'll be done by Friday and he'll leave a bill. He asked me to tell you to leave a check at the newspaper's front desk," said Yards. "He wasn't all that friendly about it, either."

Holly stared at the pea gravel under her her wheelchair. "Did he say anything about a – well, anything else?"

"Nope. That was it."

Holly knew Cutter was someone adept at holding in his outward feelings, of displaying only what he wanted the world to see – as he seemed to do Sunday afternoon on the drive back to Wolf's Run. But there was no doubt that a deep anger smouldered in him. Now it appeared she had been tossed onto that pyre as well. Having lifted herself from the car seat to her wheelchair, Holly placed her feet on the pedals, then lifted one leg to cross it over the other and smoothed her skirt. She shut the car door, hating the idea that Cutter was so deeply angry with her, and recognizing at the same time that it mattered to her a lot more than it should. *So, maybe this is for the best*, she thought – or made herself think. *What had I really expected? What could I really say to him? A lot of God talk that I wouldn't have come close to listening to at eighteen.*

She said, "I brought dinner from the Cotton Café."

Gerry Yards swayed a little as he pulled the paper bags from the back seat. "Smells great! Tell you what, I'll set up dinner on the patio. The light in the valley and on the river this time of day is extraordinary."

"Sure. That'll be fine," she said but didn't move.

"Aren't you coming?"

"You go ahead. I'll be there in a minute," she told him as she pushed around the piles. "I want to take a look at some of this stuff. There are a lot of memories piled up here. That old bicycle? That was my bicycle when I was ten. And that old TV? With the round screen. I watched Elvis on *The Ed Sullivan Show* on that TV."

There was the footboard to the white canopy bed she'd slept in until she pointed her Corvette toward the West Coast, but she didn't see the rest of it. A water-ruined cardboard box held an old china service. The top layer of plates was broken and she didn't recognize the pattern, but some of it might be worth saving, she thought, and pulled the box away from the pile. When she did, some of the junk shifted. It tumbled and clattered onto the grass as the little dog jumped back, barking her protest.

"Ooops! Sorry, Charlie."

That's when Holly saw it – the L shape of half a gold-leaf frame. She picked it up and studied the ornately carved wood. Looking at the front, then the back, then the front again, there was no doubt. This was the frame that had held the portrait of Veronique Carter, her mother. The portrait that was missing from the library.

Holly looked in the pile. Inside the shoulders of limestone that rolled up around Wolf's Run, the afternoon shadows already were deep. But after a moment, she saw another piece and pulled it free. Along the edge were tatters of canvas, as if someone had ripped the portrait from the frame.

Now she had three-fourths of it. "Come on, where are you?" she said as she moved slowly around the pile. "Yes!"

Holly pulled loose the final piece and stared at it. It was spattered with dry, brown mud or ...? She scratched a drop and lifted the frame to her nose. Immediately, she swung it away from her face and gagged. She had smelled that odor plenty of times at murder scenes, fire-blackened homes and in Vietnam. The sweet, coppery tang of dried blood was unmistakable.

Chapter 13

❦

All weekend the rumors about the future of the county's public school system and Cattahatchie High's vaunted football team swirled through DeLong like an army of dirt devils, popping up from nowhere out of a hot breeze and picking up grit and trash as they moved from street to street. The Cattahatchie County Fair opened that Saturday night. From the balcony of my room at Mrs. Fletcher's Boarding House, I could see the Ferris wheel and the lights from the rodeo arena, and when the highway and railroad tracks were quiet – which wasn't often – I could even hear the canned organ music coming from the shabby midway.

Really, the fair was like a petri dish in which the virulent and sometimes sickening rumors about Cattahatchie High's future were placed, and given the perfect environment for growth. It brought together the town people, with their baking and cooking competitions, their rose judgings and the Miss Cattahatchie County Pageant, and the rural folk, who brought their pigs, cows and horses to show in the long barns on the west side of the fairgrounds. They mingled, more or less, and talked, and in that August of '69 little of the talk was good.

In a field owned by an unabashed Kluxer across from the fairgrounds, the Klan parked a flatbed truck and set up a loudspeaker system. Those with a bent for angry speechmaking kept up an almost continuous diatribe while men and women, and even children in miniature robes, moved among the cars parked along the highway and in nearby lots placing Klan pamphlets under windshield wipers.

At their spot in the row of public service booths, National Coalition for Justice volunteers passed out their own literature guarded, always, by two deputies and several federal marshals. Sheriff's cars escorted the NCJ's old school bus back and forth to their encampment at Pickens' Ferry A.M.E. Church. None of that, however, stopped the

NCJ workers from being showered with tobacco spit from time to time and needing to duck as eggs or rocks struck their vehicle.

From a distance on Saturday night, I saw Miss Carter with the blonde reporter –her friend from Los Angeles. Miss Davis. They seemed to be enjoying the midway, but mostly they were working. Miss Davis was talking to people – those who would talk to her – and Miss Carter was taking pictures. Rumor had it that after Wednesday's editorial siding outright with the integrationists, the newspaper had lost several hundred more subscriptions.

Patti, unfortunately, caught my line of sight. "That Jezebel!" she growled. "I can't believe she has the gall to show her face in public. I *hate* that woman!"

I started to mention that hating people didn't seem all that Christian, but I had learned better than to challenge the righteous wrath of Brother Daddy or any of his clan. "She may be a cripple but she is like the prowling lion, picking off and devouring the members of our flock who stray," Patti went on, her cheeks flushed. "Only Satan could have created a woman like her. Even starting her own church!"

"The way I heard it, the Raglands and some others went to Miss Carter," I said before I could put the brakes on my mouth. "They asked her if they could use –"

Patti stared at me, her teeth grinding behind the tight knot of her lips. I knew if I uttered another word on the subject, I'd be leaving the fairgrounds alone.

* * *

On Monday afternoon, the twenty-six veterans of 1968's 13-1 Wolves football team met at the locker room beside Senator Julius C. DeLong Memorial Field. Along with eleven ninth-grade rookies we were there to get our physicals and receive our equipment for the start of two-a-day practices the following morning.

It was the first time I had seen Cutter, except glimpsed from a distance on the road, since the afternoon at Wolf's Run with Rose. As usual, he was surrounded by a knot of people wanting to talk about football or The Gin, girls or The Well or just to be near him.

I sat down in front of a locker on the other side of the room and made no attempt to cross the distance between us. He'd been seen several times since then with Miss Carter. People around town were no longer whispering about their relationship. Many were grumbling out loud. Especially now with Brother MacAllister accusing Miss Carter of "bedazzling vulnerable members of the First Denomination flock," I couldn't afford to be lumped in with her and Cutter.

At four p.m. exactly, Head Coach Gaydon Pearce emerged from his office followed by his three assistants. A big fan in one of the open windows stirred the hot, sticky August air.

"Aw'ight, aw'ight," he said in the booming, nasal baritone that had been the voice of authority in CHS football for fourteen years. "Find a place to park your backsides. We've got some 'nouncements to make. Go on. Grab a chair … and hold on to it."

It wasn't so much that at some level we all hadn't anticipated what we were about to hear, but the timing of it, the swiftness of it, the totality of it caught nearly everyone off guard – like bracing for a slap in the face and getting a punch in the gut instead.

"You rookies, listen up," said Coach Pearce. "The first rule on my teams is that when I'm ready to talk, you shut up. Got it?"

Young heads nodded in the coach's direction. He was only five-foot, nine-inches but had the massive upper body and nail-keg thighs of a college fullback, which he had been two decades earlier. Looking up from his watch, he began, "At this moment, the Cattahatchie County School Board is officially accepting the resignations of one-hundred and fifty-seven of two-hundred and nine white teachers and administrators. Including my resignation, and those of coaches Rutledge, Garrett and Parker, here."

A groan of shock and consternation rumbled across the room.

"I told you, be quiet and listen up!" said the coach. "As soon as that business is officially done, three of the five school board members will resign and leave it to the nigguhs to run as best they can. If they can.

"A few of the teachers will simply retire, but most will be signing contracts with Riverview Academy. Including this whole coaching staff," he told us. "Men, Cattahatchie football will go! It will go on just as it always has, except we'll have a new name, a new location and new facilities that are second to none at any private school in Miss'ssippi."

"Coach –?" started Kenny Dillon, but Gaydon Pearce held up his hand. "Now I know y'all probably have lots of questions. The coaches are passing out mimeographed copies of information that should answer most of those questions. Read 'em before you start askin', and take 'em home to your folks. There's information about academic scholarships, athletic scholarships – something most of you boys will qualify for – and low-interest loans at the Valley Bank that can help parents who need it.

"The main things you have to remember are that we'll have our physicals and pass out brand spankin' new equipment a week from today at the Riverview locker room. You all know where that is. You've seen it goin' up. Inside, it's gonna be a beauty. First class. We'll start two-a-days next Tuesday. School will start September 8 and we'll play our first game September 12 against Greenwood Prep."

There were nods, a few smiles, but mostly my blank, stunned look was reflected back at me. I looked at Cutter, as did a lot of others in the room, but as usual, he was infuriatingly unreadable. His icy eyes were fixed on Coach Pearce, his hands folded in his lap. I wondered if someone had given him a heads-up in advance.

Perhaps Coach Pearce was reading many of our thoughts. "And for any of you math-impaired heathens who are wonderin', Cutter's nineteenth birthday is not until September 14. That means he'll still be eighteen when school starts, so he'll be eligible for the entire season."

Many of his teammates sighed with relief. A few clapped and a couple whistled. Cutter probably was the best football player of any color in the state, but in the lily white Academy League, he would be utterly unstoppable. Some of us might have been "math-impaired heathens," but it didn't take anyone more than an instant to calculate that with Cutter onboard, the State Academy League Championship was ours for the taking if we Wolves moved en masse to Riverview.

"One more thing," said Coach Pearce. "There's gonna be a kick-off pep rally for the team and, well, the whole academy, really, at the fairgrounds rodeo arena this comin' Saturday night at 7:30. You're all expected to be there and you'll be up on stage. So wash behind your ears and practice not pickin' your nose."

Many laughed.

"Governor Broderick himself is comin' in to inaugurate things. It's all gonna be on a statewide radio hookup. We're gonna be an example for the whole state that decent white folk don't have to knuckle under to a bunch of race-mixin' judges. We're gonna show folks how to fight back ... and win!"

Chapter 14

❧

As the locker room emptied out and slowly the parking lot, too, Cutter sat in the same folding chair for a long time. Unmoving and seemingly unmoved by anything that he'd heard. Coach Pearce didn't bother to make small talk. He and Cutter didn't really get along. Cutter's legs had lifted his coaching career from the doldrums of mediocrity, or worse, to one of the best records in the state over the last three years, but Coach never felt he got enough credit. On the other hand, Gaydon Pearce wasn't foolish enough to express that resentment in obvious ways.

For his part, Cutter had little choice but to tolerate Gaydon Pearce. For better or worse, he was the coach, and football was Cutter's meal ticket for now and, more important, the future. So, he mostly kept his mouth shut and led by example.

Cutter stood and crossed the locker room. It was so quiet. No reassuring clatter of cleats on the concrete floor. No whoops of excitement, groans of pain or curses of frustration. He leaned on a locker and stared out at the field. The ghosts of games won there danced behind his eyes. In the three seasons since he'd donned a high school uniform as a freshman, the Wolves had not lost a home game. With his speed, strength and determination, Cutter simply had not permitted it. CHS was 19-0 between those red goal posts. Perfect.

Coach Pearce had asked Cutter to hang around after the announcement. Someone wanted to talk to him. Outside, Coach Rutledge was answering some final questions from players and shooing them out of the parking area. Then he left, and two minutes later, Governor Weathers' silver Rolls-Royce crunched into the gravel lot.

Coach Pearce immediately emerged from his office, stretching his shirt over his belly and stuffing it into his shorts. "Come on, Cutter," he said. "Governor Weathers wants to talk with you."

Cutter said nothing but followed Coach Pearce out to the car. The door opened and Sgt. J.D. Benoit stepped out, the bright late afternoon sun reflecting off his mirrored sunglasses. "Get in."

Gaydon Pearce hustled into the limousine like it was some new and wonderful ride at the fair. But not Cutter. "Go on, kid," said Benoit. "It's hot out here. Get in."

"If y'all got something to say to me, why don't you just say it here?"

"Boy, am I gonna have to handcuff you and put you in this car?"

Cutter flashed a quick smile – "If you can."

"What's got into you, boy?" yelled Coach Pearce. "This is Governor Weathers. He just wants to have a friendly talk."

"And this man is Tony's best friend. Anybody who's that tight with Tony is no friend of mine. And I don't care to ride in the back seat of a car with him."

Benoit balled his fists. "Why, you smart-mouthed –"

"Sergeant!" said Weathers. "Emotions run high concerning family matters. We should tread lightly.

"Please ride in front with Jerome," said the governor, indicating his black chauffeur. "Does that satisfy you, young man?"

Cutter climbed in as Governor Weathers patted the seat next to him. Gaydon Pearce sat across from them and cringed as Benoit got in the front seat and slammed the door. "Go on, Jerome," Benoit told the chauffeur. "You know what the boss wants. Give us the tour."

"Well, now! This is fine, just fine," said Weathers as the car began to move. "What a good-lookin' young man you are. And so much talent! You just don't know how proud this town is of you."

The Silver Cloud seemed to skim over the county roads that led west, through the heart of Weathers' Chalmette Plantation. Even on the north Mississippi clay and rough-quarried gravel of the side roads, it was so quiet and well balanced that it almost floated. The interior of the car was as cool as a refrigerator and smelled of old leather, expensive cigars and fresh talcum powder. Cecil Weathers was making no "common man" pretense this day. He was flexing his muscle, and demonstrating his wealth and power for all to see – especially Cutter. From time to time, Weathers pointed out something about one of the sawmills or cotton gins or warehouses they were passing. About how many laborers it took to work one of his long fields or maintain a row of grain elevators. Cutter said almost nothing. At first, Coach Pearce tried to cajole and interject but finally gave up and simply sat there, sunk in the plush seat looking like he needed to pee. After a time, they stopped on the west side of the river beside the row of cotton warehouses that was quickly being converted to classrooms and a gym. The first home of Riverview Academy while a new brick structure was going up next door to house pre-schoolers to high school seniors.

"It'll be second to none," Weathers enthused. "People will come from all over the state – *hell!* – all over the South to see what we did and how we did it. It's going to be my legacy, I tell you. My legacy!"

If Cutter was impressed by any of it, he didn't show it. During the grand tour of the old plantation and while observing the anthill of work at the new academy, he offered nothing beyond perfunctory "yes, sirs" and "no, sirs" when asked a direct question. Clearly, Cutter's silence was becoming an annoyance to Weathers.

"What about it, boy?" he demanded. "What do you think?"

Cutter considered for e moment, then – "I think it's going to be a grand place."

"Grand! Grand ain't even the word!" Weathers thundered. "It's gonna be magnificint! Nothin' but the best. And you can be a part of it, son. A big part."

After a time, Jerome put the Rolls in gear and moved on. For several minutes, no one said anything as Weathers stared out the tinted window, as if seeing it all – his legacy – come to life in the smoked glass. Then Jerome turned onto a gravel lane known as Convict Road. It climbed and dipped through the hills and eventually led to the county work farm.

As if continuing a conversation that had paused only a moment earlier, Weathers said, "Of course, you now know that Coach Pearce will be the first head coach of the Riverview Raiders, and we already have a full ten-game schedule. We've quietly approached the parents of most of your returning teammates. We have firm commitments from eighteen of twenty-six."

"Now, Cutter, you coming over to Riverview would seal the deal for a lot of folks," offered Coach Pearce.

If this was a negotiation, Cutter intended to get the most out of it he could. "What about my sister? Rose doesn't have the grades for an academic scholarship."

"As president of Riverview's board of directors and head of the scholarship committee, I'm certain a way can be found," Weathers assured him. "And without appearing immodest, I might add that I am a man of some influence with most of the universities in the Mid-South. I have endowed chairs in politics and history. I sit on any number of boards and committees, and I feel sure I can guarantee you the most complete collegiate athletic scholarship possible under NCAA rules – and then some." Cecil Weathers winked and made a tick-tick sound in the corner of his mouth. "Rose will be taken care of, too, of course."

"And my mother?"

"We can make sure that she and Rose have a nice little house somewhere near campus. In fact, a dear friend owns several well-maintained rent houses only a couple blocks off the Oxford square. I'm sure he'll be happy to give Rose an exceptionally good deal. He might well need some secretarial help in his law office, as well."

For a long moment, Cutter stared at the back of Sergeant Benoit's crew cut head – deciding how far to push. He might as well go for broke. "What about Tony? He's said he'll kill my mother and sister before he'll let them go. That's the only reason I haven't already gotten them away from here. And from him."

"Ahhh, yes. Well, Tony is a passionate man and sometimes impetuous," said Weathers. "But the things he's most passionate about are liquor, women of easy virtue and the affectation of power. He can be supplied with enough all three to console him for his loss. Isn't that right, Sergeant Benoit?"

"Yes, sir, Governor. Once I'm elected sheriff this fall, I'll need a chief deputy," said Benoit, who was so far running unopposed.

"You see, there's nothing to worry about," said Weathers. Cutter stared at him. The notion of Tony Carlucci with a badge, gun and the backing of the sheriff and the Klan made Cutter's stomach tighten into a knot but he didn't let on to the men in the car. "In the end, Tony answers to me," the governor added. "And I assure you, he will not interfere following the completion of your brilliant senior season at Riverview Academy."

The governor reached into a door pocket and held up a silver-gray football jersey with white trim and a gold 13 on the front and back. "Pretty snazzy, huh? I designed it myself. The pants are the same – gray with a gold stripe, like a Confederate officer's trousers."

Gaydon Pearce jumped in. "And the uniforms are just the start of it, Cutter. Governor Weathers and the board are sparin' no expense on Raiders football."

"Now, I'm not going to kid you, young fella. It would be a big feather in our cap to have a player of your caliber on the first Raiders team. It would probably bring into the fold a lot of holdouts. But make no mistake, son, Riverview Academy is opening next month with or without you."

"The only thing that's gonna be left at dear ol' CHS is nigguhs and white trash," Benoit added from the front seat.

Cutter drew the car's cold air into his lungs. He couldn't make himself say yes to Weathers' offer, but was afraid to say no. For several minutes they rode in silence while the governor's impatience grew. Finally, Weathers ordered, "Jerome, stop here. I think we've gone far enough."

Benoit got out and opened the back door. Cutter stepped onto the gravel without protest. He didn't like breathing the same air as Weathers and Benoit. The sergeant climbed into the back seat. "But, Governor," said Coach Pearce. "It's a six-mile walk back to town."

"Good!" said Weathers. "It'll give Cutter time to be alone with his thoughts. But just so my position is clear, young man. I love being generous with people who are on my team. Nothing gives me greater pleasure. But so help me, boy, if you screw with me on this, even if I have to endow every major college, small college and piss-ant junior college from here to the Hawaiian Islands, you will never play a down of college football."

Cutter stood still, fighting not to react to the nail of fear Weathers had driven between his ribs. ... *Without football, I'm just the son of a crazy woman and a one-legged dago drunk,* the fear reminded him even before Benoit added – "And your mother and sister'll rot up there in that shack. With Chief Deputy Carlucci. I'll make sure of it."

Gaydon Pearce looked as if he was trying to get smaller in his seat, sink into the deep leather folds. Even he was surprised and taken aback by the directness, the viciousness of the threats. In the deep blue shadows cast by the surrounding woods, Cutter stood, silent.

"One more thing," said Weathers. "We have a strict morals clause in our scholarships. I'd hate to have to disqualify you *and* your sister for you associatin' *further* with a known race-mixer, harlot and purveyor of lies."

"To put a finer point on it – from now on, keep away from that Carter woman and the rag she's printin'," said Benoit as he wadded up the jersey and threw it out the door. Cutter caught it against his chest.

"Make sure you wear that to the kickoff rally Saturday night," said Governor Weathers before relaxing back into his seat. "Jerome, drive on."

Chapter 15

෨

It was Thursday morning. Holly had three eight-by-ten blow-ups of photographs she'd taken of LeRoy Kamp spread on her desk. It had taken ten days since her conversation with Cutter – their last conversation – because LeRoy supposedly had been out of town on business. Or on vacation. Or no one was really sure. But when she called the family's car dealership on Wednesday afternoon and put on her best sugar baby accent and asked for "*Leee*-Roy," he came to the phone. Holly hung up. Fifteen minutes later, she and Julie Davis were parked across the highway in Julie's rental car.

Now Holly had the photos, but would Efram Cole talk to her? Emotions were running higher than ever now that Judge Mulberry's integration order had been upheld and she'd opined her support in the *Current-Leader*. The resignation of eighty percent of the county's white teachers and three-of-five school board members had been like tossing gasoline into a fire. On top of that, no progress – none that the public knew of, at least – had been made in catching Robert Bedford McBride or solving the murder of Ridge Bellafont and the attack on Eve Howard. Holly heard through friends in L.A. that Eve was improving but she'd be in a rehabilitation center for weeks more. Maybe months. The center had refused to put Holly's calls through. She wasn't on the approved list.

The phone on Holly's desk rang. She picked it up. Her mind and eyes still focused on LeRoy Kamp's face, she said, "Hello."

"Holly, this is John-Thomas."

"Oh, yes, John-Thomas. Hi."

"I'm sorry it's taken me so long to get the information from the Memphis P.D. The big city boys don't exactly step and fetch it when the country folk call," he told her. "But I've got it."

"Great! Thank you. Can you drop the reports by the office?"

"I can," said the deputy, letting the pause beyond after the words drag out long after the words were finished. "But I was thinking maybe I'd pass them to you over dinner tonight. Maybe Nicholls Steak House? Or we could go someplace in Tupelo."

Holly pictured the sweet, young deputy sitting at a desk in the sheriff's office, the butterflies beating in his stomach as he waited for her reply. She almost said yes. If for no other reason than to thank him. Plus, looking at him across a restaurant table would not be difficult. He was a handsome kid. *Kid?* thought Holly. *He's at least three or four years older than ...*

"Cutter ... " Holly sighed inwardly as she held the phone and John-Thomas Hinton waited for an answer. She had found herself thinking of him multiple times in each of the ten days since the picnic behind the old farmhouse. During the week that followed, he had come and gone from Wolf's Run when she was not there, done his work but left no bill. At night, when she lay down with only Charlie, her guitar and a .38 to keep her company, she rolled onto her side and imagined Cutter sleeping outside on the porch beneath her window. Then she tasted again that kiss in the strawberry field, saw his hand on her leg and imagined Cutter sleeping even closer. It was crazy and she knew it, but she missed Cutter in a way that she had never missed any man. And there had been many other men she could have missed.

Dinner with Deputy Hinton was a complication she didn't need. "John-Thomas, that's a very nice offer but with all that's happening, I'm just swamped," she said, then softened – "Can I get a rain check?"

The deputy waited a beat or two. "Sure, Holly. I'll drop the reports by in a few minutes."

* * *

Holly tried to focus on the lead story for Saturday's edition of the *Current-Leader*. It would be a preview of Saturday night's big rally at the fairgrounds' rodeo arena to kick off the opening of Riverview Academy. Like it or not, it was news. Big news. The governor coming to town. A statewide radio hook up. But Holy couldn't concentrate on the story. The pictures of LeRoy Kamp kept staring at her from the side of the desk, and just behind her Tom, Mary Nell and the kids watched her from a photo taken during a 1968 vacation to Arizona. They were standing near the Grand Canyon, trying to smile in the glare of the desert sun that glinted off the white Ford station wagon behind them. She picked up the frame and looked at the photo. Caught in that moment, they looked as if they might be posing for Norman Rockwell. The perfect American family. Except that one or perhaps both of the adults murdered her father.

The intercom line buzzed on her phone. It was Miss Frances telling her that Deputy Hinton had dropped off an envelope for her.

"Thank you, Ma'am."

"Do you want me to bring it up?"

There was much more that she could do on Saturday's edition. Much more that needed doing. But Holly said, "No, thank you, Miss Frances. I'll be down in a moment to pick it up."

"I don't mind."

"No, I'm leaving. I'm taking the afternoon off."

Holly turned the frame over on her lap, removed the back and took out the photo of the happy Carter family on vacation. She put it and the photos of LeRoy Kamp into a folder and headed for the county library.

* * *

Two hours later, Holly was lifting herself onto the side of the pool at Wolf's Run. She'd done thirty laps but was not breathing hard. Her shoulders rose and fell evenly as her heart rate slowed. She was wearing a black, one-piece swimsuit and black Bermuda shorts that hid the leg bag attached to her catheter. Julie Davis tossed her a towel and Holly toweled off before lifting her hips onto a low bench next to her wheelchair. The bench was the midway point. Holly checked the brakes on the chair and lifted herself onto the seat. Having watched Holly try to swim her tension away many times at the house in Pacific Pallisades, Julie knew better than to ask if she needed help. Holly neither needed the help nor wanted the question. Now she lifted each foot and placed the thong of a flipflop between her toes and then placed her left leg over her right.

Julie watched her friend wheel over to the patio table overlooking the hot, green August valley below and the winding brown cut of the

the Cattahatchie River. She lifted a glass of white wine to her lips. "Feel better?" she asked.

"I'll feel better when I know who killed my father," she said, placing a cube of sharp cheddar onto a cracker. She ate it and took a sip from her own wine glass then tapped a fingernail on the Memphis police reports lying on the glass tabletop. "What do you think?"

"If there's not a tie-in to your father's death, then the whole white Ford station wagon thing is one hell of a coincidence," said Julie Davis, who had put in her share of time covering L.A. cops before moving to features. "But the report seems to back up the story Mary Nell was telling around town. That she was assaulted in the store parking lot by a large, black male who stole her keys and took the car. If that's not what happened, she took a beating from somebody. According to the emergency room report the police received, this wasn't just a slap in the mouth. She was beat up. Her clothes were torn, too. But she denies there was sexual contact."

Holly nodded, but asked, "Nothing about the report seems strange to you?"

Julie looked at the report for half a minute, thinking. Then, "No. What are you thinking?"

"Mary Nell has expensive tastes in clothing, jewelry and handbags. The kind of stuff you have to go to New Orleans or Dallas to get. Or at least you have to send there for them," said Holly. "I'm thinking that if I was a strong-arm robber who took the time to beat up a woman in a department store parking a lot, before stealing her car I'd have certainly taken an extra few seconds to steal her expensive purse and jewelry. There's not even a mention of any cash being taken."

Julie nodded. "The only thing stolen was the car."

Holly let that thought rest in the humid air for almost a minute, then said, "I need to talk to Cutter. I need to get him to show these pictures of LeRoy and the picture of the station wagon to Mr. Cole."

Julie let those words rest in the air for a time as well before asking, "Is that the only reason you need to see Cutter?"

Holly looked at her friend – her best friend – for a moment and started to speak but when their eyes met, both knew no more needed to be said. Holly placed another cracker and cube of cheese in her mouth and poured each of them a fresh glass of wine.

Chapter 16

༄

It was nearly six-thirty but still terribly hot when Holly began trans-ferring from her chair into the Lincoln. Charlie jumped in ahead of her. Holly put in a picnic basket and a folder with the pictures of LeRoy Kamp and the Tom Carter clan. As she turned the key she heard a vehicle coming down the driveway and instinctively reached inside her purse to reassure herself that the .38 was handy and ready. But when she looked toward the road, she saw it was only Gerry Yards. Her former mentor was not dangerous except to himself.

Yards parked his rental car next to the garage and got out, camera in hand. His clothes looked as if he'd spent the afternoon in a steam-bath. When he walked over he smelled like beer and cigarettes. He focused on Holly. She was wearing the coolest pieces of clothing she could put together – a cap-sleeved blouson top with a loose gypsy skirt and strappy sandals over tan, freshly shaved legs. He click-click-clicked the motor drive of his camera.

"You are gorgeous!" he told her.

Holly put her hand in front of her face. "Stop it, Gerry. Please."

Click-click-click-click … click-click …"You used to love it when I took your picture. In fact, I think I'm still in possession of some pic-tures that are nothing short of – uhmmm? – breathtaking."

Holly wasn't sure if the comment was meant to be titillating, threatening or just the ramblings of a sad, empty man who now mostly got by reveling in his personal and professional past. "That was a long time ago," she said. "Are you in for the night?"

"I don't know. Are you planning to do a bed check? I hope."

"No. But Julie went to the fair. I was merely going to ask you to be sure to lock up if you go back out."

Gerry Yards threw a casual salute her way. He was clearly drunk. Holly turned the key and put the car in gear.

"Where are you and the vicious guard dog headed?"

"I have an appointment."

"Do you always take a picnic basket to an appointment?"

"It depends on the appointment."

"Come inside and have dinner with me. Just the two of us. Like it used to be."

Holly looked at her watch. "Sorry, Gerry. No can do. I'm booked."

He sneered. "That's an interesting way to put it."

Holly worked to control her temper. "Go on in, Gerry. There's plenty of food in the 'fridge. Eat yourself a good meal, then sleep it off."

"You're going to be with him, aren't you? That Cutter kid?" he asked angrily. "What does he have that I don't have? Never mind. I'm sure the answer to that question would only serve to further humiliate me."

From her wheelchair, Holly often had been the one comforting Gerry Yards as he wallowed in Scotch and self-pity, but with all she'd been through the last few weeks she was in no mood for it. "I've got to go."

Suddenly, he took a long step and grabbed the steering wheel. Charlie growled.

"Don't go to that kid. Stay here with me. Please."

"Gerry, let go of the steering wheel," Holly said as calmly as she could manage.

"You know I still love you, still want you, even though ... even though – well, you know. You're just going to embarrass yourself with that kid," he scoffed. "I mean, at your age and in your condition ..."

Holly shoved the hand control forward then jerked it backward. The big car bucked, tearing Yards' hand off the wheel. She idled the Lincoln in place and took a deep breath. "Gerry, you were good to me. You gave me a chance when no one else would, and I'll always be grateful," she told him. "But I'm sick of how you constantly find ways to intimate that I'm less of a woman than I was before ... before I went to Vietnam. That I'm damaged goods and that I'm lucky the great Gerry Yards would still be interested in poor paralyzed me."

Gerry Yards swallowed hard. He knew he'd crossed a line. "Sweetie, I'm sorry. I opened up a six-pack at lunch and –"

"Save your excuses and pack your bags," she said, throwing the car into reverse. "I expect my appointment to take about two hours. When I get back, I don't want to find you in my house.

"And in case you've forgotten, I was only nineteen when you embarrassed yourself with me."

* * *

The sky over the cypress trees was layered with lavender and pink as Holly drove west on the Pickens' Ferry Road. She turned southwest around the backside of Blue Mountain then made the sharp cutback onto the narrow road that wrapped up the hill face. It was barely wider than the tires of the big convertible, but it was cut into solid limestone, so it was firm all the way to the edge. Holly put the car's shifter in low and headed up the hill. By the time she reached the flat where the piers of the old farmhouse overlooked Moccasin Slough her heart was thumping, but she had made it. Holly stopped and took a moment to let her heart calm – at least in terms of the car's steep climb up the hill. Cutter might not even be there. He could be at The Gin. Or anywhere. But as she drove around the back of the ruins, she saw Cutter's jeep and then she saw him – and the heart that she had just calmed was racing again.

Cutter was sitting on his sleeping bag which was open atop a camouflage ground tarp. He was reading a book and had another lying next to him, his legs crossed at the ankles above his work boots. In the background, Mocassion Slough was mirroring the candy-colored sky. He watched as Holly pulled the car as close as she could and put the shifter into park. She turned off the big engine, but Cutter didn't close the book or get up.

"I thought I might buy you dinner at your favorite place," she said, lifting the picnic basket.

"How did you know I was here?" he asked, his voice even. Not unpleasant but not enthused, either.

"I tried The Well. Then I thought maybe with all that's going on you might need to do some thinking. So, I came to your thinking spot."

Cutter picked up a bookmark from the sleeping bag, placed in the book and closed it. He drew his knees up and rested his forearms on them with the hardback in his hands.

"You drove that big ol' tank up that wagon road? You're crazy."

She smiled. "You're not the first to notice."

Cutter put the book down and stood up. He was seeing the woman he'd kissed with such passion days earlier – the same one who had been on his mind every day since, but he was hearing Cecil Weathers' voice warning him to stay away from her.

"Miss Carter, I told you, this is where I come when I don't want to be bothered. I wish you'd respected that."

The words stung the smile off her face. She said, "You brought me here."

"Yeah. And we both know that was my mistake."

"Oh, Cutter, please don't say that. I had a wonderful day. And I want to explain –"

"There's nothing to explain. Let's just leave it at wonderful day. Okay?"

Holly understood why Cutter might be confused and frustrated over what had happened in the strawberry patch. So was she, but for different reasons.

"All right," she said after a moment and changed the subject. "You did a great job with the work at the house, but you didn't leave a bill. I want to pay you."

He took a few steps closer and Charlie climbed into Holly's lap and stood on the doorframe. The little dog yapped once and wagged. Cutter gave the dog a small, quick smile. "I'll figure it up and drop it by the office when I get time," he said, his tone a tad less brittle.

Holly heard the change and picked up on it. "Please do. You have no idea how valuable your work was."

Cutter took another step closer, reached out and scratched between Charlie's ears. "How's that?" he asked.

Holly told him about finding the broken frame with the tattered canvas and dried blood. "I took it to Doctor Garner," she went on. "You know, he handles all the county autopsies and he was Daddy's doctor as well." Cutter said nothing but Holly could see she had his attention. "Doctor Garner said there's no test that can determine with one-hundred percent certainty that the blood was Daddy's, but he said that the smaller drops on the frame are his type."

"The smaller drops?"

"Yes. Here's the even bigger surprise," said Holly. "On the piece of the frame that would have been at the bottom, there were several large drops that were O-negative. Definitely not Daddy's type."

The possibilities raced through Cutter's mind – questions he wanted to ask, thoughts he wanted to share, but he forced himself to remain silent. "Well, good," he allowed himself to say. "I mean, not good, but its looking more and more like you were right."

"*We* were right," she said. Then she told him about the Memphis Police reports and what Deputy Hinson had told her about notifying Mary Nell on the night of her father's death. "So, she couldn't have been part of it. Not physically."

"Then why would the killer use her car. Unless –" Cutter started but stopped himself. Holly knew what he was thinking, and said, "Unless it was Tom."

"Have you checked to see if people can place him in Biloxi that night?"

Holly shook her head. "No. The people I'd have to ask would be reporters and editors. Newspaper people. It wouldn't take some of them long to put two and two together. I don't want that until I'm sure."

"How much surer do you need to be?"

This was her chance. She handed Cutter the folder containing the pictures. "I need Efram Cole to look at these pictures," she told him.

Cutter opend the folder and flipped through them.

"Show him the one of the station wagon," she said. "Ask if there was a CHS Wolf's Football Booster sticker on the back glass? Like on Mary Nell's."

Cutter could almost smell the cigar smoke and talcum powder inside Governor Weather's limousine.

"What's this?" he said, looking at a sheet of legal paper. Mostly he was asking only to have something to say while he thought, and try to fight down a kind of lurking fear that he'd never felt. The fear that he had no control over his future – or that of his mother or Rose. That while no one owned him, someone owned enough of the world to destroy him. He barely heard Holly say, "I went to the library and looked up the Memphis and Tupelo papers for the day before my father died. Those were the top stories.

"If Mr. Cole was watching the news when the man came to the door, this might jog his memory. Maybe we could determine whether it was definitely the night Daddy died."

Cutter nodded though he hadn't really heard. He put the folder on the hood of the Lincoln. "Look, Mr. Cole said it was pitch black. He wasn't sure if he'd recognize the guy again."

"If he doesn't, he doesn't. I'm only asking that you try –"

... From now on, keep away from that Carter woman and the rag she's printin' ... I'd hate to have to disqualify you, and your sister, for you associatin' further with a known race-mixer, harlot and purveyor of lies ... Those words flashed behind Cutter's eyes like heat lightning. *... And, don't forget, your mother and sister will rot up there in that shack. With Tony.*

"No!" snapped Cutter. "I'm done with all this, and I'm done with you. I'm not sure how we got so tangled up, but it's got to stop right here. Right now!"

Holly paused, surprised. Then, "Cutter, if you're still upset about what happened between us. Let me explain –"

"No! No explanations! I don't want to hear it, because I don't care," he told her, stepping back, shaking his head. "Look, I was a jerk that first day when you and Miz Howard got run off in the ditch. I thought about it, and I, I – I felt sorry for you. And I needed to make it up. But it's gone too far and stops now."

... I felt sorry for you ... The discharge of that phrase was like someone firing a gun next to Holly's ear. It rang there inside her skull. All other sound simply disappeared and all that remained was the echo of the exploding cartridge and Gerry Yards' words – *"You're just going to embarrass yourself ... In your condition ..."*

Holly's face felt flush, ablaze with blood and heat and humiliation. She turned the key, and whipped the car around. Charlie tumbled into the passenger floor board as the car fishtailed around in a cloud of dust and nearly hit his jeep. The big convertible slid around the side of the house and disappeared. A few minutes later, Cutter saw it in the distance, its headlights flying east on Pickens' Ferry Road.

* * *

For a long time, Cutter sat under the elm with the dusty folder of photos that had spilled off the hood of the Lincoln. Soon the moon came up as bright as a dented copper plate and painted a molten strip the length of the slough. He thought of the night he and Miss Carter had watched men walk on that same moon, and knew that he'd been right. Decades from now, he'd remember where he was that night. And who he was with.

Sometime after the moon cleared the tree line, an owl in a nearby branch began asking, "Who? ... Who?"

Cutter had thought that he knew who he was – a man, plenty grown enough to handle himself and what came his way. But Weathers' threats had brought back all the little boy fear that had sent him to shivering, to whimpering and begging and crying when Tony locked him in that closet in the Old Ambrose Place. Outside, he could hear his mother babbling numbers and equations, then moaning helplessy after Tony slapped her to the floor. And he could hear what Tony was doing to Rose, and what he was making her do to him. It was happening right there, right outside the door! But he'd been too little and too weak back then to stop him.

And now he was too weak and scared to stop Tony's cronies from doing what they were doing.

After a time, the owl took wing, flapping noisily across the moon, but Cutter paid no notice. He lay under the elm in the same spot he'd shared with Miss Carter, his tears silently sliding away from the corners of his eyes, wondering who ... who he really was?

Chapter 17

∽

In my room at Mrs. Fletcher's Boarding House I pulled my number 81 Riverview Raiders jersey over my head. Without shoulder pads, it was long enough to be a dress. I glanced at my watch – 5:03. I was picking Patti up. She and the rest of the new Riverview cheerleading squad had to be at the rodeo arena early to decorate for the big pep rally. A knock at my door startled me as I pulled on my jeans.

"Just a minute," I called, knowing it probably was Mrs. Fletcher with a piece of freshly baked apple pie. The delicious aroma had wound its way up from the kitchen.

I zipped up my pants and opened the door. My father was standing in the hall, turning his hat in his hands. It had been a month since I'd seen him up close. His eyes were shot through with red veins of sleeplessness and I was sure there was more gray in his hair, which needed cutting.

When I said nothing, he asked, "Can I come in?"

"Uh, yeah, sure," I said and stepped out of the way.

Billy Wallace moved slowly around the room with its faded wallpaper and worn drapes. He stopped and looked out the screen door onto the balcony and the railroad tracks and highway beyond. "Nice room," he said with no hint of sarcasm. "The trains don't keep you awake?"

"No, sir. You get used to them."

He nodded and noticed a bookcase on one wall. He bent and studied the volumes that had been in my bedroom for years. "I saw you came and collected some of your stuff from the house."

"You weren't there."

"No, I – I don't spend much time at the house these days," he said. "Mostly I sleep at the jail. Or in my car. But Elmo Washington and his boys are doing a nice job with the farm. The cotton and beans are doin' real good. The corn's aw'right."

"Good."

My father kept his eyes moving around the room until they settled on a picture of the four of us – me and Mom, Steve and him – back when we were a family. Then they came back to the present me in my shabby boarding house room. "That jersey looks real good on you. It's mighty sharp," he said, managing a smile. "In fact, you look real good, Son. Healthy."

"Miz Fletcher's a good cook."

"I heard you found work. How's Mr. Handley treatin' you?"

"Real good. Especially considerin' how you and the feds have been harassing him and his brother," I told him, perhaps looking for a fight. If so, Billy Wallace didn't take the bait, so after a moment, I went on – "He says he could see me bein' an assistant manager in a year to eighteen months."

"What about college? I thought you couldn't wait to see what was at the other end of those railroad tracks."

"Oh, I will. You can bet your bottom dollar on that. But me and Patti may go the first two years over at the junior college in Booneville. That way, Patti can keep livin' at home a little longer and I can keep working at Handley's and save some money. That'll let us get a better start when we do go off to college."

"Is that your idea or Patti's? Or maybe Brother Mac's?"

"It was, well – it's not anybody's idea. It's just circumstances. It's just what we need to do," I tried to explain, irritated at how quickly my father had seen the truth of things. "Miz MacAllister's health isn't good. This whole mess has worn her nerves to a frazzle."

"I see."

"Speakin' of Patti, I'm supposed to pick her up in – gee! five minutes – to go to the rally. Is there somethin' you wanted to talk about or –?"

Billy Wallace set his straw Panama on his head and reached for his wallet. "No, I just wanted to see how you were farin' and give you this."

I unfolded the check and couldn't believe my eyes. Fifteen hundred dollars. "Daddy! Where'd you get this kind of money?"

"I sold Ricky Hickerson a few of those acres he's been wantin' over next to his fence line. There's enough there to cover your tuition to Riverview, your books and help out with odds and ends."

"But, Daddy, I got a scholarship. I don't need it."

"Son, take it. Please," he said. "If you're gonna go to Riverview, pay your own way. Don't let yourself be any more beholden to those people than you already are."

A bolt of anger shot through me. "Those people are my friends," I told him, pushing the check back into his hand. "And I don't want your money. I'm doin' fine on my own and I like it that way."

"Son, I –"

"Look, Daddy, I gotta go," I said and brushed past him into the hall. "Patti's waitin' on me."

"Shut the door, please, on your way out."

* * *

As the sun set and the lights of the rodeo arena were turned on, me, Mickey Ambrose and Toby Wright propped on a fence rail and watched our cheerleader girlfriends dancing in the center of the arena to Marvin Gaye's *Ain't No Mountain High Enough*, as played by Riverview's new marching band. The smell of animal dung, fried chicken, sawdust, cotton candy and sweat hung in the thick air between the highway and the river. At the north end of the arena, other former Wolves players began filling the tiers of folding chairs. The night before, Janette Wellingham had paraded there on the T-shaped stage on her way to winning Miss Cattahatchie County 1969.

One player who would not be on the stage was our quarterback, Jimmy Garner. After current Governor Broderick essentially refused to appoint a new school board until November's elections, Judge Mulberry stepped in. On Friday, he named Dr. G.P. Garner interim chairman. Mulberry also appointed to the five-member board Reverend Jean Baptiste of Roseville A.M.E. Church, and Ernie Logan, owner of the grocery recently shot up by the Klan. They became the first blacks to hold countywide office since Reconstruction.

Jimmy was a nice guy and a good leader but anyone could take a snap from center and give the ball to Cutter. In fact, if Coach Pearce was smart – and that was debatable – he'd install that new wishbone offense that they were running out in Texas and move Cutter to quarterback. That would require shifting a couple of good athletes to running back, which could open up a wide receiver slot for me. I might even start! Wouldn't that be something?

To be honest, until I saw Cutter emerge from the gap in the north grandstands and step onto the stage wearing the gold 13, I wasn't one-hundred percent sure he'd jump to Riverview. He seemed to have little room to maneuver, but as with the moves he made on the football field, Cutter could be surprising in his decisions and bold, to the point of recklessness, in his choices. Though Cutter and I had gone through a rough patch amid the agitation by that NCJ bunch and that Yankee judge, and whatever spell Holly Lee Carter had briefly cast over him, he still was my best friend. And now that decisions had been made and the county's social order was being restored, even if in exile, things would be getting back to normal, I told myself.

As I mounted the stage, most of my used-to-be and about-to-be teammates already were seated, as were Senator Wellingham, Milton Handley and Brother MacAllister. Cutter was next to Coach Pearce in the front row. I found a chair in the row behind them as Coach handed Cutter several three-by-five note cards.

"I'll introduce you," Coach Pearce was saying. "Speak clearly into the microphone. Don't mumble."

"I never do. I just don't always have a lot to say."

"Well, stick to the high points I made on the note cards. You'll be fine," said Coach Pearce. "And Cutter, you made the right decision."

"Yes, sir, I believe I have. I took a friend's advice and went to the Lord in prayer about it."

"Good for you," he said, squeezing Cutter's knee. "That's always the best way."

"Glad you think so."

Chapter 18

∽

Cutter gave Coach Pearce's three-by-five cards one more look, tapped them on his knee, folded them in half and slipped them into the back pocket of his Levi's. Over the carnival sounds of the midway, the lowing of livestock waiting to be judged and the braying of bucking horses eager to kick their hooves up and their riders off, Headmaster Larry Rhodes was saying something about how exciting it was to have the inauguration of Riverview Academy carried on a statewide radio hook-up. But Cutter wasn't really hearing him, nor seeing the Ferris wheel turning in a big neon circle at the center of the fairgrounds.

His mind was at Wolf's Run with Miss Carter. He'd been on his way to the pep rally and had not intended to talk to her about the decision he'd made to attend Riverview Academy, or really try to explain why he'd acted the way he had the other night. He had intended to simply apologize for saying he felt sorry for her. That was an out-and-out lie intended to drive her away. It had, but he had seen how badly it had hurt her. But that was it. Otherwise, he was going there only to return the photos.

Julie Davis answered the knock at the kitchen door late Saturday afternoon. She looked up at him with eyes that were no longer filled with admiration.

"Hi. I need to see Miss Carter."

"I'm not sure she's going to want to see you, sport."

"Tell her I talked to Efram Cole. She'll want to see me."

"All right. Come on in. Holly's doing her workout in the pool. I'll tell her," said Julie Davis, turning toward the French doors that led to the interior porch and courtyard. "By the way, she doesn't need your pity. She's strong in ways you'll never be."

Cutter said nothing but he couldn't hold Julie Davis' gaze. He moved his eyes away, shifting them around the room until he heard her close the door. He looked around the kitchen, remembering it warm with candlelight and Sinatra the way it had been the night after the Roseville bombing. Now the kitchen table was covered in newspapers, a ledger, an adding machine and several legal-looking documents, their edges fluttering in the wake from the ceiling fan. When he took a step closer, the seal of the State of California was not hard to read, nor were the words "Deed of Sale" in large black letters. An address on High Ridge Drive, Pacific Palisades, was typed onto a line provided in the form. He flipped a couple of pages and saw Miss Carter's signature on the line for "seller."

The heels of Julie Davis' sandals clattered on the ramp as she returned. Cutter stepped back from the table.

"Go on out," she said.

M iss Carter was settling herself in her wheelchair as he approached. She had a towel over her thighs and was wrapping one around her shoulders. He stopped on the flagstones ten feet away. Her one-piece suit, wet as it was, was almost as green as her eyes. Almost. She was quickly running a brush through her hair and Cutter thought again of the kitchen and the candlelight. That night the strokes had been gentle, even sensual, but now the movement was all merely functional. She wanted to get her hair out of the way so she could get on with this conversation. Get it over with.

The words Cutter had said had hurt her in ways she could not even explain to herself. She waited, behind her a set of waist-to-toe leg braces rested against a lounge chair. Leather straps and metal buckles were undone, and the above the ankle leather boots were unlaced.

Cutter was looking for a way to start the conversation, but Holly wasn't making it easy. "You wear those?" he finally said, cocking his chin toward the braces.

Holly pursed her lips and gave him a what-business-of-yours-is-it look, then said, "I'm supposed to. At least ten hours a week."

"What –?"

"To keep my leg bones from becoming too brittle."

"I've never seen you seen you in –"

"They just arrived from California. I didn't have room in the car," she said, but the casualness of the conversation Cutter seemed to be trying to make only irritated her more. "Look, you didn't come here to make small-talk by the pool. I hope. Julie said you talked to Mr. Cole."

Cutter put the folder down on the patio table. "Yes. I showed him the pictures. He said he's ninety percent sure LeRoy is the guy, but he couldn't swear to it in court."

Holly nodded, holding the towel together in front of her chest like a shawl. Her eyes remained hard, but they changed, too, like the clear glass of a gun sight being redirected. "What about the car?" she asked.

"It was definitely Mary Nell's car," he told her. "If you look close at the picture you can see the top part of the H and the S are missing in CHS. He noticed it that night, too."

Holly let go of the towel and her hands dropped into her lap before they balled into fists. It was what she had suspected. Still, the growing certainty that her sister-in-law conspired, in one way or another, to kill her father fell on her like a heavy weight that made it hard to breathe. But she took a breath and then another and asked, "What about the news stories?"

"No. Mr. Cole said the knock came just at the moment the news was coming on. He never saw it."

"Did you ask Mrs. Cole?"

"No. She wasn't home."

Holly nodded absently, as if hearing him from a great distance.

"What are you going to do now?" he asked.

The question seemed to bring her back to the present. "I don't know."

"It seems like it might be time to talk to Sheriff Wallace."

"Cutter, I appreciate you showing those pictures to Mr. Cole. But I'll take it from here," she said, shutting a door between them. Cutter felt it but didn't turn to leave. Instead he crossed to the knee-high fieldstone wall that guarded the edge of the courtyard where the land fell steeply away four-hundred feet to the river. Through the kudzu, briars and wild grapevine a narrow path twisted – the wolf's run. He stood there for several moments with his hands stuffed in his back pockets. Then he turned. "Look, Miss Carter, I wanted to tell you, I didn't mean what I said the other night about feeling sorry for you," he said, hurrying the words from his lips. "It was a lie. I just wanted – I mean, I-I needed you to leave. I'm sorry."

Holly studied him. She appreciated what she was hearing, especially because she could see that it was something not easy for Cutter to say. But she was cautious, too. Gerry Yards was gone back to Los Angeles but his words remained, and Cutter's angry, hurtful tone had amplified them. Now every time she looked in the mirror, saw herself in the bath or slipped into bed, alone except for Charlie, she heard them again. So it took Holly a moment to find her own voice, then – "Thank you, Cutter. It means a lot to hear you say that. I know you're under a lot of pressure to, well, to be what this town wants you to be. Believe me, I know that feeling. I ran all the way to the West Coast and crossed an ocean to get away from it. And even then, I never really did."

Cutter cleared his throat. "I guess I've always thought of myself as a pretty strong person. Or at least, if I was faced with a choice between right and wrong, I would choose to do the right thing. At least, the right thing in my eyes. But now?"

He shook his head and rubbed his hand across his mouth. Holly pushed closer, considered her words. Considering how important they might be. She blinked and in that instant asked God to give her the right words to say.

"Cutter, I truly believe that in the long run God blesses those who do the right thing as the Holy Spirit gives us the grace to understand it," she said. "But here on this earth, sometimes doing the right thing has very little immediate benefit. In fact, it can be painful and lonely, and very scary."

"Like giving up your house in California," he said. Holly's eyes registered surprise only for an instant before she remembered the Deed of Sale on the kitchen table. "The place you love most in the world."

Holly didn't have to think about her answer. She'd given the decision plenty of thought, and prayer. "There are a lot of houses in California. If God wants me to have another someday, then I will," she said. "But what I've come to see over the last couple of weeks is that I had only committed halfway to the call God gave me."

Cutter sat on the short wall so that he was level with Holly's eyes.

"Yes. I came back here when, the Lord knows, I did *not* want to. But I always had that safety net back in L.A.," she said. "The thing is, God doesn't want to us to trust Him halfway. He wants all our trust.

"So, there are moments in our lives when He asks us to walk in faith, and faith alone. This is my moment.

"Without a pretty massive infusion of cash, the paper won't last another three weeks. A screenwriter for Warner Brothers has been wanting to buy the house for over a year. Last week, he called and upped his offer again. Upped it substantially," she explained. "It's enough that we can keep the doors of the paper open and presses turning until early next year. By then, maybe enough people will have had a change of heart to keep us afloat."

"It seems to me you're taking a mighty big risk," said Cutter. "I don't know that people in this county have that much change in 'em. At least not that fast."

"It's only a risk if I don't trust God to take care of me. He may not take care of me how I expect, or in the way I would choose in my selfishness. In fact, it may be a path I wish God hadn't chosen for me," Holly said, slowly patting her bare knee. "But I truly believe God can turn anything for good."

Cutter stood and ran his left hand through his hair and rubbed the back of his neck as he stared across the broad green expanse of the Cattahatchie River Valley. A junkyard in Moore's Bridge, Alabama, still was the farthest he'd ever been from this place.

After a moment, Holly asked, "Is this about you making the jump to Riverview and taking the team with you?"

Cutter laughed sarcastically. "No. This is about the team making the jump to Riverview and taking me with them."

Then, "Miss Carter, I don't like the people running Riverview. I don't like what they stand for. I don't like the way they make me feel when I'm around them. But this county isn't coming together. It's coming apart. There's no time to start a brand new football team at the high school. And without football I'm … I'm –"

Cutter broke off the thought and the words before he could say them.

Holly looked at her watch on the patio table. "Cutter, you've got about two hours until the pep rally. You're welcome to sit here and think. No one will bother you."

"I appreciate the offer, but there's nothing to think about," he forced himself to say, remembering Governor Weathers warning about staying away from the harlot. He already had put himself at risk, and worse, his mother and Rose, by coming to Wolf's Run. Weathers' people could be watching. "But I meant what I said about not feeling sorry for you. You're a – You're a –"

"Cutter –"

"I've got to go," he said and started to turn but Holly reached out and took his hand. She squeezed it. "Wherever you're going, God will be there," she told him. "You can talk to Him. And if you open your heart, He'll talk to you."

* * *

In the library, Holly tuned the stereo to WHCI and switched off the lights. It was dusk, and cars swam like tiny silver minnows along the course cut by Highway 27. To the south, the lights of town and the fairgrounds mixed into a yellow-white glow. She wheeled to the big leather sofa, transferred out of her chair, lifted her legs and stretched out. For a moment Holly stared at the empty space on the wall where her mother's portrait had hung, then turned her mind to the more immediate. She had checked to make sure all the doors were locked, but with Julie covering the pep rally as the final chapter in her magazine piece, she was alone in the big house. She took the .38 from the pocket of her skirt and placed it within easy reach on the coffee table.

Charlie hopped up on the couch and lay against her side as she stroked the little dog's white coat.

WHCI's only real announcer, "Stonewall" Maddox, described the pageantry of the rally as if it were a royal coronation. And in a way it was, thought Holly. All Cutter had to do was go along with the River-view crowd, spend the autumn running over and past the slow-footed kids he would face in the Academy League, bring home the champi-onship trophy – and he would *own* DeLong, Mississippi. One way or another, the town's elite would make sure that Cutter got a scholarship to whichever Mississippi football power he desired.

Heady stuff when you're eighteen – almost nineteen, Holly reminded herself as she closed her eyes. "Dear Lord, I don't know if I said the right things today. Cutter is young and whatever he does tonight will change the course of his life.

"I pray that You would reach into his heart and strengthen and guide him. It's in Jesus' name I pray. Ah-men," she said, and listened as former CHS principal Larry Rhodes was introduced as Riverview's first headmaster.

* * *

The sound of his name being called over the public address system seemed distant, like the sound of a bell through water. Then it came again, and Cutter realized it was hard to hear because of all the applause, whoops, whistles and cheers.

"Cut-ter! ... Cut-ter! ... Cut-ter!"

The crowd rocked the two syllables of his name back and forth between the bleachers, from one side of the arena to the other. TV lights glared and flashbulbs glittered at the front of the stage as governors Weathers and Broderick took up station beside Cutter, waving to the several thousand locals gathered at the arena.

"Smile, son!" urged Cecil Weathers without disturbing his own grin. "Smile like you mean it."

At the Old Ambrose Place, Rose Marie Carlucci sat on the front steps holding the transistor radio Cutter had given her. Her mother was pacing the side porch repeating louder and louder the multiplication tables, until she was almost screaming them. How much Jennifer Ambrose Cutter Carlucci understood about events around her, Rose was never sure.

"First, I'd like to thank the folks behind Riverview Academy for thinking enough of me to give me a scholarship," Cutter began. "And for giving Rose, my sister, a scholarship, too. I'm sure Riverview students will get a good education."

At the far end of the arena, Tony Carlucci leaned on the rail with nine other unrobed Klansmen. One of them jovially clapped Tony on the back. The Kaptain of Klargo managed a brief, crooked smile that hid the disdain he had for the touch of any man and the distrust and contempt he had for Cutter. But mainly the curl of his lips hid a rage of jealousy boiling inside him.

Now Cutter was saying, "But I've been thinking and, at the suggestion of a friend, doing a little praying, too."

Eleven miles away, a slow smile formed on Holly's lips.

"Well, most of you know I kind of live on my own. I've worked construction. Done farm labor. Bussed tables, built fences, painted barns and done more odd jobs than I can name. And a lot of those jobs I've done next to a colored man – that is, a black man, I guess I'm supposed to say these days. Best I can tell, I'm none the worse for it."

A shocked grumble passed through the crowd. Sheriff Wallace, who had been standing behind the stage, started easing up the ramp. He had a feeling about what was going to happen.

"During wintertime, I played a lot of basketball with Tommy Ray Banks and his friends from Roseville High. I've got to say, as many times as I bumped up against Tommy or one of his cousins, I can't find a smudge of black that ever rubbed off on me."

People were booing now. At first a few here and there, then a chorus.

"That's enough!" shouted Cecil Weathers. Coach Pearce jumped to his feet as if he was ready to tackle Cutter, or try. That's when my daddy and Deputy Hinton stepped in, blocking the runway. "You wanted him to speak, now you're gonna let him," I heard daddy say.

Listening over the statewide radio hookup, Judge Mulberry and U.S. Attorney J.L. Burke clinked their whiskey glasses, shared surprised smiles and sat back in their rocking chairs on the porch of Mulberry's Oxford home as federal marshals patrolled the grounds. Over the clatter of Saturday night's busy supper rush, cooks, waiters and busboys at The Gin listened in the kitchen as they loaded steaks and catfish suppers onto plates. In the big tent outside of Pickens' Ferry A.M.E. Church, Ron Clemmer and a couple of dozen youthful volunteers from the North held their breath as Cutter went on.

"So, I've got to speak from my heart and tell you folks that I don't get it. I don't get why sittin' in a classroom next to a black kid is a big deal."

I leaned forward and held my head in my hands. I thought I was going to throw up. The dream I'd had for Cutter and I only a few minutes earlier was utterly destroyed. Brother MacAllister looked as if he was going to tear his Bible in half and Patti's mouth was twisted as she snarled words her father probably didn't even know. I couldn't pick the words out. They were caught up in the increasing howl, like heat from a fire rising in a chimney – all the heat directed at Cutter.

Miles to the north, Rose Carlucci hugged the little radio to her chest, never more proud of her brother than at that moment.

"I figure black kids probably want to learn, just like we do. Maybe more, because they've got some catchin' up to do in this country."

Instead of trying to fight through my father and his deputy, J.D. Benoit jumped down from the front of the stage, swung open the six-inch blade of his pocket knife and grabbed the microphone cord.

"I appreciate everything the people of DeLong have done for me. But my heart tells me I need to stay at Cattahatchie High and –"

The microphone went dead and Cutter's natural voice was drowned in what had become a rage of boos and profanity.

There was no point in trying to continue to talk to the crowd, but Cutter turned, pulling off the Raiders' jersey to expose a black-and-red CHS football T-shirt. He looked into the stunned faces of the would-be Riverview players and spoke. He had to shout to be heard over the jeers. "I'm going to be at the high school field Monday afternoon at 3, ready to practice," he yelled. "The season-opener is in two weeks. We'll have to work our tails off to be ready.

"If any of y'all are still real Wolves, be there!"

As Cutter walked down the ramp, someone threw a cup of soda that hit him in the shoulder. More than one person spit in his direction, and ugly voices followed him as he walked out of the floodlights and into the shadows behind the stage. He ignored them all.

"You ungrateful dago scum! ... You're done in this town! ... You're as crazy as your momma! ... And as stupid as your idiot s-s-s-sister!"

At the other end of the arena, Tony Carlucci punched the plank fence and heard the wood crack under his rage.

PART IV

Chapter 1

෪

Cutter pushed hard through the double doors at the front of DeLong Memorial Hospital. Hard enough that the glass rattled and heads turned as he stepped out of the dusky light and into the building's bright, sterile halls.

"Miz Kyle, which room is my mother in?" he asked at the front desk.

"Name, please?" asked the woman under the blonde beehive.

"Name? Miz Kyle, you've known me all my life."

"I thought I knew you, but after your performance last night at the fairgrounds, I don't think I know you at all. You're a stranger."

Cutter drew in a deep breath and let it out as slowly as his concern and a flash of anger would allow. "Just tell me which room Jennifer Carlucci is in. Please."

"I'll tell you, but I'll tell you first that God has a way of chastening those who stray from his flock. And sometimes He's quick about it, too," Mrs. Kyle told him. She pursed her lips. "South fourteen."

As soon as he turned the corner onto the south wing, he saw Sheriff Wallace leaning beside the door to the room talking to Holly Lee Carter.

"How's Momma?" Cutter asked.

"She's resting," Holly told him. "Rose is with her."

"What happened? Was it Tony? Did he do something to her?"

Sheriff Wallace straightened. "If you mean in the immediate last few hours or days, no. I heard the ambulance call this morning for the Old Ambrose Place. So, I took a run up there."

"To see who finally killed who?"

Sheriff Wallace turned his hat in his hand. "I just came back now to check on her."

"Okay. If it wasn't Tony, then what?"

"Cutter, it's a stroke," said Holly. "A bad one."

Jennifer Carlucci's son wavered as if suddenly struck by a strong wind. "Oh, Jesus," he sighed and caught himself against the wall. "How bad?"

"Well, Doctor Garner – Oh, here he is now," said Holly, as G.P. Garner emerged from a nearby room.

Cutter turned. "Doc, how bad?"

Gerald Patrick Garner chose his words as carefully and gently as he could. "She has no sensation or motor function on her left side. She's breathing on her own, which is a good sign, but her vocal cords appear to be affected. And because of Miss Jenny's, well, longstanding mental health issues, it's very difficult to determine how much neurological damage there is."

"Can I go in?"

"Of course. I'll be in to talk further with you in a few minutes."

The sheriff placed his hat on his head as Cutter stepped to the door, his hand uncertain with dread. "Son, for what it's worth, you did the right thing last night," said Billy Wallace. "It may not seem like it now, but there are a lot of people in this town who are proud of you."

Cutter nodded but could find no words with which to respond. He pushed through the door and into his mother's room.

Behind the hospital was a thick stand of woods that hid the river. In the distance, the Chalmette Hills west of town rose up. Through the windows of his mother's room, Cutter could see the late afternoon sun descending into the pine ridge that defined the horizon, melting like a red rubber ball lain amid a blacksmith's coals.

It was cool and dark in the room except for the fading sunlight, which was amber. Rose sat in a large padded chair that could convert into a bed. Not used to air-conditioning, she was wrapped in a blanket up to her neck. In truth, Rose was unused to virtually all of the physical and emotional comforts with which most people in 1969 would have defined home and family.

Cutter leaned the weight of his two-hundred-twenty-something pounds on the steel rail of his mother's bed and wondered how he had been birthed by this small, frail woman – her skin now as white and waxy as tallow. The lines around her eyes and sunken mouth were so deeply gouged that Cutter almost could see bone. In her hair, there was no longer even a hint of the golden straw color that Cutter remembered from his childhood. It was now a stark and weathered white. Her only color came from a purple spider-webbing of veins that criss-crossed each other perilously close to the surface of her face, neck and arms.

Jennifer Ambrose Cutter Carlucci was forty-six years old.

They were silent for a time, watching the IV drip as the light in the room turned from red to pink. The clear tubing looked as if it was filled with dollar wine. Without looking away from his mother, Cutter asked, "What happened?"

Rose drew the blanket even tighter around her neck and ran her tongue over her full lips. "She's been g-gettin' worse all week. Hardly sleeping or eating. By late S-Saturday afternoon, she wasn't m-mumblin' her sums or whisperin' them like usual. She was sayin' 'em out loud, then f-finally she was yellin' 'em. Screamin' the numbers out.

"I, I, I tried to calm her down. About two o'clock in the morning, I got her to stop yellin'. Or m-maybe she just lost her v-voice. I don't know. I got her to s-s-sit down at her quilting frame, but she kept missing her stitches and poking herself with the needles. So, I-I took them away from her. I gave her fr-fresh chalk to do her numbers with and she started in on the living room wall.

"I watched her for a long time. Then sometime after sunup, I, I, I f-fell asleep. When I woke up, shhhh-she was gone. I f-found her out in the b-barn like th-this," she told him and the tears burst from her brown eyes, the sobs from her throat. "I-I I'm sorry! I was *sooo* tired. I-I-"

Cutter turned and moved quickly to kneel beside his sister's chair. "Rose, this is *not* your fault. Momma has been like a pressure cooker for years. If it wasn't for the care and love you've given her, this would have happened a long time ago."

That was the truth, and Cutter was sure Rose knew it, but right now it mattered that he say it. He stood again beside the bed. "How did Miss Carter get … involved?"

"I made M-M-Momma as comfortable as I c-could, then I ran to The W-Well to find you. When you weren't th-there, I walked as fast as I c-could up to W-Wolf's Run. I-I thought maybe –" she said but broke off thought. "M-M-Miss Carter called an ambulance then took me back to the house. She's st-stayed with us all day."

It was dark outside when Cutter stepped back into the blanching flo-rescence of the hall. His knees felt weak and he didn't know which way to turn. Once again, he hadn't been there when Rose needed him. When his mother needed him. After what had happened at the pep rally, all he wanted was to get out of Cattahatchie County. He hadn't wanted to talk to anyone or explain himself. So, he drove, like he knew Miss Carter often did. Drove all night, listening to the radio. Listening to late night sounds for lonely lovers until the signal faded near Little Rock. Then he picked up the clear, clean signal of WWL in New Orleans and The Charlie Douglas Road Gang. He drove until he was too tired to drive any farther, until he had put more miles between him and DeLong than had ever been there before, drove until he was in Fort Smith, on the Arkansas-Oklahoma line. He got a ten dollar room in a roadside motel, slept four hours, took a shower, ate some breakfast and headed back to Mississippi to face whatever there was to face. But he hadn't been expecting to face this when he walked into The Gin and was handed the note left there by Sheriff Wallace. Now Cutter wavered outside his mother's room. He stepped backward. Had the hospital wall not been there to catch his shoulders, he was so off balance he might have fallen. He looked toward the nurses' station where Holly was talking to a nurse with whom she'd gone to high school. She came to him.

"How's Rose?"

Cutter stared at the exit sign, the lights, the floor. "Considering she's grown up in a madhouse and has a brother who always seems to be AWOL when she needs him the most, I guess she's okay."

"You had no way of knowing this was going to happen."

"Sure I could have known. If I stopped camping out at The Well, pretending that being there across the bean fields was some kind of protection for Momma and Rose."

Cutter released a long sigh, as if it had been the last breath holding him up, and slid down the wall. He drew his knees toward him and crossed his big forearms over them.

"What am I gonna do?" he quietly asked himself more than Holly. "Momma is gonna need all kinds of care. I've got a little money in a savings account. But it won't even cover a week of hospital bills.

"And Rose? I can't let her go back to that house."

Holly pivoted her chair and backed up next to Cutter.

"After last night, the moneychangers in this town sure ain't gonna give me a loan," he said. "I've got no way to help them. And now I don't t even have a future."

Holly felt Cutter's weight slump against her wheel. She reached and locked the brakes. With her right hand, she ran her long fingers along the side of his neck, his jaw line and stroked his hair. Silently comforting Cutter just as he had comforted her on the night after the Klan bombing ravaged Roseville and Eve Howard was found.

"You were awake? On the way back from Memphis?"

"Now and then," she said. "Enough to enjoy 'late night sounds for lonely lovers,' and the way you ran your fingers along my shoulder and neck, and stroked my hair."

"I guess I was kind of taking advantage –"

"No, you weren't. You were a perfect gentleman," she assured him as she gently kneaded the tension in his shoulder. "Besides, you didn't hear me object, did you?

A quick, tired smile moved across his face but he didn't look up. Holly was wearing jeans and white flip-flops. Her feet were well tanned and her toenails painted a shade of pink that reminded him of a tropical drink. He cupped his hand over the top of her foot. She savored his touch with her eyes, then said, "Maybe I can help. Rose can stay at Wolf's Run as long as she needs to."

Cutter glanced up and shook his head. "Thanks. I appreciate it, but no. I couldn't let you do that. I know you've got enough on your plate."

"Don't get this wrong, Cutter. I'm not offering charity. Eve Howard is, is gone and Julie Davis is leaving tomorrow. I don't need much help, but Rose could earn her keep and maybe a little more helping me the way Eve did." Cutter looked up at her again, but with different eyes – eyes that were seeing the possibilities. Holly went on – "I know Rose struggles in school. I could tutor her, or at least be there to help her with her homework. And being around the newspaper office might be good for her. It could begin to open up the world to her after being cooped up in that house all these years." Cutter was nodding slowly. "In any case, I don't want to stay alone so far from town in that big ol' house."

Cutter drew in a long breath, giving himself time to think and to find the right words. "Miss Carter, Tony would not be happy with that arrangement."

"Since when did you start worrying about Tony Carlucci's happiness?"

"Since never. But I do worry about what he might do."

"Look, I'm not making this offer with blinders on. I know what Tony is, and what he's capable of. Believe me, I *know*," she said. Cutter glanced up but saw Holly wasn't going to elaborate. Instead, she said, "Honestly, Rose would be doing me a big favor. If she's willing."

Cutter took his time, thinking, as Holly watched him gently squeeze her foot. "Can you feel your toes?"

The question didn't surprise Holly. She knew Cutter would ask something like it sooner or later. But she knew, too, that the answer entailed more than a skin-deep reply.

"Nope. I can't feel much of anything below my belly button," she said. "But when I watch you touch me like that, I think I can."

Managing a weary smile, Cutter nodded and gently squeezed again as Holly's fingers mapped the thick rope of muscle in his neck.

"I'll talk to Rose," he said.

Chapter 2

❦

Rose Marie Carlucci was surprised, relieved, frightened, excited, apprehensive, thankful and fretful as she gathered up her belongings from the only home she'd ever known. But long ago the rusty nails that held together the gray, weather-worn boards of the Old Ambrose Place had lost their hold on her. She had stayed there only because of her mother, and because the people in DeLong who were supposed to be their family had turned their backs on her and Cutter years ago.

With Sheriff Wallace sitting in his cruiser at the end of the driveway early Monday afternoon, Rose went through the house. As Cutter watched, Rose opened each compartment of an old chest of drawers. She stared into a nearly empty chiffonier. In the end, everything she had, or at least everything she wanted to take from that rotting purgatory, fit into three large grocery bags. She tucked the scrapbook she'd kept for Cutter under her arm.

"You ready?" Cutter asked as she climbed into the Jeep.

Rose brushed her dark brown hair over her ear, swallowed hard. "Y-Yes. No! W-Wait!" she told him and ran up the steps onto the porch. She quickly stripped her mother's latest quilt from the frame. There were spots of blood on the final yellow square. Rose folded it and ran back to the Jeep, clutching it to her chest.

"Is that it?"

Rose looked over the place, the rust stains cut almost black into the tin roof. They reminded her of a crying woman, her eyes red-rimmed, her mascara running down her cheeks. "W-We should b-b-burn this place."

Cutter hit the shifter – "One day we will."

* * *

Later that afternoon, Cutter drove to the Cattahatchie High School locker room. When he turned into the parking lot behind it, Jimmy Garner and Dodge McDowell already were there, sitting on the tailgate of Jimmy's pickup.

Fullback Donnie Thompson was present, as were linebackers Charlie Haygood and Chris Goodlet, defensive back Teddy Renfro and wide receiver Kyle Long. As I sat watching from an old log road cut through the dense woods south of the gym, much to my surprise, Haughton Wellingham IV, and cheerleaders Rebecca Hardin and Kathy Reed climbed out of Teddy's Camaro.

Cutter stepped from his Jeep and they gathered around him. He gave Haughton a long look. "I'd be lyin' if I said I expected to see you here today. Does your daddy know?"

"Not yet. But I'm sure he'll know soon enough," said Haughton. "He and Mother will kick about it for a few days, but they'll get over it. Ridge Bellafont was my mother's first cousin."

"What about your sister?"

"Janette?" he said, cocking his head. "She has her own set of priorities."

Cutter nodded and began counting. "Nine. Well, if you girls care to suit up, we'll have eleven. We can play football."

Dressed in her usual black shorts and red cheerleader T-shirt Becky Hardin looked up at Cutter through her big sunglasses. "I'm all for it. I've had dreams about getting all hot and sweaty, and wallowing around in the grass with you."

"Down girl," said Jimmy.

Cutter reached into his Jeep for a football. "Okay. We've got most of the offense here, so we can at least throw the ball around and run through some plays."

Jimmy Garner, the son of the school board's new president, held up a set of keys that had hung from Coach Pearce's belt. "We can do better than that. I say we suit up just like for a regular practice."

"Yeah," agreed Chris Goodlet. "We need to get the pads on."

"Darn right!" Donnie Thompson enthused.

"Then let's do it," said Cutter.

Jimmy Garner checked his watch. "I've got five till three. By three-fifteen, let's be under the west goalposts, stretching."

Dr. Garner's son stuck his hand out into the middle of the circle that had formed around Cutter. Chris Goodlett covered it and so on until there was a stack of fingers and palms.

"Come on, girls," said Cutter, "get your hands in here. You're part of the team, too."

"One, two, three – Wolves!" I whispered as I watched the knot of my one-time friends moving in pantomime. It broke apart and Jimmy opened the door to the locker room. I watched until they disappeared inside, then I cranked the truck and drove away. I already was late for the first day of practice at Riverview.

By the time Cutter and the small cadre of players made their way onto the field, two deputies were walking the south side of the practice field. One carried a shotgun, the other a high-powered rifle with a scope. They were watching the woods that rose up across a small creek and could provide perfect cover for a sniper. Everyone noticed, but no one mentioned them. Cutter's surprise announcement on Saturday night had created quite a stir thanks to the statewide radio hookup. As Jimmy orchestrated the little practice, a handful of reporters from as far away as Nashville and Atlanta began to gather under the goal posts. There was even a camera crew from a Memphis station. When practice was over, the reporters stopped fanning themselves with their notebooks and surrounded Cutter like fading, mismatched flowers wilting in the August sun. Questions were coming quickly and from all directions.

Cutter held up his hands. "I'm not going to answer any questions about Saturday night. I did what I did for my own reasons, and it's enough that I know what they are," he told them. "But I do have a couple of things I want to say.

"First, I'm really proud of the guys who came out today. And of Kathy Reed and Becky Hardin. Our cheerleaders. But we're hoping this is just a start."

"Cutter, the faces out here are still all white," noted one reporter. "Do you expect this to remain a segregated team?"

"That'll be up to the, uh, the black kids who'll be coming over here from Roseville. But we've got about twenty-five more uniforms hanging in the locker room. We need ballplayers to fill 'em."

"How about a coach?" asked someone else.

"We need one. What are you doing for the next three months?" he asked the reporter. The press corps laughed. Julie Davis stood back and smiled. For all of his strong, silent ways, Cutter was a natural in front of the cameras.

"Can you tell us –?"

"Hey, Cutter, over here!"

Cutter looked as a flashbulb went off close to his face. He tried to politely push through the circle of reporters but they moved with him.

"Cutter, Governor Weathers reportedly told the AP today that you're a turncoat against your community and your race," said a small balding man with a sunburned pate. "He also reportedly said that if he had to endow every school in America, he'd make sure you never play college football."

Cutter stared at the man but forced a smile to hide the bolt of apprehension that shot through him. "I, uhm, I thought it was from here to Hawaii," he joked. "Does anybody know if they play football in Mexico?"

* * *

Within the hour, thunderheads were dwarfing the hills and an early night fell on DeLong as the thick, black wall of rain and clouds curtained off the sunset.

After Cutter dropped his sister and her things off at Wolf's Run earlier in the day, Holly had taken Rose to the paper. She'd introduced her to those handy, shown her the offices and found her a desk, which was not hard, considering how depleted her staff remained. Now they were back, just ahead of the storm.

"I bet you could use a long, hot bath," Holly said to Rose as they paused in the kitchen. "Why don't you go relax in a hot tub, and I'll start dinner. Do you eat pork chops?"

Rose nodded. "I-I-I-I c-c-can f-f-f –" she tried then closed her eyes and covered her mouth in frustration. Rose opened her eyes, concentrated. "I, I c-can fix supp-per. Earn m-m-my keep."

"Don't worry, Rose. There'll be plenty of time for that. I'm going to be relying on you a lot," Holly told her as the first heavy droplets of rain thumped against the high eaves of the tin roof.

Forty-five minutes later dinner was ready. Holly wheeled up the hall as the rain drummed and the wind shook the pine boughs and the limbs of the big pecan trees. She tapped on the open door and Rose turned. She was wearing a long Van Morrison T-shirt that Holly had loaned her. A mist of rain-cooled air was floating in through the open windows, but the Tiffany lamp on the bed table made the room look warm and inviting. Rose already had put her mother's unfinished quilt on the room's large oak sleigh bed.

"Are you hungry?"

"Yes."

"Then come on, before it gets cold," said Holly, but Rose didn't move. "Is there something wrong?"

"I-I I'm afraid to m-move. That I'll br-break the trance and none of this will be r-real," she managed. "I-I just c-can't believe this is m-my room."

Holly pushed across the threshold. "It is, Rose. For as long as you want it."

Rose ran her hand along the fine oak of the chest of drawers. The things at Wolf's Run weren't worn out and old like at the Ambrose Place; they were antiques. Holly watched, thinking how Tony Carlucci's genetic influence was much more visible in his daughter than in Cutter. But even without makeup, Rose was a pretty girl with dark eyes and lips full enough that they balanced the considerable width of her nose and offset the roundness of her face.

Suddenly, Rose's lips quivered like a breaking dam and all the emotion of the last few days – perhaps the last few years – burst out. She ran to Holly, knelt beside her and wrapped her arms around her, the tears cascading like the rain off the porch roof.

Down the mountain and across the Old Iron Bridge above the river Tony Carlucci stood on the porch of the house now empty amid the bean fields. He had turned on no lights in the house. In his black rain slicker he was nearly invisible as the rain rolled off the roof in a cold, thin waterfall. Though the air was chilled with the deluge from the cold upper reaches of a mighty thunderhead, the sense of humiliation that had scalded him Saturday night continued to burn with the ferocity of cooking grease thrown smoking onto his genitalia.

For years Cutter had been quietly showing him up by living on his own as if he was too good to dwell under his father's roof, Tony told himself. By refusing to even own up to his last name unless he had to. And now he and the Carter bitch had stolen his daughter

The rain beat on the old tin roof and in his ears, but Tony only could hear himself making plans. Plans to regain control of his daughter – *my sweet Rose, my flower for the picking.* Now that the whole county had turned against Cutter, he could be dealt with without interference. He'd make Cutter pay for his disobedience, his refusal to honor his mother *and* his father. Why those kids always took the side of the weak, crazy, frigid old hag he would never understand. But it didn't matter. He didn't really care about understanding. Attempting to understand was wasted effort. Control was enough. In the end, control was all that mattered, and when he thought of what he would do with Holly Lee Carter when he had her under his control – if only briefly – Tony smiled. For an instant the lightning illuminated his face in the shadows. His features were as inhuman and malevolent as those of a Jack-o-lantern lit and left on the porch of the empty house.

Chapter 3

༄

Two-a-day football practices continued that week at both CHS and Riverview. I actually was working out with the first-team offense, though I had to admit our efforts looked slow and pedestrian without Cutter and Jimmy Garner in the backfield. Our defensive line seemed anemic minus big Dodge McDowell. By the middle of the week the word was around town that at least five black kids now were practicing in Wolves uniforms. That gave "Cutter's Team," as people were referring to it, enough bodies to kick off a football game and play – assuming nearly everyone played both offense and defense and very few got hurt. But for me, the biggest difference continued to be that we Raiders were not practicing under threat. Armed deputies remained watchful at every CHS practice and FBI men could be regularly seen on the hill above the field, scanning for potential shooters.

Despite all that had happened, Cutter and I had covered a lot of dirt-road miles together, and I was scared for his sake.

I had heard that Cutter was spending the nights in the sleeper chair next to his mother's hospital bed. In the mornings, Miss Carter dropped Rose off at the hospital, and in the afternoon Rose walked to the town square and helped out at the newspaper.

As it turned out, the shots fired that week were not at Cutter but at my father, among others.

Reverend Clemmer and eleven young NCJ workers were returning from the fair on Wednesday after manning a voter registration booth there. Escorted by a sheriff's cruiser in front and back, they left the fairgrounds without incident in their old white school bus. All was well until they reached a hairpin turn in the unlit dirt of Pickens' Ferry Road. There the vast swamp pressed itself within a few yards of the rising hills. As the bus started across, the plank bridge in the apex of the turn exploded, bucking the front end of the bus a good 10 feet into the air. It came down hard, nose-diving into the smoking, watery hole where the bridge had been – sending the bus's occupants flailing and tumbling. Almost before the front bumper dug into the muck, the bus and the police cars came under automatic weapons fire from boats hidden among the cypress knees in the black morass of the swamp.

Slugs stitched the side of his patrol car but my father snatched his shotgun from the rack beside the radio, rolled out beside the cruiser and returned fire across the hood. Newly hired Deputy Clint Conroy emptied his .357 twice. In the midst of all this, gas from the bus's ruptured fuel tank found the hot exhaust manifold and caught fire, sending a hot serpent of orange flame slithering across the water. At the edge of the spreading light, the sheriff saw four black-hooded men in two small boats disappearing into the deeper darkness of Moccasin Slough.

Billy Wallace grabbed the microphone on his police radio and called for assistance, "Shots fired! Shots fired!" And, "Send as many ambulances as you can to my location," he told the dispatcher. "And fire trucks, too!"

My father then climbed onto the burning bus and helped get everyone off before it was consumed.

The whole attack had lasted less than ninety seconds and the men who committed it were gone, like ghosts.

Holly's bedside phone rang about 11:20 that night. The woman on the other end was a girl with whom Holly had gone to high school. Her husband was a volunteer fireman, and the woman gave Holly all the information she had.

"Good luck, and God bless you. Not everyone supports what the Klan is doing," said Clara Franks. "But, Holly, please don't tell anyone I called you. Okay?"

"Okay, Clara," Holly said, as she held the phone between her shoulder and ear as she transferred into her wheelchair. "I won't. Thanks."

Holly roused Rose. They threw on whatever was handy and were in the car in under five minutes. Holly checked her camera bag and made sure the .38 was in her purse. "Are you okay with this?" Holly asked her new helper.

"L-Let's go."

Two ambulances already had arrived at the emergency room when Holly turned into the parking lot and stopped next to Cutter's jeep. They got out as a stretcher rolled through the doors heading for a waiting ambulance. The young redheaded man's leg was splinted from ankle to hip and an IV line was running into his arm. Holly could see at least a dozen stitches along his jaw line. Doctor Garner had walked with the stretcher to the ambulance and Holly and Rose followed him back inside.

"How bad?" asked Holly.

"Compound fractures of the right leg," said the doctor. "We stabilized him. They'll have to do surgery in Memphis. Put pins in it. But he should be all right. Eventually."

"Good, but I meant –"

"Oh, you mean overall," said the doctor. "Well, from what I was told, Reverend Clemmer missed a gear as they went around the curve so the bus came almost to a stop. It must have thrown off Mr. McBride's timing because the bomb went off in front of the bus instead of directly under it. The engine block shielded the occupants from the worst of the blast, according to Sheriff Wallace.

"Reverend Clemmer has a concussion and nasty head wound, but no one is dead at the scene. It looks like mostly broken bones and minor burns."

"Thank God," said Holly.

"Yes, indeed."

"M-M-Miss Carter," said Rose, "I'm gonna ch-check on Momma, if that's okay? I'll l-let Cutter know you're here."

"That's fine. We're probably going to be here most of the night."

Doctor Garner glanced around and motioned Holly to an examining area and pulled the curtain. After Dr. Garner told her the news about the different blood drops found on the picture frame, she'd made the decision to have her father's body exhumed for another autopsy.

"Miss Carter, as your father's majority heir and executor of his estate, you're within your rights to file for an order of exhumation and hire me as a private consultant to perform the autopsy without the involvement of the sheriff's office," the doctor told her. Holly already knew that, and he knew she knew it. He was simply setting up the second part of what he wanted say. "But I urge you to meet with

Sheriff Wallace and share with him all you know. All you suspect. He's a good man. If there's foul play involved in your father's death, he'll be the first one to want to root out the truth."

"I don't doubt it, Doctor. But before I involve the sheriff and start pointing fingers at – well, at anyone, I want some real evidence a crime was committed," she said. "I'm counting on you to give it to me."

"I'll perfom the best autopsy I can considering the amount of time your father's body was in the river," he said. "And I'll give you honest results."

"Thank you. That's all I'm asking."

"But, Miss Carter, I think you've given me the evidence to prove a crime was committed."

"What do you mean?"

"When you gave me that picture frame and asked me to check if the blood was human and if it was your father's type, that's what I did," he said. "I tested several drops, and as you know found two types of blood."

"Yes."

"As I also told you, there were more than twenty drops of blood on the frame and several smears. I didn't test every drop or the smears because I'd answered your questions and then some, but something about it bugged me."

Holly was nodding now. "All right, Doctor. You have my attention."

"I was actually in my lab at the office tonight, working on the frame when I got the call to come the hospital."

"Don't tell me you found a third blood type?"

"Sort of," he said. "I tested the smear and it was a combination of your father's blood type and the O-negative." Holly knew what the doctor would say next before he said it and it chilled her to the bone and made the heat in her neck rise at the same time. "I'm not a criminologist, but what that would indicate to me is that your father's blood and this other person's blood was put on the frame at the same time. Otherwise, they wouldn't be commingled in the way they are."

Holly was no longer looking at him, her eyes had drifted off.

"Miss Carter, I'm sorry. I'm not sure if that's what you wanted to hear or –"

The clatter of a metal hospital chart rattling against the floor just outside the cubicle startled them both. Doctor Garner turned and snatched open the curtain. Nurse Rhonda Hines was squatting, hurriedly gathering the chart back into her arms. She stood, flustered. "I'm, I'm sorry, Doctor. I didn't want to, to interrupt. I have the chart for the male Negro in Exam Four. You need to approve –"

"Yes, yes. I know," said Dr. Garner, taking the chart from the nurse and scribbling some notes. Rhonda Hines was staring at Holly, not bothering to hide her disdain. The doctor handed the chart back. "Thank you. That'll be all," he said and waited for Nurse Hines to walk away. He squatted next to Holly's wheelchair. "Miss Carter, I know you wanted to keep the autopsy a secret until it was done. Until you know more. But I think you know enough now. I urge you to talk to Sheriff Wallace as soon as possible. Meantime, I'll talk to Nurse Hines, but I won't be surprised if it somehow leaks out. I'm sorry."

"It's a small town," said Holly. "It's hard to keep anything a secret for more than ten minutes. The clothesline telegraph."

Outside they heard the scream of an ambulance siren fading away to a growl as it backed up to the emergency room dock. Standing, he said, "Sounds like they're playing my song," and hurried toward the doors.

When Holly emerged from the exam area, Cutter was leaning against a wall near the doors that led to the wards. She wheeled over.

"We're going to have to stop meeting like this," she said. "Hospital halls? Klan rallies? Junkyards? So many romantic spots. How's your mom?"

"The same. I'm glad to see you."

Holly smiled in spite of the chilling news Doctor Garner had just delivered. "Yeah. Me, too, you," she sighed, wanting to feel Cutter's arms around her or at least her hand in his. But there were patients on gurneys in the halls and dozens of white-clad people hurrying around, trying to ease another night of pain in a place that already had seen so much that summer. "Doctor Garner just gave me some news about the blood on the picture frame," she said. "We need to talk. Do you think we could find someplace quiet?"

"We can try."

Chapter 4

❀

O n Friday morning, Sheriff Wallace drove out to Wolf's Run and sat with Holly and Cutter, and Rose, too, at the poolside table overlooking the valley. My father looked about as haggard as a man can look and still be moving around. His eyes were red-rimmed and sunken under heavy brows. Wrinkles cut deep at the corners and his mouth was drawn as he ate the bacon, eggs and sausage patties on his plate, and listened as Holly and Cutter shared all they knew and all they suspected. Holly had typed up a step-by-step timeline of their inquiries and another one outlining what they thought happened the night T.L. Carter's car went into the river. At the end of it, my father wiped his mouth, put the linen napkin beside his plate and said, "I wish you two were working for me."

Holly and Cutter smiled politely, then – "So, Sheriff, you don't think this is simply a daughter's wild paranoia? Especially directed at a woman with whom – well, clearly there is no love lost between me and Mary Nell."

"Miss Carter, I have more to do than I can shake even the biggest stick at right now," said Billy Wallace. "If I thought this was a wild goose chase, I'd be the first to tell you so. At the moment, I don't have the time or patience for fool's errands.

"Now, you've laid out a good case here, though it's all circum-stantial and a lot of it is speculative. So, I'm not prepared to say I definitely believe T.L. was murdered, or who may or may not have been involved. But I can say with hundred-percent certainty, based on what you've presented, that your father's death merits further investigation."

Holly sat back in her wheelchair, crossed her arms beneath her breasts and stared out at the valley. No one spoke. "I guess there was some small part of me that hoped you'd say, 'Miss Carter, you're just letting a few stray facts and your imagination run away with you.' The wounds are already so deep between me and Tom. And Mary Nell." Holly shook her head. "But I knew. I knew."

"The wounds are only gonna get deeper from here on out," said the sheriff. "Are you prepared for that?"

Holly didn't hesitate. "Yes. I am," she said, all business again, and took another piece of paper from a folder beside her plate. "This is a formal request to exhume my father's body. I understand it has to be filed with your office at least forty-eight hours in advance."

"Yes," said the sheriff. "When does Doctor Garner plan to do the autopsy?"

"Monday afternoon."

"Good," he said. "The sooner the better, before and Tom and Mary Nell get wind of it and try to block it."

"Can they?" Cutter asked, sitting up. "Block it?"

"Miss Carter is T.L.'s majority heir," noted the sheriff. "I don't see how they could. Not legally. Not for long. But Tom and Mary Nell have a lot of friends in this county, including one who lives out at Chalmette Plantation. So, I wouldn't put anything past them. Especially if one or both of them is involved in T.L.'s death. They'll fight tooth and nail to keep his body in the ground."

Cutter grunted. "I don't doubt that."

"The law says I have to file a copy of this exhumation request with the clerk of courts, but I'm going to wait until about four-forty-five this afternoon to do it," Billy Wallace told them. "That won't give Tom and Mary Nell much time to run to court. But if I were you, I'd have the grave-diggers out there first thing Monday morning. Before the courts open."

* * *

Four-forty-five came and went that Friday, as did the five o'clock close of courts. Holly had contacted the cemetery and made sure the exhumation would begin Monday morning at firstlight. She was relieved that she'd be able to avoid an all-out courtroom battle with Tom and Mary Nell. The August air was close and hot and damp and Holly occasionally dabbed her forehead and neck with a handkerchief as she read page proofs for the weekend edition of *The Current-*

Leader. The two ceiling fans in the office turned overhead and the big front windows were open in hopes of catching a breeze that never came.

From the corner of her eye, Holly saw a woman exit the glass front doors of the courthouse and hurry down the steps, headed in a straight line for the newspaper office. Holly took off her reading glasses, laid them on the desk, pivoted and looked at the clock on the console behind her. Six-fifty-two. Then she heard someone knocking on the building's front door. Holly had a bad feeling.

Miss Frances had locked the door at precisely five o'clock and there was no one in the downstairs business offices. Holly started to send Rose down to answer the door but thought better of it and pushed across the window sill and onto the balcony.

"Can I help you?" Holly called over wrought-iron rail, though she could not see who was knocking since the balcony stretched across the entire front of the building. The knocking continued. Holly called again, louder, and a moment later a woman stepped from beneath the balcony.

Looking up through wasp-shaped glasses, the middle-aged woman said, "Miss Carter, my name is Lorene Knowles. I'm Judge Crawford's clerk. He wants to see you in his courtroom in fifteen minutes."

"Fifteen minutes?" Holly exclaimed. "This is crazy."

"I'm just delivering the message," said Mrs. Knowles. "But I'd be there if I were you."

"All right," said Holly.

The clerk turned and made a beeline for the courthouse. This was what Holly had feared. But she had not imagined that it would happen so quickly or after hours on a weekend. Holly needed a lawyer and fast. The town square was populated with their offices but it was seven o'clock on a summer Friday night. She looked around. On a balcony on the south side of the square Dan Freeman, attorney-at-law, was sitting with his tie off, his vest open and his feet propped up in a chair. He was reading a newspaper and sipping from a glass containing something the color of ice tea, but Holly knew it wasn't. Dan Freeman was a senior at CHS in '55 when she was a fifteen-year-old with a fast car. They'd had their moments at The Gin.

Holly found Freeman's number in the small phone book that contained all 5,287 numbers in Cattahatchie County. At first, she didn't think he'd answer but she let it ring. Through her window she finally saw Freeman stand up, waver a little as he folded the paper and drop it onto the table before going through the French doors into his office. He answered gruffly but as soon as he heard Holly's voice that passed. She gave him a one-minute rundown of what was going on and she hoped he was sober enough to comprehend it.

"I'll meet you there in five minutes," he said.

* * *

The three-story Cattahatchie County Courthouse was the only public building within thirty miles that had an elevator. It was there only because in the 1920s Judge Horace C. DeLong's arthritis had gotten too bad for him to climb the stairs. But for the most part, the metal gate to the ancient contraption was padlocked so that curious boys didn't ride it up and down all day. Dan Freeman tilted Holly's wheelchair and pulled her backwards up the four stone steps at the front of the courthouse. Finally, the old maintenance man with the key to the elevator was located and she, Rose and Dan Freeman stepped aboard. It groaned and rattled and tested their nerves but got them there.

"I said fifteen minutes," County Judge Lamar Crawford said from the bench. "You're late."

"We're sorry your honor," said Dan Freeman. "We had, uhm, transportation difficulties."

"Aw'right, Miss Carter. Come on up. Let's get started."

Holly pushed through the gate in the court rail and to the table where Sheriff Wallace was seated beside Doctor Garner. Tom and Mary Nell were seated at the opposite table with Brother MacAllister and an attorney Holly recognized but couldn't place. Delbert White? … Whitten? … And a woman she'd never seen before.

Judge Crawford banged his gavel. "Court is in session," he intoned and a fat stenographer, sweating profusely, hunched over his machine and began to tap the small keyboard. He reminded Rose of a chubby little boy hunched over a toy piano. "Miss Carter, you've been called here to show cause why I should not enter an order enjoining you from having the body of Thomas Lanier Carter III exhumed.

"Tom and Mary Nell here have come before this court profoundly troubled by the possibility that you intend to open T.L.'s grave without just cause. Mr. Whitten?"

"Yes, Your Honor," said the attorney, standing. "For malicious reasons of her own, we believe that Miss Holly Lee Carter is seeking to exhume her father's body, even though one of the state's most experienced and respected pathologists — Dr. Ferguson Phelps – already ruled his death to be an accidental drowning.

"My clients, and their spiritual advisor Dr. C.E. MacAllister, strongly believe this would be an unwarranted desecration of Mr. Carter's grave, in violation of their most deeply held spiritual beliefs. More importantly, in violation of T.L. Carter's religious precepts.

"They also believe that such an exhumation could permanently scar Mr. Carter's only grandchildren, Georgette Poindexter Carter and Thomas Lanier Carter V," the attorney went on. "Dr. Florence Redman, a noted child psychologist practicing in Tupelo, is here today to testify to the validity of those concerns."

"Very well. Call your first witness," said Judge Crawford.

For the next hour and fifteen minutes, the judge heard testimony as the light through the big windows faded from gold to pink to gray. The three chandeliers hanging from the twenty-two-foot ceiling were turned on but cast only weak light in a room meant for daytime use. The bottom section of the tall windows was opened and four ceiling fans turned, but the room was stifling. Mary Nell offered up long, loud sobs to punctuate many of her answers, and dabbed at her eyes with a silk handkerchief. Tom testified stoically, his expression distant, almost blank, but he looked sickly, thought Holly, beyond whatever hangover he probably was suffering. He had lost weight, but not in a good way. Then came Brother MacAllister and finally the psychologist.

With no preparation, Dan Freeman did a good job cross-examining the foursome.

After Delbert Whitten summed up his clients' arguments again, Judge Crawford asked, "Mr. Freeman, do you intend to call witnesses."

"Your honor, this whole proceeding comes as a surprise to my client," said Dan Freeman. "May we have a few minutes?"

Judge Crawford removed his pocket watch from beneath his robes. "Two minutes."

"Your honor!"

"A minute fifty seconds, Mr. Freeman."

Dan Freeman leaned in and spoke to Holly, the doctor and the sheriff – his breath a strong mix of scotch and peppermint. When Judge Crawford's gavel fell again, Dan Freeman stood.

"Your Honor," he said firmly, "we decline to call witnesses at this proceeding. Our position is that Tom and Mary Nell Carter have no standing to contest whatever actions Holly Lee Carter decides to take concerning an exhumation of her father's body.

"Miss Carter is T.L.'s majority heir and the executor of his estate. Clearly it was T.L. Carter's intention, as plainly declared in his final will and testament, that his daughter be in control of his affairs in the event of his death. That certainly would include the disposition of his final remains."

Judge Crawford gave Freeman a half smile. "Mr. Freeman, you've stated the letter of the law correctly. However, I knew T.L. Carter for almost sixty years. I cannot believe he would want his only grandchildren scarred by a frivolous witch hunt based on nothing more than the jealousy and vindictiveness of a prodigal and profligate daughter."

Holly's mouth opened but it was Freeman who spoke – "Your honor! Your bias against my client is obvious. I urge you to consider –"

"I've considered all I need to consider," scowled Judge Crawford. "I'm issuing an order enjoining you, Miss Carter, from exhuming T.L. Carter's body, and you, Doctor Garner, from performing an autopsy without the permission of this court.

"That's all," he added and banged his gavel. "Court is adjourned."

* * *

Those at Holly's table waited while Tom, Mary Nell and their group left the courtroom. Holly turned and followed them with her eyes, barely able to believe what had just happened. When she did she saw Cutter sitting in the back row of the courtroom. As he passed by, Delbert Whitten stopped next to Cutter and quietly said, "You've made a terrible mistake, son. But you might still be able to make it right. You think about it."

Cutter's gaze was connected with Holly's and he didn't even look at Whitten, who stood there for a moment, expecting some sort of – acknowledgement, at least. When he saw he wouldn't get it from Cutter, he moved on. After a moment, Cutter walked down the aisle and joined the group at the table. The growing connection – realationship? – between Cutter and Holly Lee Carter was no longer much of a secret to anyone in DeLong who was paying attention. And nearly everyone was.

"I went by your office," he said. "They told me you were here."

Dan Freeman kicked at the worn, dusty old hardwood floor. "Crawford's lost whatever mind he ever had," the attorney said, his words echoing back at him from the big room's Colored Balcony.

"But where does this leave us?" asked Holly.

"It's Friday night, so there's nothing that can be done about it until Monday. But Crawford knows that I'm right on the law and that order will never hold up on appeal."

"Then how could he s-s-say those th-things about M-Miss Carter?" asked Rose, who was sitting behind Holly in the front row.

"Because he's been in Cecil Weathers' pocket for thirty years," said Freeman. "That miserable old –"

"Aw'right, come on," said Billy Wallace. "Let's calm down. Let's not get carried away on emotion."

"I don't understand," said Doctor Garner. "If you're so certain Judge Crawford's ruling will be overturned, I assume that Mr. Whitten is telling Tom and Mary Nell the same thing. Why go through this dog-and-pony show?"

Freeman paced back and forth in front of the defense table. "I only got involved in this two hours ago, but my guess would be that Mary Nell and Tom – and maybe whoever put them up to this – were hoping one or all of you would take the stand. That way, Dilbert could cross examine you under oath about your reasons for wanting the body exhumed. They want to know what you know."

Holly laughed sarcastically. "I wish I knew what I knew."

"A proper autopsy could clear a lot of things up," said Sheriff Wallace. "I could start an official investigation and within a week or ten days probably come up with enough reasons of my own to petition the court for an exhumation order. But I'll probably get the same runaround. At least, initially."

"So, what do you want me to do?" Dan Freeman asked his new client.

Holly didn't hesitate. "Find the first district judge you can lay your hands on Monday morning, and get Crawford's injunction lifted."

Chapter 5

∾

Cutter tilted Holly's chair back and eased her down the courthouse steps. The streetlights were on and the limbs of the big oak trees cast shadows on the lawn. Cutter looked at Holly and Rose. "You two hungry?"

Rose nodded.

"I'm starving," said Holly. "I skipped lunch but I don't have time to eat. I still have a newspaper to put out."

"I'll go to the Cotton and bring something back," he said.

When Cutter returned it was almost nine-fifteen. He, Rose and Holly ate at the conference table in her office. "Are you okay?" he asked Holly. She cut off a piece of sweet white, perfectly spiced chicken breast the size of her thumb and gave it to Charlie, who was eagerly waiting beside her right wheel. Charlie yapped and wagged the tail that curled over her back. "No more, baby. We've got to watch your figure," said Holly, smiling. Then her smile faded and to Cutter she said, "I'm as okay as I can be, I suppose. From here on out, I guess it'll be open warfare between me and Tom and Mary Nell. Until I either prove Daddy's death was no accident. Or they prove I'm a nut.

"I am worried about Tom, though. He looked terrible," she said, then changed the subject. "How was practice?"

"Hot. But we had three more guys from Roseville come out today."

"How many is that?"

"Eleven blacks and the nine of us," he said. "We almost have enough players to have a full offense and defense in practice. But things are getting' ragged. We need a coach to keep things organized and keep people payin' attention, if nothing else."

"I know Doctor Garner is trying to get someone to take it on. Do you have any candidates?"

"Not anybody who'd take it," he said. "What can I do to help around here?"

"If you don't mind getting wax on your hands, Shorty Rogers can show you how to paste type on a page."

"I've had a lot worse than wax on my hands."

* * *

About the time the presses started turning at eleven-fifty-five a light rain began to fall but it did little to cool the sticky night. It was a thick, warm drizzle. The big door on the loading dock was rolled up and papers were flowing off the press. Sorters and carriers – some old but most of them new – were stuffing advertising inserts and sections together on a long table and creating stacks for delivery. Holly opened the paper and flipped from page to page, checking every headline, every photo caption one more time. It was twelve-twenty by the time she was satisfied.

"What now?" asked Cutter.

"Rose and I are going to deliver the Madison Street route," said Holly. "It's only one-hundred-twenty papers right off the square. It won't take long. Then we go home. It's been a very long day."

"I'll follow you."

Holly smiled a tired but appreciative smile and let her hand brush Cutter's without taking it. "Thanks. I'll get the car and you load us up. Four bundles. Okay?"

"You got it."

Holly pushed quickly across the parking lot with Charlie running alongside. She swung open the front door of the Continental. Charlie hopped in and Holly lifted her hips onto the bench seat. She grunted with effort and for an instant didn't notice Charlie's low growl. But as Holly lifted her right leg and settled her foot onto the floor mat, she saw that Charlie's lips were pulled back and her teeth were bared. Holly felt a chill race up her spine as the little dog barked and snapped at something under the passenger seat, then watched in horror as a bolt of black lightning emerged and struck the little dog.

"*Charlie!*" Holly screamed and reached for her companion, her very best little friend. But from another angle beneath the seat a second water moccasin sprang – this one a mottled brown and as thick as her wrist, but there was no mistaking its cotton-white mouth as it opened and plunged its fangs into the dog.

Charlie yelped and jumped but held her ground as Cutter and Rose ran toward the Lincoln.

Instinct and fear took hold of Holly and she pushed herself out of the car and over her wheelchair, both tumbling over onto the wet pavement. She landed hard, her right foot still in the car. "Charlie, come! *Come!*" she shouted, her husky voice shrill with terror. "Come, Charlie!"

Cutter leaped from the loading dock and ran toward the car.

Finally, Charlie obeyed and hurried toward the open door but yelped again as she took another hit that knocked her off her feet. But she got up and hopped out of the car as the large black-and-tan moccasin slithered over the hump in the front floorboard. Holly pulled her leg out of the car as the viper's thick V-shaped head dropped down from the car. Cutter saw it, too, and never slowed down. He slammed his hip into the door, sending it crashing shut and cutting the moccasin in two about five inches behind its head.

Rose came up, breathing hard from her run, and watched as the remainder of the snake writhed and opened its cotton mouth trying to strike. Cutter stomped the head and ground it under the heel of his work boot as Rose grabbed Holly under her arms and dragged her several feet away.

Now others noticed the commotion and came running from the loading dock and press room. Cutter knelt beside Holly and snatched off her remaining shoe. He tossed it aside and began checking her feet then her legs, front and back.

"Ch-Ch-Check her knee," said Rose.

"Just a cut. From the fall," he said, sighing with relief as Holly propped on her hands. "Charlie?" she sobbed. "Where's Charlie?"

A gap opened in the circle of workers who'd surrounded her. Charlie was sitting a few feet away, panting as if she had run a two-hundred-yard dash. She looked dazed, confused. Cutter suspected she already was blind. Through her tears Holly saw there were at least four distinct streaks of blood on her coat. "*Ohhhh*, Charlie."

Shorty Rodgers, the production manager, saw the remains of the snake and said, "I'm callin' the law. This was no accident."

"Call an ambulance, too," said Cutter. "Just in case."

Now one of the carriers was shining a big flashlight inside the Lincoln. "Holy smokes! There's another one in there. No! Two!"

Holly watched as Charlie tried to stand up but she stumbled then fell over.

"Charlie? Ohhh, Charlie! Bring her to me," Holly pleaded.

Rose picked up the little dog and put her in Holly's arms. Charlie was like a rag doll even though her breathing was very fast. Holly held the bundle of red-streaked white fur to her chest. "Oh, Charlie, you were so brave," she whispered, her lips trembling. "You saved me. Do you know you saved me?"

Charlie's eyes blinked and her breathing slowed as if she heard and understood the words, and was comforted by them. Then as Holly slowly, gently stroked her white coat – "You did good. ... You did so good, *mon chéri* ... I love you. ... I'll never forget you. Never! ... I promise."

The little dog convulsed once, then again, then Holly felt Charlie's heart go still beneath her fingers.

Three minutes later two sheriff's cars pulled into the newspaper lot. Not far behind were my father, the ambulance and Doctor Garner.

"I heard the call out on my scanner," said the doctor as he knelt beside Holly and began examining her legs. After a couple of minutes, he allowed himself a deep swallow of relief. "No puncture wounds. But I don't like the looks of that knee. We need to clean it up. You may need a couple of stitches. And there's a little swelling in your ankle."

Doctor Garner motioned for the ambulance attendants.

"No," she said, her whole body trembling. "No ambulance."

"Miss Carter, I want to keep your leg as stable as possible until we can get some X-rays and see what's what," the doctor told her. "The stretcher will let us do that."

"No. I –"

"Holly, stop it," Cutter calmly told her. "Listen to Doctor Garner."

"But Charlie?" she asked, her eyes full of pain and pleading.

"I'll take care of Charlie. I promise."

Cutter started to scoop Holly up into his arms. "No. Not like that. I want to keep her leg as straight as possible," said Doc Garner, motioning to one of the attendants. "Jack, get under her arms. Cutter, you support her hips. I'll keep her legs steady. On three. … One. Two. Three."

They lifted her onto the stretcher and quickly wrapped a blanket around her. Cutter walked with her to the ambulance. "Rose'll ride with you. I need to talk to the sheriff. I'll be up there in a few minutes."

Holly squeezed his hand and nodded before putting her arm across her eyes. The attendant closed he door.

Once the ambulance pulled away, Cutter went to the footlocker in his jeep and took out a towel and gently placed Charlie on it. He stroked the dog's blood-speckled side. "Thank you, Charlie," he mouthed then wrapped her up and placed her in his jeep.

Sheriff Wallace was standing by the back passenger door of the Lincoln when Cutter walked over. "Look here," said my father, pointing to a small, neat three-inch cut in the car's canvas roof. "That's how he got 'em in the car."

Cutter studied the small hole. "This was somebody who knows how to handle snakes," he said. "Somebody who's not afraid of 'em."

"Uh-huh," the sheriff grunted. "That's what I figure. And look at this."

Sheriff Wallace shined his flashlight onto the backseat. A sheet of notebook paper had unfolded there. Cutter had to tilt his head to read it – "Death to the hore of Babylon and the deseever of men."

Cutter said, "I've heard tell there are two or three snake-handlin' churches in the county. One out in the low country, among the moonshiners down in Hughestown. Another one somewhere in the deep woods between Pleasant Ridge and Dumas."

"And another one off the Challabeete Road on the north end," said the sheriff. "Just a couple of miles from the field where the Klux picked up that scarecrow."

"Judas Wallace?"

"That'd be the one," said my father.

* * *

A t three-fifteen, John-Thomas Hinton turned his cruiser down the driveway at Wolf's Run. Cutter followed in his jeep. The house was big and dark except for a single light in the kitchen. When Cutter stepped out, he had his shotgun in his hand.

"John-Thomas, you mind walkin' through the house with me?"

The deputy looked at Holly transferring from the front seat of his patrol car to her wheelchair. Her left knee was covered in white gauze and her ankle was wrapped in an Ace bandage. Rose was helping her.

"Sure, Cutter," he said, unsnapping his holster. "Let's go."

Once they had checked the kichen and Holly's bedroom, she and Rose came inside. Ten minutes later Cutter and Hinton had checked every room and closet, under beds and even done a quick walk-through of the massive attic. He and Cutter walked outside. The showers had passed and the moon shone here and there as a tatter of clouds drifted across the sky.

The young deputy propped on his cruiser. "She was my first big crush, you know? And even now. Even in that wheelchair ..." He shook his head, smiled. "Are you stayin'?"

"Yeah. I'll spread my sleepin' bag on the porch or out in the garage."

John-Thomas grunted. "I saw how she looked at you tonight. How you looked at her. I wish I was in your shoes," he said. Cutter made no comment and the deputy changed the subject. "You know, I've spent my whole life in this town except for the four years I went off to school, and that wasn't but sixty miles away. I've seen so many acts of genuine kindness and love among people in this county. I've always been proud of where I come from. But when I see something like this, or the other meanness that's gone on this summer – " he sighed and almost imperceptibly shook his head. "What's the matter with people?"

Cutter let the question float in the air like the scraps of cloud passing the moon.

"Well, I better get back on patrol," said the deputy, settling into his cruiser. "Take good care of her. And be careful yourself. You're one heckuva football player. The best I've ever seen up close. But you ain't bulletproof."

Cutter flashed a small, quick, tired smile. "Thanks for reminding me."

Chapter 6

෴

It was Monday morning before Holly could look up the slope of the big yard of Wolf's Run without her eyes misting. There in the cool, green shade of a massive old pecan tree Cutter had buried Charlie in a box he crafted from three-quarter-inch plywood and fourpenny nails. He put her little blanket inside, and a couple of her favorite toys.

"Nothing'll get at her," was about all he could say afterward. But all weekend, Cutter was Holly's strong, silent, sturdy rock.

Holly knew that she could never put her feet back on the floorboards of her Lincoln without seeing snakes slithering around them. So, Cutter took his toolbox to the sheriff's impound yard on Convict Road and removed the hand controls. From there he went to a car lot in nearby Holly Springs that he knew had good used vehicles. Holly told him she didn't care what he brought back, "just as long as it gets me around," she said. "I have to be able to get my chair behind the front seat. And this time, I think I'll take a hard top."

Cutter returned with a red 1966 Plymouth Fury with a white interior, four-barrel carburetor and dual exhausts. "It's not a Corvette," he'd said, "but it suits you."

Holly thought so, too, at least it suited the woman she wanted to be.

On Sunday, Holly had driven it to the prayer service at the paper. Rose went along while Cutter spent the morning stringing barbed wire in the first twist-back of the path that wound from the courtyard at Wolf's Run down to the river. Or more precisely, wound from the river up to the courtyard. He spent the rest of the day clearing an old logging road that began a half-mile around the bend from Wolf's Run then twisted it's very steep way around the top of Blue Mountain to a rock outcrop about thirty feet below the peak. It offered a good if small campsite and a near perfect observation point for Blue Mountain Road a hundred feet below, and for Wolf's Run, seventy-five yards past the white fence.

Late in the afternoon, Sheriff Wallace stopped by the house to check on Holly. Her eyes still were puffy from crying and he hated seeing her so worn down by the meanness around her. He also came to give her the name and phone number of the Memphis Electric Gate Company.

"Thank you, Sheriff, but I can't afford an electric gate!" Holly had protested. "I just had to buy a car. Every dollar I spend takes away a dollar I have to spend keeping the paper's doors open."

Sheriff Wallace's eyes had bored into Holly as Cutter propped next to the kitchen sink. "Those dollars won't do you any good if you're dead," he told her. "There's only three ways this will end. Either we'll catch McBride and the nuts who're working with him. You'll give up and leave town. Or they'll kill you."

"Then catch them, Sheriff. Catch them!" Holly told him a bit too loudly, her frustration and the strain of living under constant threat showing through her usually smooth exterior.

"Look, Miss Carter, we think we have a good solid lead on the person who placed those snakes in your car Friday night," he said. "We have the individual under surveillance. We're waiting to make an arrest hoping they'll lead us to bigger fish. Maybe McBride. Now, I can't station a car out at the end of your driveway twenty-four hours a day. Please consider this."

After Sheriff Wallace left, Cutter said, "I think the gate's a good idea. The way things are now, somebody could drive a carload of dynamite practically onto the porch before anyone could stop them. Including me."

"Cutter, I don't want to give in to … to my fear," she told him.

"That's not giving in. It's being smart."

Now it was Monday and Holly was glad to be back at the paper, glad to be busy. She interrupted her editing of stories at mid-morning and dialed the number for the gate company. They said they could have it up before the end of the week.

As Holly hung up, her private line rang. It was Dan Freeman telling her that District Judge Omar Autrey was suddenly a very hard man to get in to see.

"Isn't there another judge you can go to?" asked Holly.

"No. Not unless Autry asks for help with his docket," Freeman told her from a phone outside of District Court in New Albany. "Autrey's the next step of the ladder."

"Is he *that* busy?"

"He doesn't seem to be," Freeman told her. "But all I can do is wait. If you could persuade the Cattahatchie County prosecutor to join in the motion, it would be a big help."

"Sheriff Wallace has already tried. Jimmy Epps says he doesn't have enough evidence to go on."

"You know, of course, that Epps is one of Weathers' crew."

"I know. That's why we've *got* to have this autopsy. I'm hoping it'll give us evidence Epps can't deny," she told him. "All right, Dan. Keep me informed. Thanks."

* * *

At dusk, three men stepped out of the hidden opening to a cave that had been turned into a tunnel by Colonel John Henry Kamp more than a century earlier. It had been used by slaves to bring supplies from a tributary of the Cattahatchie into the basement storage rooms beneath the main plantation house. Over the years more tunnels had been dug until the sprawling basement was like the hub of a wheel. During the Civil War, it had been used as everything from a Confederate hospital to field headquarters for General Nathan Bedford Forrest, before and after the Battle of Shiloh.

Robert Bedford McBride liked very much the notion of treading the same ground as one of his namesakes. Sleeping in the same small room that was used by the great cavalry general and founder of the Ku Klux Klan. It made him feel even more a part of history. He hoped it would not have to be destroyed. But better that than have the Federals seize the Klavern's armory contained behind a heavy steel door in a side room.

Dressed as fishermen out for a night on the river, LeRoy Kamp led the men down an almost invisible path to where a sleek, high-powered speedboat and a small fishing skiff were hidden under an overhang of low branches. LeRoy knew the trail by heart, in the dark. It was the same way he brought in uppers, downers, even LSD, by the thousands of doses in a compartment hidden under the floor of the speedboat.

Tony Carlucci sat in front in the fishing skiff, next to two five-gallon cans of gasoline. Kamp sat at the stern with his hand on the throttle of the forty-horse outboard. And McBride sat in the middle. Under the fishing rods and a tarp were three Army-issue M-16 rifles.

Ten minutes later they were on the main river, drifting slowly south, trolling their lines like the night fishermen they pretended to be. At the entrance to Henderson Creek, Kamp turned the boat east. When they'd gone as far as the shallow creek would allow, he nosed the boat into the bank.

"The back side of the Farber property is about a mile over that ridge," said Tony Carlucci handing a rifle to each of the men and extra ammo clips. "It's not a hard walk … if you've got two good legs. I'll wait here. Besides, from what I hear, LeRoy's eager to show what a tough guy he is."

"Tougher than you, Carlucci."

"Is that right?"

"I ain't the one waitin' in the boat, am I?"

"Ladies, ladies," groaned McBride, lifting one of the gas cans by its handle. "Can we get on with this?"

* * *

Cutter wrapped the baking potatoes in aluminum foil and shoved them into the hot coals of the fieldstone grill on the patio of Wolf's Run. Thirty minutes later he had the T-bones sizzling on the metal grate. By the time he, Holly and Rose sat down to eat, the last pink light of the day had slipped away to night.

After the dinner dishes were cleared and washed, Holly returned to the patio to find the chef dozing on the double chaise lounge. "Do you mind if I join you?"

Cutter smiled. "Nope," he said, sliding over as Holly braked her chair and transferred. She lifted her legs onto the lounge. Her knee was still bandaged, covering three stitches. Once she settled, Cutter took her hand. The lights of DeLong glowed to the south. After a time, she rolled onto her side and nestled against Cutter's shoulder. He put his arm around her. She loved being near him, touching him, the smell of him.

"You make me feel safe," she said softly.

"Good. But I'm still glad you're gettin' a gate."

"Mr. Practical."

"I'll be just up the hill."

Holly was quiet for a time, then she rested her hand on his chest. "You know, I want you a lot closer than up the hill. I want you in ways I wasn't sure I could want a man again. But I do. I can. And if you walked out the door tonight and never came back, that's an incredible gift you've given me. Cutter, I want you in every way a woman can want a man" She drew in a breath and on the exhale said, "I ache for you! Please believe that."

Cutter turned his face to Holly, brushed her nose and then her lips with his, then kissed her softly. She closed her eyes and leaned her head back, then opened them and focused on Cutter. "You need to listen to me, though. There's something you have to know now before we – this goes any further.

"You asked me if I cut any deals with God when I was laying there on the floor of the Ia Drang Valley. I answered no, and that is true. But I did make a promise to myself and to God," she told him. "That if I lived, I would stop letting all the cruel, ugly, demeaning things my father said to me tear me down. That I would treat myself and my body – God's creation – with respect. That I won't use it like a, a party favor, as a vessel merely for sex. That – That –"

"That the next man you give yourself to will be your husband," said Cutter, finishing the thought. Holly swallowed, unsure of how Cutter would take the declaration. Despite all of his seeming maturity, he still was eighteen and hormones were powerful things. She wet her lips – "Yes."

"I figured as much," he told her quietly. "And I want you, too. But not like I've had other women. There's something about you. It's like there's always been a part of me missing. I've never been able to put my finger on what it is. I can't do it now either. All I know is, when I'm around you, I don't feel that way. I feel like you complete me, I guess you could say."

Holy smiled. It was if he had read her mind. "I feel the same. Exactly the same."

"For right now, it's like that river down there. We know it ends up somewhere but we can't even begin to see that somewhere from here. All we can see is what's flowin' past us now. Let's just keep our eyes on that. There'll be time to figure where it ends up," he said. "But I hear what you're sayin', and I'll respect your limits until you change 'em. Even if that means I have to sleep on rocks, instead of in that big beautiful bed of yours."

Holly leaned in and kissed him, then – "It's like you said, who knows where that river will end up one of these days."

Cutter smiled. "That's right. Who knows?"

Then she kissed him again.

* * *

Are you sure about this?" asked LeRoy Kamp as they sat in the thick woods behind the home of Olin Farber, the snake-handling, self-ordained preacher who served as the Kludd, or chaplain, of the Kattahatchie Klavern. In the house, Farber slept with his wife and five children, ranging in age from sixteen to four. To the left was the white-washed cinderblock building that Farber called a church; to the right and down the slope of the hill was the barn where Sergeant Charles Rudolph died from the gunshot wounds delivered by a Conway, Arkansas police officer. The one Rudolph had killed on his way to joining Uncle Bob. Robert Bedford McBride. Charles had seemed much better, seemed to be regaining his strength, nearly ready to rejoin him in the fight, thought McBride as he studied the barn. The long fight. For The Cause. Then bam, just like that. His eyes rolled back in his head and he dropped dead while eating oatmeal for breakfast. Mrs. Farber said a blood clot probably shook loose and traveled to his heart. And she was a registered nurse. She should know. In the end, it didn't matter how. Dead was dead.

Dynamite Bob McBride waited so long to reply that Kamp thought the famous Klan bomber had not heard him. Then, "Am I sure about what?"

"Look, I understand why we have to kill Farber," said Kamp. "Putting those snakes in Holly Carter's car was stupid. I know but –"

"He's out of control," said McBride. "Your Mr. Handley went to see him Saturday. He told your own Grand Wizard to his face that he no longer answers to the Klan. He says God's voice told him to put snakes on that woman."

"I know, but –"

"Worse than that," continued McBride, "he's talkin' about not carin' if he gets caught. About if that's God's will, then so be it."

"Yeah, but –"

"Mr. Kamp, I've dedicated my life to The Cause. And because of what I have done here in the last few weeks, and will do in the coming days, I probably will spend the rest of it on the run," he explained without rancor or emotion. "But one thing I will not do, is live out my days in a five-by-eight concrete-and-steel box. You spent four years in a cell. I'd think you'd appreciate my position."

"I do!" Kamp told him. "But the *whole* family?"

"I don't want any witnesses, do you?"

* * *

On a ridge on the opposite side of the Farber property, Deputy John-Thomas Hinton was sitting in his police cruiser. It was nearly 1 a.m., and he'd put down his night-vision binoculars only long enough to pour a cup of strong, black coffee from his thermos. He had another five hours to go on his shift. He hated stakeouts. In fact, there wasn't much he liked anymore about being a deputy. Oh, Sheriff Wallace was a good man, but John-Thomas had just about decided that he wasn't cut out for dealing first-hand with the sort of ugliness he'd seen over the last few weeks. He was thinking more and more about what Doctor Garner had said to him as interim president of the county school board, about taking a teaching job at the high school and coaching the football team.

The popping sound he heard was so distant he nearly didn't pick it out of the static from his police radio. He turned down the volume and the sound came again in a short burst. John-Thomas tossed his coffee cup out the window and grabbed the big binoculars. The deputy watched as one room of the Farber house after another was lit up as if by a quick series of flash bulbs.

He grabbed the radio mike. "Base, Base! This is Unit Five. Is Sheriff Wallace there? Over."

"Unit Five. Ten-four, but he's catchin' some shut-eye. Over."

"Wake him! Now! Over."

Thirty seconds later, the sheriff was on the radio. "Unit Five, what's happening? Over."

The deputy told him as he held the binoculars to his eyes. Then, "Oh, geez! Sheriff, the house is on fire. The barn, too!"

"All units, respond to a fire distress call at the Olin Farber farm on Henderson Creek Road, one-point-seven miles past Challabete Crossing," the sheriff said into his mike as the dispatcher hit the switch that called out the county volunteer fire department. "But, all units, be aware – there could be armed suspects on site. Approach with extreme caution. Over."

"Sheriff, the whole place is goin' up like dry newspaper. What should I – Oh, geez! – someone just jumped out the second-floor window. They're on fire! I gotta go! I gotta help 'em!"

"Unit Five, listen to me. It could be an ambush. Wait for backup," the sheriff told him. "We're on the way. John-Thomas? ... John-Thomas!"

Chapter 7

ᐤ

The headline at the top of Wednesday morning's *Current-Leader* read: Farber Family Killed in Fire ... Mr. and Mrs. Olin Farber and their five children die in blaze early Tuesday morning.

There were pictures, shot by Holly from a distance, of the scant and blackened remains of the two-story house, the big barn and the cinderblock "church." Fire had shattered the small windows and burned through the roof of the concrete structure, but most of the building remained standing. The story made no direct connection between Olin Farber, "a farmer, self-ordained minister and the leader of a small, ultra-conservative flock in the Challabete area," and the attack on the newspaper's editor; but it did note that "law enforcement officials and firemen encountered an inordinate number of poisonous snakes on the property during their investigation. ... The cause of the fire remains under investigation."

By Saturday, the Labor Day weekend edition of *The Current-Leader* was filled with stories about Tuesday's opening of schools – Cattahatchie High and Riverview Academy. Governor Weathers would cut the ribbon for Riverview at 7:30 a.m. Across town, the Klan was calling on "all right-minded white citizens to line the streets of DeLong in protest of the illegal usurpation of our public school system by the federal courts." Speeches were planned all morning on the town square.

Also in the paper that weekend was a follow-up to the fire story, saying that arson was suspected, but little else. Several family members expressed frustration in the story that the bodies had not been released for burial. When questioned about it, County Medical Examiner Dr. G.P. Garner sent a written statement to the newspaper saying that the "press of doing medicine for the living" had caused the autopsies to be delayed. He promised the bodies would be released by Monday.

Leading the sports page was the news that John-Thomas Hinton, a three-year starter for the Wolves from 1962-'64, had resigned from the sheriff's department to become football coach at Cattahatchie High. He'd also be teaching civics and American history.

Holly pulled out of the driveway at 10:10 Sunday morning. She hit the horn on the red Fury. Rose was in the passenger seat and Holly's wheelchair and guitar were in back. "Wake up, sleepyhead!" she called up the steep hill that rose above Blue Mountain Road.

Cutter caught himself against this tree and that as he came down the steep slope and stepped across a small ditch. "I was awake before you two were up and stirrin'."

"Why didn't you come down for breakfast?"

"I was reading that Truman Capote book you loaned me – *In Cold Blood*. It's really good. That guy can write. Besides, I figured I'd stay out of the way while you two primped for church. And it looks like the effort paid off," he said, leaning on the car door and admiring both the women. It was the first time since Rose was a little girl that Cutter had seen her in a real dress. On Saturday, Holly had taken her to Tupelo and the teenager had spent her first-ever paycheck on clothes – girlie clothes. And here she was, suddenly a young woman before his eyes. "You look mighty pretty. Both of you."

"Th-Thank you."

"You could come with us," said Holly.

"Maybe next week," Cutter told her. "But if you don't mind, I might hop the fence after while and go for a swim."

"Be my guest. We left you a plate on the stove," she said, looking up, her face only a few inches from Cutter's as the moment dragged on.

"G-Go on," said Rose. "K-Kiss her."

Cutter and Holly laughed as he straightened. "Later," he said.

That night the dinner dishes were put away and Rose was watching television in the library while Holly and Cutter played one cut-throat game of eight-ball after another. "That's four out of seven," said Cutter, a devilish smirk twisting his smile.

"Rack 'em again," she said.

The buzzer for the new electric gate sounded. The gate company finished the installation on Thursday. Holly had one speaker placed in the library, one in the kitchen and one on the patio, but everyone in the house still jumped whenever the call buzzer went off.

"Miss Carter, it's Sheriff Wallace," the voice said over the intercom. "Can I have a few minutes of your time?"

"Of course," she said and buzzed him in.

Cutter and Holly greeted the sheriff on the front porch.

"Can we get you something to drink? Something to eat?" asked Holly. "Have you had dinner?"

"Yes, I did. Thank you."

"Come inside, then."

He glanced at his watch. It was almost nine. "Honestly, I don't have much time, and this isn't a social call," he said, turning his hat in his hand. "But I wanted to let you two in on a couple of things before you found out on your own."

Cutter propped against a porch post. "All right, Sheriff. We're listening."

My father stopped turning his hat. "I like to consider myself a fairly honest man, so I'm loathe to lie to people I respect," he said, looking at Cutter then Holly. "But in this case, I suppose I have to use the greater good argument.

"There were two survivors of the attack at the Farber farm. The sixteen-year-old daughter, Ruth, and her youngest sister, Naomi. She's four. That night we spirited them off to a Memphis hospital. We've had them under guard there, under fictitious names ever since," the sheriff began, and spent the next five minutes explaining the events of early Tuesday morning. "The older girl was shot in the shoulder and another slug grazed her head, knocking her unconscious for several minutes. They left her for dead. By the time she roused and found her little sister hiding in a closet, they had to jump out a second floor window. Ruth's nightgown was on fire, so she has some burns, too. But not severe. She's doing better. And she's talking. The little girl has a broken arm, but she's still scared out of her wits. She hasn't said a word."

"How much has the sixteen-year-old been able to tell you?" asked Holly.

"Ohhh, quite a lot," he said. "I can't get into the details, but she can absolutely identify the shooter. He was one of two men who came to take the body away when McBride's nephew – the AWOL Army sergeant, Charles Rudolph – died out in their barn. Mrs. Farber was an R.N., as you know. She had been taking care of his gunshot wounds.

"Even more important," said the sheriff, "Ruth gave us her father's diary."

"It didn't burn up in the house?" asked Cutter.

"No, he kept it in a metal box in a hole in the concrete floor inside the cinderblock building. He called it the 'Book of Olin' and its all laid out in chapter and verse. He's been keeping it for more than twenty years. Aside from his own lunatic ramblings about religion and the end times, it's a history of the Kattahatchie Klavern since he came back from World War II."

"That's great!" said Holly. "So –?"

"So, starting about one a.m. my deputies, the FBI and U.S. marshals will be serving eleven arrest warrants for the leaders of the Kattahachie Klavern and another seven search warrants that we hope will give us McBride. Or at least flush him out."

Holly thought about Tuesday's start of schools. "I have a feeling the timing of this is not coincidental."

"Well, here's how it is," said the sheriff. "Some of the charges may or may not stick. But even with the kind of lawyers Milton Handley and Walter Kamp can afford, it'll be Wednesday or Thursday before they can be arraigned and bond out of the federal lockup in Memphis."

"In the meantime," said Cutter, "school gets started with the Klan leadership behind bars and out of the way. Pretty smart."

"It wasn't all my idea. But, yes, we're hoping that without their leaders, the rank-and-file Klansmen'll be like – like chickens with their pointy heads cut off when the school buses roll Tuesday morning," said Billy Wallace, allowing himself a quick smile. "We'll see."

"Is Cecil Weathers' name on one of those warrants?" asked Holly.

"No. I'm afraid not," the sheriff told her. "Farber mentions Weathers plenty in his diary. Like he's the patron saint of the KKK. But there's nothing overt. We have no doubt Weathers pulls a lot of the strings, but the ol' fox has been careful to not to directly connect himself to Klan leadership. The only way we'll get Weathers is if Handley rolls on him."

Despite her frustration with the news, Holly nodded her understanding

"What about Tony?" asked Cutter. "Do you have a warrant for him?"

"Yes, son, we do."

"Good."

Billy Wallace looked at Cutter for a long moment, sad that any son would have such feelings for his father – despite the righteousness of his feelings. He thought of me and him, and hoped somehow the distance between us could be healed before it became a similar chasm. Then, "Look, we're going to be bringing these men to the county jail for processing, then putting them in a school bus and taking them to Memphis before dawn. If you want pictures for the paper, be at the jail starting around two a.m."

"Thanks, Sheriff," said Holly. "I wouldn't miss it for the world."

Billy Wallace smiled. "Glad to hear it. Consider it a present. A thank you gift from me and Mr. Burke for all you've done."

Holly returned the smile. "My pleasure."

* * *

By 3:15 a.m., the moon was low in the western sky and the high banks of the Cattahatchie cast long, black shadows over the river, and the small boat where Tony Carlucci pretended to fish while waiting for Dynamite Bob near the Old Iron Bridge. Dressed in camouflage, his face covered in lampblack, McBride was almost invisible until he got within a few feet of the spot where the boat was tied to a spindly willow tree. Tony caught sight of him out of the corner of his eye as he emerged from the small trail that wound steeply up the hill's face to the courtyard at Wolf's Run.

"Something's wrong," said McBride, quietly, calmly.

"What? Did someone see you?"

"Of course not," he replied as he lay on his stomach and dipped his hand into the river. He began washing the lamp black off his face.

"The charges are all planted and the fuses run. Everything's ready. Toss me that towel.

"All that old wood?" he said as he rubbed his face. "All I have to do is press a button and the place'll go up like a Roman candle."

"Then what's wrong?"

"Follow me – quietly," said McBride.

Tony climbed carefully out of the boat and onto a sandbar, then followed McBride up the narrow path. In late summer, the top of the bank was at least twenty feet above the river's surface. As soon as he got there, McBride pointed east past the Old Iron Bridge and the bean fields that were Jennifer Cutter's inheritance. At least three police cars were parked at the Old Ambrose Place and every light in the house was on.

"Shhhit!" growled Tony.

"Shit, indeed," agreed McBride.

After watching in silence for several minutes, they walked down to the river and settled into the boat. McBride said, "It strikes me as unwise to return to the Kamp mansion."

"I have some other places lined up," said Tony, turning the boat so that they headed south. Before dawn they could be in the swampy backwater southwest of Hughestown. "If the law moves in, I hope LeRoy remembers what to do."

"It's not his memory I'm worried about, Mr. Carlucci. It's his guts."

Chapter 8

⁓

In the parking lot behind the North County Farmers' Cooperative building on the Kossuth Road, my father was standing over a diagram of the old Kamp Plantation property. He, six of his deputies, and four FBI agents were studying it in the glow of their flashlights. Off to one side were the members of an Army demolitions team that had driven in from Fort Polk, Louisiana.

The Book of Olin described the Kamp place as the "altar and arsenal for the knights of the Empire." This part of the sweep Billy Wallace would handle himself. The FBI didn't like it, but the sheriff had the blessing of the U.S. Attorney.

"LeRoy Kamp's house is here but there's no direct access from the road. We have to go down this dirt road here, then into his yard. The ruins of the old main house are back here, two hundred yards or so, against this hill," my father was pointing out. "There are several outbuildings down through here. A barn and old gin. A tractor shed. A sizable creek runs behind the whole place. Deep enough to float a boat most of the year.

"According to Farber's diary, they've been using that creek and the tunnels that run all under this place for years to bring in illegal weapons, ammo and explosives. So, our goal is to go in hard and fast, take the small house here and LeRoy, then bring in the Army team.

"If LeRoy gets down into those tunnels, my guess is he'll pop out back here on this creek somewhere. I flew over the area yesterday with Jack Yancy in his crop-duster. I didn't see a boat. Still, I'd bet there's one there. That's why I want you two on this bridge," he said to deputies Ingram and Cauthon. "LeRoy has to pass under it to get to the river. Now, I want him alive, if possible. So, don't go blastin' away at the boat if you don't have to. String you a line or two of that half-inch cable across the creek to stop a boat if it comes through."

"Question, Sheriff," said one of the FBI agents. "There's only one road in. It's going to be awfully difficult to get close without being heard or seen. Don't you think it would be smarter to work our way up through these woods and take him by surprise? It looks like only a quarter mile, maybe, from the road here to the house."

"Well, Agent, uh –?"

"Martin."

"Agent Martin, from what we've learned, Robert Bedford McBride has been around this place, on and off, for more than a month. With time on his hands and plenty of supplies, there's no telling what's in those woods. Trip wires? Homemade land mines? Bouncing Betties? If you'd care to lead the way, I'll be happy to follow – at a distance."

Everyone laughed except the young FBI agent.

LeRoy Kamp was asleep – that is to say, passed out – in his bedroom when the roar of car tires coming hard over gravel jarred him from his stupor. He rolled over, snatched the M-16 from beneath his bed and flipped the safety off as he ran to the living room. Through the bay window he saw two sheriff's cars sliding to a halt in the front yard, their red lights flashing. He glanced over his shoulder and saw more red lights out back.

Everything was happening so fast.

He had to – *to?* – set the timer! The timer!

When Kamp started to swing around toward the kitchen his nervous hand clamped on the trigger of the automatic rifle. Suddenly, he was spraying 5.56 millimeter slugs through the front window and the door. He stared at his hand and the gun as if they both belonged to someone else. He wanted to stop shooting, but it seemed as if his finger was cramped on the trigger and he had no control over it. Suddenly, slugs were coming back through the walls, he saw, as if in one of those slow-motion dreams. Dozens of holes opening up filled with flashing light the color of blood.

This was all happening too fast. Simply too fast.

The pain in his leg snapped him from his half-dream and the jolt of his shoulder blades landing on the floor nearly knocked the breath out of him but he rolled over and started crawling toward the kitchen. He had to get to the timer, then get out of there. Get to the boat.

As suddenly as the shooting had started, it stopped and things were terribly quiet. LeRoy could feel the crunch of broken glass under his hands and knees as he crawled. Outside, he heard the sound of fresh rounds being chambered.

"LeRoy!" a voice called. "This is Billy Wallace. There's no way out. No place to run. If you give it up, I promise no one will hurt you."

Keeping low, LeRoy reached onto the kitchen counter for a simple egg timer. He and McBride had timed it. Two minutes was enough to get through the trapdoor in the hall closet and through the tunnel to the main basement and down the side tunnel to the boat. Plenty on a dead run. But the pain in LeRoy's leg was awful. In the flash of the red lights he could see a large hole ripped in his thigh and something that looked like black paint oozing from it.

"I cain't do that, Sheriff," he called back. "No surrender!"

"LeRoy, don't be a fool. Don't make us fight our way in there."

Two minutes? Two minutes was enough on two good legs, running hard. But now? LeRoy wiped a sheen of sweat from his face. No. He'd need four – no five.

"If you try to bust through that front door, this whole place is gonna go up like an atom bomb," LeRoy yelled. "Bob McBride does good work."

"If we go up, so do you."

"I'm ready to die for The Cause," LeRoy lied as he twisted the timer and scuttled as quickly as he could toward the closet. He pulled open the trap door and headed down the steps, firing one final blast from the M-16 as he descended. As he hustled into the tunnel, he heard the muffled sound of gunfire above and behind him.

"Cease fire!" the sheriff yelled. "Cease fire!"

Billy Wallace sat with his back pressed to his cruiser listening in the silence that followed. After a minute or so, Agent Martin asked, "What do you want to do? Do you think the place is really wired?"

"I don't know, but I'm not eager to kick the door and find out," he said. "Let's ease up close and see if we can't slip in through that bay window." Motioning to the men behind the other car, he said, "Cover us."

The sheriff and Agent Martin quickly worked their way up to the shattered front window. The exchange of gunfire had exploded all the glass and most of the woodwork.

For a few moments they listened as the seconds ticked silently away on the timer. ...3:39 ... 3:38 ... 3:37 ...

"I don't hear anything," said Agent Martin. "Do you think he got down in the tunnels?"

"Maybe. I'm gonna try to ease in. Keep your eyes on that hall."

My father stepped inside, onto the crunch of broken glass. He could feel his hand sweating on the slide-handle of the shotgun. He secured a position behind a large recliner and told Agent Martin, "Come on in."

Once both men were inside and had cover, the sheriff flipped on the light switch behind him. Most of the bulbs were blown out but one or two ceiling lights were intact. The room lit up and they could see the blood trail leading to the hall closet. The sheriff motioned the other team inside and they quickly went from room to room, securing the scene before snatching open the closet door. The blood trail stopped at the big trap door.

Agent Martin reached for the handle. "No!" said the sheriff. "Let's wait until the demolitions boys can check this whole area."

"But Sheriff, he's a suspect in five murders –"

"I know what he is. I also know who he is and that he's wounded," said Billy Wallace. "LeRoy'll turn up. I'm more interested in preserving the evidence than catching him right now."

"It's your show," snapped Martin, "as per the U.S. Attorney. But I have orders to call Mr. Burke and give him a full report on what went down here."

"Go ahead, if the phone is still workin'. But don't mess up any fingerprints."

The FBI agent gave Billy Wallace an arrogant smirk and walked off toward the kitchen.

"I'll radio for the demolitions team," said Deputy Jackson.

After a moment, Billy Wallace strolled into the kitchen, careful to step over the large splotches of blood on the linoleum floor. He hadn't been able to eat all day and now he felt hungrier than he could remember feeling in a long time. The smell of liquor was all in the house and he badly wanted a drink – a stiff one that would dull his senses. Instead, he looked in the refrigerator and saw a plate of cornbread and bottle of milk. He took both out as the young FBI agent began his report to J.L. Burke. It wasn't very flattering, emphasizing that LeRoy Kamp had escaped.

The sheriff leaned against the sink eating a wedge of cornbread. As he lowered the milk bottle from his lips, he saw the egg timer behind the agent, counting down under a minute. Way under a minute!

Billy Wallace put down the milk and pushed aside the startled agent. "Hey! What are you doing?"

The sheriff took a quick look behind the timer, then snatched it off the counter, pulling it free of the two electrical leads screwed into the back.

As the stunned agent held the phone on one hand, my father slapped the timer into the other. The agent looked at it. There were seven seconds left.

As Agent Martin stared silently at the device they all heard the blast in the distance, in the direction of the creek behind the property, and out the back window saw the fireball roiling up into the night sky.

Chapter 9

◌◌

Had the stakes not been so high, it would have been comical to see robed Klansmen marching on the town square carrying signs complaining that the civil rights of their leaders were being violated. *Their* civil rights? But as Holly watched from her office, that's what she saw early Tuesday morning – the first day of school, 1969. Mercifully, the Klux were outnumbered by reporters and FBI agents. Down on the highway, almost no one turned out to harass black youngsters and poor whites as the buses turned onto the road up to Cattahatchie High School. It was soon obvious that a larger-than-expected group of white students had stuck with the school. Much of it thanks to Cutter and the football program.

Even out in the most rural parts of the county, the buses rolled with only minor incidents here and there – rocks or eggs being thrown, trees cut down on a couple of roads to block the buses. Of course, the fact that each bus traveling the country roads had some sort of law enforcement escort was part of it. That couldn't go on forever, but it would continue for at least the first two weeks of school, the newspaper told us.

The strategy that my father and J.L. Burke put together, and that Judge Mulberry quietly approved, worked almost to a T. With the major leaders of the local Klavern either hauled away to the federal stockade or in hiding, members of the Klan's rank-and-file were confused and frightened. Most hunkered down and stayed out of sight, hoping FBI agents or sheriff's deputies didn't come to their door next with a warrant to search or arrest.

For the most part, "The Sunday Night Massacre," as Klansmen were calling it, was bloodless. The only fatality was LeRoy Kamp. He made it to his hidden speedboat, fired it up and raced toward the river. He saw the two sheriff's cars sitting on the bridge, red lights flashing, but instead of easing back on the throttle, he stood tall at the controls and slammed it to the max – which gave him no time to react to the cables strung across the creek, if he ever saw them. Tied off two large, deep-rooted trees on either side of the creek, the bottom cable cut through the boat's fiberglass hull like a bandsaw and the upper strand sliced through LeRoy's neck like a scythe. Moments later a severed fuel line found a spark and the deputies dove for cover.

Later they would say they saw LeRoy's head spinning in mid-air, "like a flipped coin," before it splashed into the creek. It had not been recovered.

The only other injury was to an FBI agent named Martin, who got too eager to explore a barn on the Kamp property before it was thoroughly checked by the Army demolitions team. He hung his foot on a trip wire and the place went up. Fortunately, his injuries were minor.

E ven though three of its board members were in the federal stockade in Memphis dressed in prison uniforms, Riverview Academy opened Tuesday morning as planned, but with a much smaller turnout than expected. There was a ribbon-cutting by Cecil Weathers, but due to another sudden family illness Governor Broderick did not attend. Weathers was sweating so copiously in his cheap man-of-the-people suit, that I almost felt sorry for him.

After Brother MacAllister gave the invocation to open the first-day celebration for Riverview, Weathers took the mike and launched into a speech so vicious and venomous that even some mommas and daddies who were true-blue believers in segregation, now and forever, were taken aback.

I knew right then that Riverview Academy would fail, or maybe survive but only a much smaller scale than Weathers and his bunch envisioned. Really, I didn't care either way. No more than I ever really cared if I went to school with blacks, whites or space aliens, as long as Patti and I stayed together.

* * *

A t a few minutes after seven Tuesday night, Sheriff Wallace entered *The Current-Leader* building through the loading dock and went upstairs to Holly's office. She, Cutter and Rose were eating fried chicken at the conference table.

"You're just in time," said Holly. "Won't you join us? Or is this not a social call, either?"

"It's not, but I'll join you anyway," said my father and pulled up a chair.

"How was school?" the sheriff asked.

"Tense," Cutter told him. "There was some pushin' and shovin' here and there, but nothing serious that I saw."

"Good."

"Did all the afternoon bus routes go all right?" asked Holly.

"Yes. Thankfully."

"Sheriff, what you and Mr. Burke cooked up?" she said. "It was brilliant, and it probably saved many injuries and maybe even some lives. This county owes you a huge debt of gratitude, and I'm saying so in tomorrow's editorial."

Billy Wallace finished a crispy thigh and wiped his mouth with a paper napkin. "Well, that's kind of you, but we're not out of the woods yet," he told her. "We missed two of our main targets."

"Tony and McBride," said Cutter. It wasn't a question.

"Maybe they're on the run," said Holly, more for Rose's sake than because she really believed it.

"Maybe," said the sheriff. "Anyway, that's not why I came by."

"Then –?"

"When we searched the Kamp property, we found something – interesting, let's say, for lack of a better understanding of what it means," the sheriff told them. "We found a 1968 Ford station wagon. When we ran the plates, they came back to Mary Nell."

Holly and Cutter looked at each other.

"Does the right front fender have damage?" asked Cutter.

"Yes. Just like Mr. Cole described."

"I knew it!" said Holly. "What about fingerprints or blood?"

"I'm afraid that's the bad news," my father told them. "You probably heard about an FBI boy settin' off one of McBride's booby traps and burning down a barn out there." Holly and Cutter looked at him. "The car was in it. So anything like that is gone." Holly groaned and slumped back in her chair. "The FBI techs are still going through things, starting with LeRoy's house, the basement and tunnels, and then working their way out as the Army demolitions guys clear the way. Maybe they'll turn up something else when they process the wagon."

Holly pushed back from the table, staring at the pictures on the table behind what had been T.L. Carter's desk. Most were of Tom, Mary Nell and the grandchildren in some combination. The more certain she became that Mary Nell, at least, was involved in her father's death, the more she wished it was not so.

"There's one more thing," said the sheriff. "We only found a few sets of fingerprints in LeRoy's house. Apparently he didn't have a lot of friends."

"Were McBride's among them?" asked Cutter.

"Off the record, yes. But as it relates to our discussion, the techs found several sets of fingerprints that they believe to be female because of the size and shape," the sheriff told them. "Including on the laminated wooden slats in the headboard of LeRoy's bed."

There was a pause, and everyone got the picture.

"And you're thinking Mary Nell and LeRoy were lovers?" asked Holly. "I can't see it."

Billy Wallace cocked his head to one side. "Wife, mom, Sunday school teacher gets bored with the PTA and running Daughters of the Confederacy bake sales? Mary Nell wouldn't be the first woman like that to go for a walk on the wild side."

"All right, Sheriff, assumin' that's true, it still doesn't explain why they would kill Mr. Carter," Cutter pointed out.

"Could be plain old greed," he said. "If Mary Nell thought Tom stood to inherit. Maybe she promised LeRoy –"

"Wait a minute. We're getting ahead of ourselves," Holly interrupted. "Can any of the fingerprints in the house be matched to Mary Nell?"

"As far as we can tell, Mary Nell has never been fingerprinted. And we don't have enough for a judge to compel her to give them to us. Especially in this county," the sheriff explained. "Speaking of judges, what's happening with that exhumation order? I'm sorry, I've lost track."

"You've been a little busy. I understand," said Holly. "Judge Autry finally ruled for us on the law last Wednesday, but stayed his order until Tom and Mary Nell could take it to the State Court of Appeal.

That hearing is tomorrow morning in Tupelo. Dan Freeman swears there is no way we'll lose. And Doctor Garner says he can do the autopsy Thursday afternoon."

"Good. I'll try to be there," my father said, lifting his hat off the table. "Maybe the techs will have something else by then. Thanks for dinner. Cutter, would you mind walking out with me?"

In the parking lot, they propped against my father's cruiser.
"How's your mother?"

"They moved her to the nursing home on Saturday," said Cutter. "But there's no real change. To get better from something like that, I think you have to have a real will to do it. Tony broke Momma's will a long time ago. But you didn't get me down here to ask that."

"No, I didn't. This is going to have to come out eventually, but I didn't want to mention it in front of Rose yet," the sheriff began. "When we searched the barn on your property, we found Tony's stash of Klan gear, including a whip with nine cords. It's called a cat-o-nine-tails. Back during the days of pirates and the Royal Navy and such, they were used to flog sailors who got out of line. Nowadays, they're pretty unusual."

Cutter's expression was neutral. "I'm listening."

"We didn't release the information to the public, but a cat-o-nine is what was used to whip Ridge Bellafont to death. The FBI lab found blood on Tony's whip that was consistent with Mr. Bellafont's. Tony is goin' down for capital murder."

Cutter rubbed the back of his neck. His throat felt tight. "Okay," was all he could manage.

"I'm sorry, son."

"Don't be."

My father clasped Cutter's shoulder. "There's one more thing. Tony may be a lot of things, but he's no fool. He'll know we searched his place, and he'll figure we found his gear. That means he knows he has nothing to lose, and that makes him more dangerous than ever.

"Until we catch him, or know he's long gone from here, I'd stick pretty close to Rose and Miss Carter," he said. "And watch your own back, too."

Cutter nodded. "I plan to."

Chapter 10

༙

Early Thursday evening Cutter sat opposite Holly and Rose outside of the morgue at DeLong Memorial Hospital. On Wednesday, the state appeals court had, indeed, vacated the stay without comment. My father and Deputy Ingram oversaw the exhumation on Thursday morning, but an emergency appendectomy had delayed Doctor Garner another couple of hours.

Cutter leaned back in the chair and stretched his long legs as far as he could across the hallway until he was almost touching the foot pedal of Holly's wheelchair. "How you doin'?"

Holly looked up from a story she was editing for the weekend paper, and took off her glasses. "I'm okay," she said, rubbing the bridge of her nose. "Part of me wants Dr. Garner to find evidence of a murder so that my father's killers can be brought to justice. Another part wants him to come out here and say, 'Miss Carter, this was a big waste of time.'

"The thing is, if Mary Nell is involved, I don't see how she could have covered this up without Tom knowing. Or at least suspecting. I'd hate for –"

"There she is! There's that woman!" Mary Nell Carter yelled as she strode toward Holly, her four-inch heels pinging off the tile floor like two tack hammers. "This is all your doing," she hissed, bending down and grabbing the frame of Holly's chair – she shook it and tried to tilt it.

Cutter grabbed Mary Nell around the waist and lifted her off her feet with no more effort than he'd need for a rag doll. She flailed her arms as he put her down, keeping himself between her and Holly.

"How dare you lay hands on me!" yelled Mary Nell. "You all saw it. That boy assaulted me! That Carlucci boy!"

Cutter said nothing, merely held his ground as Rose pressed herself back into a corner. She hated fighting and screaming. She'd lived with so much of it.

"Mary Nell, you need to calm yourself," said Delbert Whitten, her attorney.

"Don't talk to me like I'm a child! Do your job."

Hanging farther back was Tom. Holly could see he'd lost even more weight, as if he'd been on a liquid diet of sour mash and barley malt. His eyes were sunken under his prominent brow, yet red and swollen. His shoulders sagged and sweat rings wrapped from under his arms around the front of his shirt. He smelled of beer and nicotine, and maybe even urine. No matter what he'd done, Tom still was her brother, and seeing him that way made Holly want to cry and curse and pray, all at the same time.

"Hurry up! Get in there and serve that court order," Mary Nell told Whitten. "Have them stop this, this – this desecration. Now!"

It was at that moment that the two men and a deputy emerged from the morgue.

"Sheriff, I have a stay here issued by State Supreme Court Justice Miller, ordering you and Doctor Garner –"

"I'm afraid you're too late, Mr. Whitten. The autopsy is complete," said Sheriff Wallace.

Mary Nell Carter was steaming like a teapot with a too-tight lid. She stamped her feet looking for somewhere to vent her rage. "In that case, I want this boy arrested for assault. This woman and that – that girl will lie for him, I'm sure. But my husband and Mr. Whitten are witnesses."

"It's over, Mary Nell," said Tom. "Let's just go h—"

"Shut up, Tom!" she snapped. "Mr. Whitten will verify that –"

"Mrs. Carter, please," tried the attorney. "Your husband is right."

"You're weak! Useless! Both of you!" she snarled as she straightened her dress. "I'll go to the county prosecutor. Mr. Epps is a man of quality. His great grandfather served gallantly under General Longstreet during numerous engagements. His wife is on the Daughters of the Confederacy State Committee with me.

"I'll show you a thing or two," she said, whirling to leave.

Everyone except my father was too stunned by Mary Nell's manic outburst to say anything. "Mrs. Carter, wouldn't you like to know the results of the autopsy?" he asked.

Mary Nell stopped, turned, lifted her chin with all the imperiousness she'd learned as one of the Vicksburg Poindexters, as Senator Poindexter's daughter. "Not at all. I consider this an unholy desecration of my father-in-law's grave. We all know what happened. That girl even saw it."

"Her name is Rose Marie Carlucci," Cutter told Mary Nell.

"Yes, well, in any case, this was a senseless mutilation of T.L.'s body, and I have no interest in –"

"I do. I'd like to hear the autopsy results," said Tom.

Holly felt a spark of hope flash inside her. Maybe he really didn't know. Maybe he wasn't in on it, at least not consciously. Maybe …

"Tom, darling, it'll only upset you," said Mary Nell, taking his arm, attempting to turn him. "You know how close you were, how close we all were to your father. T.L. drowned in an unfortunate accident. That's all there is to it. Anyone who says anything different is just out to, out to –"

"Out to what, Mary Nell?" asked Tom.

"Why, out to, to smear our family name. To bring more scandal on us."

Tom shook off his wife's arm. "Go ahead, Doctor Garner. I'd like to know if Daddy drowned."

The oxygen seemed to empty from the room. Everyone held their breath.

"Yes, Tom. Your father drowned. That would be the official cause of death," said the doctor.

Holly and Cutter looked at each other and then at Sheriff Wallace, whose expression changed not at all as he observed Mary Nell. She drew in a deep breath and the color that had momentarily drained from her cheeks returned. "You see, Tom," she almost gasped. "I told you."

"However," Doctor Garner continued, "prior to his death, Mr. Carter received a severe blow to his forehead that resulted in a skull fracture and sudden and intense bruising of the brain."

Mary Nell cleared her throat. "I'm not surprised. T.L. was in an automobile accident."

"Did the wound match the steering wheel from Daddy's car?" asked Holly, the surprise showing on Mary Nell's face.

"No. And from the amount of bruising to the brain, it's easy for a competent pathologist to see that the injury occurred at least two hours prior to his death," said Doctor Garner.

Tom seemed not so much surprised by the news as simply saddened, as if someone had added one more brick to a heavy load he already was carrying. Holly's emotions were so mixed and mottled she didn't really feel anything.

"In fact, we believe we have the weapon that delivered the blow," said Sheriff Wallace. "Deputy, would you fetch it, please?"

"Mr. Carter also suffered a compound fracture of the left femur and a severe dislocation of the left shoulder *prior* to death," added Doctor Garner. "So, he could not have possibly driven himself to the bridge that night."

Mary Nell waved as if she'd been hit by a strong wind, but reset her high heels and maintained her composure.

The sheriff quietly said something to the deputy, who stepped into the morgue and quickly emerged with a fireplace poker bearing a unique bronze wolf's head handle. The whole thing was wrapped in plastic. Holly recognized it as part of a set in the library. She had not noticed that one piece was missing.

"About noon today, FBI technicians processing the scene at the Old Kamp Place found this inside of the spare-tire well in a Ford station wagon registered to you, Mrs. Carter," the sheriff said.

"The end of this poker, shaped like a wolf's paw, is a perfect match for the wound to Mr. Carter's forehead," said Doctor Garner.

"Would you care to explain that, Mrs. Carter?" asked my father.

Mary Nell fought to keep her chin high as her lips trembled.

"Mrs. Carter, don't say a word," advised her attorney. "Are you arresting my client?"

"Not at the moment."

"Then we'll be going," said Delbert Whitten.

"Yes. I need to call my father, Senator Poindexter. His counsel always has been wisest. And he has many friends in high places."

"Good, because you're going to need them," said Sheriff Wallace.

Holly could see the Mary Nell's knees were shaky, but she managed to stiffen her back and march away. Tom gave his sister a long sorrow-filled look, his exhausted eyes heavy with regret, then followed his wife out.

"I'm sorry, Holly," said Billy Wallace. "I didn't mean for you to hear it like that."

"Why didn't you tell me about the poker?"

"I didn't know about it until right before the autopsy."

"It doesn't matter. She did it. She killed my father," Holly said with certainty. "She and LeRoy. Why didn't you arrest her?"

"Because I still don't have anything that directly ties her and LeRoy together," he said. "She has a police report that says that car was stolen in Memphis. And Wolf's Run was empty for weeks after T.L. died. The defense will claim that the poker could have been taken at any time, by anyone."

"The FBI couldn't find any fingerprints on the poker or in the car?" asked Cutter.

"No. The fire destroyed any fingerprint evidence there might have been."

"But if that car really is crucial evidence, why did LeRoy keep it around?" asked Doctor Garner.

"Maybe for insurance, in case Mary Nell ever tried to turn him in," said the sheriff. "Maybe for blackmail. If Mary Nell's fingerprints were on that poker or your father's blood was in the car, then as long as LeRoy had it, he owned her."

"Somehow we need to put them together. We'll start questioning friends and –"

"Wait!" said Holly. "If we could put Mary Nell in LeRoy's bed, that would be perfect, wouldn't it?"

"Of course, but until I can get a warrant to take her fingerprints –"

"No. She just gave them to us," Holly told him, pointing to a length of metal tubing that connected the foot pedals to the wheelchair's frame. "She grabbed my chair. Right there."

"And nothing holds a nice print like a beautiful hunk of stainless steel," smiled Billy Wallace. "Deputy, go get a fingerprint kit. I'll lift 'em myself."

Chapter 11

❧

Sheriff Wallace placed a car in front of the Carters' home on Jackson Street. By ten Friday morning the FBI had matched the fingerprints taken from Holly's wheelchair to those found in LeRoy Kamp's bedroom.

Meanwhile, Doctor Garner had done some detective work of his own. He remembered that Mary Nell Carter had led a Daughters of the Confederacy blood drive for the Vietnam war effort. He checked with the Tupelo blood bank and they gave him Mary Nell's blood type. It was O-positive, the same as that spattered on the picture frame along with blood of the the same type as T.L. Carter's.

When the sheriff returned from testifying in federal court in Oxford late that afternoon, the doctor passed the information along. Billy Wallace was eager to get an arrest warrant or a least a search warrant for the house on Jackson Street, but County Prosecutor Jimmy Epps said he didn't have enough evidence to take to a judge.

"I thought you might feel that way," said the sheriff, looking at his watch. The phone rang on the prosecutor's desk. Epps leaned back in the chair, looking smug and letting it ring. "I suggest you pick it up, Jimmy," said my father. "It might be the most important call of your life."

After another three rings, Epps lifted the receiver. On the other end of the line was the United States Attorney for Northern District of Mississippi. "You're going to get onboard with this, Mr. Epps, or I'm going to open a full-scale investigation into your office and your personal finances," J.L. Burke told him. "Believe me, I'll have IRS investigators turn over every rock and look in every hiding place in Cattahatchie County, including the crack of your ass, if you get in Sheriff Wallace's way on this."

Billy Wallace saw the Adam's apple in Jimmy Epps' throat jump like a bobber on a fishing line that had been jerked hard. "You, you can't threaten me," Epps managed but it was a half-hearted effort.

"In that case, I hope you've kept good records," said Burke and hung up the phone. The line went dead and Epps forced his gaze to meet the sheriff's.

"Anytime in the next two hours'll be fine, Jimmy," Billy Wallace told Epps and turned for the door. "If I'm not in the office, the dispatcher'll know where to find me."

* * *

From the balcony of my rented room I watched the Cattahatchie High team bus pass by, headed south on Highway 27 to the Wolves' opener against New Albany. John-Thomas Hinton – Coach Hinton, now – was driving, and black faces outnumbered white in the windows. I had heard that there were twenty-eight players, including freshmen and Roseville kids who never had participated in organized football.

Instead of the two or three "spirit buses" and dozens of vehicles that usually followed the CHS team bus, there were only a handful of cars. Including the red Plymouth Fury Miss Carter now was driving. I saw Rose Carlucci's face in the passenger window and I was glad for her. To my knowledge, she never had been to a high school football game. Never seen her brother play.

Riverview didn't open its season for another week, and it looked like I would start at wide receiver. Start in my white-and-gold uniform with my pretty cheerleader girlfriend shaking her pompoms and high kicking to encourage me. So, I turned my back and stepped inside as the old screen door squawked its rusty call. I needed to get ready for my date with Patti.

* * *

If cheering loud and hard could earn a football team a victory from the stands, then Rose Marie Carlucci's efforts would have given the Wolves a three-touchdown win. It was as if Rose was making up for all the games she missed.

TV stations from Memphis and Tupelo, along with at least ten print reporters, including Holly, were there to capture the moment in history when the Cattahatchie Wolves kicked off their first-ever season as an integrated team. To be sure, many who had been following the story of the Wolves hoped for a fairy-tale season. But it quickly became evident that such was not to be. The Bulldogs scored on their first five possessions and CHS was down 34-6 at the half.

Cutter ended up rushing for 281 yards and four touchdowns, but it wasn't nearly enough as New Albany exploited the inexperienced CHS defense for 675 yards of total offense and a 64-28 win ... as Holly Lee Carter told Managing Editor C. Michael Morton when she phoned in her story.

* * *

By Saturday morning the Carters' house on Jackson Street had been thoroughly searched. Mary Nell Carter was in custody, and Tom Carter and their children were hospitalized. In his small hospital office, Doctor Garner and my father met with Holly and Cutter. Rose was at the nearby nursing home with her mother.

"When administered in very small doses, arsenic builds up in the system and causes the jaundiced condition you saw in Tom on Thursday," explained Doctor Garner. "Eventually, it causes liver failure and death – especially when exacerbated by a heavy and regular intake of alcohol."

"What are Ton's chances?" asked Holly.

"Not good, I'm afraid. Not good at all. Preliminary tests indicate he's on the verge of liver failure," said the doctor. "If the poisoning had continued another week, I think he'd have been dead. As it is, he probably has a few weeks. If he doesn't drink, then maybe three or four months. At the outside."

Holly was stunned, almost to the point of being numb. While she had come to believe and at some level accept that Mary Nell had been involved in her father's death, the notion that she would poison her husband and children? It was almost beyond comprehension, beyond evil.

"What about Georgette and Lanny?" asked their aunt.

"Apparently, Mary Nell only recently started slipping them the arsenic. Physically, they should be all right in time. But God only knows what all of this will do to them emotionally."

Holly turned as best she could in the small room, staring out into the bright sunlight of a beautiful September morning. She wanted to see the light in all this. God's hand. His plan. But all she could see was Mary Nell Poindexter's pinched, hate-filled face as she was loaded into the police car, her hands cuffed behind her, her friends from Jackson Street, First Demonination and the Daughters of the Confedracy crowding the sidewalk. Most whispered, some called words of support, a couple of them cursed the sheriff as he got in the car. They called him "a worthless drunk" and "an embarrassment."

After a time, Holly asked Doctor Garner, "When can I take Lanny and Georgette home?"

My father and the doctor shared a look. "Holly, I don't think that would be a good idea at the moment," said G.P. Garner. "Tom and especially Mary Nell have been poisoning their minds – no pun intended – against you for months. Years, even. They're frightened. They're confused. And they're angry. And unfortunately, a lot of that anger is directed at you."

"I'm still their aunt."

"Mr. and Mrs. Poindexter are on their way from Vicksburg," said the sheriff.

Holly whirled, banging into the doctor's desk. "No!" she told him. "Absolutely not! I will not have those children going to live with the people who created that woman. If I have to find a judge today to –"

"All right, Holly," said the sheriff, raising his hands in mock surrender. "I can get the state welfare folks to take temporary custody. They can place them with a neighbor for now. Several have already volunteered."

Holly let her anger roll back like a tide she could only barely control. "Thank you."

"In any case," said the doctor, "I want to keep them here for another day or two at least just for observation."

Cutter looked at the sheriff. "How could Mary Nell think she could get away with killing her whole family?"

"I don't believe she was thinking that far ahead," said my father. "No one wants to see Mary Nell walk away from this, and the murder of Mr. Carter, on an insanity plea. Least of all me. But its hard to tell where hatefulness leaves off and pure crazy starts with her. Maybe when she comes down from all the pills she's on, she'll be more lucid."

"Don't count on it," said Doctor Garner. "This is out of my field, but I can tell you that if she isn't properly weaned from the cocktail of barbiturates, amphetamines and painkillers we found in her blood, she easily could slip into a psychotic state from which she might never recover."

"A psychiatrist from the state hospital will be here on Monday to evaluate her," said Sheriff Wallace.

"What does she say about all the pills you found in the house?" asked Cutter. "You told us earlier that LeRoy's prints were all over the bottles and baggies."

"Right now she's not really saying anything, under advice of counsel. Except ordering the deputies around like they're chambermaids."

"At least we know now how Mary Nell and LeRoy were connected," said Cutter. "He was her supplier."

"And her lover," added Holly. "That combination probably explains how he got involved in killing my father. Sheriff, do you think he knew about Tom and the kids?"

Billy Wallace turned his hat in his hands, the way he did when he was thinking. "Apparently, LeRoy was a much nastier guy than we ever suspected. The FBI found evidence in the tunnels under his place that he was, at the very least, involved in planning the attack on the Farber family. That's five counts of capital murder. Including three children between the ages of six and fourteen. So, would I put anything past him? Not at this point."

That thought gave everyone in the room pause. After several moments, the sheriff said, "We've got Mary Nell cold on three counts of attempted murder, plus all sorts of drug possession charges. I'm convinced she and LeRoy killed Mr. Carter, but we're still a ways from proving it beyond reasonable doubt."

"The timeline," said Holly.

"Yep. The timeline," he said. "There's no way she could have gotten from Lawler Bottom to her house in time for Deputy Hinton to notify her that night. And with LeRoy dead, unless Mary Nell gives it up we may never know exactly what happened that night at Wolf's Run."

* * *

Five minutes later, Holly stopped outside the door to her brother's room, unable to make herself push any farther. Cutter gently rubbed the knots in her shoulders. "Do you want me to go in with you?" he asked.

"No. This is something I need to do alone. But I'm glad you were with me this morning. For all that," said Holly, reaching across her chest to squeeze his hand on her shoulder. "When I think of how things were when I was five or six or seven. Before Momma left. And I look around now and see how things have turned out." Holly exhaled a long, tired breath and rested her head on the boilerplate of Cutter's ridged stomach. "It just makes me sick. I mean, we were a family once. You know?"

Then she straightened. "I'll see you later. Okay?"

"Later," Cutter agreed.

When Holly pushed into Tom's room, the heavy curtains were almost closed, but the one long shaft of sunlight that entered was as bright as a laser and made the rest of the room look all the more black for it.

Up close, Holly could see that Tom's hair was thinner, much thinner. His eyes were sunken and his skin was as dry and yellow as parchment. From his right wrist almost to his elbow, where an IV needle entered his arm, was a terrible rash. Tom was only seven years Holly's senior. Only thirty-five. He looked closer to seventy.

Holly slipped her hand into his. "Tom?" Her brother opened his faded brown eyes with great effort, but it only took one look. "*Ohhhh-hhh*, Sister, I'm so sorry!" he moaned as the tears burst from his eyes. "What have I done? What I have done?"

And for the longest time, as Holly held hand his, he cried like an abandoned child who'd finally found his way home.

Chapter 12

༄

My father pulled his police cruiser into the lot between the Randleman Cotton Warehouse and the Emerson Grain Storage elevators on the west side of the river. The lot was directly across from
the rear of *The Current-Leader* building where more than a hundred
and twenty people were gathered for the Sunday morning "downtown
prayer meeting," as the service was coming to be known. Cars filled
the newspaper lot and spread out down River Street and up the hill
toward the town square.

Billy Wallace parked next to Cutter and got out. Cutter was sitting
on the hood of his jeep wearing his black-and-red letter jacket. The sun
was beaming warm from a perfectly clear sky, but in the shadow cast
by the warehouse the air was unseasonably cool and free of humidity.
Holly was leading those gathered in a rendition of *Blessed Assurance,*
her voice so pure and sweet that it seemed to travel not on waves of
sound but on pathways of sunlight.

"Mornin', son."

"Mornin', Sheriff."

"Chilly for September."

"Yes, sir."

"Supposed to get even colder later this week. Almanac says it's
gonna be an early winter."

"Looks like it's right again."

"How come you're not on the other side of the river?"

"I guess me and Jesus still have some things to work out," Cutter
told him. "But I'm close enough to feel the Spirit."

"And to hear Miss Holly sing? She has an amazing voice."

"She's an amazing person."

"Yes, I think so, too. I think any man would be lucky to have her,
and luckier still if he can handle her," said Billy Wallace, offering a
quick smile. "Wheelchair or no wheelchair."

Cutter returned the same quick smile. "I think you're right."

Then, the sheriff got to it. "Mary Nell wants to see Holly."

Cutter stared at him with those blue-white eyes. "For what?"

"She says she'll tell what happened at Wolf's Run, but only to Holly."

Cutter thought about that for a moment. "Are you sure it's not just some game to – I don't know – to get at Holly?"

"Honestly, I don't know what it is," my father told him. "But don't worry. Mary Nell will be shackled. There's no way we'll let her hurt Holly."

"I'm not thinking about physically."

"Cutter, this may be our best chance – it may be our *only* chance to find out what happened to Mr. Carter and why she tried to kill her family. You know, she fired Mr. Whitten?"

"No. I didn't."

"Her father – Senator Claudius Poindexter 'of the Vicksburg Poindexters' – came up yesterday, spent an hour with her and left looking as white as a Klansman's pillowcase. He didn't even inquire with me about his grandchildren. I think he cut her loose, for whatever reason," explained the sheriff. "Mary Nell is right on the brink of either giving it up or shutting down completely. Maybe for good."

"All right, I'll talk to Holly. When do you want to do it?"

"Two o'clock. My office. The FBI's wiring the place right now," he said. "We'll be able to hear everything and record it, too."

After the prayer service ended and the parking lot had mostly emptied, Cutter told Holly what the sheriff had said. Of course, she agreed to do it. There was no question. Cutter knew there would not be. Still, he was uneasy.

As planned, Holly, Cutter and Rose went to lunch at The Cotton Café. Mostly Holly could only pick at her food, her stomach in knots thinking about being in the same room alone with her sister-in-law. Not because of physical fear, but because the notion of being in the proximity to such abject wickedness repulsed her almost to the point of nausea. But she knew she had to do this for her father, and for Tom, Georgette and Lanny. There could never be an adequate explanation for what Mary Nell had done, but perhaps there could be an intellectual comprehension of her motivations. Whatever that meant.

A t ten minutes to two, Sheriff Wallace pointed to a large supply closet adjacent to his office in the jail. "We set up the tape recorder in there," said Billy Wallace. "We'll be recording and listening."

"We're not violating her rights?" asked Holly. "I don't want her to tell me everything and have a judge throw it out."

"Absolutely not," said J.L. Burke, who'd come up from Oxford. "Mrs. Carter asked for the meeting. You're not her preacher and you're not her attorney. She can have no expectation of privacy. We're fine."

"What if she claims later she was so messed up on all the drugs in her system that she made it all up?" asked Cutter.

"We'll deal with that in court if it becomes an issue," Burke told him. Then, squatting beside Holly's wheelchair, said, "I believe she wants to tell you her story. She wants to justify her actions. But if you come off as too confrontational, she could back off. I know this will be difficult, but try to talk to her like you would for a newspaper story."

"Let Mary Nell think she's in control," said the sheriff. "Control is very important to her."

"All right," said Holly, pushing into the office. "I'll try."

"You sit here, Miss Carter, on this side of the conference table," said an FBI agent. "The prisoner will be across from you. She'll be shackled to the radiator. So there's no need to be afraid."

"Okay. I'm not. But could I have a couple of minutes to myself before we start?"

"Of course," said Burke. "But I think it's important to start at the time she set. Control."

I n the closet, an FBI tech sat at a small table with a big reel-to-reel recorder in front of him. My father, J.L. Burke and Cutter were with him. Sweat, cologne and testosterone were thick in the room. Through the small speaker the men could pick up a word or two as Holly waited for two deputies to bring Mary Nell down.

"What's she doing?" asked the tech. "Who's she talking to?"

"Never mind," said Burke. "Just make sure everything's working. We don't want any screw-ups."

It was one minute until two. "Amen," said Holly.

A t exactly two, the deputies marched Mary Nell into the sheriff's private office. Despite being in a red jail jumpsuit, her wrists locked to a heavy leather belt at her narrow waist and a stout chain connecting her ankles, Mary Nell Poindexter Carter held her head with the imperiousness of a queen suffering house arrest. She seemed to navigate with her pointed chin as she shuffled across the room, the chain scuffing across the tile floor with a soft rattling sound.

Deputy John Ingram pulled the chair for her and she sat as if he were a waiter at a fine restaurant while the other deputy connected the leg chain to the radiator. "Might you unfetter my wrists?"

"No, ma'am, Miss Carter."

"Carter?" she asked. "Deputy, I don't want to have to remind you again, my name is not Carter. It's Poindexter, of the Vicksburg Poindexters. Please don't force me to report you to your superiors."

John Ingram stared at her for a moment, then, "Yes, ma'am. I'll try to remember."

Holly had to force herself to look at Mary Nell without showing in her face the revulsion she felt. Maybe she could someday forgive Mary Nell in Christ, as a lost soul, but not now. "You asked to see me."

"Yes, well, I thought you should hear it from me before I make your family's filth public to the entire community."

"All right, Mary Nell. I'm listening."

The woman drew back and focused her hard, gray eyes down her perfect nose. "You will please address me as Miss Poindexter. Or if you prefer, Miss Mary Nell."

Holly had to bite her tongue. "Mary... Miss Mary Nell, what is it you want to tell me?"

"Filth, filth, filth," Mary Nell repeated. Holly stared at her and said nothing, remembering Burke's instructions. Finally after almost a minute, Mary Nell spoke. "You know, of course, your mother, Veronique Dupre, was born and reared in New Orleans – a place of decadence and fornication."

"I'm aware my mother is from New Orleans. Yes."

"What do you know of your mother's blood?"

"My mother's 'blood'? Not much," admitted Holly. "She was an only child. Her parents died in the Great '27 Flood. The rest of the family was scattered."

"So your mother wanted her poor husband and children to believe."

Holly felt her breathing become shallow, growing more uneasy by the moment. "What does that mean?"

"In a safe deposit box in my name at First United Bank of Vicksburg you'll find a file gathered by a private investigator in 1949 outlining your mother's complete genealogy – and thus that of you and your brother."

"And why is this important?"

"Oh, it's terribly important. It's, it's – well, it's all that matters, really. Your blood. The sum of all the generations that came before you," Miss Poindexter told her. "You see, you and your brother were tainted from the womb. If it weren't so disgusting, I could feel sorry for you. Like idiot children born to a syphilitic whore. It's not really the fault of the children, but that fact makes them no less idiots."

Holly fought to control both her temper and her dread. "I'm sorry, Miss Poindexter, I don't understand."

"Then understand this: your grandmother was a mulatto. Half Negro. A high-yellow who hooked herself a fine, rich Louisiana planter as her lover, her provider." Holly felt herself stop breathing. In the other room Cutter and Burke and my father looked at each other. "Your mother was a quadroon who could pass for white, and did so to marry your father. That makes her offspring octoroons. One-eighth colored. Under the laws of genetics and this state, you and your brother are as much Negroes as the naked savages who came babbling their African gibberish off a slave ship two hundred years ago.

"You're nothing but colored filth!" growled Mary Nell Poindexter as she drew her mouth into a knot and spit across the table.

Cutter snapped toward the door to the small room, but my father blocked it – "No! Wait."

His fists clinched, Cutter's eyes burned into the sheriff's, but after a moment he let out a breath and stepped back. In the office, Holly reached into her purse for a tissue and wiped her face. She thought of her own dusky complexion. Of some of the vile things her father had said to her when she was a teenager – things that bordered on what she now knew was the truth. Holly clinched the tissue in her fist and asked, "How long have you known?"

"Since the weekend prior to T.L.'s demise."

"And that's why you killed my father?"

"Why, yes," she replied without hesitation or emotion. "T.L. showed Tom and I the detective's report. He told us that Mr. Weathers commissioned the inquiry in the late 1940s after hearing rumors from business associates in New Orleans. To his credit, when Mr. Weathers showed the evidence to your father, T.L. immediately drove the conniving Negress from his home and all the way out of the state."

Holly was trying to fight through myriad confused emotions – remembering the terrible day she came home from school and her mother was gone. No note, no explanation, just gone.

"Some of Mr. Weathers' associates made sure she never returned," Mary Nell added. Holly's eyes fixed on her, fearful. "What does that mean?" Holly demanded.

Mary Nell settled back into her chair and gave Holly a knowing smile, but said nothing.

"Tell me," said Holly, ashamed of the plea she heard in her voice.

Mary Nell only smiled, savoring whatever control she could maintain despite her shackles. Holly fought to control her breathing and get her mind back on track. She thought of how her father despised Cecil Weathers and yet refused to openly challenge him in the pages of *The Current-Leader*. Now she knew the reason. What she did not understand was – "Why did Daddy show you and Tom the report after all these years? Twenty years"

"Because he said he was going to Los Angeles to, among other things, tell you. And when he returned he planned to integrate the pages of *The Current-Leader* and change its editorial policy concerning the race-mixers," Miss Poindexter explained. "Worse than any of that, he planned to publicly disclose the truth about your mother, so that Mr. Weathers could no longer hold it over his head. Of course, that was entirely out of the question."

Holly understood the impact that series of events would have on the people of Cattahatchie County, but especially on Tom and Mary Nell, who made their home in DeLong. "So you decided to kill him?"

"No. Truly, I did not," Mary Nell insisted. "But Tom fell into a useless state of drunkenness and denial, and drove off to that convention in Gulfport. So, I went to Wolf's Run to reason with T.L. privately. Though I suppose I was prepared to do whatever was necessary to prevent such utter humiliation from befalling my family."

"Georgette and Lanny ..." whispered Holly, almost to herself, sympathetic to how cruel kids could be, and surely would be once their mixed-race blood became common knowledge. But Mary Nell heard and told her, "No! Not Georgette and Lanny. They're Carters. They carry the same taint as you and your brother. I'm talking about my parents, Mr. and Mrs. Poindexter. And siblings. We'd be the laughingstock of the state, of the entire South, if it were disclosed that I, Mary Nell Poindexter, was impregnated by a Negro."

Holly stared at Mary Nell. She felt as if she was in a horrible dream, but she knew the only way to awaken was to ask the right questions. "What happened at Wolf's Run?"

The chains rattled on the floor as Mary Nell tried to cross her legs but, of course, could not. She sighed and settled. "I had slept very little since T.L. told us of his plans on Saturday afternoon. Not even the strongest of my nerve pills had any effect," she remembered. "I was crazed. Desperate.

"When I arrived at Wolf's Run the electricity was out. T.L. showed me to the library where he had a fire going. I tried to talk to him, to reason with him. But he wouldn't listen. No, no. He just wouldn't listen," she remembered. "He crossed the room to fix me a drink. To calm my nerves, as if that was the problem. My fragile nerves. But there was your mother's portrait. I saw her smiling at me in the firelight. Mocking me! That lying Negress! It was all her fault.

"T.L. had been cutting some stories from the Memphis paper. I grabbed the scissors from the coffee table and began slashing the portrait. T.L. ran across the room, tore the scissors from my hand and threw me down. He just stood there staring at the painting, mumbling something about being sorry.

"I looked at my hand and I was bleeding. It was all so wrong! I, I simply – exploded. I grabbed the first thing I could put my hands on and I swung it. He turned just as I did. It took only one blow. He went down hard. Blood went everywhere."

For once, Holly was glad she was sitting. She felt physically and emotionally sick. But there still were things that needed to be learned. She swallowed and pressed on. "Daddy wasn't dead, though."

"Oh, I thought he was. I couldn't hear a heartbeat. I was sure I'd killed him."

"How did LeRoy Kamp get involved?"

"Well, you see, Mr. Kamp, who is, err, *was* from a very fine old Miss'ssippi family, excellent bloodlines – was an acquaintance. I thought that he might be wise in such matters. I started to use the phone, but thought better of it. So I drove to his house for counsel. I felt that it would be imprudent to allow T.L. to be discovered in such a state. A thorough investigation might lead to the discovery of his wife's true ... nature."

"I see," was all Holly could manage.

"Out of, uhm, friendship, Mr. Kamp followed me back to Wolf's Run. But as we were going down the driveway in the pitch-black night, there was T.L. staggering toward the garage."

"And you hit him?"

"Yes."

"On purpose?"

"Why, yes. He *had* to be stopped. In any case, he went onto the hood and hit the windshield. The damage to my car wasn't terribly serious, but it was a shock to my system. To our utter astonishment, the old fool was *still* breathing," Mary Nell went on, shaking her head.

Holly wanted to reach across the table and slap her or choke the life out of her. Instead, she asked, "Whose idea was it to put Daddy in the car and drive it into the river?"

"Mr. Kamp suggested that it might be a workable scenario," she explained matter-of-factly. "I went inside and tidied up. I cleaned the blood from the floor. I tore the rest of that woman's portrait from the frame and burned it in the fire. I discarded the frame in the old greenhouse, with the rest of the trash. Where it belonged.

"It all would have worked perfectly if that demented Carlucci girl not been traipsing through the rain." Holly bristled, but told herself, *It's nearly over.* "With T.L. scheduled to leave for Memphis and then California first thing the next morning, he might not have been missed for days. Who could say when the car went in the river?"

Holly nodded. "But Rose did see it and you knew that she would get to a phone as quickly as she could."

Mary Nell studied not so much Holly but a space in the air beside Holly as if she could see it all playing out again in some vaporous TV monitor. Grudgingly she conceded, "Yes. Just a piece of bad luck. By the time LeRoy returned to Wolf's Run and told me the accident had been seen, the police already were at the bridge."

"So, you and LeRoy had to go around the back side of Blue Mountain."

"I was following Mr. Kamp in the station wagon but my wheel slipped off into a flooded ditch. Mr. Kamp was so kind. He understood that I needed to be home in case visitors came to call. So he gallantly allowed me to take his truck," she said. "When we discussed the matter later, he told me about the need to employ a local rube to extricate my station wagon from the ditch. We decided it might be best if the vehicle disappeared. Mr. Kamp suggested a ruse involving an out-of-state theft could help in that regard. He surreptitiously drove me to Memphis a few days later."

"It was LeRoy who beat you."

"Yes. We had to make the theft appear genuine. But I must ask you to cease calling Mr. Kamp by his Christian name. Please show the proper respect for the departed. And for your betters," said Mary Nell, a sneer crossing her lips, but Holly pressed on.

"Where was Tom during all this? Did he know?"

"Who knows what a drunken Negro knows? Or can comprehend? But he certainly could not be trusted in this matter."

Holly realized she was breathing through her mouth. Trying to get enough air into her chest. Her ribs felt as heavy as ironwork, pressing on her lungs. All the oxygen was being sucked from the room. "If the purpose of all this was to keep my mother's ancestry hidden, why are you disclosing it now?"

"Sadly, I've undergone an unfortunate change of circumstances. Mr. and Mrs. Poindexter feel it appropriate to maintain a certain, uhm, distance in this matter. Allowing myself to be deceived by the Negro Tom Carter has put our family in a sordid and scandalous position. So, it is up to me to clean up my own mess," she explained. "Once I tell a jury of *white* men how I was duped into becoming a Negro's wife, they won't send me to prison for any of it. They'll give me a parade down Main Street."

Holly had only one more question. "When did you decide to kill Tom and the children?"

"Why, as soon as T.L. revealed the report to us. You see, T.L.'s death really was an unfortunate moment of circumstance. Of his refusal to listen to reason," explained Mary Nell, straightening her shoulders. "But the notion that I would continue to share my bed with a Negro and raise his pickaninnies – well, such a thing is simply out of the question."

That was it. That was all Holly could listen to. She whirled and headed for the door as Mary Nell sprang to her feet, the chains rattling. "Stop! How dare you turn you back on me!" she screamed. "I didn't dismiss you! You dirty, filthy –"

Cutter stepped out of the nearby storage room as Holly came through the door. Mary Nell was still screaming, the chains clattering. Holly didn't stop or speak until she was outside next to the red Plymouth. Rose stepped out from the car's front seat, concerned. Holly's chest rose and fell as she drew in one long breath after another, trying to clear her lungs of the poison Mary Nell had spewed into the air of the conference room.

"Can you drive?" Holly asked Cutter.

"Sure."

She wheeled around the passenger side. "Rose, do you mind riding in back?"

"N-No. Of course not."

Holly transferred into the car as Cutter got behind the wheel.

"Do you want to go home?" he asked.

"No."

"Then –?"

"Anywhere, Cutter," she said, laying her head on the seat back and closing her eyes. "Just drive. Anywhere. Anywhere but here."

Chapter 13

❦

At twilight, they ate dinner at a floating restaurant on the Tennessee River near Perryville. They were all shaken and ate little. Really, it was merely an excuse to stop and take a break before returning to DeLong. To face all that Holly had to face there.

When they pulled in the driveway at Wolf's Run it was almost ten. Rose excused herself and went inside. One light after another came on until most of the east wing was lit. Holly hadn't spoken about what had been said in the sheriff's office since they left the jail parking lot. In fact, she hadn't said more than a hundred words total. On the way back, she lay on the wide bench seat and rested her head on Cutter's thigh. He drove and stroked her hair and occasionally brushed a tear from her cheek. Now she was sitting up next to the passenger door.

"My jeep is still at the paper," Cutter said after a time. "Can I catch a ride with you in the morning?"

"What makes you think I'm going in tomorrow morning?"

"Because you are."

Holly looked at him across the wide front seat. The golden summer moonlight painting and shadowing his face at the same time. "Cutter, you think I'm a lot stronger than I am."

"No," he said. "You just don't give yourself enough credit for how strong you are."

Holly shook her head, amazed by Cutter's confidence in her, unsure if it was deserved. A large part of her wanted to go inside, climb into Meemaw Carter's bed and stay there until the mess was over. Until all the crap had hit the fan and spattered wherever it was going to spatter. And another part of her wanted to pull Cutter right into that bed with her. To feel his touch, his caress and then his weight. She slid her hand across the seat and Cutter covered it with his. "Did you ever think you'd be with a black woman?"

"How do you know I haven't been already?"

"Touché."

"Holly, the whole thing is ridiculous. It's stupid."

"Yes, but it is the law. In this state and most states in the South, legally I'm as black as anyone in Roseville." When Cutter said nothing, Holly told him, "This isn't something that can be kept under wraps. I'm going to have to deal with it in the paper."

"I figured that. I don't doubt there'll be some ugly talk. But there'll be plenty of people who'll stand with you."

Holly nodded, knowing there was no need to state the obvious – that there'd be a lot more who would not.

"Would you get my chair out for me?"

Cutter walked around, lifted the chair from behind the seat and positioned the cushion. Holly gathered her strength and transferred. Cutter squatted and placed her feet on the rests. When Cutter stood, he could tell her mind was far away. "What are you thinking?"

Holly bit her lip and let it go in that way she had when she was deep in thought. "I suppose I was thinking that if this had come out in 1949 it would have utterly destroyed my father and the newspaper. The whole family."

"Then you think Mr. Carter did the right thing driving your mother away?"

"No. I don't think it was right," she said. "The part of me that is Veronique Dupre's daughter hates him for it. Hates him for not standing by his wife. The mother of his children. My mother! For letting Cecil Weathers and maybe his own racial prejudices steal her from us. But the part of me that is T.L. Carter's daughter – the part that has been sitting behind his desk this summer understands the responsibility he felt to five generations of Carters. To the paper and the people who work there. Even to the community."

Cutter looked at her, uncertain.

"Don't get me wrong," said Holly. "I'm not excusing it. I don't have that have that kind forgiveness in my heart tonight. But I know God does. And I hope Mamma and Daddy are together now, and happy. Because I know he never had a happy day on this earth after she was gone."

Holly turned, sniffling, and pushed toward the kitchen door. Cutter walked beside her. She stopped next to the ramp. He squatted beside her. "As awful as this afternoon was, Mary Nell gave me a tremendous gift," she said, her eyes glistening in the moonlight. "All these years, I've thought my mother abandoned me and Tom, and Daddy, too, because she simply woke up one day and decided she didn't love us anymore. That out there, someplace, there had been someone or something she loved more than us. Now to find out that she was made to leave? That she probably even thought she was protecting us by leaving? It changes a lot of things."

"The truth always changes how you look at things," said Cutter.

Holly reached out her hand and gently caressed the side of his face, letting her long fingers slide off the square of his chin. "Are you sure this truth doesn't change how you look at me?" she asked.

Cutter didn't answer in words. Instead, he caught her hand and drew her palm to his lips. He gently kissed her there and on her fingertips without ever taking his eyes off of hers. Then he slipped his hand behind her neck and drew her toward him. His lips touched hers and parted. When they kissed, Holly had the answer she needed.

Chapter 14

෬

I started hearing the rumors at Sunday night's choir practice about what had transpired at the jail that afternoon. And those rumors flourished on Monday and Tuesday as Mary Nell Carter was arraigned before Judge Crawford for the murder of her father-in-law, the attempted murder of her husband and children, and multiple drug-related counts. With her new attorney, a Lattimer fellow from Ashland, Miss Poindexter, as she asked to be called, entered no plea. Bail was denied and she was returned to jail to await trial.

In Wednesday's paper, however, Holly Lee Carter addressed the issue head on. She acknowledged Veronique Dupre Carter's lineage and wrote that "just as I am proud to claim the English part of my heritage, which provided this nation with its concept of law and justice; and the French in my blood line that turned the Louisiana frontier into one of the great Colonial empires of the New World; I am proud, too, to claim the blood of the strong black men and women upon whose scarred backs was built most of what we treasure today as the physical heritage of the Old South – from Chalmette Plantation to my own home, Wolf's Run."

By Wednesday night's prayer meeting, the talk about Miss Carter at First Denomination was so vicious and hateful that, I swear, I half-expected the sanctuary roof to collapse from the weight of all the ugliness. And almost wished it would. The attendance for Sunday morning services had been dwindling for weeks and the drop-off was even more pronounced at practice for the youth choir and prayer meetings. Thus those who attended now were the staunchest in their commitment to The Cause of racial separation. The notion that an "octoroon," as people of one-eighth black blood were classified, was running the newspaper infuriated them almost beyond measure.

Brother MacAllister preached a sermon that stopped only a hair short of advocating violence against Miss Carter. With a copy of

Wednesday's *Current-Leader* in his hand, he stomped and sprayed spittle and beat the newspaper against the fine mahogany pulpit until it was tattered to rags. My darling Patti hung on every word. Afterwards in the parking lot, she remained rapt in her father's righteous judgment.

"Well, we certainly see now why Miss Holly the Whore sides with the nee-grahs," she was saying. "She's one of them! I don't believe for a minute that she just found out. This was all part of their scheme. The race-mixers. And now they're trying to blame poor Miss Mary Nell. Lies, lies, lies!"

I stared at her, holding her gaze as long as I could, hoping to see something else there – some greater comprehension? *something?* – but there was nothing else. I pecked her on the cheek and headed for my truck as Brother Daddy watched from the church door.

"Don't be late pickin' me up tomorrow night," she said to my back. "The captain of the cheer squad has to set an example."

* * *

It had turned unseasonably cool during the week, and in the mornings a column of fog rose from the river and settled into the low spots of the land in white drifts, like snow. On Thursday night, pep rallies were held around bonfires at CHS and Riverview. The Wolves' home opener was scheduled for Friday and the Raiders were set to play on the road at Greenwood. When the team was introduced, I stepped forward as one of the starting wide receivers. Me!

Across the river, Coach Hinton and Jimmy Garner made brief speeches while Cutter stayed out of the limelight as much as he could. The Wolves were going to lose and badly to a very good Baldwin team on Friday, and Cutter knew it, but it didn't matter as much as seeing Rose clapping and cheering, wearing the spirit T-shirt she'd made with Holly's help. Just as the fire radiated light and heat, Rose's face radiated a joy and a hope for the future that made the blood run warmer through his heart. She hooked arms with some other girls – black and white, and they kicked up their legs and sang some silly song, and they laughed.

Holly parked at the edge of the road next to the field where the bonfire blazed. She rested her elbows on the door and clicked away with her camera. Now and then she and Cutter caught each other's eye and shared a private smile.

As Cutter stood there in his black-and-red letter jacket, washed in the warm, moving light of the bonfire, he wished his mother could see her children now. Away from Tony, and happy for the first time in years. Yet, the ugly force of Tony's style of hate pressed in around them, held at bay by deputies cradling shotguns at the edge of the light – the flames glowing on black, oiled steel of the gun barrels. Out beyond them in the dark were FBI agents and U.S. Marshals scattered in the hills that rose to the south of the high school, on the lookout for Klansmen with deer rifles. Cutter wasn't unaware of the dangers, but didn't let himself dwell on them. Instead, he allowed himself to enjoy the moment with his sister – and with Holly, too – wondering if this was what normal felt like.

* * *

The twisty-turny road to where Cutter was now making his camp up the slope from Wolf's Run was barely that – a road. It was more like an overgrown wagon path. There was no way my truck could have negotiated the steep parts, so I was glad that I had left it around the curve and out of the way. Even on foot it was a difficult walk, especially in the dark, and I felt like I was carrying sixty pounds of sharp glass in my chest. My shoulders sagged and my feet barely found enough lift to take the next step. When my shin hit a tripwire I heard the rattle of rocks inside tin cans. The sudden *clack-clack* of Cutter chambering a round into his .12 gauge froze me in the moonlight.

"It's me!"

"Nate?"

"Yeah, yeah. Take it easy."

"Are you alone?"

"Yes."

"All right. Come on up." I climbed the last 30 feet onto the plateau. Through a natural gap in the trees, the precipice offered an unobstructed view of Miss Carter's property – the newly painted fence and the new electric gate. Farther down the slope, the outline of Wolf's Run was visible behind a screen of pecan, walnuts, pines and oaks.

"That's a good way to get yourself killed," said Cutter.

"It used to be a fella could drop by your camp for a beer or conversation without worrying about getting his head blown off."

Cutter said nothing, just clicked the shotgun's safety on and reached into an ice chest sitting next to the jeep, which held a precarious perch. "Coke's the best I got. You want one?"

"Sure."

Cutter handed me a can, walked over and sat on his sleeping bag. The clearing was small, much smaller than the area around The Well. He propped the shotgun on a large rock and leaned back next to it. I sat down across from the coals of a small fire. It wasn't chilly enough to see my breath, but it would be before morning. Fall was rushing into the Cattahatchie Valley.

"What time is it?" he asked.

I tilted my wrist in the light of the half moon until it glinted off my watch. "1:52."

"I've got a football game to play tomorrow night, and so do you. What are you doing here? In fact, how'd you know where to find me?"

"I called Miss Carter from the pay phone outside Gibson's Grocery."

"When?"

"About thirty minutes ago."

"At one-thirty in the morning?"

"Yeah. I told her I had to see you."

"What? Did Miz Fletcher throw you out?"

I had wondered how I was going to tell it, but I opened my mouth and it just came out. "Patti was in on what happened to Miss Howard and Ridge Bellafont."

Cutter stared at me through the moonlight. I'm sure I must have looked ghostly in the sheer white glow from the heavens. I felt like all the blood had been drained out of me. I went on before I lost my nerve. "We had a pep rally tonight. The band was there and the cheerleaders. I took Patti. She never looked prettier or sweeter. Like an angel," I told him, and looked away for a moment, seeing her in that moment before I knew. "Afterwards we went parking out in Clark Creek bottom. But she and Janette Wellingham had smoked a bunch of pot, and instead of calming her down, she was all worked up about what Miss Carter wrote in Wednesday's paper. She said, 'At least my conscience is clear. I'm a good girl. I did my part to stamp 'em out. Nobody can say I didn't.'

"I asked her what she meant. She reminded me about our fight at the Klan rally and how she'd walked off. It turns out she spied Eve Howard beside Mr. Bellafont's car. Patti turned her in. She told the Klargo."

Cutter didn't seem surprised and I suppose he wasn't. He always had understood what Patti was capable of in a way that I had not, or at least would not allow myself to believe until that night. Cutter understood elemental evil, because he had lived with it.

When he said nothing, I went on – "She told it like she'd tell about how she did on a, a, history test or, or what she had for lunch. Like it was nothing. I tried to make her see what she'd done. What I saw under that car the next morning. About how Miss Howard's skin was so cooked it came off in, in –" I stared at my hand but I couldn't say the word. "Patti just looked at me like I wasn't – I don't know – getting it?

"Then she said, 'Nate, it was just a nigger.'"

In the woods and not far away a bobcat squalled. A shiver crawled up my spine like a six-inch centipede and I drew my knees to the gold 81 on my jersey and wrapped my arms around them. I felt my chest heave with a deep sob. When I'd forced my own emotion back into my chest, I said, "Right that minute, I took her home, opened the door and told her to get out. She sashayed up the driveway and said, 'You'll be back.'"

The quiet of the night settled around us for a time. Then, "Will you? Go back?" Cutter asked.

I thought about it for a bit. "I hope not," was the best I could do. "Can I keep camp with you for – I don't know, a few nights until I can kinda, kinda …?" I didn't have the words to finish the thought or the strength to consider my future, but I did know something about my past. "Cutter, I'm sorry about all that's happened between us the last few weeks. If you don't want me around, I understand. I've been a sorry excuse for a friend."

He used a stick to stir at the fire coals and threw on another log. "You're gonna be a might chilly before mornin' without a sleepin' bag."

"I got one. I left it down the hill a piece."

"Then go fetch it and settle in," he said, sliding down into his bag. "I don't want to be up all night."

Chapter 15

∾

Next morning a small, wind-up alarm clock began to rattle at 5:50 a.m. I had slept on the rocks near Cutter's jeep and felt as if they'd worked their way inside my skin. It was still dark, only the slightest hint of pink in the eastern sky. But Cutter rousted me up and within ten minutes had his camp area clear, the fire embers doused and was ready to roll. That was his way of things.

"Let's get some breakfast," he said, his breath coming out white in the brisk air, and I climbed into the Jeep's passenger seat. When he cranked the vehicle and downed the clutch I nearly dove out. The Jeep looked as if it would go right over the edge of the outcrop. After that, there would be almost nothing but a steep slope between the front bumper and the front porch of Wolf's Run. But he backed up, maneuvered and headed us down the narrow lane.

The lights already were on in the kitchen at Wolf's Run and what I guessed were a couple of bedrooms. Cutter tapped on the door and walked in without waiting. Rose was frying bacon and scrambling eggs at the stove.

"G-Good morning," she said as Cutter passed by. I hung back in the shadows of an alcove that was lined with shelves and glass jars filled with fruit preserves and locally canned vegetables. "Are you r-ready to w-win tonight?"

"Oh, yeah. I'm ready. What about the coffee?"

"A little gr-grumpy this morning?"

"I sleep on rocks. I'm grumpy every morning."

"N-N-No you're not."

Cutter grunted noncommittally over the sound of a radio from up the hall. The Memphis news was on. He walked over to a corner of the counter near the hall and started pouring a cup. "Do we have enough fixin's for one more plate?"

"One more? For who?"

"Nate, come on in here."

Rose looked at me as I hung back in the shadows. She smiled. "H-Hi, N-Nate. Come on in. W-W-We have plenty."

"Thanks," I whispered, touched that Rose seemed genuinely glad to see me.

It was just then that Holly Lee Carter wheeled in from the hall. Her long hair was up and wrapped in a towel. She was wearing a white terry cloth bathrobe. She hooked the long fingers of her left hand into one of Cutter's hip pockets and left them there.

"Hey, you. How about pouring me a cup?"

It wasn't what Holly Carter said, but the husky, sleepy tone she used and the easy familiarity with which she approached Cutter and touched him, that told me all I needed to know. I just didn't know how to feel about it.

"We have company," he said, and Holly withdrew her hand from his pocket.

I cleared my throat and stepped into the light of the kitchen. "Miss Carter."

"Nate, well – hi!"

"I'm sorry I woke you last night."

"That's all right. I'm happy to see you found Cutter," she said. "Won't you sit down and join us for breakfast?"

"Yes, ma'am. Thank you."

* * *

After we ate, Cutter took a quick shower. I was in the courtyard by the pool when he came out. The light in the valley floor was moving from gold to white as the sun fully cleared a thin ribbon of silver-tipped clouds that feathered above the eastern hills. At the bottom of the steep bluff that fell away from Wolf's Run, the Cattahatchie was flowing south, its brown skin veiled in mist. In the distance traffic hummed its busy Friday song on Highway 27. Pickups, cars, tractor-trailer rigs and school buses moved along the faded blacktop as if on gray rails.

Cutter approached. "Great view, huh?"

"Yeah. Gorgeous," I said. "It looks like you've found your paradise. In more ways than one."

Cutter allowed himself to admire the valley for a time. Or maybe he was thinking of Holly Lee Carter and the home Rose and he apparently had found with her, in different ways. I studied him and wished I had the kind of clarity that he and Miss Carter seemed to possess. I didn't but, by God, I intended to try to get it.

Cutter said, "We're all gonna have to hustle to get to school before first bell. Let's go."

"I'm not goin'."

"You've got a game tonight. You're gonna start."

"To hell with the game. I'm not goin' back to Riverview."

Cutter sat down on the knee-high stone wall that guarded the patio's edge.

"Nate, you've been through a lot in the last few hours. Heck, the last few weeks. Don't make any snap judgments you'll regret."

"This isn't a snap judgment. It's been building up, one of Patti's lies on top of one of her meannesses for a long time," I told him. "Now this with Miss Howard and Mr. Bellafont?"

"Nate, Patti couldn't have known what they were going do. She did wrong but –"

"But what? She helped the Klan kill someone, like you'd slaughter a hog. And they meant to kill Miss Howard. Crushed to death or burned alive. They didn't care which. And Patti *still* don't care. I'm sick to death of it!"

Cutter stood and put his hand on my shoulder, squeezed it.

"Do you think Miss Carter would mind if I just sat here for a while and drank another cup of coffee?"

"No. I can guarantee she won't. She likes you, Nate. She likes you a lot."

"But she loves you."

Cutter looked at me for a long moment, but he didn't contradict me. Attempt to deny or dismiss what I'd seen or the depth of what was going on between them. He was, as ever, at ease with who he was and choices he'd made, and committed to the course he'd set. That was as clear to me as it had ever been. He pushed his aviator shades onto his nose. "I've got to go."

"I'll walk back to my truck in a little while."

"If you aren't goin' to the Riverview game, come see the Wolves play. But I warn you, it may not be pretty. We're still mighty ragged."

"Maybe I'll do that," I told him. And that's how we left it that Friday morning.

* * *

As it turned out, I never left Wolf's Run that day. I didn't want to be anyplace where Patti might track me down, or Coach Pearce or anyone else from Riverview might find me. I hadn't slept more than a couple of hours the previous night, so the jolt of morning coffee quickly wore off. About ten o'clock I fetched my sleeping bag from the truck, and spread it in a warm, sunny spot on the interior porch of the big house. A spot where I could see the Cattahatchie Valley, but no one in the valley could see me.

I fell asleep and didn't open my eyes again until late that afternoon when Rose knelt beside me, shaking me gently and asking if I was hungry. I was. Starving, in fact. I got up and ate cold pork chops and hot macaroni and cheese like I'd been asleep for a week.

Miss Carter and Rose invited me to ride to the CHS game with them, "if you're going?"

Honestly, I didn't know if I was. So, I thanked them but fired up my truck and went my own way. For an hour or more I simply drove around. I slowed at the boarding house and at our farm on Pleasant Ridge Road, but didn't stop. The sweet yellow light of late afternoon was spreading across every road and field. The cotton and beans and corn were standing high now in neat rows. Soon it would be harvest time. The sides of nearly every bottomland road in the county would be so white with cotton fiber blown from full-to-the-brim wagons that it would look like snowfall. The county's eight gins would start running twenty-four hours a day, their gears and lint cleaners resting only on the Sabbath – like the farmers and field hands and bale press operators who tore their livelihood from the land and the cotton bolls it fed.

The Riverview buses, carrying the team, cheerleaders and band, had left on the one-hundred-and-fifty mile trip to Greenwood hours earlier. But I had to fight the urge to turn my truck south and race toward Leflore County, to somehow beg forgiveness from Coach Pearce and my Raider teammates, and most of all Patti.

Finally, I turned my wheels onto the pavement of Highway 27 and pointed my old truck toward CHS stadium. It was only fifteen minutes until game time, and I drove north expecting to hit traffic as soon as I passed the fairgrounds. Often late-arriving fans had to park on the shoulder of the highway and walk nearly three-quarters of a mile to get to the grandstands. But not on this night. Not for this team. A sheriff's deputy stood beside his car, his red strobe vibrating in the dusk, but he had little traffic to direct. I turned up the drive toward the school, circled around the side and parked close enough that I could have stepped out and hit the back of the press box with a baseball.

At the main gate a black deputy – one of my father's new hires – stood next to a black man, whom I did not recognize, and collected my two dollars. I ambled inside. During the "Cutter Era," in which the Wolves had gone 33-6, spectators often ringed CHS field and gate receipts showed crowds in excess of five thousand – more than twice the population of DeLong. On the opening night of the Wolves' 1969 home season, there were perhaps two hundred people occupying the plank bleachers that usually overflowed with fifteen hundred or more. In fact, Baldwin fans on the opposite side of the field outnumbered those in the home stands at least three to one.

I spotted Miss Carter's Plymouth parked just outside the west end zone near the locker room. When the Wolves jogged back to the locker room for final instructions and a prayer, I walked down.

"H-Hi, N-Nate. I'm gl-glad you c-came," Rose told me. She looked pretty in new jeans and a black pull-over sweater.

Moments later we heard the shout from the locker room. The door opened and the reincarnated Cattahatchie High School Wolves charged out for their first-ever home game. They all wore green-and-gold patches on their black jerseys, honoring Roseville High's traditional colors. That had been Jimmy Garner's idea. Cutter smiled at me and Rose as he went by, running toward the sideline where Miss Carter had positioned herself with her camera and notebook.

"Nate!" Jimmy Garner called as he went by. "You better have your skinny ass out here for practice Monday."

"Or I'm gonna kick it clean to Tennessee," added Dodge McDowell.

I smiled and gave them a little wave, but at that moment I didn't know where I'd be on Monday.

* * *

Cutter had let his boss at The Gin know that he wouldn't be back for awhile, not wanting to be far from Holly and Rose come nightfall. But he had lined up a day of construction work with some guy he knew in Holly Springs, and had to be on the road by six a.m. Saturday to be there for the seven o'clock start of the work day. He said I could stay or go, and I went mostly because I didn't trust myself to remain in DeLong without running back to Patti. As it turned out, they had plenty of work for me, too, and by sunset we'd both earned a decent wage. But even as we worked and listened to the Ole Miss game on the radio, I could not help but marvel at Cutter. He'd taken a tremendous pounding the previous night, with the Bearcats keying on him on every down. Despite that, he'd recorded fourteen individual tackles, gained 280 yards and scored three touchdowns in the 52-26 loss. Then, with about six hours of shut-eye, rolled out of his sleeping bag into a cold camp and put in a ten-hour day toting cinderblocks and roof shingles on a construction site.

But even Cutter was mortal. As we were walking off the site, one of the masons clapped him on the shoulder and I saw him fight not to miss a step or let the flash of pain turn into something more than a grimace on his face.

"Next year," the man said, "we're gonna be listening to you on that radio playin' for the Rebs."

"That'd be nice," Cutter managed, his right arm hanging at his side.

"Nice? It'll be great! With you and Archie in the backfield, Bear Bryant and the Crimson Tide are all washed up," said the man, laughing at his own word play. Clearly, the man did not know how shaky the dream was for Cutter. Cecil Weathers was not a man for idle threats.

"Yep, that'd be nice," Cutter said again as the man walked off. "Nate, you mind drivin'?"

Back at Wolf's Run, I took a quick shower but Cutter stayed in a hot bath in Miss Carter's bedroom for almost an hour while she and Rose fixed a spaghetti dinner. When he came out and sat down at the kitchen table I could see that he could move his arm again. The pasta and meat sauce steamed on the candlelit table in front of us and the sharp scent of garlic filled the air.

"Are you all right?" asked Holly.

"We got the snot beat out of us last night," he said gruffly and took a pull from the longneck beer next to his plate.

"I meant your arm. Nate, would you please start passing the pasta?" she asked. "I know losing a game is frustrating to you, but there are other ways to look at it."

"No, Holly, there's only one way. Fifty-two, twenty-six? Geez!" he grumbled, always one to take any loss hard and personal. "Anyone who thought this story was going to have a Cinderella ending was mighty mistaken."

"It's amazing that Cinderella is even showing up for the ball," she told him. "That's a moral victory in itself."

"I don't believe in moral victories," he told her.

"S-S-Sure you do," said Rose. "Or you, you'd have been playing for R-Riverview last night."

The three of us stared at her, then Cutter laughed, his face holding a broad smile.

Holly smiled and extended her hands. "Nate, would you please say the blessing?"

And I did.

Chapter 16

༸

The Sunday morning of Cutter's nineteenth birthday rose clear and beautiful and crisp, but not as unusually cold as the previous couple of sunrises. Still, with the first breath of autumn lingering, the coffee at Wolf's Run was a hot blessing, and a shower nearly as hot as the coffee knocked the chill off.

Cutter had agreed to go with Holly to prayer services at the *Current-Leader*, sort of a reverse birthday present. His gift to her. Rose said I might as well go, too, and I agreed.

When Cutter emerged into the kitchen in his only white button-down, jeans and oxblood loafers, Holly handed him a large box as she reached up and gave him a hug.

"Happy birthday," she said and kissed him warmly on the cheek.

He smiled. "I thought we were celebrating my birthday tonight."

"We are," she said. "But I thought I'd give you this early. For church."

"Is this my surprise?"

"No. I'm saving that for tonight."

Cutter opened the box and in it was a classic, single-breasted navy blue jacket. Holly and Rose had driven to Tupelo on Saturday and picked it out at Reed Brothers. He slipped it on and it fit him perfectly, as did the look. I'd never seen him so pleased by anything, or look more happy or at ease as he drove Holly Lee Carter's Plymouth toward town.

We passed the Burger Den, Kamp Motors and the hospital. Holly smiled nervously at Cutter. As usual, she was to lead the singing but was ready to turn it over to someone else if need be. This would be her first real public appearance in DeLong since the article acknowledging her racial heritage. She had grown up in a world of country club privilege, in which everyone, without question, thought of her as white. One of *them*. And, of course, Holly had thought of herself the same way, and still did. But according to the laws of Mississippi, she was a Negro. In DeLong, such distinctions always had been as crucial as the air one breathed and as unchanging as the Ten Commandments.

When we started up the hill toward the courthouse, Holly's chin quivered and her chest tightened. Cutter reached over and took Holly's hand in his. To our surprise, the perimeter of the square was nearly ringed with cars.

"What in the world?" I asked.

We turned down Commerce Street and left on River. Cars lined the route and stretched out on down the street past The Cotton Café. Vans from the Tupelo TV station and a couple from Memphis were parked along River Street. Mary Nell's case and Holly's acknowledgement had made the regional news earlier this week and even got a mention from Walter Cronkite. The only place where there were no cars was in the newspaper parking lot. It was filled with people, standing. When Cutter turned in, they parted. Men with notebooks and cameras scribbled and took pictures.

As we passed, people tapped on the car and leaned in from nearly every angle. They were saying things like, "God bless you. ... We're with you, Holly. ... Hang in there, girl!. ... God loves you and we love you."

By the time we eased up next to the ramp, riverlets of tears were flowing down Holly's cheeks. She looked at Cutter. "Did you know about this?"

"The doctors got together with Sheriff Wallace and decided we needed to show the TV folks that not everyone in DeLong is behind the Klan," he said of doctors Dale, Garner and Ragland. "They've been working the phones all week. Doctor Garner told me in the lockerrom Friday night that they were expecting a big turnout today, and that I shouldn't miss it. Or let you miss it."

A couple of minutes later, Holly was pushing up the ramp to the loading dock that served as a dais. The applause began and did not stop for a long time as she looked out on the several hundred gathered in the parking lot, including some surprise faces, such as that of Senator Haughton Wellingham III and County Prosecutor Jimmy Epps. To be sure, it was a ninety percent white crowd but there was a smattering of black faces as well, something that would have been unthinkable only a few weeks earlier. Ron Clemmer led a delegation of support from Pickens' Ferry A.M.E.. Mrs. Harriett Houston, the former principal of Roseville High and the principal at CHS was there, too, as was Miss Winona St. Julian and a dozen members of her family.

Holly wheeled next to the microphone and tried to quiet the crowd, but they – that is to say, we – went on as she opened her guitar case and rested the instrument on her leg. "Does someone have a tissue or a handkerchief, please?" she said, leaning away from the mike.

Mrs. Frances Ragland handed her a lace hanky. Holly wiped her eyes. Then into the mike said, "Thank you. Thank you all so much. You all have no idea how much this means to me. But ..." she cleared her throat. "But I sure hope you didn't come this morning just to clap for me.

"I don't know if you'd call what we have here a church, but on Sunday mornings it definitely has become a place of worship. So, let's start worshipping the Lord this morning with one of my favorite hymns," she said, finding the proper chord on her guitar. "We don't have hymnals, but I think you'll all know this one.

"*He's Got The Whole World in His Hands*. Okay? ... One ... Two ... Three..."

* * *

At six o'clock that night, Cutter began answering the front door at Wolf's Run as invited guests stopped by to wish him a happy birthday and to enjoy a double chocolate cake that had been delivered from the best bakery in Tupelo.

Some of the attendees Cutter expected – Coach Hinton, Dodge McDowell, Jimmy Garner, Haughton Wellingham IV and other CHS teammates and Wolves cheerleaders, including some who had come over from Roseville; along with doctors Garner, Ragland and Dale and their wives; "Shorty" Rodgers from the paper; Gil Clanton, the owner of The Gin; and my father. The surprise guests were U.S. Attorney J.L. Burke and U.S. District Judge Oren Mulberry. Spreading out on the property were half dozen deputy U.S. Marshals. Their protection detail.

By 6:20, the only person not in the courtyard was Miss Carter.

"Where's Holly?" he asked me.

"Inside, still gettin' ready. Rose is helping her."

Five minutes later, Holly came down the ramp to the courtyard without her wheelchair. She moved slowly, swinging both legs stiffly between a set of metal crutches clamped tight on her forearms. The boot-like shoes that showed beneath the hem of her long skirt were heavy and black and connected to steel bars that fit just in front of the thick heels. And yet, for all of it, Holly Lee Carter carried herself with such dignity that no one noticed the awkwardness. Especially Cutter.

By the time *Happy Birthday* was sung, nineteen candles were blown out and presents were opened, the Cattahatchie Valley was growing purple with shadow and the air was fresh and alive with the foretaste of autumn. Finally, Cutter and Holly had a chance to step off to the side. He looked her over from toe to head and back. She was almost as tall as him.

"Is this my surprise?" he asked.

"It's one of them," she said, leaning on her crutches. "Do you like?"

"Very much. You're tall. Really tall."

"Yes. I hope it doesn't bother you. Doesn't intimidate you. It does some men."

He smiled, chuckled. "Not a bit. I think you're what I've been looking for – a woman who can stand up and look me in the eye. Besides, it'll make it all the easier to kiss you."

They shared a smile that would have melted brass but kept a distance between themselves. Everyone by now knew that they were a couple, for lack of a better word, but because of Holly's position and the age difference, they'd agreed not to flaunt it. When Holly noticed my father and the U.S. attorney approaching, she asked Cutter, "Have you talked to Judge Mulberry yet? Or Mr. Burke?"

"Yes. A little. But I still don't understand why they're here."

"I invited them. They're powerful players in this state and I thought they'd be good for you to meet," she explained. "Cecil Weathers isn't the only person in this town with friends in high places."

"Thanks. But I can't believe two men that important don't have better things to do than come to my birthday party."

"Cutter, they were eager to come. To thank you," she said looking straight into his eyes. "I don't think you have any idea how important it was – what you did at the fairgrounds. And sticking with the CHS team. But they know."

Just as my father extended his hand and said, "Happy Birthday, Cutter," I found myself next to them, handing Holly a cup of punch. I had done my best to stay away from Daddy, making wide circles around the patio when necessary. I didn't know what he knew about me and Patti and Riverview, or what to say to him about it.

"Son," he nodded.

"Daddy."

"Nate, can you excuse us a minute?" he asked. "We need to talk to Cutter and Miss Carter about something in private."

"Is this about Tony?" asked Cutter.

"And McBride," said Burke.

"Then Nate can hear it," said Cutter, and I felt both proud and embarrassed. Proud that Cutter would vouch for me and ashamed that he had to – with my own father. But there it was, and considering the people I'd held fast to over the late summer, it was no wonder.

"Aw'right, then," said Billy Wallace. He saw Rose and motioned her over, too.

"We think we have some news. Some very good news," began Burke. "Working with the FBI and the Royal Canadian Mounted Police, we think we've located McBride and your father on a remote lake in southern British Columbia.

"A float-plane operator tipped the Canadian authorities that he flew two men fitting their descriptions into a hunting cabin four days ago."

"The place is only accessible by float-plane or horseback," said my father.

"The FBI and the Mounties have a team working their way in now," Burke told them. "We should know something by noon tomorrow."

"How sure are they?" asked Holly.

"Sure enough that the team is going in with automatic weapons and all the firepower they need to handle whoever they find," Burke told us.

Everyone looked at each other and then at Cutter, not knowing quite how to react. But Cutter knew. "Good," he said. "If you catch 'em that would be a great birthday present. If you kill 'em, that'd be even better."

Burke and my daddy shared a look but had no words for a son so distanced father.

* * *

By nine-thirty the cars and people were gone and Rose and I were finishing the dish washing in the kitchen. From the window above the sink, we could see Cutter and Holly stretched out together on the big chaise lounge. He was thumbing through his other birthday gift from Holly, a leather-bound edition of Harper Lee's *To Kill a Mockingbird*.

"It seemed appropriate for you," she was saying.

"So, who am I? Jim? Or Atticus? Or maybe Boo Radley?"

"Don't forget Scout. She was a tomboy and a fighter," said Holly. "You're as good and brave as any of them, all of them. And you're real."

Cutter closed the book and laid it on the table next to them. He rolled onto his side, propped his head in his hand and looked at her. "I liked seeing you tonight, standing."

"These braces are a pain. But it was worth it to be able to stand beside you."

Cutter lay back on the chaise. "When I turned eighteen, this sure isn't what I expected nineteen to look like."

Holly smiled. "Considering how sweet you were to me that first day I came back, I'm a little surprised, too."

"I was a jerk," he said without hesitation. "But seeing Tony use his one-leggedness to excuse every kind of ugly, sick –" Cutter struggled to find a word that captrured it – "demented thing he did. Every hurt he inflicted on Momma and Rose."

"And you," said Holly.

"Yeah, but it was different with me," he said, looking up at the stars in the clear black sky. "The night I actually caught him on top of Rose, I should have killed him."

With the heavy braces girdling Holly's hips and legs, she couldn't roll onto her side, but she wrapped her arm around Cutter's. "No one, including Rose, blames you for the things Tony has done. No one but you. And you need to let that go."

Cutter said nothing to that but gripped her hand in his, gently, firmly. He thought of Rose and twisted his head toward the kitchen. He saw the way Rose and I were smiling at each other, standing closer than we had to be to wash dishes.

Holly looked across him. "They make a cute couple."

Cutter growled. "Nate had it out with Patti MacAllister the other night. He's all depressed and needy about it. I don't want him using Rose on the bounce. She's never had a boyfriend. Never even been on a date."

Holly rested back. "I'll talk to her. Gently. You talk to him. But your first crush can be a powerful thing."

"It *sure* can!" he agreed a little too enthusiastically.

"What does that mean?"

Cutter gave her a look, up and down, then settled his smiling eyes on hers. "Don't forget where I grew up. When I was seven or eight or nine – before you left DeLong, my mother still owned the land all the way to the river. It was our land. And I hunted and fished every inch of it, and across the river, too." Holly guessed where this was going and felt her cheeks starting to warm. "I played everything from pirates to Davey Crockett along that stretch. I built forts and I knew every hidy hole within a half-mile of The Well."

Now the blush was spreading into Holly's neck as she remembered the many times she'd descend into the frosty water in pursuit of a cold beer or simply to cool off from the swelter of another Mississippi summer day. Sometimes she'd brought a bathing suit. Sometimes she'd gone in wearing her bra and panties. Sometimes only her panties. Sometimes she'd worn nothing at all. And sometimes, she wasn't alone.

"Ohhh, Cutter, I – I mean, if I'd known anyone was watching –"

He laughed. "If you'd known, you probably wouldn't have done a darn thing different. I don't think less of you for it," he told her, smiling. "After I left the house and started makin' camp at The Well, I've crawled into my sleepin' bag many a cold night thinking of you. With no idea I'd see you again, except in my memories."

Now the blush was pink on Holly's cheek and neck and the tops of her breasts. "Cutter, I –"

"You knew who you were and what you wanted, and that impressed me as much as – well, anything else."

She stopped him. "You're wrong. I knew what my body wanted, and I knew how to get it. But I had no idea who I was. I didn't find that out until Vietnam. Until I really let Christ into my life. And I'm still working on it. Especially after Mary Nell's little bombshell," said Holly, looking into Cutter's eyes now with more concern than embarrassment. "I truly am a different person now. Raised up a new creation, to walk in the light. If you're thinking I'm the girl you saw by The Well ten years ago –"

"Stop," he said, rolling back onto his side. "That's not what I'm saying at all. I wouldn't trade the woman I know today for the girl I saw back then for anything."

"Then –?"

"I just want you know that you were my first crush," he said, leaning in and gently brushing Holly's lips with his. "And I intend to make you my last love."

"Ohhh, Cutter …" she sighed as she opened her lips to his and wrapped her arms around him. *He's still so young!* she thought even as she felt in her lips the hot, powerful pulse in his neck. Far too young to make that kind of commitment, that kind of a promise. And far too young for her to believe it. But she wanted to believe it, and silently prayed that it was true.

* * *

Less than an hour later, Cutter had a low fire going on the small outcrop of rocks above Wolf's Run. In the courtyard hidden in the U-embrace of the house, Rose spread a blanket over Holly.

"It's g-getting ch-chilly. I thought you m-might need this."

"Thank you."

"You're not c-coming to bed?"

"Not yet. It's such a beautiful night," she said, looking up at the amazing glitter of stars in the black satin sky. "It's like I don't want to let it go."

"I-I know. It's been a w-wonderful day. W-Will you need help with your br-braces?"

"No. They're a lot easier to get out of than into, and I've had lots of practice," she said. "Go on to bed, if you want. I'll be in soon."

Up at our camp, I slipped down into my sleeping bag as Cutter propped against a boulder, thumbing through the novel Holly had given him. He had the radio on, the volume low, and he looked as content as I had ever seen him, though I noted that he still had his .12 gauge propped close at hand.

I was exhausted. Not just by the day, or Saturday's long hours of hard construction labor, but by everything that had happened that summer. "Good night, Cutter. I'm glad I was with you and Miss Carter today. And Rose."

"Me, too," said my best friend as an old Nat King Cole tune whispered from the radio – *Unforgettable*. Before it ended, I was asleep.

Chapter 17

∾

When Rose awoke in the quiet of her room, she blessed the darkness. For years she had slept with a light on by her bed at the Old Ambrose Place signaling Cutter, warding off her father, and the demons he left in the corners of her room and her heart. The light, though, caused years of shallow sleep devoid of rest. Now she could safely disappear into her pillows and the deep tunnels of sleep and luxurious corners of cool darkness that the big rooms and high ceilings of Wolf's Run provided.

Rose drowsily rolled onto her side, her mind both fighting to ignore and explore the sound of boards creaking in the hallway.

Is Holly just now coming to bed? She wondered. *What time is it?* She asked herself, but she twisted onto her stomach and snuggled into the down. The clock beside her bed said 1:17.

Rose listened, expecting to hear wind moving in the trees, causing limbs to tap-tap on the tin roof. Or maybe rain. But there was none of that. And yet the house seemed to be moving, something applying pressure to planks, creating a whisper of movement in the air. Something? *Or someone?* Panic lodged in her chest like a knife. *It couldn't be Daddy!* She told herself, willing it to be so. *He was in Canada ... With McBride ... The FBI was ...But what if –?*

Her eyes flew open, wild at the thought, but it was too late. The scent of dried sweat and stale clothes, motor oil, testosterone and dirty hair filled her nostrils. They flared and her mouth opened to form a scream, but before she could empty the sound from her lungs, a calloused hand shoved her face down into the pillow. She flailed, but his weight was on top her. She felt the wire stubble of his beard against her shoulder and the side of her neck. His fingers were claws that threatened to crush her skull.

"Stop wigglin'," Rose heard her father growl, but she fought through the pain and paid him no heed. "Stop!" he told her again.

She couldn't breathe but she kept swinging her arms, kicking her legs. "Stop! Be quiet and go with me, and the Carter woman lives. Otherwise, I'll leave you both here – *dead!* "

Rose's lungs felt as if someone had dumped hot coals down her throat, and her head would implode in the crush of her father's hand. When it did, she'd be gone and then Tony would kill Holly. Rose let her limbs go limp.

"That's Daddy's girl," Tony Carlucci said into Rose's ear, then stuck his thick, rancid tongue inside. His daughter's body convulsed and bile churned hot in her throat before falling back into her stomach liked poisoned water. "You didn't think I was gonna leave you behind, did you?

"Noooo. We're goin' out west. To the high country. To the deep woods. You need a daddy, and I need a wife," he told her. "This is all gonna work out just fine."

A chilly breeze on my face and neck brought me awake. I slipped my hand from my sleeping bag and used a stick to poke at the coals where our little fire had collapsed to embers, and barely even those. That's when I heard them. Men. Grown men. Trying to talk in whispers. But tension and adrenaline caused their voices to become brittle and crack like ice on a winter lake. I eased up onto my elbows, my ears straining to hear.

Silence.

Was I mistaken? Or maybe dreaming?

Then I heard the door of a vehicle open and softly close, and the rattle of a tailgate being gently lowered. I bolted up, scuttling on my hands and knees toward the edge of the rock. I got there just in time to see two men going over the white plank fence in front of Wolf's Run.

My heart was pounding so hard against my ribs that I was certain that the two men standing behind the truck could not keep from hearing them rattle, but neither looked up the steep hill to the promontory. They continued to look one way on the road then the other, floppy fishing hats hiding their faces. One cradled a deer rifle, but I couldn't place either one. Whoever these men were, I knew as sure as my soul they were there to do no telling what to Rose and Miss Carter, and then kill them.

I pushed away from the edge and crawled to where Cutter lay, pouncing on his sleeping bag with my hand covering his mouth. His body bucked and nearly threw me off, but I held fast until his eyes focused on my face.

"They're here!" I whispered. "Four, I think."

He blinked once, twice, then I saw the comprehension in his eyes as surely as moonlight.

Tony Carlucci took a greasy rag from a pocket of his dark green coveralls, whipped it into a tight cord and strung it between his daughter's teeth. Rose groaned and tears popped from her eyes as he knotted the cloth behind her head, stretching it, almost tearing the corners of her mouth. Then he pulled a nylon rope from his other pocket, snatched Rose's arms behind her and tied her wrists tight. When he pulled her from the bed, her bare legs were shaking. She recognized McBride as the man from the posters she'd seen around town. The way he and her father looked her over in her light blue panties and the snug black T-shirt made her want to vomit.

Tony dragged his daughter through the bedroom door.

"All right, Mr. Carlucci. You've got what you want," said McBride. "Let's take care of the Carter woman, blow the place and get out of here."

"You're darn right I'll take care of her," said Tony. "I intend to send her to her grave with my face in her eyes and my –"

The words sizzled in Rose's ears. She began to jerk and writhe, and tried to kick. But Tony slapped her so hard across the face that it sounded like a whip crack. Rose's knees buckled and blood dripped from her nose as Tony shoved her into McBride's arms.

"If the Carter woman didn't hear that, she's paralyzed *and* deaf," said McBride. "Get to it."

Rose struggled. She had to do something to warn Holly. But McBride jerked the rope around her wrists, and she thought her arms would separate from her shoulders. She could do nothing but watch as Tony held his prized Luger next to his cheek and cracked open the bedroom door. With the other hand he searched the bedroom wall for a light switch. He found it and flipped it on.

The room was empty. "Damn it!" Tony growled, charging inside.

Holly's wheelchair sat beside a bed that was still made. He searched the bathroom. The closet. Looked under the bed. There was a .38 on the bed table but there was no sign of the woman. Tony cursed as he returned to the hall, to Rose. "Where is she?" he demanded, grabbing her hair.

Rose thought of the chaise lounge. She was too frightened to let her eyes laugh at Tony as she wanted to do – laugh for joy that Holly was not in her bed. Instead, Rose stared up into her father's bulging, bloodshot eyes, shaking her head, refusing to give anything away. "Show me!"

"Maybe she's with your boy, wherever he's makin' camp these days," said McBride. "Or shacked-up with him in a motel."

"But her car's here."

"She could have rode with him," McBride persisted. "She could be anywhere."

"No! She wouldn't have left her wheelchair," insisted Tony. "I'm telling you, she's here!"

"All right. She's here. When this place goes up, so does she."

Rose sucked in a breath and tried again to jerk away but it was no use.

"Take the girl to the truck while I set the detonator," McBride told Carlucci.

In an instant, Cutter was out of his sleeping bag, pulling on his jeans then his boots and tying them tight around his ankles, getting ready to run on rough ground. From where he sat, he could see the truck and the men milling around it.

"All right, Nate. I need you to do *exactly* what I tell you," he whispered as he got to his feet, shotgun in hand, and hustled to his jeep. He reached into a compartment under the seat and pulled out a box of .12 gauge buckshot. He stuffed a handful into the front pockets of his jeans and quietly poured the rest into the little fire pit.

Cutter reached in and knocked the jeep out of gear.

"Get on the other side," he told me. "Help me push it over." I stared at him for a second then understood. We were about to launch a ground-to-ground missile. I took hold of the cold metal. "I'm going down right behind it," he whispered. "You get to your truck and hightail it to the nearest phone. Call the law, and tell 'em to hurry."

"But –?"
"Push!"

Down below, the man with the deer rifle crouched beside the truck, focused on the house. The other man sat on the tailgate trimming his fingernails with a pocket knife.

They heard the groan of metal but no engine sound. As J.D. Benoit looked up the hill, I recognized him. He got the impression of something large and solid and heavy speeding down the steep slope. He dove off the tailgate, but long before the man behind the truck could react, the Jeep slammed into the pickup, knocking it onto its side in the ditch.

Cutter reached the road less than three seconds after the Jeep. Benoit was on his feet, reaching for a pistol in a shoulder holster when a blast from Cutter's shotgun knocked him backward onto the gravel. Running around the truck, Cutter aimed the gun but didn't fire. I still was trying to hold onto tree limbs and saplings on my way down the hill when Cutter hopped the fence and ran toward the house.

On the patio, Holly had dozed off on the chaise, cozy under the heavy blanket Rose had brought to her, but the sound of crashing, groaning metal punctuated by the shotgun's thunder jerked Holly upright. She twisted so that she could see the house behind her. The light was on in her bedroom. At first, that was all she could see. Then her eyes widened, her heart raged as she saw a man – *Tony Carlucci!* – drag Rose through the light spilling into the long hall of French doors.

Instinctively, she felt in her pocket for the pistol she'd been keeping close. "Oh, no!" she gasped, remembering she'd left it in her bedroom before the party. She had to move. She had to help. She had to do *something!* She used her arms to swing her braced legs off the lounge and plant her booted feet on the flagstones.

McBride swung his M-16 off his shoulder and clicked off the safety as he jogged to the front of the house. Tony pushed Rose into the kitchen as he looked out the side window into the yard and car park.

On the patio, Holly pushed herself up on her crutches. The braces locked at her knees and at her hips, holding her upright.

McBride entered the kitchen.

"I don't see any red lights flashin'. So, what do you want to bet it's your boy?"

Tony seethed but said nothing.

"Whoever it is, it looks like they ran something into the truck," said McBride. "We won't be leaving that way. The river is our best option."

"No," said Tony. "We'll take her car."

As if Cutter could hear them, a shotgun blast bellowed from somewhere near the garage and the left front tire of the Fury flew apart. The next blast hit the kitchen door, shattering window glass, splintering wood and spraying preserves all over the small alcove.

"Like I said, the river is our best option," McBride told Carlucci, handing him the M-16. "Gimme three minutes to set the detonator and cut us a path through that barbed wire."

"All right. Three minutes. But take her with you," said Tony, handing his daughter off to McBride. "She's mine, or she's nobody's," he snarled.

"Fine," he said, and tossed Tony something that looked like the remote control for a TV. "As soon as you get over the wall, blow the house. Then get your ass down to the river double quick or you'll be swimmin'."

I stood in the road staring at the shattered chest of Mississippi Highway Patrol Sergeant J.D. Benoit. One boot still was planted at the spot where the buckshot hit him. I thought about doing *exactly* what Cutter had told me to do. About getting to my truck and to the nearest phone. But everything was happening too fast. All of that would take close to ten minutes. By the time a sheriff's car got here? Another five or ten minutes.

No! I already had let down Cutter and Holly and the newspaper – and my daddy and myself – in so many ways. This was one battle I was not going to leave Cutter alone to fight. I edged over around the truck. The deer rifle was lying in the grass next to – to? – Coach Pearce! – who was pinned under the truck. He was trying to say something but his mouth was too full of blood.

I picked up the rifle and jumped the fence. Moving from walnut to pecan, I reached the last row of trees in front of the house just as I saw Cutter dart from the garage to the side of the Plymouth. Slugs thump-thump-thumped into the side of the car facing the house, glancing off the hood and shattering the windshield.

"I think I hit him," Tony yelled over his shoulder. "I'm gonna finish him."

It was then that the first shotgun shell exploded up the hill. I ducked, forgetting for a moment about the ammo Cutter had tossed into the coals. Another boomed, then another.

Tony cursed, fired another long blast from the M-16 then hunkered down as Cutter popped up and pumped three blasts of buckshot into the kitchen. I fired two shots through the front door, to announce my presence to them and Cutter.

"He's not alone," Tony called to McBride.

McBride shoved Rose ahead of him down the ramp onto the patio and then across the flagstones until he found the spot where he'd hidden the detonator. He pulled a pistol from a shoulder holster and told Rose, "Kneel." She did. "I'm going under the house for a minute. But I'll have the gun on you the whole time. You move, and I'll kill you. I don't give a damn what your daddy wants. You understand?"

Rose tried to ignore him but he grabbed her hard around her chin, his fingers digging into her cheeks. "Do you understand me?" he demanded. Finally, Rose nodded.

"Good," said McBride and rolled under the house. With a small flashlight in his mouth, he quickly found the arming mechanism he'd planted days earlier along with enough plastic explosive to level Wolf's Run. He twisted two screws down upon their corresponding wires and spent five seconds double checking his work. He was back out in under a minute.

Holly was trying to get to the porch steps near the library. If only she could get into the house and get to a phone … but trying to hurry in the braces was like trying to run in lead boots. McBride saw her and threw Rose down hard. Blood oozed from her chin and one knee. He was almost on Holly but Rose managed a guttural groan against the rope cutting into the corners of her mouth. Holly heard the sound and caught a glimpse of McBride coming out of the darkness. She brought the right crutch up hard and fast, the metal slamming into the side of his head. He went down hard and Holly jammed the tip into his stomach. He doubled but grabbed the crutch that was supporting her and snatched it out from under her.

Holly toppled onto her side, groaning as her shoulder hit hard on the stones.

McBride shoved Holly onto her back and was on top of her. He snatched a ten-inch survival knife from a scabbard on his leg. "You are a spitfire, aren't you?" sneered McBride as he pressed the razor-sharp blade to her neck and she felt a sharp pain and a small trickle of blood. "We could have some real fun together."

"Then let Rose go," Holly told him. "Take me."

"Sorry, honey, we've gotta travel light and move fast. You're just dead weight," he said, rolling away and grabbing up her crutches. He threw them over the wall. "But there's somebody who wants to say good bye to you. He'll be out in two shakes. So, don't you run off."

Cutter was as startled as his father to hear a rifle shot come from the tree line near the front of the house. If it was friendly fire, good. Or maybe Coach Pearce had wiggled out from under the truck? Either way, he knew he couldn't worry about it.

"Let us pass, boy!" Tony shouted from the kitchen window, trying to buy time.

Cutter could feel the drum beat of his pulse change in his neck. So, Tony wasn't hiding in Canada after all. He wasn't surprised, and neither was I, I suppose as I knelt behind the trunk of a big pecan tree.

"No way!" Cutter told him. "We settle this here! Tonight!"

"Your sister's blood'll be on your hands! The woman's, too!"

"If you hurt either one, I'll cut you up an inch at a time. I swear!"

More shells blew up on the plateau and Tony ducked.

From somewhere inside the house – no, the courtyard – I heard Miss Carter's voice – "Leave her alone! Let her go! You let her go!"

I didn't know what I was going to do but I knew I had to do something, so I ran to the west side of the house. The boards came so close to the kudzu and the limestone wall that a man much bigger than me could not have fit. But I hustled through the narrow gap thinking I might be able to get behind the men in the house. Then suddenly I found myself staring almost straight down at Dynamite Bob McBride. He was quickly using some sort of utility tool to snip through strands of barbed wire as Rose knelt on the path, her hands tied behind her back.

The view from my perch was dizzying, the river and the valley nearly four-hundred feet below at the foot of the steep incline littered with big rocks and sharp briars. I pressed my back to the clapboards of the house, chambered another round and prepared to take McBride down. But as I peeked over the ledge I saw Rose spring up with all the force she could muster, her bare legs uncoiling and her shoulder slamming into McBride's back in the same way her linebacker brother might deliver a textbook tackle. Only Rose didn't hold on. Couldn't if she wanted to. But neither could McBride and the impact catapulted him sideways and off the path. He fell a long fifty feet before slamming into a rock and crumpling onto the path. I stared into his dead eyes.

When I refocused, Rose was looking right at me. Her face and legs were bloody. Her momentum had carried her into the barbed wire and it now was tangled around her. I slung the rifle over my shoulder by its strap, grabbed a wild grapevine as thick as my wrist and started down the forty feet to her.

Tony fired another burst from the M16 until the clip was empty. Cutter popped up and Tony dove for the floor as another spray of buckshot tore the kitchen wall. He cursed and came up firing with the Luger but he knew the advantage now was with his son. And Cutter knew it, too. He waited a beat and came out from behind the car in a sprint as Tony ran for the courtyard, swinging his left leg in a wide arc. When Cutter got to the ramp he fired a shot that knocked the kitchen door off its hinges and went right in behind the blast. He gave the hall a quick look.

When Tony ran onto the patio he saw Holly pulling herself up on one of the patio chairs. The stiffness of her legs made it obvious she still had the braces under her skirt. Tony wished he had time to find out what else she had under her skirt, as he'd planned, but this was going to be even better. She was going to be his ticket out of this mess, and when it was over she and Cutter both would be dead.

I swung open the blade of my pocketknife but it wouldn't even begin to cut through the barbed wire that was twisted around Rose, digging into her flesh. "I can't get you loose," I said as her eyes implored me. "It's gonna take wire cutters."

Her eyes were practically screaming for me to do something, I could see. So I did the only thing I could, I slipped my hands through the wire web and cut the gag from her mouth. She swallowed and ran her tongue around her lips, tasting the blood at the corners of her mouth.

"H-H-H-Help, C-C-Cut-Cutter!" she told me.

"I gotta help *you*!"

"N-N-N-Nooooo!" she struggled. Then, she closed her eyes for a few short seconds, focusing all her energy on what she needed to say. When she opened them again, she said with the clarity and diction of an English teacher, "Tony is going to kill Holly and Cutter. *Go!*"

Cutter darted onto the courtyard porch and a slug tore into the wall next to him. He dove over the railing and landed hard but rolled over behind the big stone fountain as a slug sparked on the flagstone where he'd been.

"So, it's come down to this, huh, boy? You and me," yelled Tony. "Just like it ought to be."

I crouched, easing up the path. I peeked over the stone wall. Tony Carlucci was sideways to me, next to the pool. He had Holly upright, his arm tight around her, the Luger to her head. I'd have only one chance. One shot. If it wasn't perfect it would pass right through Tony and into Holly.

"Tony, there's no way out," said Cutter. "Let her go and drop the gun."

"'Tony?' You smart-mouthed, know-it-all brat. You call me Daddy or Papa or Dad or Blessed Father, but don't you dare call me Tony again," he snarled, pressing the gun to Holly's temple. "You acknowledge me right this second as your father, or so help me God I'll –"

"All right … Dad … Take it easy."

"That's better, *son*."

Cutter let things settle for a moment. The breech stood open, smoking and empty. The acrid smell of cordite hot in his nostrils and on his clothes. He reached for his pocket to chamber another round. No more shells. He held the gun close.

"Okay, Dad, put down the gun and you live to walk away from this. But if you hurt her, I'll blow you in two," he bluffed. "You *know* I will."

"Live to do life in prison? I don't care much for that deal," said Tony. "Tell you what we're gonna do instead, *son*. You throw that shotgun into the pool and I go over that wall. Everyone lives happily ever after."

"No, Cutter," Holly called out, her voice strong and steady. "Don't do it! McBride has Rose. He'll kill us anyway."

I brought the deer rifle to my shoulder and looked through the scope. The crosshairs met just behind Tony's ear. All I had to do was squeeze lightly on the trigger and his head would disappear ... unless he moved or twitched or jerked. Then it would be Holly's head.

Tony Carlucci laughed – a hot, humorless laugh against the back of Holly's neck, like the sound of bellows stoking the fire in a crematory. "She might be right. Or she might not, but let's up the ante," he said and suddenly shoved Holly into the pool as he ducked behind the stone barbecue. I cursed myself. My hesitation had caused me not to take the shot and now Holly was in the pool, in those heavy braces. She wouldn't have a chance. And I no longer had a shot.

"What'cha gonna do, hero?" his father taunted. "No stands full of people cheerin' for you. Chantin' your name. You gonna stay back there where it's safe while your girlfriend drowns? Or you gonna come help her?"

"Just me and you now! Come on, boy! What's it gonna be?"

Cutter squeezed his eyes shut. "Lord, help me!" was all the prayer he had time for as he sprang from behind the fountain and sprinted toward the pool, using the empty shotgun as a prop. When he got within a few steps he tossed it and dove for the water.

Tony stood and fired three quick shots, and watched with glee as one of the slugs hit home and spun Cutter around in midair. The water began turning pink as soon as he splashed into it. He saw Cutter sink toward the bottom, motionless. For a moment, Holly fought the water and the weight of the braces to get to him, bubbles escaping from her mouth, but then she was still, too. Standing at the bottom of the pool, her arms floating beside her. Cutter was motionless. His arms and legs spread inside a growing pink cloud. Tony smiled and spit on the water and sneered, then turned for the stone wall. I ducked back and edged down the path, the deer rifle against my shoulder.

Out on the highway, Tony could see three police cars racing up the valley. There'd been enough shooting that someone had called the law. It was time to go. McBride was right. It was good to have a backup plan, even if that wolf path would be hell to get down with his bad leg. There was a boat waiting, tied to the willow at the foot of Blue Mountain. Tony dropped the Luger into his pocket and took out the detonator as he swung his leg over the wall. I backed down the path a few more steps. Then he saw me, and past me he saw Rose lay-ing in the tangle of barbed wire and McBride dead on the rocks below.

"D-Don't move," I said, but the words came out as more of a plea than an order.

Tony Carlucci smiled an ugly smile. He had one more card to play, and I saw it in his hand – a remote detonator. His thumb was over the button.

"I ain't goin' to jail," he told me.

My finger settled on the rifle's trigger as I heard a splash.

"Holly!" Cutter gasped as he burst the surface. I heard Holly cough. "It's okay! I've got you! It's gonna be okay."

Tony glanced toward the pool and back at me, and the smile became a sneer. I felt the sweat trickling down my neck, the tightness in my chest and my left hand cramping as I steadied the barrel.

"Okay, boy," he said looking right at me as he raised the transmit-ter. "Show me what'cha got."

I felt the weight of the trigger resisting my finger, my finger insist-ing, and the trigger giving way. The recoil thudded against my shoul-der and in the scope my friend's father disappeared behind a white flash.

Epilogue

January 1973

⌒

The night was overcast and cold, and a frost-filled northwest wind prickled like a thousand needles through the fabric of my Class A Uniform. I could see my breath in front of me as I hustled up to the ticket window at the Rebel Theater.

I glanced at the prices behind the glass and said to the heavyset young woman making change, "A dollar, huh? Last time I was here, it was 75 cents for adults and a quarter for kids."

She looked me over in my Marine greens and asked, "You from DeLong?"

"I used to be. But I haven't been home in – let's see, three years come May."

She didn't pursue my history or my reasons for leaving, and I was glad.

"I reckon it costs more now to rent the movies to show," she said pleasantly, her dumpling-shaped cheeks red from the cold seeping in from the half oval hole at the bottom of the glass. "But you're late. You've done missed the cartoons and the movie's already started. I'll just charge you fifty cents," she said, sliding two quarters back through the slot.

"No, no. Please. I wasn't complaining. Just commenting on how things change."

"I guess they do," she said. "But they sure take their time about it around here. Tell you what. Come on in, I'll get you a hot popcorn on the house."

"All right. That'd be top notch."

I entered the small lobby, which, thankfully, was warm. It smelled of salt and butter, Coke syrup and pine-scented cleaner as it always had but was completely remodeled since the last time I was there in the spring of 1970. The lobby carpet was new, the concession area had been rebuilt and expanded and there was a fresh coat of paint on the walls.

"Things certainly have changed here," I said, looking around.

"Yeah?" she asked, looking around now, too. "Been like this since we been in DeLong. But that's only a year. Moved down from Middleton when daddy lost his job."

I nodded, finishing my once-over of the lobby. "The movie any good?" I asked, waving a hand toward a poster for *The Last Picture Show*.

"It's aw'right," she said as she scooped popcorn into a square cardboard cup. "Kinda slow in places. And it's in black-and-white. Don't know why they done that. Ain't no movies in black-and-white no more."

I put 25 cents on the counter. "Could I get a Co-Cola, too, please?"

She filled a large cup for me instead of the medium I'd paid for, fitted a plastic lid on top and slid a straw through the hole. "You see, it goes in easy as pie. You in town long?" she asked, her smile making her cheeks blow up like balloons.

"No. I'm catchin' the bus for New Orleans at 0-700 hours. Then a plane to San Diego," I told her. "In fact, I'm shippin' out overseas next week. Vietnam."

"Well, that's a shame. That you're leavin' so soon," she said, another small disappointment in a life full of them. "I had a cousin from Alabama who went. He got killed. I didn't know him much, though. Hey, I thought President Nixon said the war was over?"

"We don't officially have combat troops there anymore. But there are still a lot of Marines on the ground and a lot of fightin' to do," I told her. "Thanks for the popcorn."

"Sure. Be careful over there."

I nodded, smiled and stepped through the curtain into the nearly empty theater. Jeff Bridges and Cybill Shepherd were twenty feet tall on the screen, and their moving images lit everything in front of me in silhouette – including a wheelchair about halfway down the aisle. A couple sat next to it, he with his arm around her, she with her head on his shoulder.

My heart thudded and I cocked my foot as if preparing to execute a classic military about-face, but instead I just stood there, staring. This was exactly what I had wanted to avoid, why I'd told no one of my visit home and arranged it to be as brief as possible. Drop in, drop by to see Daddy at the sheriff's office – which I had done – and take the first bus out the next morning. That was the plan. Or was that all a lie I had told myself? Hadn't I really wanted to see Cutter? Needed to see him? Otherwise, why was I standing frozen in his place of business?

Someone in the back corner cleared his throat in complaint. I looked around for where to sit, as if I didn't have my choice of three-hundred-and-fifty seats. It was a cold Thursday night and the audience was small. I slipped into the closest row to my right and hunkered down next to the wall.

So much had happened since the late summer of 1969, since men landed on the moon and Holly Lee Carter returned to DeLong. As I sat there in the flickering semi-darkness, ignoring the movie and staring at Cutter and Holly, I hardly knew where to begin cataloging it all.

That night at Wolf's Run, when Cutter and I sent his jeep crashing down the hillside, marked the end of the most violent and ugly period in our county's history since the Civil War. The chore that remained was cleaning up the literal and figurative wreckage.

As I squeezed the trigger that September night, Tony Carlucci's thumb struck the button on the detonator. A wall of debris-filled fire exploded white over the top of the stone wall then roared red up into the night in an extended thunder-clap. Some claim to have heard the blast fifteen miles away and people out late in DeLong saw the fireball.

The impact nearly bucked me off the narrow path, but I dove for the ground and hung on. Cutter pushed himself and Holly to the bottom of the pool and they looked up as the flames sizzled across the top of the water, protected from the blast and the heat. When Cutter used most of his remaining strength to get Holly back to the surface and to the steps at the shallow end of the pool, they saw that all that remained of Wolf's Run was burning debris piled atop a handful of brick piers and the stone fountain. The century-old house was completely leveled and in the front yard many trees were on fire as three police cars – led by my father's cruiser – slid to a halt around Cutter's jeep, the overturned truck and the body of J.D. Benoit.

Dynamite Bob McBride was dead, and good riddance. I believe God made Hell for men like him.

Tony Carlucci's corpse was never found. Had I hit him with the deer slug? Had he thrown himself from the wall in the instant before he pushed the detonator? His prosthesis was discovered several weeks later, half-buried in a sandbar about two miles south of the Old Iron Bridge. It was an area notorious for undertows and water moccasins.

Coach Pearce survived being pinned under the truck but was a quadriplegic. He cut a deal with prosecutors for his testimony. He testified in two state conspiracy trials against Grand Wizard Milton Handley, Walter Kamp and former Governor Cecil Weathers. Both trials ended in hung juries.

J.L. Burke, who by then had been named a Deputy U.S. Attorney General, was going to have a go at them in federal court on civil rights charges, but before the prosecution could be mounted, Coach Pearce died.

Not a single Klansman ever did prison time for the violence that took place that summer. But multiple investigations, prosecutions and a final wave of public outrage broke the back of the Kattahatchie Klavern.

Mary Nell Poindexter Carter never stood trial. While undergoing evaluation at the state mental hospital at Whitfield, she hanged herself.

Over the fall of '69, Tom Carter slowly recovered from the physical and spiritual toxins that his wife had been feeding him. Most people, including Doctor Garner, termed it a miracle. Not only did his long hospital stay allow him to detox his body from the rat poison, but it also allowed him to kick the booze habit.

Miss H.L. Carter remained editor and publisher while C. Michael Morton used *The Current-Leader*'s journalism prizes – many of which were national in scope for the paper's coverage of the events of August and September 1969 – to propel himself to a job with the, by gosh, *New York Times*.

Despite the national awards it garnered, *The Current-Leader* struggled for many months in the wake of all that had happened, and barely survived. But thanks to the efforts of Holly *and* Tom Carter, it now had a larger circulation and advertising base than at any time in its history. Mister Tom's name was back on *The Current-Leader*'s masthead as general manager.

Eve Howard recovered from her injuries, though, obviously had to learn to walk with a prosthesis. Holly helped her get on at the *L.A. Chronicle*, and she now was considered one of the paper's top photographers. Once the dust settled, Eve also remained one of Holly's closest friends.

Reverend Ron Clemmer also recovered from the injuries suffered during the attack on the NCJ bus. He wrote a bestseller about the events of that summer in DeLong, then moved on to become a community organizer in Chicago.

And in November 1969, William T. "Billy" Wallace was elected to a full four-year term as sheriff of Cattahatchie County.

One of the bullets that Tony Carlucci fired as Cutter dove into the pool to save Holly shattered his son's left knee. The finest, quickest, fastest, most gifted high school football player I ever saw never played another down.

Cutter was in a cast from hip to his foot for almost two months and it was well into the following spring before he could walk without a cane. But he and Rose and Holly attended almost every CHS game that fall. Cutter offered encouragement, tips and even helped call many of the offensive plays. I never returned to the team, but in the end the Wolves finished 2-8.

If Cutter was bitter about the loss of a scholarship, the fame that a college football career could have brought and the money that might have awaited him as a professional, he hid it from everyone – especially me.

We graduated together from Cattahatchie High School in the Class of 1970. Me, Cutter, Rose, Jimmy Garner, Dodge McDowell, Haughton IV, Paula Simpson and twenty-six others, who, by one troubled and frightening road or another, made our way through the minefield of integration. Once done, it was never again an issue in the halls of CHS. But my friendship with Cutter and my budding relationship with Rose was never the same after that night at Wolf's Run. Not because of anything they did, but because of what I knew about myself. I could not look into Cutter's eyes, or those of Rose or Holly, without seeing my own guilt reflected back even when they turned sincere and open smiles my way.

After high school, Rose continued to live with Holly in a house she rented two blocks off the square. Rose attended junior college in nearby Booneville, so that she could stay close to her mother. During that time, Holly taught Rose the guitar and encouraged her about music, and to everyone's surprise discovered that Rose had a beautiful voice and did not stutter one lick when she sang. After Miss Jenny died in the nursing home in the spring '71, Rose couldn't leave DeLong fast enough. Holly helped her connect with some people in the Los Angeles music scene, and Rose had a small apartment in West L.A. She was working pretty steady in neighborhood bars and coffeehouses while honing her skills as a songwriter.

Two weeks after the attack at Wolf's Run, Brother Charles Everett MacAllister was ousted from the pulpit at First Denomination. The congregation brought in a young minister who talked about inclusion in God's kingdom, not exclusion based on race and political beliefs. Cutter and Holly regularly attended, sharing the pew with Tom and his children.

Now Patti MacAllister was dead, but I thought of her nearly every day, and supposed I failed her as well. Although I never repeated to anyone, aside from Cutter, what Patti told me about Eve Howard and Ridge Belladfont and the Klan rally, whatever love I had given her had not been enough to tear her away from the demons of her father.

Brother MacAllister retreated deeper into his own twisted theology and moved himself and his family into the mountains of rural north Alabama. It was a place of steep dirt roads and family trees that branched little, and where snake-handling churches were not uncommon.

Patti – the pathologically loyal daughter – died at age 20 when she was struck in her carotid artery by a three-foot rattlesnake. Her father said it proved she was a sinful and evil girl. He would not preach her funeral or allow her to be buried in his churchyard.

Janette Wellingham wept when she told me about it, which she did over several drinks at the Decatur Street bar where I was working in New Orleans. She was in town for the Ole Miss-LSU football game. I was living in a garage apartment off the Rue Montegut and attending Tulane on a journalism scholarship that Holly helped me get; but by the fall of my sophomore year, I was a part-time student and bartender, and full-time drunk. So, I quit before I flunked out and started working the shrimp boats out of Delacroix – hoping, I suppose, that the scalding sun and scouring salt of Vermillion Bay would somehow scrape my insides clean. They didn't. But in the late summer of '72, I sobered up long enough to realize I needed some sort of order in my life and a place to release the murderous anger that seemed to be always twitching at the corner of my mouth. The Marines and the last agonizing engagements of the Vietnam War seemed the places to deal with both. So I volunteered.

Almost before I realized it, another Hank Williams tune was playing over the movie credits. The lights came halfway up as Holly transferred back to her wheelchair. Cutter stood straight, his shoulders as flat and broad and hard as they'd ever been, his waist narrow, and I felt something like panic in my muscles. I hustled down the row and into the lobby. I heard Holly laugh, her voice husky and weightless at the same time. The sound of a mature woman who'd endured enough pain to know real joy when it came her way.

The men's room was to my left and I pushed through the door.

For several minutes I stood at the urinal, pretending to focus on my business, then tucked myself back into my uniform. I washed my hands and my face and leaned my weight on the sink to keep my knees from giving way. I was so ashamed that I wanted to cry, and that knowledge made me even more ashamed. Yet, more than anything I knew I had to talk to Cutter. Talk to him before I took off for Vietnam – maybe not to return. I needed to tell him how sorry I was about ... about everything.

Finally I dried my face, straightened my uniform, took a deep breath and stepped into the lobby. The theater had quickly emptied out. I was alone and the lights were already dimmed. Through the glass front doors I saw Cutter waving to Holly as she pulled away from the curb in a new red Thunderbird. It suited her. The wind had picked up and snow was falling, blowing at an angle down Main Street and starting to collect on the brick sidewalks of the town square.

When Clifton Reese died in the late spring of 1970, Doctor Garner and couple of partners bought the Rebel Theater from Mr. Reese's daughter. Cutter applied to manage it for a little salary, the right to live in the small apartment upstairs and a cut of the profits. Despite commuting to Ole Miss, taking a full course load and pulling a 3.85 GPA in American history/pre-law, Cutter had made the Rebel more successful than ever. His share of the profits was enough to pay for his schooling and help Rose out, too.

Cutter watched until Holly's car was away, then turned and hurried back through the doors, blowing into his cupped hands. He tilted up his eyes and then his face and stopped in his tracks, his black hair flecked with snow. Then he charged.

"Nate!" he yelled, and before I could respond, he had his big arms around me in a bear hug, lifting me off my feet. "When did you get here? How come you didn't let me know you were coming? You just missed Holly.

"Gosh! It's good to see you."

We went upstairs, past the projection room and the small balcony that used to be labeled Coloreds Only, and into a single room. It contained a desk, an old refrigerator and cook stove, a single bed, and an overflowing bookcase. To the side was a small bathroom and tiny closet. Through the window, I could see the snow falling past a streetlight on the square. Big, thick flakes. "Angel feathers," my mother called them.

"It's not much, but it's a lot better than sleepin' on rocks, huh? You want a beer? Something to eat?"

"I already ate. But I'll take a beer."

He got two from the refrigerator.

"The theater looks real good," I said, by way of conversation.

"Thanks! I did a lot of the work of myself. And you know what? Holly helped!" he enthused, laughing. "Never saw a woman take to power tools like she did."

I smiled. "I'm surprised you and Holly aren't already cohabitatin'."

"Don't think it hasn't crossed my mind. But she's a woman of strong convictions, and that's one of the reasons I love her. Even if it's about to drive me crazy! But that was our pact, I guess you'd call it. No marriage and so no – uhm – full-on cohabitatin' until I finish school. So, I've crammed four years of college into three. I graduate May 7, and we're getting married the next weekend. And that woman better be ready to spend a month in bed," he said, smiling. Then his voice changed. It softened and glowed as if warmed by firelight. "You know, Nate, I never expected to be this crazy about a woman. Until Holly came along, I never even knew this kind of love existed. I sure never saw it between my folks. I can't wait to wake up next to her."

The admission was so unguarded and honest, and thus so intimate, that it almost made me blush. I lifted my bottle in a toast – "I'll drink to that."

Cutter and I talked our way through the night and a six pack. Mostly about old times, where high school friends were and what they were doing. He told me about his plans for the future with Holly.

"We're gonna move a double-wide onto the Wolf's Run property over on the side by the garage," he told me. "Then we're going to start building a new house around the courtyard and the pool. We've already got the plans drawn up. We'll contract the heavy-duty stuff, but Holly and I are going to do as much as we can."

I arched my brows. "That's impressive."

"I don't know about impressive. Probably more like downright crazy," he told me smiling, then more seriously. "It'll be something we can hand down to our children and them to theirs, and as long as it stands it'll have our sweat and blood, and our dreams in it." For a second I thought I saw the glint of moisture cover Cutter's eyes, and that surprised me for I remembered him as one of the least emotional and sentimental people I had ever known. But he blinked and it was gone. I smiled, stood and walked over to the window overlooking the square. My smile faded and I took a long swig from my fourth beer. Then with the same clumsiness I'd shown as a wide receiver and a farm hand, I asked, "Do you think Tony's dead?"

Cutter stood and joined me at the window watching my mother's angel feathers gathering on the courthouse lawn and around the monument to the county's war dead. After several moments, he said, "Tony was the hardest man I've ever seen. But the impact of the explosion? The slug from a 30.06 at near point blank range? It –"

"I'm not sure I hit him!" I blurted.

Cutter turned to face me and put his hand on my shoulder. The shrimp boats and then Marine basic training had made my muscles hard and bigger than they'd ever been, but under Cutter's hand I still felt like the scrawny third string wide-receiver I had been for a team that had only two real strings.

"Nate, it doesn't matter," he told me, those eyes of his fixed on mine. "Tony wasn't your demon to kill." I looked away, nodding almost imperceptibly. Then he grunted, and forced a mirthless laugh. "Shoot, the fall alone would have killed him."

"Yeah," I agreed, forcing a smile. "Yeah. You're right."

Then, noticing the clock beside his bed, Cutter said, "Five-thirty. Miss Winona should be heatin' up the griddle. I know she'd like to see in your uniform. You want to get some breakfast before your ride gets here?"

"Sure. Reckon the bus'll run in this weather?"

"I guess we'll find out."

We went down the fire escape to the adjoining lot where Cutter's truck was parked. It was new – at least new to him – a '61 Ford. And he told me about how he'd fixed it up.

"I left my duffel at the jail," I said, closing the door behind me as the windshield wipers threw off the layer of snow.

Cutter made a slow loop around the square, mostly for my benefit, I think. DeLong looked as if it were covered in white velvet trimmed with crystal. The streets were as beautiful, quiet and serene as I had ever seen them. It is how I would remember DeLong ... and Cutter.

"Pretty, isn't it?" he asked.

"Yeah. It sure is."

Cutter eased down the hill toward the jail, the river and the Bilbo Bridge over to Roseville. Businesses had been rebuilt in the place of those wrecked in the bombing, and *The Current-Leader* had led a civic push to create a memorial park on much of the block destroyed by fire. But I won't attempt to calculate or pretend to comprehend the pain and anger that lingered behind the cotton warehouses on the other side of the river. That summer of '69 had been moved on from, but it had not been erased from the lives of anyone of us who lived through it.

At the jail, we picked up my bag and then went to The Cotton. Paula Simpson was away at college and her mother no longer waited tables on the early shift, so the girl chewing gum behind the counter was new. An acne-pocked blonde, she didn't fill out her pink uniform nearly as well as her predecessor. But Miss Winona came out of the kitchen and gave me the once-over with her milky eyes and welcomed me home as if I'd already been to war.

"Why, Nate Wallace! You've just growed up to make the handsomest young man!" she crowed, resting her strong old hand on my forearm. "And look at you in your uniform. Nothin's too good for our soldier boys. Breakfast with all trimmin's is on the house. "

We sat at the same spot at the end of the counter that we had on so many Sundays, including the morning on which Cutter and Holly had met on such unfriendly terms, three-and-a-half years earlier.

"Guess Miss Winona doesn't remember the side I took that summer," I said.

"Oh, I'm sure she remembers," he said, warming his hands around the steaming coffee cup. "But like a lot of people, she'd rather live today in forgiveness than dwell on three-year-old upset and ugliness."

I didn't know what to say to that, so I said nothing.

Miss Winona's pancakes, sausage, bacon and hash browns were delicious, and the snowy morning made The Cotton's coffee taste even better, but after a third cup it was time to go. I excused myself to the men's room and when I came back I said, "Guess I better get outside. If I'm not there to flag down that old gray dog, the driver's liable not to stop on a mornin' like this."

Cutter walked out with me. He was wearing his CHS letter jacket. The wind was light but still out of the northwest and as sharp as razor blades. The snow had slacked up but continued to lightly fall from a sky that gave little hint that dawn was only minutes away. We shifted and waited and stuffed our hands into the pockets of our pants as we huddled behind the corner of the café, using it for a windbreak. The green-and-white neon glow of a blooming cotton stalk lit us and the snow around our feet.

"I'm sorry you're not going to be here for the wedding. I can't think of anybody I'd rather have as my best man," he said. When he saw my chin quivering, he went on, trying to save me from embarrassment. But what he said then touched me in a place that only he could. "Be careful over there. Don't go gettin' yourself killed to prove something that don't need provin'. You're not a coward, Nate, and you never were."

The flakes touched my face like frozen tears and melted on my cheeks.

"You saved Holly's life and Rose's, too," he went on. "If you hadn't been there that night and done the things you did, Holly and Rose – well, all I'd have now is memories of them. And that would be killin' me by degrees every day."

My chin shook. "But I could have killed Tony the first time I had him in my sights. If I had, he wouldn't have been alive to –"

"Yeah or you could have hit Holly," he interrupted. "Or Tony could have squeezed that pistol's trigger on reflex and killed her."

"But your leg!" I gasped, a sob bursting from my throat. "You were the best football player I ever saw. The best anybody around here ever saw! You could be a star at Ole Miss right now. Bigger than Archie! On your way to the Heisman. You could be headed to the pros. New York or Chicago or –"

Cutter grabbed me by the shoulders. "Nate, stop it!" he told me. "That was *your* dream. That was this town's dream. But it was never mine. All I ever wanted out of football was a way to get Rose and Momma away from Tony, and an education.

"And you know what? I got all three, and I got Holly, too."

I stared up at him, my face streaked with snowflakes and tears, hearing but not comprehending. *How could anyone not want –?*

"Nate, stop feelin' guilty for the death of something that was never real in the first place," he said, imploring me with the grip of his fingers on my arms and the way his eyes held mine. "I'm livin' the best dream I could ever imagine. I wouldn't trade the life I'm livin' now and what's ahead with Holly for a hundred Heismans and twenty Super Bowls." He shook me a little. "Do you hear me?"

I nodded and stepped back from him, wiping my face as the bus rumbled down River Street, the driver shifting gears, the snow crunching under the big tires. I stuck my arm up and waved. The airbrakes on the Greyhound hissed.

"Nate, let it go," he said. "Don't throw your life away. Come home to the people who love you."

The door to the bus swung open. Cutter and I embraced until the driver bumped his horn. "Let's go soldier boy," he said. "Daylight's comin' and I need to put this burg in my rearview."

I rubbed more tears from my cheeks, grabbed my duffle and climbed aboard and found a seat where I could see Cutter. He stood there in the cold and the snow next to the neon bloom of The Cotton Café sign waving until the bus was out of sight.

The driver did a loop around the courthouse to get the bus pointed in the right direction. We went past the theater and *The Current-Leader* building with what looked to be its freshly painted logo on the brick near the roofline –

Cattahatchie Current-Leader
The Conscience of the Community since 1836

Then the driver maneuvered off the square and pointed us south on Highway 27. I'd been awake for more than 24 hours and my mind was giving way to both fatigue and relief. My hands were cold but my belly was full, and my eyelids felt as heavy as tent canvas.

As we passed Mrs. Fletcher's Boarding House and the fairgrounds, the sun was breaking through small cracks in the leaden clouds. To our right, the Cattahatchie looked like a wide black ribbon lain on a white linen tablecloth. To the left, the east, the fallow fields of winter were glistening like cake frosting laced with diamond dust. As we approached the short bridge where Holly and Cutter met, a shaft of light as defined as a glass tube and as pure and golden as liquid platinum painted the creek, the ditch and the nearby field. It glittered on the bus and through the windows and onto the souls wrapped in blankets, snuggled on small pillows and sleeping around me. Unaware.

Though we quickly passed out of that sunbeam's singular radiance, it hung there on that spot for as long as I could see.

The bus picked up speed and as quickly as it could put the quiet acres and snow-frosted miles of Cattahatchie County behind it, until there were no more. Then I settled down in my seat to sleep, certain that such a perfect stream of golden light was what the finger of God looked like when He chose to touch the earth.

THE END

Acknowledgments

❧

The first fragment of the idea that became *Wolf's Run* was scribbled into a reporter's notebook while covering a Bolivar County (Ms.) Board of Supervisors meeting in Rosedale about 1980. Since then I have sought and been blessed with the input of countless people. Many deserve a mention here and will not get it because of my poor memory, note-keeping and the confines of space. To each of you I want to say a heartfelt thank you and offer a heartfelt apology if your name is not mentioned.

However, there are a handful of people who were invaluable in this multi-decade process and I am pleased to acknowledge them.

First and foremost, I want to again thank my wife, Joyce, for her incredible patience, support and encouragement throughout the twenty years of our marriage.

Also I want to thank:

Greg Akins, my best friend, for his consistent encouragement and faith in me even when I lost faith in myself.

Eddie Galey and her children, Ben, Amy and Shannon Downs.

Jane Berkey, one of New York's finest literary agents, for her guidance and insight into the publishing world.

Maureen Rung Simonson, Milita Dolan, Liz Winkelaar, Lenore Castro and numerous other spinal cord injured individuals who shared with honesty and openness about their lives in wheelchairs; and, of course, my wife, Joyce, who did the same.

David L. Maxwell of Everest & Jennings wheelchairs.

Bill Bowen and Jodi MacNeal, my editors on this project; and April Elizabeth Williams Milner (www.coconutcircle.com), who shot my author photos. Great job! Thank you!

Maretta Corey, Greg Akins, Maureen Rung Simonson, Julie Burks, Pat Sherlin, Mike Schlechter, Sam Dworkis, Paul Blythe, Jane Berkey, Anne Boles Levy, Jennifer Patzius, Lois Pickens and all those others who over the years have read one version or another of *Wolf's Run* and given me excellent feedback.

Dr. Darrell P. Orman, senior pastor of First Baptist Church in Stuart, Fla., and Gary and Marianne Ruffin, of First Baptist Church of Lafayette, La., who were lights for me during a very dark time – leading me back to a walk with Christ.

My grandmother, Bettie Belle Pickens, who worked tirelessly – and for the most part thanklessly – to plant in me the seeds of Christian values that somehow took root and decades later have flourished into a faith for which I will be grateful throughout eternity. "Mamma Bettie" I'm looking forward to seeing you again one bright morning.

My mother, Louise Park, and Mrs. Valerie Boyd Howell, who instilled and nurtured in me a love for the written word.

The Pickens, Akins and Reno clans of north Mississippi who, at one time or another, took me in as one of their own and gave me a sense of family that I would not otherwise have had.

Randy Windham, for all the dirt-road miles we turned together in that ol' brown pickup.

Jason Johnson.

Dana Carter McCormick.

John Grisham, for making a lot of us believe it is possible.

And finally, Mrs. Allie Gaddis, her daughter Paula and girls everywhere in Tuff-Nut overalls.

www.ingramcontent.com/pod-product-compliance
Lightning Source LLC
Chambersburg PA
CBHW031050260626
47172CB00001B/14